KNIGHTS TE

CW00505363

THE WINTER KNIGHT

by S.J.A. Turney

1st Edition

For Paul and Lou,

Always and forever

Published in this format 2019 by Victrix Books

Copyright - S.J.A.Turney

First Edition

Also by S. J. A. Turney:

The Templar Series

Daughter of War (2018)
The Last Emir (2018)
City of God (2019)
The Winter Knight (2019)

Tales of the Empire

Interregnum (2009)
Ironroot (2010)
Dark Empress (2011)
Insurgency (2016)
Emperor's Bane (2016)
Invasion (2017)
Jade Empire (2017)

The Ottoman Cycle

The Thief's Tale (2013)
The Priest's Tale (2013)
The Assassin's Tale (2014)
The Pasha's Tale (2015)

The Praetorian Series

Praetorian – The Great Game (2015)
Praetorian – The Price of Treason (2015)
Praetorian – Eagles of Dacia (2017)
Praetorian – Lions of Rome (2018)

The Damned Emperors (as Simon Turney)

Caligula (2018)
Commodus (2019)

The Marius' Mules Series

Marius' Mules I: The Invasion of Gaul (2009)
Marius' Mules II: The Belgae (2010)
Marius' Mules III: Gallia Invicta (2011)
Marius' Mules IV: Conspiracy of Eagles (2012)
Marius' Mules V: Hades Gate (2013)
Marius' Mules VI: Caesar's Vow (2014)
Marius' Mules VII: The Great Revolt (2014)
Marius' Mules VIII: Sons of Taranis (2015)
Marius' Mules IX: Pax Gallica (2016)
Marius' Mules X: Fields of Mars (2017)
Marius' Mules XI: Tides of War (2018)
Marius' Mules XII: Sands of Egypt (2019)

Roman Adventures (Children's Roman fiction with Dave Slaney)

Crocodile Legion (2016)
Pirate Legion (2017)

Short story compilations & contributions:

Tales of Ancient Rome vol. 1 (2011)
Tortured Hearts Vol 2 (2012)
Tortured Hearts Vol 3 (2012)
Temporal Tales (2013)
Historical Tales (2013)
A Year of Ravens (2015)
A Song of War (2016)
Rubicon (2019)

For more information visit **www.simonturney.com**

You can also follow Simon on:
Facebook Simon Turney Author aka SJATurney (@sjaturney)
Twitter @SJATurney
Instagram simonturney_aka_sjaturney

Schloß Renfrizhausen

1 Main Gate	5 Chapel
2 Guardroom	6 Stables
3 Main Range	7 Dormitory Range
4 Kitchens	8 Well

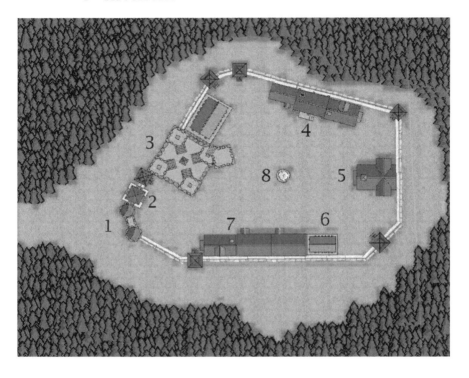

A man apostate, a man unprofitable, is he who goeth with a wayward mouth; he beckoneth with eyes, he trampeth with the foot, he speaketh with the finger, by shrewd heart he imagineth evil, and in all time he soweth dissensions. His perdition shall come to him anon, and he shall be broken suddenly; and he shall no more have medicine.

Six things there be, which the Lord hateth; and his soul curseth the seventh thing.

High eyes
A liar tongue
Hands shedding out innocent blood
An heart imagining full wicked thoughts
Feet swift to run into evil
A man bringing forth lies, a false witness
And him that soweth discord among brethren

My son, keep the commandments of thy father; and forsake thou not the law of thy mother. Bind thou those continually in thine heart; and encompass to thy throat. When thou goest, go they with thee; when thou sleepest, keep they thee; and thou waking, speak with them. For the commandment of God is a lantern, and the law is light, and the blaming of teaching is the way of life

Proverbs 6:12-23

THE WINTER KNIGHT

The door to the castle's great hall slammed shut somewhere far back, and the greasy smoke and dancing orange flames of the three torches along the corridor walls each guttered and flared momentarily, throwing eerie demonic shadows around the grey stonework. For a heartbeat the flittering illumination picked out details in the great tapestry that hung on the wall opposite, a treasure from the time of his great grandfather, the story of the fortress and his family.

A flare: Henry the Lion with sword raised, heroic and larger than life as he stands alongside the fearsome beast that is his namesake, the pair facing the dread crimson wyrm as it breathes its fire at them in great billowing clouds. Guttering back into darkness.

A flash: Burkhard von Zollern in his mail shirt with a sword large enough to cleave giants, standing atop a rock in the shape of a curled dragon, his new castle rising strong and noble behind, imposed against a bright sky. And then darkness.

A flicker: Hildiger von Ehingen de Rottenburg standing between Frederick the One-Eyed and a young princeling the family proudly claimed to be Frederick Barbarossa. A trinity of steel-clad warriors and nobles representing the great power of the Hohenstaufen dynasty and their allies.

The angry figure stomped past the tapestry and its glorious scenes, past the torches as they once more settled into a quiet guttering, sinews of black smoke rising to add to the sooty coating of the ceiling, hiding its once rich, now faded paintwork. The torches entirely failed in any aspect of their purpose. The light they gave off did little more than highlight how gloomy the corridor was by throwing small patches of it into clarity, and any heat they produced was immediately smothered by the bitter cold, carried along the passageway on a wind that cut like the talons of a wyrm.

Anger. Anger and frustration. Anger over the rifts that were endemic in the family, over the idiocy of the argument that had led to his storming out, over the pig-headedness of the old man, refusing to accept that there could be any view but his own. Anger over a world where such a noble family could be brought so low,

low enough that arguments over minutiae shattered the peace, when they should be above such things.

Frustration that his own manner was so impulsive and hot-headed that he had so readily failed to keep control of his temper in the face of the argument. He should have been able to rise above, but he couldn't. He simply couldn't. He was a man of fire, like his father, not one of ice, like his uncle.

Would that Lütolf was here now…

Trudging along the corridor, still aswirl with anger and regret, he made for the square of blue-white ahead, the open door into the courtyard, passing through into the antechamber on the way. Two more torches entirely failed to illuminate this small room between the wide corridor and the courtyard exit, the bottom of a spiral staircase presenting a black maw to the left; to the right was bare stonework with pegs for cloaks. Half a dozen thick robes hung there, and he made his way towards them

Through that doorway the world was a wintry blue-white. So cold that the world felt as though it might snap or crack. The blizzard had stopped for now, and the moon had put in a rare appearance, lending the world a silvered glow. The dazzling light on the white landscape below made the world as bright now as it could ever hope to be on the sunniest of days. White-blue and perfect.

He reached up and grasped the thick fur collar of the hooded cloak on the end peg – the fleecy thick wool garment rich burgundy in colour, picked out with silver thread designs, a grand garment for a once grand family. His fingers, becoming raw with the cold already since leaving the comfort of the great hall with its roaring fires, closed on the fur.

He was aware of the movement behind him for just a fraction of a second before it happened. Something hard came down on the back of his head, scattering his wits in a flash of terrible pain. His hand went instinctively to his waist, fingers wafting across the pommel of the dagger as he tried to grip it to defend himself against this sudden and unexpected threat. Nothing happened. The fingers danced on, twitching, uncontrollable. Years of martial training rendered ineffective by a critical blow to his head. His mind was a blur of pain and panic. If he'd been able to think, to move, to react to the blow, he'd have reached up and tested his scalp. He felt sure even in the swimming nausea of agony that he would find the skull cracked and loose, blood welling up into his thick lion-mane of hair.

He fell forward as if poleaxed, almost putting his eye out on one of the cloak pegs as his face slammed into the stonework, a blow that would have been painful in itself if he could have felt anything over the agony in his scalp.

Warm blood ran down his forehead and into his eyes. He tried to blink it away, tried to think, tried to move. His body felt useless, as though it belonged to someone else. Even every ounce of will he could summon, which was almost nothing, could not even lift his finger. He slipped. He felt certain he should be falling, but seemed to be being supported. Someone was lowering him to the ground.

Thank the Lord. Thank you, kind friend.

He was on the floor now, but not on the hard cold flagstones of the antechamber. He was lying amid the comfortable folds of the cloak, the fur of the collar under his head, soaking up the blood flowing over his face. It was in his eyes, in his nose and mouth. He choked and coughed out the viscous liquid of his life, groaning and shaking.

The figure was there, just a silhouette. A darker shape within the hellish gloom of the chamber. It was probing him, moving him. It was in his garments now, feeling, pushing, grasping. What was it doing?

He tried to shout, his wits slowly returning. He had been almost knocked out completely by the blow, but he was made of hardy stuff and already he was beginning to recover from the shock, master the pain. His fingers gripped into a fist, gathering a fold of the cloak in them. The other hand went feeling for the hilt of the dagger once more, groping wildly in his slow recovery, but now they found only the empty mouth of the sheath. The blade had been removed. Blood sprayed from his lips as he tried to speak, but a hand was suddenly clamped over his mouth. He struggled. Panicked.

He was recovering his wits and even his mastery over his limbs, but not his strength. The pain and the nausea were still there and were a combination far too powerful for his potency to override them. He had been a strong man and deadly with a blade, but the suddenness and well-placed violence of the attack had unmanned him in an instant. Now he was weak, at the mercy of the figure. As he struggled and tried to rise, tried to slip out from under the gagging hand, he felt his head lifted slightly and then smacked back against the stone floor.

The thick fur beneath his skull did little to dampen the blow, and once more he felt his wits scrambled with fresh waves of pain. He threw up, the bile seeping through the fingers of his attacker, adding volume to the blood coating his face and the cloak upon which he lay. The figure was no longer probing. No longer searching, prodding, testing. The hand came away from his mouth, but he couldn't shout or scream now anyway. His mouth was full of blood and vomit and his mind was awhirl with pain and confusion.

What was happening? What had he done?

Lord help me!

But the Lord was not helping him tonight. The Lord's gaze was elsewhere.

He was being half-lifted, half-dragged, on the cloak. Where was he being taken? He could do little more than moan now, as they paused at that entrance to the wide, white world. What were they waiting for? There was silence. No movement. Nothing. Just the frantic beat of his heart and the laboured breathing of his otherwise silent attacker.

Then they were moving again. From the gloom of the antechamber they suddenly emerged into the dazzling silver world outside. The icy cold hit him like a wall, immediately driving deep into his marrow, through his hose and shirt, filling him and adding to the twin miseries of pain and nausea. His eyes blinked away blood and were blinded with the sudden light as he stared up at the moon in its blue-purple sky.

He was still moving. His feet bounced and skittered on the stone. No fleecy white snow cushioned him, for the servants had recently shovelled the drifts away and brushed the courtyard, clearing it for passage between the various doors. They were moving quickly now. There was no one else here, just attacker and victim.

He tried to cry out. Perhaps someone would hear. The Lord had forsaken him, but perhaps *someone* might yet hear. The pain, the confusion, the weakness and the thick, tin-tang of blood in his mouth made it impossible to utter more than a moan or a gurgle.

They stopped again.

He realised now that they were at the centre of the castle courtyard. He looked around desperately. No lights showed at the windows, each shuttered against the cold and the threat of fresh snow. Only the chapel shone, its windows high and largely impenetrable to more than that quiet glow, formed of small coloured panes between lines of lead. There was no one.

He was being lifted again. God, no. Not that.

Fresh nausea and more blood as he was rolled onto his side, still half-wrapped in the sodden cloak. He felt the stone of the well top, jagged and unforgiving under his shoulder and ribs, eyes blinking away blood and treating him to a view of the terrifying black maw of the well. He could see nothing but blackness in there, and the frost-coated line of the rope descending deep into the earth.

He managed just a gurgling noise that was supposed to be a plea. But he was not to be simply abandoned. To be tipped into that deep mausoleum was not to be his entire fate, for something else happened first.

He saw the flash out of the corner of his eye as the moonlight caught the blade, which then moved with a hunter's speed. His own dagger, for the love of God! The pain and nausea he'd already suffered he thought could not be matched, but he was wrong. Fresh agony and terror assailed him as the blade dug in close to his ear and then cut across his throat, catching here and there in its passage.

He could hiss now and nothing more, though it made no difference. He was a dead man already, just counting the heartbeats until he passed. He would have no last rites. No service. No mourners. No comfort. Just agony and cold eternity.

He felt his shuddering, bleeding body being pushed.

He was falling now, plummeting into the darkness.

Would it all be over before he hit the bottom?

CHAPTER ONE

ROURELL, CATALUNYA, NOVEMBER, 1208 AD

𝔄rnau de Vallbona stepped back. The sweat ran down his forehead and into his eyes, and he reached up, brushing it away with his forearm. The air was still temperate for the time of year – comfortable, if a little chilly at times – but the exertion of training made him as hot and tired as he would have been in the heart of the Aragonese summer.

He coughed, the dust cloud from their latest bout settling slowly.

Arnau's gaze rose to the gateway of the preceptory. Balthesar and Ramon stood beneath the arch, their white mantles with the red crosses stark against the honeyed stonework of the monastery walls and the brown of the parched earth around them. Both men looked faintly amused, which irritated Arnau intensely. Why couldn't they find something useful to do and leave him alone?

'You're still dropping your guard, Felipe,' he said. 'Your attacks are better every day, you're fast and accurate and intuitive, but you simply cannot rest upon your laurels after an excellent strike. The chances of you disabling an opponent with that one blow are ridiculously small, and unless you do, stepping back and taking stock is just opening yourself to a counter-attack, as you should now be very well aware.'

The young man in the black surcoat rose from the dirt, coughing in the dust and swaying slightly, using his blade to support his weight as he rose.

'And don't do that to your sword. Think of the damage the stony ground will do to the tip. You'll have to sharpen it very thoroughly this evening, and you *really* don't want to break the blade.'

His face a picture of chagrin, Felipe staggered straight. Arnau sighed. He'd hurt the lad's feelings now. Honestly, it was like having a puppy, and whenever he had cause to bring Felipe up on anything it was a little too like kicking a puppy for comfort.

'Like the brother at Montpellier,' Felipe said sheepishly. 'The one who broke a sword and was sentenced to losing his habit.'

Arnau nodded, trying hard to remember what rule that was. Two hundred, he thought. The young squire spent every free moment studying his copy of the Rule, as intent on following every stricture as he was with the Bible, though unlike the Good Book, which sat in grace in the chapel, Felipe had his own copy of the Rule. It had surprised Vallbona that the young man had his letters at all, as a poor farm lad, even if he only spoke Aragonese.

'Give the boy a chance, Vallbona,' Ramon said from the gate. 'His attacks are improving, and you can't expect him to learn everything at once.'

Arnau shot the older knight a look loaded with irritation. 'Do you mind, de Juelle? Have you nothing better to do? And anyway, *I* was expected from the start to learn everything at once.'

Memories of the repeated instances of landing flat on his backside in the dirt with the severe figure of Brother Lütolf looking down at him disapprovingly swam into his memory. How many times had he struggled before he could even hope to hold his own against the man?

'*You* were expected to learn everything at once because you were already a knight, Vallbona,' Balthesar replied. 'You'd had years of training, in bad habits admittedly, but you were passing competent with a mace and had tasted the bitter fruit of battle. Felipe is years younger than you were, with no training behind him. Go easy on him.'

Arnau threw a look of warning at the older knight, who shrugged his indifference and fell silent.

Felipe was steady now, standing well, feet braced a step and a half apart, one foot forward slightly, both hands on the hilt of his heavy sword, a sword that had once belonged to Matteu. A good soldier's weapon.

'Perhaps if I had a shield?' the young man said hesitantly.

Arnau sighed and stepped back, eying the young man. Felipe was perhaps sixteen summers now, hopelessly enthusiastic and over-helpful in everything he did. In truth, he was already an excellent squire with only three months of experience. And they were lucky to get him.

Political manoeuvrings were once more troublesome in the region. Following a period of prosperity when they had brought a 'relic' back from the Moorish island taifa, when they had afforded to rebuild the damaged preceptory and attract new brothers, things had begun to tail off once more. At least their lands were well-worked and profitable, but the popularity of Rourell began to descend once more, and it took some investigation and pulling of strings to discover that the Baron Castellvell was once more in residence in his homeland and stirring up trouble. Some fresh dispute between he and Preceptrix Ermengarda had led to him doing what he could to blacken her name afresh.

But still they received the odd donat or associate brother. Felipe's parents had died in a landslip on the farmstead they worked near Vilaverd during the previous winter, when the floodwaters of the Francoli had carried away a sizeable part of their farm. The young boy had been sent by the local landowner to Rourell, penniless and broken. Perhaps it said much about Rourell and its unconventional mistress that a stray waif might be assumed to be taken in by them. Perhaps it spoke of the preceptrix's charity and humanity, of her adherence to the Order's raison d'être as a force to protect and shelter the needy. Or perhaps that they were simply seen as a gaggle of eccentrics who might take in a charity case. Either way, Felipe had come, hands wringing, and Ermengarda had seen something in him, enough to take him in.

Certainly he had the muscle for a warrior, grown through early years of labour, and his instincts seemed good, even in wild grief.

Voices had been raised in concern, but the preceptrix had overridden them and set the task of convalescing the lad. It had taken months to heal his spirit, to the stage where Felipe had latched on to the preceptory and decided that Templar life was for him.

Clad now in the black of a sergeant, he had been given to Arnau to train, to take as a squire. There was a general feeling that the young knight had more than proved himself in that disaster at Constantinople, and Ramon had declared him every bit the knight of the Temple. Thus, finally he had been granted all those things that proclaimed him a full brother: his mantle, three horses, lance, and now a squire.

If only Felipe would follow instructions instead of trying to do what he thought was best. Arnau had to fight down that annoying little voice that suggested the older brothers had probably said almost exactly the same of him a few short years ago. Probably still did, in fact.

Felipe was looking longingly at the black and white shield with the perfectly painted red cross, as yet unmarked with dents and scratches, lying in the dirt ten paces from where they trained.

'When you have mastered using a blade without falling over or trying to impale yourself, we'll throw a shield into the training. Until then concentrate on what you have in hand. And let go with your left. How do you intend to wield sword and shield if you insist on holding the sword with both hands?'

Looking abashed once more, Felipe removed his left hand from the grip, putting it behind his back and balling it into a fist, where he would not be too tempted to use it. The sword dipped immediately, and Arnau remembered just how young and new the lad was. He might have muscles, grown large through years of labouring over the plough, but there was a difference in the type of strength a man needed for most labours and the strength needed to hold a sword forth for any length of time.

'Two more tries and we shall take a break,' he told Felipe with a touch of sympathy now in his tone. The lad smiled with relief.

The pair stepped back into position, facing one another fifty paces from the preceptory's gate on the dusty lane between fields. A breeze whispered across the flat farmland, bringing the chill and the faint salt tang of the sea eight or nine miles south. Arnau shivered. It might still be relatively warm for November, but the cold still got to him the moment he stood still and the sweat cooled. Only a few birds gave desultory hungry croaks in the silence, no hum of summer bees and cicadas now.

'All right, Felipe,' he said, changing posture. 'I shall give you an advantage, but I need you to finish and be prepared. I am going to close my eyes and you will try and strike me, though when you fail, be prepared for the consequences.'

'But if I...' the young man began.

Arnau was shaking his head. 'If you wound me, then I do not deserve to be wearing this surcoat. Do not worry about me. Just concentrate on yourself. Attack me, and make sure to be ready this time, as there will be a counterstrike, and I will not hold back.'

He straightened, lowered his blade and closed his eyes.

He could hear Felipe, could even hear in the silence that followed a strange doubt and nervousness. He heard the creaks and shush of mail as the lad changed position and lifted his sword ready. He heard the distant whispered murmurs of Balthesar and Ramon, which made him grit his teeth. He took a deep breath. Lütolf would have been proud to see him now. He almost laughed at that. Who was he trying to kid? The old German would still have found something wrong with him to pull him up on.

He heard the sound of the disturbed grit as the young squire's boot moved. He heard Felipe begin his attack. The lad was nine paces away. Arnau counted. Three. Two. One.

As Felipe leapt, sword coming out into a powerful lunge, Arnau brought his own blade up in a wide sweep from left to right, low to high. It connected with Felipe's blade at chest height and knocked the sword aside. Arnau stepped to his right, turning. His eyes opened.

Felipe had fallen forward a little and was staggering, desperately trying to bring himself back into a position to defend against an attack. Arnau continued to bring his sword up and right, and then swung it back down and across with the speed of a striking cobra.

The young squire had to leap out of the way, and only just managed. Arnau had deliberately pulled his blow so that should Felipe fail to defend he would not break a leg, and yet the way the squire had stepped, he almost walked straight into the blade regardless.

Arnau flashed a look around at the older knights in the gate as he pulled back his sword and lowered it. Both were wincing, and Arnau felt the frustration rising once more at being watched so. He was half tempted to complain to the preceptrix that if they had time to watch himself and Felipe training, then they were slacking in some other duty somewhere. The mistress of Rourell would take them to task over it, he was sure.

Heaving in a breath and sweating once more, he stepped back. Felipe was straightening.

'Once more. This time I shall allow you your strike, but watch for me upon your recovery. That is where you need to concentrate. *"Therefore be ye ready, for in what hour ye guess not,"'* he quoted. 'Matthew twenty-four.'

'Isn't that about the coming of the saviour?' Felipe asked quietly.

'In this case about the coming of the blade. Be ready.'

Felipe stepped away and straightened, grasping his sword in both hands. Arnau simply cocked an eyebrow until the lad's left hand pulled away from the hilt as though it suddenly burned hot, and jammed it behind his back once more.

'Come at me.'

Felipe did. To his credit, it was a good strike. He leapt forward but, with a speed and grace that surprised Arnau, halfway through the advance he changed foot with an odd skip and now came from a slightly different angle. Moreover, where his sword had been pulled back ready to slam forward in a simple lunge, as he changed footing, so did he change his grip, and the blade came in a sweep, right to left, at waist height.

Arnau blocked the blade with relative ease, but could feel the force of the blow from his fingertips to his shoulder, reverberating through the blade. Felipe quickly danced out of the way, and Arnau was on him, sword up and sweeping around at neck height.

Felipe was doomed. With no shield, all he had to save himself were his sword and his legs. His blade was too far down to parry, having not yet recovered from his low cut, and his footing was wrong to sidestep. Arnau had been extremely careful with his blow. The last thing he wanted to do was break the squire's neck in training, but he really had to be more prepared for counter-attacks.

Arnau's blade came in, and he pulled the blow hard so that it would stop an inch or so from Felipe's neck, but that neck wasn't there by the time the blade approached. Arnau blinked. Unable to leap out of the way or parry in adequate time, Felipe had simply dropped below the strike.

He looked down. The squire's blade had been low enough for his own counter, and the tip hovered threateningly a hand's breadth from Arnau's groin. He blinked. Heavens, but the lad had been quick.

'Now *that* was a counter-attack,' Ramon said from the gate, and Arnau looked around irritably to see both knights clapping their hands in appreciation. 'Perhaps you could teach Brother Vallbona it next time.'

Arnau felt his lip twitch in irritation and straightened, stepping back.

'Excellent, Felipe. Much better, and ingenious at that. You have earned a good half hour's rest now. Go deposit your gear in the dormitory and find yourself a cold drink and a seat somewhere. I will call for you in due course.'

The squire, grinning from ear to ear, rose and hurried back into the preceptory. As he passed through the gate between the older knights, Balthesar clapped his hand on the young man's shoulder in approval.

Vallbona spat out more dust and gathered up his rag, wiping the dirt from his sword before sheathing it and striding back towards the arch.

'He's good,' Ramon said. 'For his tender years and lack of experience, he's *very* good. In a year or so, he'll be excellent. Better than any of us were at that age.'

Arnau nodded. The man was right, of course. Arnau still had the edge, but then he had more than a decade of practice over the lad. In a year Felipe might well be just as good as him. It was something about the young man's combination of strength, speed and endurance, earned through years of farming, but also to do with confidence, which the lad seemed to be gaining daily.

He huffed.

'Training would be a lot easier without an audience.'

'There is so little entertainment to be had in winter,' Balthesar smiled. 'But we were not here on an idle whim. The preceptrix has asked for you.'

'And it took the two most senior knights in the house to find me and deliver the news?'

'So *little* entertainment,' repeated Balthesar with a grin.

Arnau followed the two older knights into the preceptory, noting with a roll of the eyes that Felipe had paused on his way in to lean against the well and leaf through his copy of the Rule, searching for some new minutia of conventual life about which to worry. With an oddly paternal smile, he passed the lad and the belfry, heading past the church and into the chapter house, Ramon and Balthesar at his shoulders. He paused at the doorway.

'Any reason I am not alone?'

'Moral support,' replied Balthesar, just as Ramon put in, 'Curiosity.'

Sighing, Arnau entered the chapter house. If anything this large hall, which was in many ways the heart of the monastery and the centre of the preceptrix's power, was now grander than it had been when he'd first arrived. After the siege that had damaged so much of the place, the rebuilding had been thorough, but there had been no real damage to the chapter house, barring a few scratches and dents in the doors. Regardless, Ermengarda d'Oluja, the undisputed mistress of Rourell, had had new cushions made for the stone benches that ran around the edge, and one of the new sergeants, who had proved to be a talented artist, had painted upon the rear wall a grand red tree, each branch carrying the name of one of the brothers or sisters of Rourell, living or departed. Ermengarda herself, of course, was the bole that supported it all. Lütolf was there, and Matteu, and everyone who had passed away in that awful battle. And on one, until recently empty, branch: Sebastian.

It still made Arnau twitch to see all those names, and the latter in particular. He had never touched a mace since that day in Constantinople, his favourite weapon lost to him for the horrific memories it carried.

The preceptrix sat in her high seat beneath the painted tree at the opposite side of the room, austere and yet in an odd way imperious, a woman holy and far removed from the base world of men, like some Madonna made flesh. The door to the church was closed, and apart from the preceptrix, the only other occupant was Jayme, another recent arrival to Rourell the previous year and now the house's scribe and clerk.

At a glance from the preceptrix, Balthesar turned and closed the main door behind them, shutting out the winter sunlight and throwing the room into a deep gloom. As Arnau's eyes adjusted they strode across the room to stand before the preceptrix, heads bowed in respect. He shivered once more. Now with exercise done, the chill of November was much more noticeable, especially away from the feeble warmth of the sun.

'Vallbona, good,' the preceptrix said. 'I am afraid I have a somewhat laborious and tedious task for you, which will take you from our walls for a time.'

Arnau frowned. If pressed, he would have had to admit that he was starting to feel a little bored and trapped with conventual life after more than three years since their return from the east. Admittedly, his last two journeys had been more than a little eventful, searching a Moorish island realm with Balthesar and enduring the dreadful sack of Constantinople with Ramon, and yet the very idea of setting forth into the great unknown once more made him itch with anticipation. He tried to force down the sudden growing excitement. It was not seemly. Moreover, a brother of the Order should not seek for self-indulgence, and he knew that above all. Still...

Balthesar and Ramon were sharing a look.

'It is, I am afraid, little more than the job of a courier or dispatch rider. I need something delivered, checked, and then hopefully returned.'

'What of the rising threat at home, might I humbly ask?' Arnau said quietly.

There had been a lull in the war with the Moor across Iberia as the Almohads secured their possessions, including Mayūrqa, sadly. The new Almohad Caliph, al-Nasir, had temporarily turned his attentions away from his Christian enemies to put his own house in order in the Maghrib. Consequently, the kingdoms of Iberia had breathed easy for a while, regrouping and preparing. But the Maghrib, it was said, was now settled. It was also said that al-Nasir once more turned his gaze north, towards Aragon, Castile and Leon. Rourell, as every other noble or religious house, knew that the time was coming for war once more. That the Almohads would soon begin their final push to control the whole peninsula. The end days were coming for one people, for Iberia could only be one or the other: Christian or Moorish.

It seemed odd to send away a knight, even a relatively young one, on some administrative duty when the enemy might turn north at any time.

The preceptrix nodded her understanding. 'It is the considered opinion of the Aragonese court and our mother house both that when al-Nasir decides upon his return to Iberia, the time it will take for his forces to assemble and prepare will be more than a year. We will have adequate warning. And while your task will take you far from home, it should not take a great length of time. I anticipate your return by the spring. I will, of course, keep your two brothers here at Rourell, against an unexpected call to arms.'

Arnau still fretted. 'But Brother Jayme—' he began.

'No, Brother Arnau. Jayme is a valued member of this house, but his experience with arms is limited. This is the job of a knight, for the documents are valuable, and must be well guarded.'

Now Arnau frowned again. Jayme stepped towards him at a gesture from the preceptrix. He held out a letter, sealed with wax and bearing the twin knightly figures sharing a horse – the Order's symbol. He peered at it. It did not seem much to require a knight's protection. He looked up.

'No, Vallbona, this is not your burden. This is simply instructions for the clerk at the mother house at Barberà. You will take your squire and all you require for a considerable journey. Jayme will supply you with appropriate funds to last. Journey to Barberà, and there use this document to retrieve a set of deeds. The mother house is, of course where we lodge records of all donations to the Order. There you will acquire the documents relating to the gifts of Lütolf von Ehingen.'

Arnau blinked. What in the world could those documents be needed for? As if reading his mind, the preceptrix leaned forward and gestured at the letter.

'We have received word through the mother house that Brother Lütolf's nephew, at a place named Renfrizhausen in Swabia, has produced a will, purported to be that of our beloved and missed brother, which promises to his nephew those lands currently held by the Order. Needless to say, the Order is far from keen to return to the family lands that have been in our possession for years, but there are niceties involved. The Order has little influence in the lands of the Germans, and they are a strange and unknown people. Their relationship with the west is troubled, their king often at odds with the great kings of Aragon, France and England.'

'Surely, sister, our status as Knights of the Lord must overcome mere lay divisions?' Arnau said.

'The division goes deep, Vallbona. Our Order fought in strength alongside England and France in the Holy Land, while the Germans largely turned back at their emperor's death en route, and few of our people helped them in their difficult time in Turk lands. Some of the eastern lords have close alliances with the Teutonic

Order at the cost of our own connections. Our holdings within the German Empire are obscure and small, and favour is given to their own orders.'

Ermengarda leaned back in her seat. 'Even their Crusaders usually join a German-only order, shunning the established ones. We must be seen to abide by the very letter of the law. If it turns out to be true that our departed brother had, indeed, promised those lands to his nephew, and our bequest has been superseded, then we will be forced to relinquish them, which creates many headaches.'

Arnau nodded. He could imagine how those lands and funds had been moved around, divided up, changed and exchanged in twenty years. They almost certainly were not in Rourell's keeping, for a start. He sucked his teeth.

'I am no lawyer, Preceptrix. Not like Brother Ramon.'

Ramon snorted. 'This is very straightforward, Vallbona,' the older knight replied. 'As long as the documents are genuine, then it is simply a matter of dates. If their documents are real, then they will be sealed with the stamp of Lütolf von Ehingen, which remains with his few personal possessions that are kept in this very preceptory. If they bear any other seal, then they are fakes. If they are genuine, then they will also be dated. Very simply the latest date holds the precedence. If this new will postdates our bequeath and it is genuine, then we must give up the lands and finances to the nephew. If the date on the document you carry is newer, then we retain the bequest, and the family have no claim.'

Arnau straightened. 'This is a great deal of responsibility.'

'That it is, Brother Vallbona,' the preceptrix agreed. 'You are one of my knights. One of a trinity in whom I place all my trust and faith. Do not tell me that my trust and faith are misplaced. I charge you with this task. Collect the documents from Barberà, convey them to Renfrizhausen and compare them there with the new will of this nephew, one Rüdolf von Ehingen de Rottenburg. With the grace of God, our cause will be upheld and you will be able to return immediately with our holdings intact. If they are not to be held so, then you will leave our records with the family along with our apologies and return empty-handed. Jayme will find you

Brother Lütolf's preserved personal effects, which should perhaps be returned to the family.'

Arnau nodded slowly and straightened.

Swabia. Far-off German lands, away in the north. He shivered, and only partly with excitement.

THE WINTER KNIGHT

CHAPTER TWO

RENFRIZHAUSEN, LATE NOVEMBER, 1208 AD

rnau brought his horse wearily to a halt as the road wound between copses of larch, oak and linden, all boughs drooping and low, heavy with packed snow. The drifts of white at the edge of the woods were almost as tall as a man, denying any hope of access to foresters and hunters. Winter here seemed to be a different beast entirely to the slightly chilly winters in Catalunya. At least the road was relatively clear, having been kept so by repeated pressure of feet, hooves and wheels travelling between Renfrizhausen and the river.

He shivered and pulled the entirely inadequate white mantle around himself slightly tighter, a futile gesture in this freezing world.

Sülz.

He had enjoyed Sülz about as much as every other town since they had left the valley of the Saone and begin to climb.

Catalunya was his homeland, and travelling to and beyond Narbonne had been comfortable and familiar. Then, for the rest of that journey, into the third week, it had still been easy enough. They had been content, skirting the highlands of south-central France and sticking to the lowlands and valleys with little wintry difficulty. Arnau spoke French. Everyone at court spoke French, and in Catalunya many of the low-born were proficient in that tongue too.

Then they had passed through the county of Toulouse and the Auvergne region, through the Duchy of Burgundy and into increasingly high hills, leaving the territory of everything remotely familiar. As they travelled higher and higher through Belfort, Mulhouse and Freiburg, everything changed. The architecture became more severe, austere and angular, the names jagged and unpronounceable, the landscape hard and unforgiving. And the people?

No one seemed to speak French. In truth, Arnau was fairly sure that many of them could, but none seemed inclined to regardless, addressing the travelling Templars in their own unfamiliar and guttural tongue. Once they left the French lands, where the Order had its true origins, they lost all the benefits of their house, for these high, jagged German lands had no contact with the Order, and Templars were to them no more important than any other foreign knight.

It was, he suspected, not so much a case of the locals not liking them as not understanding or trusting them. Perhaps it was understandable in some ways. Not very long ago, lords of the Holy Roman Empire, of which all these lands were part, had been in furious conflict with Richard of England and the men of the red cross. There was a cultural divide that was clear, yet, Arnau hoped, not insurmountable.

He had paused for a whole day early in their journey, halfway through their own lands, at the monastery of Santa Maria de Ripoll, famed across the region for its library. There he had read all he could find and plumbed the monks for information on the lands of Swabia and the Holy Roman Empire, all while Felipe prayed and saw to their gear and animals. What he had discovered was not encouraging. The few books that held odd nuggets of information were largely geographical and historical, though the monks seemed oddly, given their nature, to have more current political and social information for him.

They had left Ripoll with Arnau slightly better informed, and thus had begun the long journey's odd tit-for-tat conversations. Throughout the ride thereafter, Arnau would speak of what he had learned of their destination, while Felipe would question him instead about the Rule of the Order. It was a tiring business, and after the first few days, somewhat uncharitably, Arnau began to ride just far enough ahead to make conversation difficult, leaving Felipe studying his book in the saddle.

'It seems that the king there is not a hereditary role such as those of Aragon or Castile, or even the Counts of Barcelona,' Arnau had said as they passed the mountains in the north of Catalunya. 'Their king is elected by a gathering of nobles and churchmen. It would seem that there is an odd friction between church and state there, and the nobles and the Pope's men each vie to put their chosen figure on the throne. A peculiar arrangement.'

Felipe had nodded and then frowned, pointing at the small inn for which they were making for the night. 'Brother Arnau, the seventieth rule states that we should not eat or drink in a tavern. We have already done so on two separate occasions, and we are only a short distance into our journey. Should we be so blatantly breaking the Order's Rule?'

Arnau had sighed and turned in his saddle. 'The sad fact is that we cannot spend each night within monastic walls. There are houses we can turn to in places during our journey, but if we are to achieve our task, then we must needs make use of base accommodation and do such penance as is required later. Were it high summer I would camp in the open and abide by the Rule without question, but it is deep winter and rule seventy can hang if it means a roaring fire and a solid roof above us.'

That had earned staunch disapproval from Felipe, but he had gone along with it anyway, trusting in the senior brother.

Such conversations had been the norm throughout the southern lands.

'The nobles of Swabia seem to be called "*Graf*" from what I have read. They seem to work on a system of patronage, with lesser nobles owing to greater all the way up to the king who, strangely, is elected by even the lowest of them.'

'Brother Arnau, I do not think I could take penance for staying in low inns if it meant losing my habit. The 119th rule states that in such a case, we would be lodged in the Almoner's house, not granted access to the chapel, and say our hours and work with the slaves.'

Arnau had sagged in the saddle once more. 'If I remember rightly that same rule states that if the habit is taken from a man, he is quit of all his penances. You are worrying about legal minutiae, Felipe.'

'But it is the *Rule*, brother. It is the unbreakable law of the Order.'

Arnau turned, irritably. 'The laws you continually quote are from the Aragonese Rule, Felipe, and from additional clauses, rather than the Order's general monastic Rule. How you came to be given the book is beyond me. Such manuscripts are usually kept only among the masters, in order to prevent just such confusion and distress among brothers.'

'But it is still the Rule.'

Arnau had become angry then, turning once more. 'Felipe, many of these rules were imposed by some Aragonese master while serving in the east, possibly even in Cyprus. Half of them do not even apply to life in Iberia. Should a brother be known to break rules, it is not those same masters who sit in judgement over him, but the brothers of his own house. Ramon, Balthesar and the preceptrix herself will judge our actions upon our return, and each of those three great brothers and sisters of the Order are well aware of the fundamental difficulty in following every last tiny rule in circumstances such as these. Now for the last time will you please stop prattling on about losing your habit and think about Swabia and what lies ahead for a change.'

Two days had passed after that without a social word exchanged until Arnau had finally relented to the puppy-like misery of his travelling companion and tried to make up with him. Once he had finally cajoled Felipe back into conversation, he immediately regretted it.

'I think I should call you commander, brother, instead of brother.'

'What?'

'Rule 144 states that if we're on business and there is no commander among us—'

'For the love of God, Felipe, close the book.'

'Why are there no German Templars, Brother Arnau?'

The sudden tangent in conversation threw Arnau completely and he floundered for a moment. 'I… I believe it's simply a matter of nationality. Since the days of the first great expedition to the Holy Land, the knights of the Empire kept to themselves, even tending their own hospitals. When our own illustrious Order was founded, it was done so by Frankish knights with no German blood, and they continued to work in their own hospitals and groups in the Holy Land thereafter. Finally, some two decades ago they were granted their own fraternity by Papal Bull. With the Teutonic Order now growing in strength, there is little chance that our Order will ever gain brotherhood and influence in their lands. Indeed, Brother Lütolf having joined Rourell is extremely unusual, and I have never entirely understood the reason for it. Perhaps we might learn of it while we are here?'

Felipe had nodded and begun to leaf through his book again. Spotting this, Arnau had deliberately ridden ahead once more.

And so it had gone all the way, until they climbed into the mountains that seemed to separate the Frankish world from the Germans, and the cold had silenced them both, for to sit with mouth open was too much toothache to contemplate.

Finally, they had passed through the standoffish Germanic towns where they had been forced to rely upon inns each night for there seemed to be no monastic foundations. In these places all communication had been achieved by gesture and repeated trial and error, for no one seemed to want to speak a tongue they knew, and neither of the travellers could understand even one iota of the local language.

Sülz had been the worst of the lot, for they had known now that they were close to their destination. Thus far, since leaving Burgundy, they had managed to glean directions from town to town simply by using the next name on their proposed route. Now, though, Sülz had been the last town on their journey, and only the fortress of Lütolf's family remained. They had tried in the inn last night in Sülz.

'Renfrizhausen?' Arnau had asked, pointing off in what he hoped was an easterly direction.

'*Ja*,' the bearded, pot-bellied man behind the counter had agreed, a word Arnau had learned through its association with nods to mean 'yes'. 'Renfrizhausen *dorf und die kirche von Heilige Georg. Nehmen sie die linke strasse, vorbei am kreuz und über die kleine brücke. Oder suchst du die schloss?*'

Arnau had stepped back, flabbergasted by the stream of incomprehensible German.

'Renfrizhausen?' he had tried again, trying not to look embarrassed.

The innkeeper had beckoned him out into the snow, which had begun to come down in a fresh fall at dusk, and had stopped in the square, pointing past the small stone cross at the centre to the left hand of two roads.

'*Hier*,' he had said simply.

Arnau had nodded his thanks and had paid above the odds at the end of the night.

'Seemed a lot of verbiage to simply say "left",' he'd later grumbled to Felipe when they were alone.

They had set off at dawn the next morning. The snow had not stopped during the night, though now it had thinned out to a light shower of delicate flakes in a lead-grey sky. Felipe had fetched Arnau's horses from the stables. Marte, his chestnut destrier, had been a recent acquisition and had been unburdened during the journey, barring an hour or two of granting the other beast rest. No knight rode his warhorse on a long journey, saving the animal for when it was needed. And so he had ridden his palfrey, Canción, leading Marte and his pack pony Bixcocho. As a squire, of course, Felipe had only his pony Picante, who lived up to her name, his gear being packed with Arnau's.

They had set off through the light flurries, down that leftmost of the two roads. Crossing a narrow bridge over some unnamed stream that ran like black water between gleaming white banks, they left the houses of Sülz behind, skirting a hill to the north, keeping parallel with the great River Neckar. They could see the other road out of this side of the town, heading south between hills, but, like this road, once it left the urban area the night's snowfall made it almost impossible to trace the route.

This road was only visible with concentration, and only because of hedges, lines of trees, and the gentle camber. In every other respect it was indistinguishable from the white ground to either side.

Still they had plodded on, following the road along the low slope of the hill, tracking the river eastwards until some two or three miles later they had reached a fork in the road and found a small hamlet where one of the more helpful strangers they had met on their journey had directed them south with a single pointed finger.

Now, a mile or so from the river, they had emerged from between trees and reached Renfrizhausen, a fact confirmed by a squat, misshapen stone cross standing close to the road, with the name carved crudely in the horizontal shaft, peeking out from beneath the settled snow like a lurking homunculus.

'At least they're God-fearing Christians,' Felipe murmured.

'Of course they are. After all, Brother Lütolf came from here.'

But in truth he did not feel half as confident as he had tried to sound.

'Where now, Brother Arnau?'

The older knight sat astride Canción, peering through the almost-stopped fluttering snow at the squat, dark town that lay before them. In truth, 'town' was being a little over-generous. It was really little more than a rural village with delusions of grandeur, timber structures with black roofs covered in thick white, nestled in the unforgiving blanket of winter. Arnau could see the tower of a small church, but nothing that might be a castle.

Frowning, he looked about in the eye-watering pale world. Castles in this land, he'd noted, tended to be built high on crags and peaks, unlike the fortresses of Catalunya, many of which would sit on good arable land. He couldn't immediately identify a potential castle-like shape on any of the surrounding hills, but then they were covered with trees and half-hidden by threatening snow cloud.

'I think we had better seek directions in the town.'

Kicking his horse into motion, they moved on down into Renfrizhausen, a higgledy-piggledy collection of narrow streets and squat, square buildings. The roads were deserted, it still being relatively early in the day and the weather such as to discourage emerging from warm hovels. There were marks in the snow, though, signs of the passage of men and beasts.

Shivering once more, and wishing his mantle were ten times its actual thickness, Arnau made for the tower of the church. Hauling on his reins outside the graveyard, he noted two hunched, miserable looking figures busy digging a familiarly-shaped hole in the white ground. Calling to them, he leaned in the saddle, and then suddenly realised he had no idea what to say. He was already at Renfrizhausen, and these men would be very unlikely to speak French.

Chewing his lip as the two men downed tools and crossed to the gate in the wall, he prepared himself and slipped from the saddle, handing the reins to Felipe.

'Castillo de Renfrizhausen?' he hazarded. 'Er... *Castrum*? *Chateau*? Castle?'

The men shared a look of incomprehension and then shrugged at him in unison.

'Graf of Renfrizhausen?'

The men frowned, but it looked as though he was onto something now.

'Graf von Ehingen?' he tried.

'*Ehingen und Rottenberg*?' one of the men asked.

'I think so, yes. Er... *Ja*.'

'*Auf dem südlichen hügel*,' he said authoritatively.

Arnau winced. With a sudden thought, he drew his dagger, at which the men lurched backwards until he waved them down. Crouching, he drew a crude battlemented wall and tower in a patch of pristine snow. Pointing at it, he said 'Graf *von Ehingen*?'

Tracing his battlements with the dagger tip, he said 'Castle. *Castillo. Castrum.*'

The heavier set of the two men nodded. '*Schloss*,' he said flatly, then grabbed a stick from near the wall and crouched, tracing those same battlements. '*Schloss.*'

Arnau smiled and nodded back. '*Schloss*. Castle is *schloss*. Good. Now where?' He gave an exaggerated shrug and pointed in half a dozen directions.

The man took a breath and pointed behind him to a forested hill south of the village. '*Sehe*,' he said, a command in his tone as he found a new patch of snow and began to draw with his stick.

'*Hier. Hier ist Renfrizhausen, ja?*' He drew a stylised church and a few squares. Arnau nodded. '*Hier*,' the man repeated, and drew a line, snaking from the church in a south-westerly direction. Frowning for a moment as he paused, he reached across and scooped up a huge pile of snow, dropping it in a heap and then shaping into a bulbous Y shape. He then pointed at the lump and at the hill to the south. Arnau nodded his understanding. The man drew a series of curving lines around the hill and a few stylised trees to make its forested nature clear. Then he jammed the stick in the top of the mound of snow and pointed to Arnau's drawing. '*Schloss.*'

Arnau grinned. 'Thank you. Thank you so much, my friend.'

He retrieved a few coins from his purse, more than he could really justify giving a man for directions, but he was simply so pleased not only to be shown a clear path, but to have found helpful locals, that he was feeling especially generous. Leaving the two pleased-looking gravediggers behind, he mounted once more and gestured to Felipe, with a last, lingering look at the map in the snow.

They left the village on that south-westerly road, grateful as the last flakes fell from the sky, leaving only brooding low cloud and a crisp cold. Arnau had memorised the map well, and was sure of his directions, but as they began to climb and the trees closed in about them it became harder and harder to identify where they were, there seemingly being more side paths than he'd anticipated.

By the time they were way out of sight of the village and had been riding half an hour, he was lost. Still, he reasoned, the castle was at the summit of this spur of the hill. As long as they kept climbing, in theory they would eventually find the place.

He lost heart for a while when they seemed to have doubled back on themselves without noticing and revisited their own tracks, but biting down in the disappointment, they pressed on. It was hard going in the snow here in the narrow tracks between the trees, and even though they remained mounted it was looking increasingly like they'd soon have to drop to the ground and travel on foot, for the trails they snaked along were becoming increasingly small.

He harrumphed with irritation, then shuddered with the cold. Behind him, Felipe said something, but the creaking of laden boughs and the howling of the wind through the forest dampened all other sound and Arnau couldn't make out what was said. Frustrated, he turned sharply, leaning back in the saddle to ask his squire to repeat himself, and that simple and chance action saved his life.

The arrow thrummed through the air so close to Arnau's neck that he felt the rush of wind with its passage even over the ever-present breeze. For just the blink of an eye he had no idea where it had come from, but instinct swiftly took over. The arrow had gone past right to left, across his horse, so the archer had to be in the trees to the right.

He threw himself from the saddle with little grace but every available iota of speed.

By the time he'd rolled, grunted, stood and shook his head to clear the snow that had covered his face with his landing, they were coming. Four of them, shapes of black emerging from the dark grey beneath the tree canopy. He noted in passing that the thick blanket of snow was working to his advantage, for it had cushioned a pretty poor fall, and was now hampering the approach of the four men as they laboured through the knee-deep drift.

'Dismount,' he bellowed at Felipe. This was no place for mounted combat, with only enough room for single-file horseback travel, and treacherous branches hanging low to either side. And there were the horses to worry about, also. They were a long way from home and would need all four beasts for the return to Rourell. Plus, as Felipe had undoubtedly mentioned more than once from his little book, losing a horse could be a serious offence for a brother, though only if neglect could be proven.

As Felipe dropped from his saddle and grabbed his sword hilt, yanking the thing free with difficulty, Arnau drew his own blade and weighed things up. The four figures had split apart. Two were coming for him, the dangerous target, one for Felipe and the other was heading to the rear. To the pack animal. Damn it.

Their shields were packed for travel, and Arnau settled himself for an attack without, feet planted apart in the snow, toes already becoming numb as the freezing damp settled into his boots. The two men were unarmoured, though wearing heavy leathers and furs that might well turn aside a blade simply though their thickness. They each held a single weapon, one an old, plain sword, the other a stout ash cudgel. Both men wore cowls that hid their features.

Not professional warriors, Arnau surmised. Opportunists? Bandits and thieves? Well, they would regret their actions this day.

'This is the word of the Lord,' Arnau bellowed into the muted snowy air, 'not in a host, neither in strength, but in my spirit, saith the Lord of hosts.' He let his lip curl into a feral snarl that he knew looked fearsome with his beard. 'And my spirit is as great as the Lord's fury.'

Sword man came at him first, sword lancing out inexpertly. Arnau would have performed a perfectly neat sidestep, but this terrain was unfamiliar to him. He had never fought in snow this deep, and found that it inhibited his movement far more than he'd expected. In the end the man's sword only just missed him, and his response, which would have been perfect on dry, flat dusty ground, barely connected. Oh, he drew blood from the man's left bicep, and it hurt, because the German gave a bellow of pain, snarled something unintelligible in his growling tongue, and staggered back.

Arnau left him to it, turning to the second man, who was busy swinging his ash club. Arnau dropped beneath the sweeping blow, not having to move his legs to do so, and therefore not troubled by the snow. His hand came out, heel first and still gripping his sword. The pommel smashed into the club-man's face and he screeched as bone broke beneath the heavy iron globe.

With time to breathe, Arnau took two difficult paces back, standing beside his charger, who stood passive, untroubled by the violence going on about him. Flicking his hand around, he lunged at the staggering, half-blind club wielder. The blade sank between layers of fur and plunged deep into the man's torso.

Arnau turned to spot the other man. He took precious moments to locate the shadowy shape, where the bandit had disappeared beneath the trees once more, and as his eyes adjusted enough to pick out details, he felt a moment of panic. The shape he could see was that of a man drawing the string of a bow, an arrow glinting in the dappled light.

He moved right a pace. To his relief, the arrow tracked his motion. Thank the Lord. He was sure he'd survive, but he had to get away from Marte, lest that arrow put down his destrier for good. Two more hurried sidesteps, each tracked with the arrow, and he was out away from the horse.

He took a deep breath, watching carefully.

The man released his missile.

Unlike a crossbow, which has an impressive turn of speed from the outset, an arrow picks up momentum for a moment as it leaves the bow, and there is the precious space of a heartbeat as the string snaps tight and the arrow departs. Arnau had seen it enough to recognise the very moment the archer's fingers twitched free.

He was in a roll in the snow by the time the arrow hummed through the freezing air towards him, then looked this way and that as he rose once more. He wouldn't be able to avoid arrows all day. The archer was busy drawing a new one from his quiver, but there were other problems too. Felipe had managed to hold his own against a swordsman. He'd even wounded the man, but he was on the defensive now and in an almost comedic manner was backing around his pony in a circle, with the enraged and bloodied German stomping along in his wake and shouting demands in his guttural language. Beyond him, the fourth man was busy rifling through their bags on the pack pony. Damn it, but the *documents* were in there. He couldn't let the man get anything. The man seemed to be unarmed, though. Arnau looked this way and that, knowing he was needed in all three directions.

Gritting his teeth and praying he didn't take a stray arrow, he ignored his own opponent and leapt at the man attacking Felipe. It was not difficult for he took the man in the back. His sword entered the bandit's side near his kidney and punched in so hard he felt the tip come out free through his belly. The man screamed, the noise swiftly descending to a gurgle, and Arnau hurriedly twisted and freed his blade, the fuller helping prevent the sucking wound from holding onto it.

As the man fell, Arnau was already moving. Felipe was staring at him with a mixture of relief, pride and shock. Arnau was pointing over his shoulder. 'Stop that thief with our bags,' he bellowed, then turned to go after the archer.

He left Felipe to it. The thief had seemed unarmed, and the squire should be able to deal with him, or at least frighten him off. But then, they did not seem so easily deterred. In Arnau's experience, bandits tended to abandon their attack and flee the moment it looked as though they would not win with ease. These men were fighting hard, though. He had to remind himself that he knew little about these Germanic peoples and their tough, mountain ways, and winters such as this would make even a coward desperate enough to fight for a warm meal.

He could see the man now. He had given up with his arrows and was leaving the shadow of the trees. Arnau gritted his teeth. Though he knew it was foolish, he gave chase. The man was on the run, and by rights Arnau ought to go back and help Felipe, to save the gear. Yet something about the very idea of letting this man get away with what he'd done sat badly with Arnau, and he found himself growling like a wild beast as he sprinted as best he could through the deep snow after the fleeing robber. The man emerged onto a side path and started to run that way, and Arnau turned off his own road in pursuit. They were almost of a match, speed-wise, and the man remained consistently twenty paces ahead. Worst of all, he continued to turn down new routes, and Arnau tried hard to remember the directions as he followed, aware how easily he could get lost here.

The bandit's fate was a matter of pure serendipity. He suddenly went down like a sack of grain, issuing an awkward squawk. Likely his foot had caught in a rabbit hole or suchlike. Arnau's could so easily have done as much too, but he'd managed not to, through fortune and the favour of the Lord.

The man struggled to get upright, though his ankle was turned, and he immediately fell once more with a cry. Before he could rise a second time, Arnau was on him, sword coming round in a swing.

The man bellowed as the blade bit into his neck.

The Templar paused then, heaving in breaths, praying that Felipe had managed with the fourth man. He approached the fallen bandit, dispatched him with a quick blow for mercy, which he probably didn't deserve, then straightened once more.

As he looked up, he blinked.

The Lord's great plan truly was beyond the ken of mortal man.

At the end of this latest wide path, a heavy, stark stone gatehouse rose, beyond it a fortress of unforgiving grey, its black roofs covered with thick snow, banners snapping in the wind, too mobile and high up to make out well.

The castle. Bandits so close to the demesne of a lord and his soldiers seemed odd, but then it was the depths of harsh winter, and desperation drove men to unexpected acts of violence. And, Arnau once more had to remind himself, the red cross of the Order was unlikely to make them popular even with the law abiding Germans.

'Thank you, you godless animal,' he said to the body of the bandit with an air of satisfaction, then turned and, grasping the man's belt, began to drag him back through the forest. He'd had no idea how long he had been chasing the man through the woods, but it took him around half an hour to make it back, though he had to admit to taking two wrong turns on the journey, despite their tracks in the snow.

He was immensely relieved to find Felipe leaning against a tree trunk and drinking from his flask. The body of the fourth robber lay in the snow close by, and all four horses were tethered.

'Excellent work, Felipe,' he announced as he approached, dumping the archer's body in the snow with his friends. As the lad broke into a tired but satisfied smile at the complement, Arnau bent and looked at the body, which lay on its back in the thick white.

It *was* excellent work, too. The man had been killed with a single blow to the throat, and from the front, so Felipe had not simply surprised the man from behind. As the squire grinned and proffered the flask, Arnau couldn't help but join in the smile. The lad was just too damn likeable. He took the flask and lifted it to his lips, taking a gulp.

He stopped, lowered it, frowning. 'Wine? I thought it would be water.'

'Water is no comfort on a day like this, Brother Arnau. Wine warms the soul.'

Arnau laughed and took another pull. 'Aren't you lucky that only custom limits wine to our evenings, and not the Rule?'

Felipe chuckled. 'Many of these rules were imposed by some Aragonese master while serving in the east,' he quoted, 'possibly even in Cyprus. Half of them do not even apply to life in Swabia.'

Arnau couldn't help but laugh. 'Well, as it happens, chasing these low villains brought me right to the door of the castle. The *schloss*. And in good time, I think.' He looked up. 'These clouds belly heavy with further snow. Let's get into safety before we are buried afresh.'

THE WINTER KNIGHT

CHAPTER THREE

WEDNESDAY MORNING

The gates of Schloss Renfrizhausen stood resolutely closed, a great barrier of iron-studded oak in a grey stone façade that defied all approach. Windows were visible but only high, the lower reaches showing only narrow slits. This was no palatial home built for comfort and display like the Castillo of the Counts of Barcelona, but a stark fortress, constructed with an eye only for defence and strength. Already, despite the earliness of the hour, golden glows of fires and torches issued from the upper windows, warding off the bitter chill of the white, snowy world.

Approaching, cold and weary, as the latest snowfall began to settle upon their shivering forms, Arnau slipped from the saddle with a shush of chain, handing his reins to Felipe, who also held those of the destrier and the packhorse. Slapping his hard leather gloves together to remove the snow, he stepped over to the gate and reached up. The great iron knocker that hung from a hinge on the door set within the gate was in the shape of a curled dragon, and Arnau frowned at the strange demonic imagery as he lifted it and cracked it against the timbers three times before standing back.

There was a prolonged silence, made all the more noticeable by the snowfall that suppressed all the background sounds of nature. He was about to reach up to the knocker again when he heard the clack of three bolts being withdrawn and the rattle of keys. Finally, the door swung inwards.

'*Ja? Wer bist du?*'

Arnau sucked his teeth. Damn it, but he'd not contemplated that the man at the door might not understand him.

'Me Arnau de Vallbona. Knight of the Temple. Templar, see?' He pulled back his cloak to display openly the red cross that had been folded in as he huddled in the garment for warmth. 'Templar. With Lütolf of Ehingen.'

The guard, for that was clearly what he was, in a padded gambeson with a basic kettle hat, a plain sword at his waist and all overlaid with a heavy fur-lined cloak, huffed. He wore a short beard and his hair was long, poking out beneath the helm, his expression suspicious, eyes glittering like coal. He chewed on his lip and peered at Arnau, then at Felipe and the horses.

'*Warten sie hier.*'

Whatever that meant, the door was suddenly shut once more and a bolt thrown. Arnau presumed he was supposed to wait, and stood in the gradually thickening snowfall, arms wrapped tightly round his chest as he shivered. He was reaching up for the knocker when the door opened once more. This time, the man at the door wore a surcoat, though Arnau couldn't make out the design beneath the heavy cloak of wool and fleece. His head was bare and he had short-cropped white-blond hair and a neatly cut short beard of the same colour. His face was weathered and worn, for he was not young and was clearly a warrior as a few lines of old scars marred the skin.

He stared at Arnau, then tapped his lip.

'You speak the language of the Franks?' he asked in good, if accented, French.

Arnau nodded, relieved. 'I am Arnau de Vallbona, a knight of the Temple and frater of the late Brother Lütolf of Ehingen. I have been sent by the Order to compare the will of the late brother with the one purportedly held by his nephew, one Rüdolf of Ehingen.' He glanced up and snowflakes landed on his eyelashes, making him blink. 'Look, I don't mean to be rude, but might we come in. The weather is becoming increasingly poor.'

The man frowned and looked up at the sky as though he had no idea what Arnau might mean and that this was the balmy norm for the area. Arnau hoped that wasn't the case, though it might account for the generally surly nature he had noted in the populace, and the severe personality of Lütolf.

'Very well. Please wait.'

The door closed again, and the bolts and rattle of keys were audible before the gate itself opened, wide and high enough to admit the horses too. Arnau stepped inside and joined the white-blond man in the cover of the gate arch, while the guard held the gate open for Felipe and the horses.

'It is not that someone was not expected,' the man said. 'We knew someone from the Temple would come, but the timing is not good. Very unfortunate, in fact.'

Arnau frowned. 'Oh? How so?'

'The family has suffered a tragedy. I—'

A dry, scratchy voice in the German tongue barked out something, and the man turned, looking up at a woman of advanced years leaning out of a window, holding the wimple of her headgear over her like some kind of awning, fending off the falling snow.

'*Hier ist ein Tempelritter, Euer Hochwohlgeboren.*' He flashed an apologetic look at Arnau and then turned back to the old woman. '*Er spricht kein deutsch.*' Then to Arnau. 'I explain who you are and that you do not speak our language.'

Arnau nodded gratefully.

The woman threw him a look she probably usually reserved for diseased rodents, and sneered. '*Dann, was nützt er?*'

Throwing him that look again, she retreated inside and slammed the shutters tight.

The man shrugged. 'The high lady Ute von Ehingen.' His voice dropped to a conspiratorial whisper. 'It is said that if she had been born a man, she would have wrested the crown from its owner's grip and ruled the world.' His brief smile slipped away swiftly.

Arnau jumped as the gate slammed shut behind him. The blond man issued instructions to his man as he fastened the bolts and lock once more, and the guard nodded and took the horses' reins from Felipe, waiting for the squire to dismount and join Arnau.

'I have told Anselm to stable your horses.'

Arnau nodded, then held up a hand and hurried over to the beasts. Swiftly, he unfastened one of the bags and heaved it over to Felipe, handing it to the squire. 'My personal effects and the important baggage for our visit,' he explained. 'I cannot let it out of my sight, I am afraid.'

The man shrugged, nodded, and then waved the guard called Anselm away with the horses and the rest of the baggage.

'I am Bernhard Bulstrich. I am what you will call, I think, the marshal of this *schloss*. I command the guards and all matters of security for the family. And you are Arnau of Valbony?'

'Vallbona. This is my squire, Felipe.'

Bernhard issued a curt bow from the neck only. 'I had the honour to meet a few knights of your Order in the south in the days of the emperor Barbarossa and his son. We did not see Jerusalem sadly, but I fought alongside the red cross against the Turk.' He looked apologetic once more. 'Many of my countrymen do not trust the knights of your Order, sadly. They see the Temple as allies not of Rome, but of the ruthless warmonger Richard of England and the dangerously expansionist Phillip of France. Our noble houses prefer to show favour to their own Teutonic knights and not see their profits wend their way back to France.'

Arnau nodded. He'd expected as much. 'With luck, my visit will not be extended and disruptive. A comparison of the wills and confirmation of which takes precedence, and I will leave. I had the greatest respect for Brother Lütolf, who trained me within the Order, and I have no wish to cause problems for his kin.'

Bernhard winced. 'As I said, your timing is poor. I understand your mission, but we have suffered a tragedy.'

Arnau's eyes narrowed. 'Might I ask who? What?'

The marshal nodded. 'Hochwohlgeboren Rüdolf, Graf von Ehingen de Rottenburg, passed away not two days since. The family is in mourning.'

Arnau stepped back, shocked. 'The nephew of Brother Lütolf? The heir of the castle?'

Bernhard nodded. 'It was a great shock. A bad end, also.'

Arnau felt the hair on the back of his neck rise, his skin prickling. 'Foul deeds?'

'Yes. His throat was cut.'

Arnau took a deep breath. 'That is terrible. And, I have to say, more than a little suspicious, given my imminent arrival and the matter of contested wills.' His grip on the bag with the precious document and Lütolf's personal effects tightened suddenly.

'It is a strange coincidence, is it not.'

'With the loss of the graf, who rules here now? Who inherits after Graf Rüdolf? I will need to speak to the most senior family member about this matter. Would it be the lady... Ute, was it?'

Bernhard shook his head. 'The graf's father is head of the household, Dietmar von Ow.'

Arnau sighed, already having to repeatedly mutter the names under his breath to commit them to memory. It would be bad enough meeting a castle full of new people, but with their strange Germanic names and honorifics, it was going to require a major feat of memory to get through the next few hours.

'Might I speak with this Dietmar? I do not wish to impose in such a time. If we can compare wills, I might even be able to depart today and reach town by nightfall.'

Bernhard shook his head again. 'Only a fool would attempt to strike for town now, Master *Tempelritter*. The snow is getting heavier once more, and from the clouds I cannot see it stopping before dawn. The ways down through the forest will be extremely hazardous.'

'And there's the bandits, I suppose,' Arnau mused.

'Bandits?'

'Yes. We were attacked by four robbers in the woods. They went for our possessions, but we managed to fight them off without too much trouble.'

Bernhard seemed shocked, his brow creased. 'They took nothing, I hope? You are uninjured?'

'No. Nothing taken, and we escaped unharmed. But perhaps you are right. If we might impose upon you for shelter until the weather lets up, then we will not risk bandits and becoming lost in the forest and the snow.'

'Of course. And you are not dressed for this weather. Your name... you are from Sicilia?'

'Aragon,' Arnau replied. 'Iberia, in the west.'

'Your weather is like that of Outremer. Hot and dry. You are not prepared for a Swabian winter. We shall see to that.'

'Perhaps I might meet with this Dietmar?' Arnau pushed again. 'The matter of the wills is of some import.'

'The graf is in mourning, *Herr Tempelritter*. He will emerge from his rooms perhaps this afternoon, and then we will see what we can do. For now, I shall see you settled, warm and housed. Come.'

He beckoned to Arnau and Felipe, and they followed on. Felipe looked nervous, though whether due to the strange place or the news that the man they had come to speak to had apparently been murdered, Arnau could not say.

They left the shelter of the arch and emerged into a courtyard, roughly pentangular in shape and with a wide, stone-walled well in the centre, a windlass and rope housed beneath a small roof of grey slates. Arnau's gaze played here and there as they walked, taking everything in through the falling white, which was beginning to settle upon the courtyard that had obviously been recently cleared.

To the right of the open flagged space stood a range of buildings two storeys high with many shuttered windows, several doors and one maw of a staircase leading up into the gloom. At the end stood the glowing arches of the stable, where even now the guard named Anselm was busy taking their horses. At the far end of the courtyard sat a chapel with coloured glass windows – barring the shutters painted with black and yellow chevrons, the only visible colour in this monochrome world. To the left of that sat a small low range of buildings from which smoke poured through heavy chimneys, and to the left of that, almost next to the gate once more, having turned full circle, stood the main block, containing what had to be the noble apartments and great hall.

Bernhard led them straight across the courtyard and into that stairwell opposite. A straight flight of steps led up directly from the courtyard, with no door, and to a second storey which seemed to consist of a single corridor lined with doors to either side. Torches guttered and danced along the walls, giving off a greasy light and curling, acrid smoke. There was no decoration, and the place looked severe and austere. With surprise, Arnau realised that the corridor was not enclosed in permanent darkness as he'd immediately presumed, but that the windows to either end, closed up with shutters, were so coated outside with packed snow that hardly a trickle of weak light passed through the cracks.

They paused at the entrance to the corridor.

'We have two spare rooms. Your squire can be housed in this one here, and yourself at the end, *Herr Tempelritter*.'

Arnau chewed his lip. 'One room would be more than adequate, marshal, thank you. In the monastery we are accustomed to dormitory accommodation. Could you have a cot added to the one at the end?'

The marshal looked momentarily put out, and Arnau wondered whether he had broken some unspoken rule or fallen foul of local tradition or some such, but Bernhard eventually nodded. 'It shall be done. Come.'

He led them along to one of the doors at the far end of the corridor, and pulled it open. 'Please.'

As they entered, Arnau smiled his satisfaction. It was as plain and austere as the rest of the castle, yet in truth it was more than adequate for their needs, the pair being used to the ascetic life of the monastery. As Felipe unloaded their bag in the corner and stretched his sore shoulder, Arnau strode over to the window. Shutters once more closed this one; he unhooked the catch and pushed them open with a little strain. The weight of the snow coating the outside made them heavy, and he shivered at the icy blast that hit him. The snow that fell from the shutters dropped onto the roof below, causing a small avalanche that slid down the tiles with a low rumble and ended with a thump as the large pile of snow dropped to the courtyard below. Shivering, he closed the shutters again and latched them. At a sudden thought, he turned with a hope which was swiftly dashed. There was no fireplace in the room. Instead, the bed was laden with numerous blankets all covered with what had to be the pelt of a bear from its size.

'You are, I think, dangerously unprepared,' Bernhard said. 'I shall return.'

He disappeared from the doorway and returned a minute later with two thick, heavy woollen cloaks draped over his arm. These he cast onto the bed. 'These will help prevent the freezing illness.'

Arnau thanked the man and picked one up. It was almost as heavy as his chain hauberk, but with the fleecy lining and the fur hood it would certainly help keep him warm. He wondered for just a moment whether the cloak, also, was made from a bear. It certainly smelled as though it might be. And only recently made too.

'Thank you, Bernhard. You are most generous. Might I ask about the castle. Are you the only man to speak Frankish?'

The marshal shook his head. 'The family speak the tongue, though some will be reticent in doing so, especially around an outsider. Some of the guards and staff do, particularly the more senior.'

'The family consists of this lord, Dietmar, and the lady, Ute, then? Are they husband and wife?'

The marshal frowned. 'No, no, no. Graf Dietmar is the master of the *schloss* now. Lütolf was his brother. Hochwohlgeboren Ute is their mother, the *Grand Dame*. The graf's wife died some eight years past, and the *dame*'s husband the following winter. The only other family member in the castle is the lady Gerdrut, Lütolf's sister, also a widow.'

Arnau found himself thinking rather privately that only the most unlucky seemed to be born into the family, given the number of widows and widowers and the record of recent murder and self-imposed exile. He fought not to say something pithy, and barely succeeded.

'There are my guards and the servants, of course, as well as Michael Trost, the seneschal, and Father Oswald. Oh, and you are not the only guest. The graf's old friend, a Hungarian minstrel, has been staying with us through the winter.'

Arnau nodded. Wonderful. A collection of dour widows and widowers with weird, unfamiliar names, and now a Hungarian thrown into the mix.

'Please make yourself comfortable,' Bernhard said. 'I will have an extra bed brought in and will inform the family and staff of your arrival. The noon meal will be served in a little more than an hour. I will send for you before then.'

Arnau thanked the man and took a deep breath, placing his hands on his hips as he took in the cold room once more, wishing for a fireplace. As Bernhard made to leave, Arnau turned, a look of curiosity on his face.

'Where was the body of Graf Rüdolf found?' he asked, hoping that it wasn't in this room. He had no great fear of evil spirits and ghosts, but better to make sure that he wasn't sharing a room with one anyway.

Bernhard paused at the door, a look of pain crossing his expression. 'One of the serving girls went for water and couldn't bring up the bucket from the well. When we managed to haul the rope with the help of two of my men, the young master's body had snagged on the bucket.'

Arnau nodded, wincing at having drawn such information from the man. Bernhard gave him an odd look for a long moment, and then left, closing the door. As soon as he heard the man's footsteps diminishing along the corridor, Arnau opened the door, took the key from the outside, and put it on the inside, closing and locking it.

Felipe had noted the activity and his breath caught in his throat. 'You don't fear a murderer would come for us, Brother Arnau?'

He shook his head. Actually, he'd not considered that, although now the notion suddenly seemed horribly plausible. 'No,' he reassured the squire, 'but we have Brother Lütolf's will here, as well as his personal effects. We have been charged with protecting the former, and I would rather be cautious with the latter until we are sure to whom we should pass Lütolf's things. Better safe than sorry.'

Felipe nodded, though his expression suggested he still pictured murderers lurking outside their door.

'The killer must still be here,' the squire said.

Arnau nodded. That had occurred to him too. Whoever had killed Rüdolf von Ehingen was surely someone within the castle. Unless anyone had left since yesterday, that meant they had to still be here.

'Likely, though, it is some private family matter and is, in truth, none of our business. All we should do is make the most of their hospitality until we can speak with this Graf Dietmar, compare the wills, and transfer to the appropriate recipient Lütolf's effects. Then, once those simple tasks are complete, we will depart as soon as the weather permits and make immediately for Sülz and then home. If we push hard, it is possible we might be back in Rourell in time for Epiphany.'

He felt a sudden rush of guilt that he had been so ready to travel and leave the monastery on this journey, and yet the conditions, the standoffishness of many of the denizens, and the tidings of a grisly killing that might hinder their task had already made him yearn to be back in the warm simplicity of the house of Preceptrix Ermengarda.

'Perhaps it was bandits?' he mused. 'If they are desperate enough and brave enough to attack travellers so close to the castle, might they be hardy enough to attack their local lord?'

Felipe looked unconvinced, and Arnau had to admit that it sounded far-fetched to him too. How did they get in, after all, to kill the young lord and dump the body in the well?

'They might come after us,' Felipe said with a touch of trepidation.

'No,' Arnau shook his head. 'No, I do not see why. This is the family's business. We were not even here. We were not even expected.'

The squire straightened. 'But *someone* from the Order was expected,' he corrected Arnau. 'And given than we carry a will that grants considerable family lands and funds to the Temple…'

He left it hanging, and Arnau tried not to see the perfect sense in it. He shivered and crossed to the window once more. Throwing open the shutters, he flinched at the chill wind. The snow was coming down thick again now, and the courtyard below was already becoming a white carpet, a threatening demonic maw of a well at its centre, a deep hole that had swallowed a young man's life. His next shiver was only partially because of the cold.

His gaze played across the other buildings. A serving girl hurried out of that low range with numerous chimneys, carrying a basket covered with a checked cloth. Possibly bread, Arnau suspected, and mentally labelled the range over there the kitchens, cellars and buttery. His gaze was immediately drawn back to that well.

He'd already quoted the verse once before he even realised he'd done it. From behind, he heard Felipe question what he'd said. Arnau turned.

'"But if thou doest evil, dread thou; for not without cause he beareth the sword, for he is the minister of God, venger into wrath to him that doeth evil." Romans thirteen. The Lord reminds us that the ministers of God are the agents of his vengeance, bringing the sword to evildoers.'

Felipe frowned. 'You don't mean…'

Arnau sighed. 'It is, in one very important way, none of our business. But as warriors of His Church, it is in another way our business above all others. The word of the Book should always take precedence over temporal matters, Felipe.'

'Interference might not be popular, Brother Arnau. I do not think they like us.'

'They do not have to *like* us. Just to respect our authority within the Church. It might be a matter of duty that we apprehend the evildoer and visit divine judgement upon him.'

Felipe joined in the shivers now. 'Be careful, Brother Arnau.' He tapped his precious book of the Rule. '"Every brother of the

Temple should be believed to the benefit of the Temple and our house, and the brother should be careful what he takes upon himself, for if the thing is not as he says, he should be judged to have committed a fault." Rule 150.'

Arnau turned back to the window. Beneath that canopy and the ever-present snow, the dark circle of the well seemed to be taunting him, sneering that it had eaten the young lord who was the very reason for their visit. He clenched his teeth. 'I can live with committing a fault, but whoever cut an innocent man's throat and attempted to hide the body in such a despicable way? He *deserves* the vengeance of the Lord.'

His eyes rose to the apartments opposite, just in time to see a hooded figure in one of the windows looking straight across the courtyard at him, then disappearing within and slamming the shutters tight.

Damnation, but this place vexed him already.

CHAPTER FOUR

WEDNESDAY AFTERNOON

The second bed had not yet arrived, and Arnau had stopped Felipe unpacking their gear when a knock announced the arrival of the messenger. Arnau unlocked the door and pulled it open, his hand instinctively going to the pommel of his sword as he stepped back. A serf in black and yellow livery stood in the corridor, eyes downcast.

'*Bitte*?' he asked. Though he had no idea what the lad had said, Arnau assumed he meant them to follow, for he gestured along the corridor with one hand. Beckoning Felipe, Arnau followed the man out into the corridor, locking the door behind them, and then allowed himself to be led back down the stairs and into the courtyard. As they stepped out into the falling white, Arnau was glad of the cloak he had been given, pulling the cowl down over his forehead and wrapping it tight about himself. He felt sure there was some rule about not covering the cross but displaying it openly, though he couldn't remember the detail and was hardly about to ask Felipe about it. A glance at the squire revealed a disapproving face as he too wrapped up tight, though that might be as much to do with the cloaks' smell as covering their crosses.

They were led across to the doorway of the main block. Inside lay a small antechamber with cloaks much like the ones they wore hanging on pegs, a staircase winding up into the second floor, and a corridor ahead. Three torches along the right wall illuminated a grand tapestry on the left and, as they were led down that passage,

Arnau examined the old hanging with interest. It was exceptionally well made.

He picked out numerous scenes, and was taken by the appearance in it of a dragon on no less than two occasions, once in the form of a curled drake-shaped rock beneath a castle – this castle? – and once a great beast fighting a knight and wolf together. It was only as they reached the far end that he realised the tapestry seemed to be telling a tale, but he had begun at the wrong end. The dragon appeared to be the beginning. As the door ahead was opened, throwing extra light out into the gloomy corridor, he vowed to examine the story later in the correct order.

For now, they were led into a wide stone hall. Two long wooden tables lay parallel, with benches at both, a higher table a step up at the far end. All were set for dining, the room lit by numerous torches and a single great hearth filled with a roaring fire of great pine logs. The walls were given a little colour and life by tapestries of lesser quality than that great tale in the corridor, and by banners hanging from the blackened timber rafters all around the room. Black banners with a single gold chevron. Clearly the family's arms.

The top table had been set with five chairs, the central one larger and more ornate, though only three were occupied. At the left end sat a middle aged woman with a perfect, alabaster, chiselled face and ice blue eyes, her clothing dark and severe. Arnau could see the close resemblance the lady shared with her brother, the departed Templar Lütolf. She was quite striking, and any man might consider her something of a catch even in her advancing years. Beside her sat her mother, the *Grand Dame* Ute, as cold and disapproving as she had been when she'd first leaned from the window to see Arnau at the gate. The main chair and the one beside it sat empty, while at the far end a man loafed in a rich, dark blue shirt and crimson hose, red suede boots clearly on display as he lounged in the seat with his legs crossed, feet up on the table in the most insolent manner. His hair was black, long and very curly, his neat pointed beard similar. His face was tanned and relaxed and, though he currently bore an expression of sombre mourning, the lines at his eyes spoke of a man usually given to good humour. Despite the man's clear arrogance and insolence, Arnau couldn't help but immediately form a positive impression of him. He was too young to be Lütolf's brother, and must be the Hungarian minstrel. The master was conspicuously absent then.

The other tables were filled with men and women in either the family's livery or drab serf's tunics. There was a solemn air to the room, and Arnau had to remind himself that the castle was in mourning, and he should not expect too much life from the populace, though in truth they seemed little different to many of the Swabians he had met on his journey.

Their guide showed them to two seats at the top end of the left hand table, close to the two ladies, and Arnau bit down on the disappointment of being placed near the disapproving *Grand Dame* rather than the easy looking Hungarian. Bernhard was seated at the far side of the hall, opposite them and far from conversational reach, along with a man in a long black robe with a yellow chevron across the chest that clashed oddly with a gold chain and medallion hanging around his neck, together creating a strange saltire cross. He was an older man with long grey hair and a clean-shaven face. The seneschal, Arnau decided, who looked after the administrative side of castle life as Bernhard did the military. The only other character who stood out was clearly the priest in his white cassock, his hair straight and as white as his garment, and his expression dark.

Arnau removed his cloak and handed it to a serf who hovered nearby, three sodden dripping robes already in his arms, and Felipe did the same as the pair sat. The sudden revealing of their white and black mantles, each bearing the Order's red cross, sent a hush across the room, as almost every eye turned to them, suspicion in each face.

Arnau felt somewhat irritated at the odd sense of disapproval and accusation he received from the castle's occupants. After all, he and his squire were innocent servants of God, here on a legal matter, while someone in this room – perhaps the absent cook or the lord himself – was a base murderer. How dare they judge him so?

Conversation resumed slowly, like a creeping tide, and it was uniformly in unintelligible German. He couldn't pick out any specific comments, not that it mattered with his total lack of comprehension, but the tone suggested that many exchanges were about the two Templars, and were far from flattering.

Arnau sat silent as the noon meal was served. The salted pork was tough, and Arnau suspected that he and Felipe had been given the poorest offcuts, even after the castle's serfs. The top table were served with soft white bread and cups of wine, while those at the other great trestles, the Templars included, were treated to tougher dark bread and mugs of frothy beer. All, however, were given copious helpings of some sort of vegetable medley in a soggy, briny, pickled heap. Felipe stared at it in horror, though Arnau tried it and found that once the initial shock of the unusual taste settled, it was surprisingly palatable. The beer would have been refreshing had it been a warm summer's day, but the cold frothy beverage did little to warm on a day like this.

The Templars finished the meal in silence in a room crowded with the German tongue, and remained at their places as first the top table and then the rest all filed out. As Bernhard rose, Arnau gestured to Felipe and they stood and crossed the room, but before they could speak to the marshal, a guard joined him and the pair left together, deep in conversation. Arnau paused, wondering what to do next until a voice spoke just behind him.

'You seek an audience with the Hochwohlgeboren von Ow, yes?'

Arnau turned to find the seneschal standing behind him, brow puckered into a V.

'Yes,' Arnau replied simply. 'Yes I do, thank you, master...'

'Trost. Michael Trost. I cannot guarantee that the graf will see you, I am afraid. He is not of a mind to meet with others presently, as you will have noticed. Come, and we shall see.'

Arnau shared a look with Felipe and the two men followed Trost from the room, along that corridor and to the chamber at the entrance. On the way, he glanced once more at the tapestry, but had too little time to study it in depth. In the room they entered the spiral staircase and climbed to the next floor. There they were led through corridors lined with doors and lit with torches to one forbidding looking portal. Trost rapped twice on the door and stood back. After some time there was a call in German, and the seneschal opened the door and entered, waving the other two in.

This was a private chamber, well-appointed if perhaps past its glorious best. It was also unkempt, with platters and cups on a great cabinet to one side. Dietmar von Ow sat slumped in a large chair with a black cushion, close to an open window, the icy blast seemingly not bothering him at all as snowflakes drifted in and eddied before falling to the floor and soaking the drapes to each side.

The lord frowned, his face pale and drawn, and barked something at Trost, who answered quietly and in a measured tone. 'Speak, and be brief,' Dietmar finally said, turning his hollow gaze on the two Templars.

Arnau cleared his throat. 'My apologies for the intrusion, my lord. I have travelled from the preceptory of Rourell in Aragon, to compare the document lodged with the Order against the will claimed by your late son.'

He shivered. The room was freezing cold with the window open and no fire in the hearth, but he could swear the temperature dropped noticeably in the moments following his words. The lord rose from his chair slowly, and although there was no visible change in his expression, he suddenly exuded anger like some roused Titan. Arnau found himself taking a step back, and trod on Felipe's foot.

'The arrogance of the red cross is staggering,' growled Dietmar von Ow. 'What care I how many miles you have ridden to claim my family's precious inheritance?'

He took a step forward and his finger came up in an accusatory manner, stabbing out at Arnau as though to impale him.

'I wallow in grief, my only son and heir cruelly torn from me so recently that his body barely be cold, and you come here speaking of wills and claims? The audacity. The sheer putrid nerve of it. Begone, *Tempelritter*, and leave me to my mourning, lest I send my dear Rüdolf company in his afterlife.'

As if to underline the threat, Dietmar's eyes shot across to a stool upon which lay a misericorde, gleaming. Arnau realised with a start that the vicious dagger was unsheathed and wondered whether the lord had been contemplating joining his son in death, though to do so would deny them their bond anyway, since self-murder would see Dietmar burning in hell. Perhaps that was all that had stopped him, for the painful grief in the man was clear.

In the moment he had stepped forward, the fury seemed to drain from Dietmar as though a plug had been removed, and with it went all strength and spirit, leaving once more the hollow shell of a man they had seen upon entry. Dietmar von Ow staggered and then slumped back into his chair.

'Begone,' he said again, this time in little more than a croak.

At a small gesture from Michael Trost, the two Templars backed swiftly from the room, bowing. Arnau left the apology unsaid. It seemed so insignificant in the face of the misery they had witnessed. Despite the threat and the anger that had poured forth from the castle's master, Arnau found that he genuinely felt sorrow for the man.

He ground his teeth. In bringing up the matter so soon, he had hoped to get it out of the way and intrude on the family as little as possible. Now, he realised how short-sighted and foolish a decision it had been. He should have approached much slower and with more sympathy.

As they left, the lord called for Trost, and the seneschal turned to them.

'If you could see your way back to your rooms?'

The two men nodded and Trost returned to his master's chamber, closing the door behind him and plunging the passage into gloom once more, lit by a single flickering torch. Arnau sighed and turned to his squire.

'We shall not be leaving this day, Felipe, even if the weather clears. It has become obvious to me that our visit must be extended. I very much doubt we shall be back for Epiphany.'

'It may be weeks before the lord is in such a mood as to deal with the will, Brother Arnau. Months, even.'

Arnau shook his head. 'I think not. I see changes coming in Dietmar von Ow. While our meeting might have been inadvisable, in the end I suspect we will have done some good even in angering him.'

'Sir?'

'The father wallows in sorrow for his son, and he is the master here. Nobody in Renfrizhausen will dare to do ought other than allow their master his grief. In prompting him to fury, I believe we will have shown him the first step out of misery. Anger is often a bad thing, but as an alternative to misery it can still be positive.'

'So we wait for his mood to improve enough to see us again?'

Arnau nodded. 'And while we wait, we find out more about this death. Little would give more solace to the lord, von Ow, than the apprehending of the man responsible for his son's death.'

'Or the woman.'

'Quite,' agreed Arnau.

With that they set off once more. As they set foot on the staircase Arnau turned, thoughtfully. 'Perhaps we could speak to the sister? She seemed to be the least—'

He stopped sharp as his descent brought him face to face with a cloaked figure climbing the stairs towards him. Spinning back, he slipped on the wet stone and skittered down two steps. His shoulder knocked the climbing man, who fell back against the wall of the staircase, gripping the stonework to prevent falling himself.

As Arnau righted himself, Felipe reaching down to grab him, the stranger bridled. His cloak fell back and his ruddy face radiated fury between the short, spiky, red hair and beard. His livery and armament labelled him as one of the castle guards, and his fist came up threateningly. He snapped something at Arnau in his native tongue.

Had the Templar even a hope of deciphering the words, still he would not have been able to, for he had only just arrested his fall, having almost gone tumbling down the rest of the stairs, and was consequently a little winded and stunned.

The guard barked out that same phrase again, with an upturn at the end, suggesting that it was a question. Another guard was now coming up the stairs, shouting questions in German. Arnau stepped back, aware that he was at a loss and that this situation was in danger of becoming out of control.

'Look, I apologise,' he said in Frankish, holding out his hands in a supplicative manner. 'It was accident, pure and simple. I was not looking where I was going.'

The guard snapped something angry once more, his pointing finger gesturing at Arnau's red cross. Then, in a speedy move that the young knight could not possibly have anticipated, the hand came up and gave him a sharp crack on the jaw that sent him sprawling against the curved wall, where the back of his head connected painfully with the stonework. His hand went down to his sword hilt on instinct, though his head was now swimming with the blow and his thoughts had scattered.

Felipe was there quickly, gripping him, preventing him from falling again. Through the blurring whirl of his painful wits, Arnau realised the red-headed guard had gone for his knife and felt a moment of panic. He could probably still fight back, and possibly even win, but if he did, then their reputation in Renfrizhausen would be lost for good.

Fortunately the second guard was there suddenly, his hands going to restrain the red-head, shouting at him in German. This second man turned to Arnau even as he gripped the other's dagger hand tight. 'You go,' he snapped in halted, heavily accented French.

Arnau needed no repeat and, with Felipe's support, staggered down the stairs. As Arnau leaned against the wall in the antechamber at the bottom, slowly recovering his wits, the squire went to the hall to recover their cloaks. Arnau felt around the back of his head, but there was no blood. There would probably be an impressive lump later, but it was not serious, and his thoughts were clearing now. He gingerly tested his jaw, opening and closing his mouth and moving it this way and that, then prodding and feeling it. Nothing had broken, but again there would probably be a good bruise. Thank the good lord the man had been barehanded, and not wearing hardened gauntlets.

Felipe reappeared and draped the damp cloak over Arnau, then the pair, finally recovering and attired for the weather, stepped through the door and out into the courtyard, where the snow was now coming down thick, the stone flags already half a foot deep since their arrival. As they crossed to the stairway in the guards' building, a serf appeared from somewhere with a great flat wooden shovel and began to clear paths across the courtyard.

In moments they were back inside. They climbed the stair and headed across to their room, where Arnau unlocked the door and they entered, closing it behind them. He looked at the window, which had clearly already been caked with snow outside, given the lack of light between the shutters.

'We are, I think, stuck here anyway,' he said with a sigh. 'Even if we had swiftly resolved the issue of the will and felt good to depart, I would not remotely fancy any attempt to make it through those woods back to civilisation in this. I fear the forest goes on for some way to the south and west and onto other hills. If we lose our way, which we surely would, we might walk halfway to Austria before we freeze to death.'

Felipe nodded. 'But I fear we must do something, Brother Arnau. We arrived unpopular, and our reputation declines by the hour. Only the marshal seems to hold us in any esteem, and that is only because he has fought alongside the Order in the Holy Land.'

Arnau sighed and crossed to the windowsill. 'Quite right. We must do what we can to build bridges with these people. We need to start with Bernhard and with Trost, for they can speak our tongue and they have influence with those both below and above. And perhaps then we might speak to the ladies and to Dietmar von Ow once more.'

'And avoid red-bearded guards,' added Felipe.

'Well, quite.'

'Shall I unpack, brother?'

Arnau nodded. 'I think so. We will be here at least one night, likely several.'

As the squire began to remove their gear from the bags, Arnau stretched for a time, tested his jaw once more, then removed his sword and slipped from his mantle in order to remove the chain hauberk below. The cold hit him afresh as he stood in just shirt and hose, and he hurriedly dressed once more without the armour.

He turned as Felipe removed a smaller bag from within the larger one. With a look of reverence, he passed it to Arnau, who strode across to the window and undid the string. Little remained of Brother Lütolf's former life. When a man joined the Order, he forsook his worldly goods, but there were instances when a brother might later leave the Order and return to their former life. Any bequests he'd made with his donative would stay, but many a preceptor would keep the very personal effects of a brother against the day they might leave. Such was the case with Lütolf and the Preceptrix Ermengarda.

With care and respect, Arnau withdrew an old and musty yet high quality surcoat in black and gold, neatly folded, and placed it upon the windowsill. On it, he lay a set of ornate spurs which, he noted with interest, had dragons etched upon them. There was a small liturgical book, a ring set with a ruby, a small loop of three keys, a second ring, this one a signet with a chevron and a dragon, a knotted prayer rope of silver material, and a single gold coin of great antiquity, bearing the image of an ancient emperor with a spiky crown and of some heretical deity wielding a spear. A strange set of effects, but each had either intrinsic or personal value, clearly.

As Felipe began to remove the rest of their own personal gear from the bag, there was a knock at the door. Arnau stepped away from the window and called for the visitor to enter. The door groaned open to reveal Bernhard, who gave a troubled smile.

'I gather your audience did not go so well. I am sorry for that, though I might have predicted it. It will be some time before the master is receptive once more, I fear.'

Arnau shrugged. 'For now it would appear we are going nowhere, courtesy of the Swabian winter. Perhaps there will be a better chance.'

'I am sure.' Bernhard stepped in and to one side and at a gesture, two men struggled and fought to angle a second cot through the doorway, then carried it across and placed it on the opposite side of the room. The men left swiftly and a maid hurried in, head bowed, with an armful of linen and blankets. She quickly made the bed, as Arnau addressed the marshal.

'The rest of our luggage?'

'Will be with you shortly. It will be brought up.' Bernhard frowned and gestured past Arnau at the windowsill. 'The von Ehingen colours. A surcoat?'

Arnau nodded. 'The personal effects of Brother Lütolf we have brought from Rourell.' For a moment he wondered where the all-important will was, but a side glance caught Felipe holding it behind his back, out of sight. Good lad.

Bernhard sighed a sad sigh. 'While the former graf might have left under something of a cloud, he is still regarded in high esteem, and his loss was felt most keenly. I owe my own position to him, for one. I would, at some point, appreciate the chance to talk of his time in your Order. We have heard so little.'

'Of course. I'm sure there will be time. I doubt we shall be taking the air or engaged in sword practice too often in this. Does your priest maintain the liturgy of the hours? I am unfamiliar with Swabian custom, and our Rule commands us to attend such services where at all possible.'

Bernhard nodded. 'Indeed, Father Oswald holds every service. You will hear the bell, I'm certain, and I shall see you there for, as a former Crusader myself, I ensure that I am at every service. You will find attendance from the others sporadic, I am afraid.' His tone dropped to a near whisper. 'Personally I blame Father Oswald's tedious sermons for that.'

Arnau gave a short laugh, the first since their arrival, and a most welcome release.

'Would you like me to have those effects placed in secure storage in the castle?'

Arnau shook his head. 'Until the matter of the inheritance and the will is sorted, and I feel comfortable with whom I am handing such treasured possessions, I think I had best keep them secure. But thank you.'

Bernhard smiled. 'You do your Order credit, master *Tempelritter*. I hope things become easier for you, and I shall expect to see you at nones.'

With a nod of the head, the marshal left. As Arnau turned to his squire, he noted the maid, busily tucking the top blanket in, her eyes on the documents held behind Felipe's back. Realising she was being observed, the maid averted her gaze once more and finished up, turning back to the door. As she left the room, she bowed. '*Bitte*,' she said, and then trotted off along the corridor.

Arnau crossed to the door, closed and locked it, and then looked around the room. A heavy oak cupboard against the far wall had two keyholes but no key in evidence. Nothing else looked particularly secure. He couldn't say particularly why he suddenly felt as though security might be a concern, though he remembered the oddly suspicious look in the maid's eye as she peered at the will in the squire's hands.

'Would that we could carry those documents around with us, but with the wet snow, I fear for their survival. They must stay in the warm and dry. I shall speak to Michael Trost as soon as possible about a lockable container, or perhaps the key for that cupboard. Until then, pass me the will.'

Felipe did so, and Arnau slipped it between two folds in the black surcoat on the windowsill. Putting all the effects, with the hidden will, back into the bag, he slipped it under his bed, pushing it into the far corner, away from the centre of the room.

'That, I fear, is about as safe as the will can be made for now.' He chewed his lip. 'It can still be more secure, though. One of us can remain in the room at all times until a lock is made available. I hereby release you from the command to attend all services. I shall do so, and you may rest here. And when you feel the need for the latrine or suchlike, make sure I am present. The preceptrix charged us with protecting the document, and I shall not fail in my duty.'

Felipe looked concerned. 'Brother, such dispensation to miss services can only be given by a convent of brothers or a commander. It is stated in rule—'

Arnau held up a hand. 'I think it is time to revisit rule 144 of which you made note on our journey. "If any brothers go on any business, and there is no commander among them, they may elect one among them as commander." Kindly elect me, Felipe, and then I will give you dispensation. Neatly done, I think. See how the Order's Rule becomes flexible even in itself?'

Felipe continued to look unconvinced as Arnau flopped down onto his bed and ran through everything they had seen and heard in a few short hours. Despite the remoteness and winter-driven closeness of life at Renfrizhausen, he was already convinced that their sojourn here would be far from boring.

Danger lurked within the foreboding stones of Renfrizhausen. It had claimed the heir of the family's name and inheritance, and threatened all within its boundaries. His memory slipped back to those bandits in the woods close by. Not just within its boundaries, either.

Trouble. The man to whom he had been sent to compare wills had been killed, and he was not sure how to proceed. One thing was sure, however he proceeded, it would need to be with care. There was a killer in Renfrizhausen, and this problem was not one that would be solved with the tip of a blade.

Fretting quietly, he turned it all over in his mind again and again until finally he nodded off into a sleep filled with ominous dreams of dragons.

THE WINTER KNIGHT

CHAPTER FIVE

THURSDAY MORNING

The service ended with a blessing, and Father Oswald performed his benediction with two fingers sweeping the cross over his minimal congregation. A flock of five seemed poor to Arnau, but when he thought back upon his life before the Order, there had rarely been many folk to be found at the early morning services in the castle, and he had just become used to a full chapel in a monastery where it was part of the natural daily routine. Here in Renfrizhausen castle, many of the denizens would be too busy at dawn to attend the service, and the older nobility might not be expected to rise from their cot until it was fully light. And so the congregation had consisted of one serf, two guards, Bernhard and Arnau.

As the small flock emerged from the church, Arnau gestured to the marshal. The light was only now beginning to make its presence felt through heavy layers of cloud that promised a fresh blizzard soon, and torchlight still illuminated much of the world. A serf was busy clearing fresh paths across the courtyard once more.

'Bernhard, I know it is something of a delicate situation, and our last meeting fared rather dismally, but I wonder if you might convey my apologies to the Graf Dietmar and politely request another audience?'

He winced at the marshal's expression. 'More a job for Michael, I think,' the man replied.

Arnau chewed his lip. 'Perhaps, but I fear the seneschal holds us in no more esteem than most of the castle's occupants. *You* know that we mean well. I suspect you can be the most persuasive if you have a mind to be of help?'

The marshal nodded slowly. 'I shall see what I can do, *Herr Tempelritter*.'

'Thank you. And is there somewhere a little... private... where we could engage in a little training, my squire and I?'

Bernhard pursed his lips. 'The castle is not large, and privacy is generally limited to small rooms and apartments. Guard training is usually conducted outside the castle or in the courtyard, but the former is difficult with the weather, and the latter far from private. My best suggestion would be the *Roterdrachenturm*,' he turned and pointed up to the largest of the castle's towers, looming over the main range and close to the gate.

Arnau smiled. 'Perfect. Thank you.'

With a wave of farewell, he left Bernhard to his work and hurried back across the courtyard into the staircase and up to his room. A swift rap on the door, and Felipe opened it. As Arnau entered and closed the door behind him, the squire held out a hand.

'Ten more minutes and I'd have been able to join the service,' Felipe sighed.

Arnau peered at the lad's hand. He held a small but heavy iron key.

'It was delivered by a serving girl half an hour ago,' Felipe noted as Arnau took the key. 'With the complements of Michael Trost. It is the key to the cupboard here. I have put all the items of value inside and locked it. A bit of poking and prodding, and I'm fairly sure that no one is getting in there without the key.'

Arnau nodded. 'I'll keep this in my purse then. Let me know if you need it.' He did so, and straightened once more. 'I was intending to give you a set of training exercises to perform, but since we can now safely leave the documents we can *both* go. Arm yourself, Felipe, and follow me. Leave the cloaks, though.'

As Arnau belted on his sword and picked up his shield from the corner, where the rest of their gear had been left since its delivery from the stables, he continued. 'Hopefully today I will get to speak to Dietmar von Ow once more. Then we'll know whether it's worth unpacking fully or not.'

Once Felipe had his sword and shield in hand too, Arnau led him out, pausing to lock their chamber and then making their way along the corridor and down the stairs to the courtyard. Father Oswald was leaving the chapel at the far side, and Arnau called out a greeting, hoping to make a bridge with the priest at least, but the old man ignored him, crossed the newly-swept path and disappeared into the kitchens.

'What hope have we when even the Lord's own ministers will not acknowledge us?' Felipe muttered.

Unable to refute the words, Arnau held his silence as the pair crossed the courtyard, past the well, which again brooded evilly and drew Arnau's gaze. Reaching the open door of the main range, they entered that small antechamber, turned and began to climb the spiral staircase, hoping not to bump into the red-headed guard this time and paying careful attention to their climb. They passed the first floor with the graf's room and continued their ascent, past a second floor of apartments, then up a long flight that seemed to wind its way to the heavens, and finally reached a door around which a freezing blast blew, indicating that they had reached the top.

Arnau took a deep breath and lifted the latch, heaving against the door. The snow had built up on the far side into a deep drift and the Templar struggled against the weight, grunting as he pushed. Felipe lent a hand, and slowly the door crunched further and further open until there was room for a man to pass through into the bitter cold, white-blue world.

Once they had both emerged onto the tower top, Arnau closed the door again and busily used his shield as a makeshift shovel to move the worst of the drift away from the door.

'Sweet Lord above,' Felipe said in a breathless voice, and Arnau turned to see that the squire had crossed to the battlements and was looking down. Wading through the foot deep snow, Arnau joined him, and felt the pit of his stomach turn over at the view. Perhaps a hundred feet below, the courtyard looked so small, the well at its centre and radiating spokes of grey in the white blanket where the serfs had cleared paths. Below the tower directly stood the steeply sloping roof of the upper floor apartments, grey tile covered with thick fleecy white.

Arnau stepped back. 'I have faced the Almohad menace, escaped burning buildings and stood on a wall as Frankish forces launched artillery at me, and I don't mind admitting that I've rarely felt as nervous as I do looking down there.'

Felipe nodded his agreement and stepped back. 'An excellent view, though.'

They plodded slowly through the deep snow, taking in the view. Arnau had to admit that it was impressive. Now that the blizzard was in abeyance and the cloud lifted enough to allow a view of some distance, for the first time Arnau could appreciate the position of this powerful fortress. To the south and the east, wooded hills stretched into the monochrome distance. To the east they could see the wide valley of the Neckar heading away towards Sülz, and to the north he could make out the squat huddle that was Renfrizhausen village, through which they'd travelled, and the road marching off towards the river.

It seemed such a simple matter to get from here to there when looking down from such a height. But then it had seemed simple looking up at the hill from the village, too. Once in among the snowy woods, it had proved much the opposite.

He returned to looking down at the courtyard. In his mind, he pictured two figures, one animated and urgent, the other still and lifeless. A dead man being dragged to the well. Yes, he thought, poor Rüdolf could not have been killed at the well. It was too open a position for such nefarious deeds. An excellent place to hide a body, but not to commit a murder. There was far too much chance of being spotted. And with a cut throat there would be much blood, which would show up too readily on crisp white snow even if it had been snowing. No, he was killed somewhere else and then dropped down the well, so the killer had dragged the heir across the courtyard to the centre, quickly and while no one was looking. The actual murder had happened somewhere else. From which door was he dragged? He looked at the spokes of that wheel of cleared paths. One from the stables. One from the guards' dormitory below Arnau's room. One from the staircase to that last. One from the chapel. One from the gate. One from the kitchens. One from the main block above which they stood. Seven paths. And assuming that the serfs rarely if ever varied their clearing of snow, then only those doors could harbour the site of the death.

Arnau frowned, wondering if he might have the leisure to do some poking around. Perhaps he should have been doing that instead of training, but then training was commanded in the Rule, and God forbid he give Felipe something else to fret about from the Order's rules.

'Brother?'

He turned to see the squire standing at the centre of the tower, waiting. With a sharp breath that sent the freezing air seemingly into every corner of his being, he shivered and stepped over to meet Felipe.

'A short stint, this morning. Ten bouts. It is simply too cold for more.' He settled into position and raised his sword and shield. 'First, I will come at you high, and I want you to knock the blow aside with your shield and respond quick and low. All right?'

A nod.

'And be very careful not to go straight past me and over the parapet.'

Another nod, this time more emphatic.

'Good. Let's begin.'

Taking a chilly breath, he leapt forward in a deft strike, sword held high and sweeping down in a chop. Or at least, that was how it was *meant* to be. In fact, the foot-deep snow around his boots clung to him and prevented him leaping athletically. In reality, he more staggered forward until his blade was within reach, when he brought it down.

Felipe caught the strike with his shield, knocking it away, though Arnau could see from his expression that the blow had numbed his arm and reverberated right up to the shoulder. By the time the squire had spun aside and brought his own blade around in a backhanded slash, Arnau had recovered his stance well, and his own blade caught Felipe's sword and knocked it aside.

They staggered back, and Arnau had to be careful to keep his footing. The snow was treacherous, and where their feet had begun to compact it, it was all the more slippery and dangerous. He looked across at the parapet, which came up to around his lower ribs. He didn't have to do much calculating to work out that if he hit the edge at speed, he would almost certainly tip over it before he could stop himself. He remembered that view down into the courtyard and shivered.

'A backhanded strike. Very clever. Not what I was expecting, and put me off my guard, made me use my sword to block instead of my shield. Good. Right,' he said, his voice croaky with the cold. 'Now you come at me, however you like.'

He stepped back to their starting position and readied himself. A moment later, Felipe danced towards him, blade slashing this way and that, angling high to low across his chest as he went, shield clutched to the side out of the way.

It was a forceful attack, and with the continual change in angle of attack as he approached, Arnau was having difficulty anticipating where he needed to be. As Felipe reached him, his blow was coming backhanded again, and Arnau was in a position where his shield could not be brought to bear. His blade clattered against the squire's, knocking it away once more, but this time he punched out with the shield, catching Felipe full in the chest, winding him and sending him sprawling back into the boot-compacted snow.

'The sword is not your only weapon, Felipe. Remember that.'

The squire nodded as he stood, wincing and breathing deeply, staggering back to his starting position.

'Good. Now my turn. Eight more bouts to go.'

He readied himself and raised his sword.

***

In actual fact, they had managed only six before they were interrupted, the door at the tower top creaking open to their sudden surprise and bringing them both to a halt. The face of one of the castle's guards appeared. Arnau fought for the name, the man who had first opened the gate when they arrived and taken their horses.

'Anselm?' he said.

'*Ja, Herr Tempelritter. Die marschall* Bulstrich, has me sent. You meeting *ja* with graf. *Komme.*'

Arnau nodded, pleased that despite the uncomfortable muddle of Frankish and German that tumbled from Anselm's mouth, he was at least trying.

'Thank you,' Arnau said, wiping his sword to remove the excess moisture and sheathing it as Felipe did the same, and the pair crossed the tower top, the deep snow now well-trodden down with their exertions. As they entered the stairwell, shivering with the cold, they shook their feet to remove the snow from their sodden boots and stamp life back into their toes.

Anselm set off down the staircase and they followed quietly. On the descent, Arnau pondered briefly the possibility of trying to strike up a conversation with the guard. Being on friendly terms with someone other than Bernhard could be of great value, but he simply couldn't decide what to say that would be simple enough for the man to grasp with his limited command of French. In the end, he decided against it for now and followed in silence as they reached the first floor and followed Anselm along to the now familiar door of the graf's room.

The guard knocked and at a call from inside announced their presence. At a reply, Anselm swung the door open and stepped between them and the room meaningfully. As Arnau paused with a frown, the guard pointed at his sword. Arnau nodded and unbuckled his sword belt, motioning for Felipe to do the same. Handing them over and now unarmed, they were escorted into the room. The window was at least shut this time and the room was a little warmer, though only embers burned in the fireplace from the night before.

Lord Dietmar von Ow sat in that same seat, one hand wrapped around a cup, the other on his knee, eyes on the newcomers. He motioned for Anselm to leave, and the guard bowed his head to the Templars and departed, closing the door behind him.

'Please allow me to apologise for yesterday,' Arnau said immediately, trying to pour as much honesty into his voice as he could, laced with strong sympathy. 'I truly did not mean to open wounds. I thought to wrap up my business as fast as possible and thereby cause as little trouble for your family as I could. I felt like something of an intruder. I still do. I was foolish, though it was a mistake made with honestly the best intentions.'

There was a long silence, and Dietmar finally nodded. 'Your apology is accepted, *Tempelritter*. And I offer one of my own in return. Since my son... I have not been myself. My mood rises and falls, never rising very far and often falling too deep. I should not have agreed to see you yesterday. My sister spoke to me at length last night after the evening meal. She called me something quite cruel, in fact.'

Arnau gave a weak smile. It sounded as though perhaps he had another ally after all, in Lütolf and Dietmar's sister, the striking and handsome lady Gerdrut. And perhaps now in Lord Dietmar too? Arnau silently resolved not to ruin this chance. *Tread carefully.*

'Now, then, perhaps I might offer my deepest condolences over your loss, fresh and raw as it is. Though I never met your son, and I only knew your brother for a short time, Lütolf became a friend to me, tutoring me in the ways of the Order. I held him in the very greatest esteem, an esteem in which I now find myself holding your honoured self.'

He wondered for a moment whether he had gone too far, been just too fawning in his manner. Dietmar gave a weak smile. 'It is said that the knights of your Order are uniformly arrogant. That you care about nothing outside your service to the Church and your own kind. It is an attitude you will find common in Swabia. Bernhard has tried to persuade me otherwise, for he has experience of your Order. I think perhaps we sometimes see only the red cross and forget that it is being worn by men.'

Arnau smiled in return. 'Lord Dietmar, I have brought from Rourell the personal effects of your brother, which have been preserved since his arrival at the house. I was not certain to whom they should pass with Graf Rüdolf not present, but I think that now, perhaps they ought to be given to you? At least until the matter of the wills is concluded.'

Dietmar waved a hand dismissively. 'Keep them, for now anyway. I have enough to deal with, in the castle and in my heart, with the passing of my son. I have no wish at this time to be pressed into fresh mourning for my brother.'

Arnau winced. Damn it, that was clumsy. Still, it did not seem to have angered the lord, merely to have made him sag into himself just a little more. Ah well, since he'd raised the subject and not been shouted down...

'On the matter of the will,' he said hesitantly, 'I hope that it will be a quick task to compare the documents and resolve the matter. I appreciate that it is your family's property of which we speak, and were it not for the fact that the Order has already been administering them for so many years it might seem...' he tailed off. 'I am sorry about this. The timing is poor.'

Dietmar shrugged. 'After your visit, and that of Gerdrut last evening, I sent for the will, but it seems to have vanished, and no one appears to know what happened to it. The one man who would definitely know, of course, is my son.'

Arnau sighed. 'What is to happen with the graf, Rüdolf?

'He is lying in state in the vault below the castle. He will be eulogised and then interred at the church in the town when the snow allows. We have no mausoleum here and the family are all at the church in Renfrizhausen. The weather has prevented swift dealing with the matter, unfortunately.'

Arnau pictured the two gravediggers who had directed him to the castle. Had they been preparing a hole for the young lord? He shook off the notion. If the weather had kept the family here, it seemed unlikely the village church would yet know of the death.

Besides, surely a man of the graf's standing would be interred in a proper mausoleum or in the church itself.

'It would seem that we are similarly trapped here by the elements,' Arnau sighed, 'but I would consider it an honour to attend the service when the weather clears, before we depart.'

The lord simply nodded and drank from his cup, placing it on the table beside him.

Arnau's mind was racing now. The will was missing. The young lord murdered just a couple of days before the arrival of the document that would prove or disprove the inheritance, and then the will that it all hinged on had vanished. In a way that made things unpleasantly easy for the Templar. The lands would have to remain in the hands of the Order. But it complicated matters at Renfrizhausen, too.

'My lord,' he said, troubled, 'it seems odd that the will should disappear so. I have no wish to see the family lose out simply through such an unfortunate mishap.'

Dietmar nodded. 'I have men searching for the will. It must still be in the castle. Bernhard is overseeing the search, though he has his hands rather full, since I have also charged him with uncovering the truth behind my son's death.'

Arnau drummed his fingers on his hip. 'Have you any idea who might have reason for such a black deed, my lord?'

'I am hopeful that Bernhard will conclude, as we suspect, that an interloper happened upon Rüdolf and killed him in a struggle. The family and the castle's staff are beyond suspicion, each and every one, and the morning after it happened, the main gate was found to be unlocked. It is the simplest explanation, and one that I can put down to the will of God without any deeper melancholy.'

Arnau nodded. It was possible. Especially with bandits in the castle's proximity, of course. But somehow he didn't believe a word of it. A passing bandit slips into the castle, stumbles upon the young lord, kills him, steals his will and drops the body down the well? Whatever the graf thought of his family and staff's loyalty, Arnau was convinced that one of them was somehow responsible.

'If the will is missing, it seems likely that this entire business is over money and land, my lord,' he said hesitantly. 'That being the case, it is perhaps likely some impoverished acquaintance who would have most to gain. Your noble self and your family are surely powerful enough to be able to shrug off the loss of a few acres to the Order?'

He wondered if he'd gone too far then, for that familiar flare of anger from yesterday shone once more in Dietmar's eyes, but it quickly burned out, and the lord sighed. 'Would that it were the case, *Tempelritter*. Sadly, our family is not as wealthy as once we were. By the standards of our peers we are a poor cousin indeed. Any generation that loses lands makes the family progressively poorer. When our cousin ran off to join the Swabian Hospitallers in Outremer, then helped found the Order of the Teutons, my grandfather was furious. His decision was in the end accepted because the connections he made among our countrymen in the order were valuable in themselves.'

He seemed to sag inwards once more. 'But when Lütolf ran off to join a foreign order at the other side of the world and gave away valuable farms and tenant lands, he was cursed from every mountain peak in Swabia. Your very presence with that red cross on your chest reminds everyone of that day. In some ways you represent loss for the family.'

Arnau nodded. 'I can only apologise and offer my sympathy. In fact, I understand your plight more than most. My own family had become poor vassals of the Counts of Barcelona and I fear that we would not have survived another generation without losing our lands and castle entirely. I entered the Order in desperation. A title is not always supported by heaps of gold.'

The lord gave him an appraising glance. 'Perhaps there is more to you than anyone expects, *Herr Tempelritter*. I shall be sure to send for you if the will is found, or when there is progress on my son's funeral. In the meantime, Bernhard will no doubt keep you abreast of matters. For now, I feel the need to rest once more. My nights are filled with demons and sleep comes only in tatters these days.'

Arnau bowed. 'I am pleased that we have been able to speak thusly, Lord Dietmar. Once again, you have my respect and my sympathy, and if there is anything I can do, you have but to ask.'

The lord of Renfrizhausen's eyes narrowed. 'You want to help? Find the blackguard who killed my son.'

Arnau, unsure of what else to say in response, simply bowed his head. 'I will help however I can.'

With that, he stepped back and opened the door, ushering Felipe from the room. Just outside, as he closed the door once more, Anselm waited with their swords, handing them out. For a moment, Arnau was filled with suspicion. Had the guard been standing outside the chamber with his ear pressed to the wood, listening to their every word? Had he reason to hate his young lord or envy his lands? He chided himself over his overactive imagination. Whatever Anselm's motives, he would learn little from listening at the door with his clearly limited understanding of the language they had been speaking.

Thanking the man and belting on his sword once more, he and his squire marched out from the corridor, down the stairs and into the antechamber. Spotting Bernhard just outside in the courtyard, he made for the door but paused in the archway for a moment, recognising the red-bearded form of the guard who had struck him on the stairs speaking to the marshal. He waited until the pair's conversation ended, watching the surly brute head for the stables. Before the marshal could stride away, Arnau emerged into the cold and waved to him.

'Bernhard, good morning again. Thank you for the introduction to the lord, Dietmar. Our exchange was considerably more agreeable this time. I think I begin to understand, also, the unpopularity with which I have been greeted on the whole.'

The marshal gave a curt snapped nod of the head. '*Herr Tempelritter*. Yes, times here are tense and the red cross is not well looked upon.'

'You wished to hear of Lütolf's time with the Order,' Arnau said, carefully. 'Perhaps in return you might enlighten me as to why he came to us in the first place? I spoke to Lütolf about it a little, and he intimated that there had been some sort of argument.'

Bernhard nodded. 'It is not a conversation to hold here, though. Perhaps tonight. For now I have much to do.'

'I understand. Dietmar has you looking into the loss of the will and the death of Rüdolf both. You must be run ragged.'

'In truth, I am far from sure where to even start with that last,' Bernhard sighed. 'Come.' Quickly, he led them from the courtyard and into a doorway in the range below their room. It appeared to be a small guardroom of sorts and was currently empty. As Arnau closed the door behind them, Bernhard stirred up the fire in the grate and tossed a few more logs upon it. Finally, rubbing his hands over the flames to warm them, he resumed.

'This is another conversation best not held in the open, master Arnau. It is important, of course, that a man in my position be seen to be efficient, in control and a step ahead of everyone. Sadly, I can claim none of those things today. I am a soldier and a commander of men, not some shrewd investigator of criminal acts. In the matter of the missing will, I have searched the castle with the aid of my men, paying as much personal attention as possible. Indeed, I searched the graf's chamber myself, under the watchful eye of the Hochwohlgeboren Ute. I can find no sign of the will, and have interviewed everyone but the lord and ladies, to no avail. It has vanished.'

'When was it last seen?'

'There was a discussion about it around a week ago. Since then, as far as I know it was kept by Graf Rüdolf. He and his father argued the night of his death, I understand. Perhaps the will was involved, but I know not.'

Arnau frowned. An argument? This was news, though not *welcome* news. He could not believe, especially after seeing the old man's reactions, that he might be somehow responsible for his son's passing. But an argument the night of the death was too coincidental to be ignored.

'And what of the death?' he asked.

'I have made little progress,' admitted Bernhard. 'It is too difficult and delicate. The gate was found to be unlocked. Had there been snow, footprints might have clarified matters, but the courtyard is regularly cleared of snow, and so there were no marks to identify. In truth, I am very much hoping that all evidence points to an interloper so that I can discipline the man who left open the door and be done with it. At least then the matter will be closed and further suspicions can be allayed.'

Arnau nodded. 'I understand. I will be most surprised, however, if the evidence points to that. It seems so happenstance and unlikely. My heart tells me there is more to it. If you are amenable, I would like to try and help you unravel this tragic mystery? We are more or less trapped here by the weather, and Felipe and I can offer an objective view on matters, being strangers.'

'In truth I would be grateful for any assistance,' the marshal said. 'I am so very perplexed by the entire matter, and I do not enjoy digging into such a miserable subject. How would you suggest we proceed?'

Folding his arms and chewing his lip, the Templar thought it through. 'I would like to hear everything that is known about the death. Then we can speak to each and every person within the walls and learn what they were about at the time of the death. Someone was with the graf when he died. We need to try and pare down the facts until we can work out whom.'

Bernhard nodded. 'I will arrange for the entire castle's staff to be available for interview tomorrow. Today I have them performing a second search for the will. Perhaps I can leave it to you, *Herr Tempelritter*, to speak to the family. It is not my place, and I am more than a little uncomfortable in what amounts to an interrogation of my own master and mistresses.'

Arnau agreed, unfolding his arms and coming to join him at the fire, warming his fingers. 'Then perhaps I should introduce myself to the ladies?'

'There will be ample occasion for that at lunch,' Bernhard said.

As they fell quiet, Arnau looked into the dancing fire.

Where were you killed? He asked the shade of Rüdolf von Ehingen amid the flames. *Who by, and where?*

CHAPTER SIX

THURSDAY AFTERNOON

𝔄rnau and Felipe secured their room, the knight pocketing the key, and strode along the corridor, wrapping their heavy wool and fur cloaks about them in preparation as the chimes continued to ring out, calling the castle's occupants to the hall for lunch. Down the stairs they went and out into the cold courtyard, crossing to the main range.

The clouds had lowered noticeably once more, thickening and darkening, ready for the next scattering of white. The pathways that had been cleared across the stone had become part-frozen now and were treacherous, so one of the kitchen staff was busy throwing hot ash upon them from the fires left after the meal's preparation. Other colleagues of hers were busy ferrying baskets and trays of food across the courtyard, while other guards and staff descended upon the door.

On the way down the long corridor with the tapestry, Arnau reminded himself to examine it more closely at some point. Though he should have plenty of time to do such things, it seemed to keep filling up without warning. They pressed on, into the hall.

A serf stood waiting to take their cloaks, and Arnau handed his over with a nod of thanks and then made his way forward. Where they had been seated the previous day there was now only one empty seat, a worn-looking and slightly wall-eyed guard sat in the second one. Arnau scoured the room for Bernhard, but caught sight of Michael Trost, the seneschal, instead. He made *where should I sit* motions, and at the man's smile turned to realise that the serf with his cloak was gesturing for him to follow. Of course, the fellow wouldn't speak French.

'*Bitte*?' the man said, pointing with a hand poking out from under the garments.

Leaving Felipe with a little regret and considerably more trepidation, he followed. The squire was seated where he was yesterday, next to that guard, who gave him the sort of look a man might reserve for a stinking garderobe. Arnau followed the serf, who led him unexpectedly around the top table. Once more there were five seats there and the two ladies occupied the left two, the lounging minstrel the right. Arnau was shown to the seat next to the Hungarian, and sat with a nod of gratitude, feeling his nerves rising.

The top table, with the family! Clearly his audience with the lord had gone far better than he could have hoped. He must have made just the impression for which he had hoped. All he could wish now was that the Graf Dietmar would join them for the meal, presumably in the high chair at the centre.

The hopes of that faded though, as the last of the castle's denizens came in and took their seats while the central chair remained empty. The food was served, and seemed to be a cut above yesterday's fare, though whether that be a true change or simply something to do with the top table, he couldn't say.

A small plate was placed before him with some curled pastry sprinkled in white, while something pinky-brown in a thick sauce was placed beside it. Arnau peered and took a sniff. It smelled rich, meaty and peppery. The pastry smelled sweet.

'Deer liver,' said the man beside him. 'Eat the pastry first, then the starter. It is one of Dietmar's favoured dishes.'

Arnau turned to the man, who grinned. 'Karolus Kovacs, friend of the graf and troubadour to the great houses from here to Strigonium and beyond.' His accent was exotic and eastern and bore an odd resemblance to some of those Arnau remembered from Constantinople, which soured the experience a little.

'Well met, master Kovacs. I am—'

'Arnau de Vallbona, Aragonese knight and brother of the Temple. Yes, everyone in Renfrizhausen is well aware of who you are by now. I have been waiting for a chance to speak to you. With the exception of Bernhard there is a great tendency for the folk of Renfrizhausen to be inward-looking and suspicious of anything that happens beyond the next valley. I fear it is something to do with the remoteness of the estate, a certain mountain nature that I often see in my homeland too. But it will be nice to speak with someone who carries tales of the outside world. I have missed almost four months of life beyond the River Neckar.'

Arnau gave an apologetic shrug. 'I fear perhaps I am not the greatest bearer of tidings. My very nature means that I mostly see the inside of our monastery in Catalunya. My few topics of conversation will be poor fare compared with yours, sadly.'

Kovacs laughed then. 'Perhaps it is a good thing that I love the sound of my own voice and the tales tumble from my lips like dice from a desperate man's hand. I do miss easy conversation, and I am not built for mourning. These sad events of the past few days have torn all the joy from Dietmar, and though I visit him repeatedly, our talks are strained and troublesome, where we have always before been as thick as thieves and as scandalous as unfettered boys.'

Arnau smiled as he took a bite of his pastry. Kovacs was clearly going to be something of a relief in this dour place. After he had swallowed, he cleared his throat. 'Being as I am something of a stranger here, perhaps you might be able to tell me something about the place and the family?' He lowered his voice to a conspiratorial whisper. 'The graf has charged me with helping Bernhard uncover the culprit of his woes, and anything I learn may be of value.'

Kovacs finished chewing and Arnau blinked. Both the man's plates were empty and he'd barely paused in his conversation. How had he managed to eat all that so swiftly?

'Stories are, of course, my stock in trade. You have seen the grand tapestry?'

Arnau nodded, caught in mid-mouthful again. 'Mmmff. Yes, but not in detail. I keep planning to study it.'

'It tells the tale of the fortunes of the von Ehingen. Are you familiar with Swabian politics?'

The young Templar shrugged. 'A little. It seems complex and murky even by Iberian standards.'

Kovacs nodded. 'You eat, I will talk. Our specialities,' he grinned. 'In these Germanies, high in the mountains, the two dynasties of which you should be aware are the Welf and the Hohenstaufen. They are at the heart of the rift in this family.'

'Lütolf?' managed Arnau through a mouthful of extraordinarily rich and tasty deer liver. He began to hurry as serfs were already removing the dishes and bringing out another course.

Kovacs nodded. 'The old graf and all the von Ehingen going back, including the de Rottenburg and the von Ow, were bound to the Welf, sharing their fortunes. As the tide of politics changed, many houses began to favour their opponents, the Hohenstaufen. While Lütolf and his father held true to their Welf allegiance, Dietmar favoured the Hohenstaufen. The family is not wealthy, as you might have noticed, and in the Hohenstaufen Dietmar sees the future fortune of the von Ehingen, while Lütolf would rather be very nobly poor. The rows they had upon their father's death led to your friend storming away from Renfrizhausen and seeking a life free of such politics. The matter was further complicated by the fact that Dietmar and Lütolf were twins and the order of inheritance in the family is purely arbitrary.'

Arnau leaned back, issuing an accidental belch. 'I can picture Lütolf with his chin high and resolute. That is very much the man I knew,'

'Then he did not change much.'

'The tapestry,' Arnau said. 'You were going to explain it?'

Kovacs turned and steepled his fingers. 'The Welf are part of it. You know of Henry the Lion, the Welf duke?'

Arnau shook his head, leaning back for more steaming food to be placed before him.

'It is said that Duke Henry fought alongside a lion, the pair of them destroying a great fire-breathing dragon. Dietmar's grandfather was one of Henry's close supporters. The old man once told me that the dragon had only been overcome, not killed, and that Henry had the von Ehingen build the fortress atop a cave in which the dragon slept, to keep it contained. Such you will see on the tapestry. It is a proud statement of their Welf ties and the tale of Henry's dragon.'

Arnau frowned. 'I am always troubled by dragons. In my childhood they were the stuff of tales and legends, and seemed both glorious and entirely fantastical. Yet I have met holy men and knights alike who claim to have seen the beasts and consider them aspects of the Devil himself.'

Kovacs laughed. 'Fantasy or Devil, they make for great stories, my friend. Renfrizhausen is full of such tales. I have gathered many stories over my visits here, which I will then sing to other nobles when I travel, just as I tell their best tales here.'

Arnau smiled. 'There are many legends?'

'Do not let the Hungarian fill your ears with detritus,' came a scratchy voice, and Arnau turned to see the old *dame*, Ute von Ehingen, glaring at the pair of them. 'There is no dragon here and there never was. It is a fiction of my father's. He was given to flights of fancy, just like this peddler of dross. Drakes are evil things, and such a creature could not exist here. Father Oswald would know of it, for it would not be able to withstand the presence of the cross over its heart.'

'Thus speaks the voice of reason,' grinned Kovacs, bowing his head to the owl woman. 'My life would be uneventful and impoverished if I kept my tales to the ordinary. And, dear lady, Renfrizhausen is so full of great stories.'

'Lies.'

Kovacs shrugged. 'Perhaps not all. I might challenge you to disprove the burial mound.'

The old woman snorted and turned away, and Kovacs leaned closer to Arnau. 'There are many ancient burial mounds around here. I can show you some when the snow lets up. They are no fiction. It is said, though, that the castle is built upon the levelled remains of one such ancient tomb, and that a ghost can be found wandering the halls, disturbed from its eternal rest by the destruction of its grave.'

'Idiocy,' Lady Ute snapped. 'The first rule of building a castle is to do so on good rock which cannot crumble away. Not an ancient mound. And I am as old as the mountains themselves, and have never seen such a thing. No one in my lifetime has seen a ghost here.'

Before Kovacs could answer, she had turned away again. The minstrel shrugged and whispered to Arnau. 'She is mistaken. I have spoken to three people in this room who claim to have encountered the ghost. And there is the tale of the Roman gold.'

'Piffle,' snapped the old woman, without even turning to face them this time.

Arnau frowned. 'Go on.'

'Dietmar's father used to talk of a hoard of ancient gold coins. He believed that they were the treasure of some Roman lord who was overrun by the German tribes, which were brought back and hoarded. He claimed that the gold was the source of the von Ehingen's fortune.'

Lady Ute snorted again and turned so sharply that Arnau jumped a little. 'Do you think we would be scraping around for money if we had a fortune in Roman gold? Would the family be torn, my son running off to join foreign wolf packs like this man's brethren, if we were not holding on to our remaining lands so tightly that we might snap our fingers? You talk nonsense as usual, singer.'

Kovacs laughed again. 'Stories. My stock in trade. But I tell you that all legends contain at least a grain of truth.'

Arnau nodded. A touch of excitement crept into him now. The dragons in all the von Ehingen images started to make sense. He did not particularly enjoy the notion that a devilish, fire-breathing drake might live in the rock below him, but his mind had furnished him with one image that shone through, past that worry. In Lütolf's personal effects: a single gold coin bearing the image of a god and of some long forgotten emperor. A grain of truth in every legend.

'How do you come to be here,' Arnau asked, changing the subject. He peered at the rich mutton dish with the strange pickled vegetables before him, and noticed that his fork was stained with old food, badly washed. He paused, wondering whether it would be acceptable to swap with the fork in the lord's setting, since he clearly was not coming.

'I have known Dietmar since the days of our youth,' Kovacs smiled. 'Once, he travelled. He went on pilgrimage, and we met on the border of the Sultanate of Rum as part of a group of like men under the protection of a party of Hungarian knights. By the time we returned to my homeland we were fast friends. Dietmar stayed at my father's court for some time, and when he returned home I went with him. I have been visiting ever since, all the more since the recent troubles.'

'Troubles?' Arnau prompted, putting his fork back down.

'I am tied to the Hungarian court during my summers, and King András is locked in an ongoing campaign to seize control of Halych, while my ancestral lands along the coast are ravaged with troubles. Nothing at home has been easy since Zadra.'

Arnau frowned. 'Zadra? The Byzantine city?'

A sudden anger flashed across Kovacs' eyes, and Arnau reeled at the change, so unexpected was it in the easy-going minstrel. The Templar's elbow caught his plate of mutton, which went spinning from the table and fell to the floor with a clatter, soaking Arnau's ankles in rich meaty sauce.

The entire room fell silent at the noise, all eyes turning to the top table. Arnau was almost cowering back in his seat as Kovacs had risen, his face white with anger, eyes flashing dangerously.

'Do not *mention* that collection of stinking Greek heretics in my presence, master Vallbona. Zadra is a *Hungarian* city, and the lands of my forefathers. The Venetian pigs ravaged our lands, and those Greek animals have the audacity to be outraged, when the Empire had failed to protect Zadra from invasion, and the city had renounced Venice and placed itself under the protection of the king of Hungary almost two decades ago.'

Arnau stared.

Kovacs was waving a knife at him, and his hand was shaking. The minstrel stopped, breathing heavily, then turned, realising that the entire room was staring at them. In a flash, the anger was gone, and Kovacs shrugged to the room.

'And this mutton is too good. Surely there is magic afoot in the kitchens. Eat, people of Renfrizhausen, lest in my hunger I come round the tables and swipe up all your meals.'

There was a strange silence, and slowly the murmur of conversation returned. Kovacs seated himself once more and turned to Arnau. 'Apologies, Templar. I am one of nature's most gentle creatures, but there are subjects that still grate on my heart, and the fate of my beloved homeland is I think almost as raw as the graf's sorrow, though in a different manner, of course.'

Arnau, still shocked, straightened.

'No apology is necessary. A man *should* be so proud of his home. And whoever claims the grief for Zadra, I feel we can all be bound together in hatred for the Venetians who sacked it.'

'Hear, hear,' Kovacs agreed, tucking into his mutton.

Arnau turned back to his place setting. All he had now was the bowl of strange briny preserved vegetables and warm, damp ankles. He wondered whether he might be treated to a replacement portion, and shuffled aside in his seat to look down. His food was scattered across the timber floor below the table, the platter upside down, and a rough-haired hound was busy wolfing down the mutton with glee.

Arnau sighed.

As he caught the eye of one of the kitchen serfs, who nodded, he took a deep breath. The change in Kovacs when angered had been so sudden and horrifying he had almost fallen from his chair with the force of it. No one here in Renfrizhausen was a simple character, he decided.

'I understand that Bernhard has his men searching for the missing will this afternoon,' he said to the minstrel, quietly.

'Tomorrow I intend to aid him in speaking to the entire population of the castle in an attempt to shed some light upon the passing of the Graf Rüdolf. Would you object to such a thing?'

Kovacs shook his head, his mutton already gone. How did the man eat so swiftly, yet stealthily? 'By all means call upon me and I will tell you everything I can.'

With a nod, Arnau turned to the ladies across the central chair. 'Might I prevail upon you ladies for a little of your time tomorrow?'

The *dame*, Ute, graced him with a look of disapproval, but Lady Gerdrut leaned past her and smiled, and it felt as though her whole being lit up when she did so. 'Most certainly, master *Tempelritter*. Mother and I will both make ourselves available, will we not, Mother?'

Dame Ute turned to her daughter and hissed a stream of words in their own tongue. Gerdrut replied with a sweet face, though her tone carried steel in it. Among the unintelligible stream Arnau caught the name of Graf Dietmar several times. In the end, the old woman turned to Arnau with an expression of grudging ice. 'That would be acceptable, if you are brief.'

Arnau thanked the two ladies and leaned back a little, seeing that a serf was bringing him a replacement plate. He shuffled his heavy chair back a little out of the way as the serf approached, clutching the plate tight. He smiled apologetically as the girl stepped close, and almost fell once more as she suddenly screamed and dropped the plate, a second dish crashing to the floor beside Arnau and sending fresh waves of meaty liquid across his legs. The girl recoiled, stepping back, still screaming and Arnau, brow creased, leaned down to look under the table.

The hound lay on its side, shaking, back legs twitching spasmodically, eyes rolled up showing the whites, and a mix of snotty froth and blood issuing from its jaws and nostrils. Arnau lurched back from his chair, coming to his feet in shock and with a yelp.

Kovacs was standing beside him now and Bernhard and Michael had risen from their places and were hurrying this way.

'What can have happened to the poor beast?' Kovacs muttered.

'Poison,' breathed Gerdrut from the far end of the table. 'My poor Aldo. Who would do such a thing?'

Michael Trost was here now, dropping to a crouch. 'Surely not poison. Likely he ate a bone that punctured his innards. I have seen such things.'

Bernhard pursed his lips. 'It *looks* like poison, Michael, I have to admit. And the *Tempelritter* here is not uniformly welcomed in the castle.' Very briefly, so short as to be noticeable but easily denied, his accusing gaze fell upon the old *dame*, Ute.

Arnau was shaking, he realised, as he stepped back, close to the serf, who was still screaming, ignored by everyone. Suddenly his appetite had shrivelled to nothing. Trost sounded content that it had been unhappy accident, that the dog had simply injured itself on a bone. Arnau was not so easily convinced.

'Well the dog has eaten the whole plate,' the seneschal said. 'There is no easy way to confirm whether the bones are the cause or some other more nefarious thing.' He turned to Arnau. 'I can have a third platter delivered?'

Arnau shook his head. 'Suddenly I am quite replete,' he said, as his stomach gurgled with a mixture of hunger and nerves.

'I shall see you back to your room,' Kovacs said in a friendly, helpful tone. 'You will want to change your hose, I suspect.' Arnau nodded, and now Felipe was there too, having retrieved both of their cloaks. Huddling into his, the Templar followed his squire back along the corridor, taking no interest this time in the tapestry and with the Hungarian minstrel following close behind, accompanied by a serf and a guard. They passed out into the courtyard and hurried across it as the first flakes of the new snowfall began to drift down from the leaden sky.

As they entered the staircase and made their way up, Kovacs waved away the guard and followed the others along to their room. Arnau unlocked the door and entered where, still shaking, he crossed to their packs and searched for a spare pair of hose. Finding them, he removed his boots and began to change quickly.

Kovacs pointed to his soaked, stained boots and addressed the serf that had accompanied them. 'Have those cleaned and dried as fast as you can and returned to the brother here.' As soon as Arnau had stripped off his filthy hose, Kovacs nudged them over to the serf with his foot. 'Same with those. Quick as you can, and off with you now.'

The serf scurried out, carrying the clothes, and Kovacs crossed to the door, closing it behind them and turning the key in the lock.

'While I would prefer to believe that providence had simply called the dog to its end,' the minstrel said, 'I cannot help but agree that poison seems more likely. It would be far too much of a coincidence that you drop your food and the dog dies eating it, when you are the distrusted outsider.'

Arnau nodded as he pulled on his clean hose. 'This entire sojourn is filled with unpleasant but undeniable coincidences, Karolus. That the dog should die eating my food is the least of them. That Rüdolf von Ehingen should die mere days before I arrive is another. That the will should go missing even more so. Something is afoot in Renfrizhausen, and the passing of the young lord was not the end of it, but perhaps just the beginning. I hate to connect them all in motive, but there is a clear link.'

'Oh?'

'The will. The bequest. I carry documents that sign over a sizeable portion of land and wealth from the family to my Order. Rüdolf von Ehingen had a will to the contrary. That the young lord be killed and his will taken is wicked enough, but think that perhaps now here has been an attempt on my life. Are the documents I bear awaiting a similar fate to Rüdolf's will?'

'Then perhaps you need to keep the document safe?'

'I cannot make it any safer for now,' Arnau sighed, tying up his hose and lowering his shirt, turning back to the room. Quickly, he fumbled in his purse for the key and withdrew it, crossing to the heavy oak cupboard.

Felipe flashed him a warning look, and Arnau momentarily worried about the wisdom of letting Kovacs see in the chest. The man seemed perfectly reasonable, and Arnau could not immediately come up with any reason the foreign minstrel might have for committing any of these deeds, but the memory of that sudden violent change in him at the talk of Zadra yet made him nervous.

Still, he had something he wanted to do.

Unlocking the cupboard, he bent in. Careful not to disturb the folded surcoat in the folds of which lay the documents, he found the bag containing the rest of Lütolf's effects. Crossing to the windowsill, he tipped them carefully out, one by one into his hand. Kovacs watched with interest each treasure tumbling from the opening, until Arnau came to the coin, which he held in the flat of his hand, turning to the minstrel.

'From Lütolf's effects and in light of your story of the Roman gold,' he said, and proffered the coin.

Kovacs hesitated for a moment, and then reached down and picked it up carefully, turning it around and around in the poor light, squinting.

'D N VALENTINIANUS P F AUG,' he read. 'Our Lord Valentinian, the pious and lucky emperor. Not so lucky if his coins end up in the hands of a German tribe, I might say. And look, here is a picture of the armoured emperor.'

He turned it over. 'This winged goddess is Victory, which I feel is another ironic sight in the circumstances. She holds a long cross. You should be pleased. An ancient coin that bears your own symbol.' He smiled. 'If I remember my lessons, this is Valentinian the *third*, a hapless emperor who was one of those that ruled a shadow of old Rome in its latter days. By his time already the tribes from these lands were claiming territory all over the Empire. It is no surprise to find that coins have made it back here over the years.'

Arnau nodded. 'You know your history, Karolus.'

'It is something of a requirement in my business, master Templar, but I hail from a noble family, albeit through a concubine, and I was educated at court. There is, of course, no indication from this one coin that there was ever a real hoard of treasure.'

'It is a hint, at least.'

'That it is. It may be that Lütolf kept it as a good luck charm. Such superstition is rife in the mountains, and it does rather openly display the cross, after all. It may be unconnected, and certainly as long as I have known them the family have struggled to maintain themselves, which would be unlikely had they a store of gold.'

'Perhaps the castle has a resident dragon and a ghost, but they *protect* a huge pile of gold,' Arnau said, with a wry smile.

'And a murderer,' threw in Felipe from the corner, his face deadly serious. 'It has a murderer.'

'Yes,' Kovacs agreed quietly, 'despite Dietmar's hope that the blame can be landed upon passing vagabonds, it seems a given that someone here is capable of the most despicable deeds.'

'Perhaps tomorrow will turn something up,' Arnau murmured.

'Quite.' Kovacs handed the coin back and Arnau replaced everything in the cabinet, dropping the key back into his pouch once he had locked it.

'I will speak with Dietmar about what has happened. I shall see you later, master de Vallbona.'

Arnau nodded and watched as Kovacs unlocked the door once more and left the room.

'I do not like this,' Felipe said. 'We should leave.'

Arnau felt a strange lurch, picturing himself saying just that to Bochard in the imperial palace a few years earlier. This was different, he told himself. This was not something he was about for his own vanity. This was a duty he was performing, and he could hardly leave until the will was found and the comparison made, anyway.

'You might as well attend the services for the rest of the day in my stead,' Arnau sighed.

'Brother?'

'No shoes,' he smiled, and sagged down onto his bed.

***

Arnau sat on his cot, polishing the hilt of his sword carefully and peering at the gleaming iron, when the door reverberated to a knock. He frowned. Who it might be he couldn't imagine. He had spent the rest of the afternoon and evening in their room, mostly alone.

He had missed services and the evening meal without footwear to brave the courtyard. A serf had brought the meal to him, and had offered to eat some to prove it was safe. Arnau had waved him away. Since what had happened at lunch the kitchen staff would be very much on the alert and no one would have a chance to mess with any other meal now. Consequently, he had eaten without great worry and had not collapsed on the floor coughing up blood.

Felipe had wanted to stay with him, but he had sent the squire to the hall for food, and to the chapel for all services. Then, during the evening, while the squire had been enthralled with a performance by Kovacs in the main hall, Arnau had had a visit from Bernhard. For a refreshing hour they had talked not of wills and murder, but of Brother Lütolf, during his days as the master of Renfrizhausen, and during his time at the preceptory, of which Arnau could only tell the last year in any detail. Finally Bernhard had retired, having admitted that despite another full search, they had still been unable to locate the missing will, and Arnau had settled in to polishing his sword.

For a moment he wondered if the knock was Felipe returning, but realised that the squire would be at compline, as the bell for the service had rung only half an hour after Bernhard had left.

'Come,' he said, sitting up straight.

He blinked as the door swung in to reveal the looming shape of the hulking red-bearded guard. Arnau's hand snaked round the hilt of his sword, ready to lift it, but the big man entered with both hands raised in peace.

Arnau released the hilt and placed his sword on the bed.

'Can I help you?' he asked, coldly. His jaw still felt painful, as well as his head, and both bore bruise and lump from the assault on the stairs.

'I… be Matthias,' the man said in thick, German-accented Frankish.

'Yes?'

'I not like you. You not right here. *Verstehe*? Understand?'

Arnau nodded. 'I had formed that impression, yes. Did you drop by just to hate me, or is there something else?'

Matthias' lip wrinkled. 'I not like you. But I not kill you.'

'Well that's encouraging.'

'*Verstehe*. I am warrior. Sword, yes? I want kill you, I kill you. In open. In light. With sword. Not like…' he made a throat-cutting motion and then mimed being sick. 'Understand? *Verstehe*?'

And Arnau did. He nodded. 'It is, in a very odd way, comforting to know that if you suddenly decide to you will attack me in the courtyard with your sword.' He nodded as the man glared at him. 'I understand. You might be an unpleasant man, but you are one with principles. You will not use poison or a knife in the dark. And while I cannot say I like you any more than you like me, I find that I believe you.'

Matthias frowned as he translated and slowly digested this. With a nod of agreement, he turned and opened the door.

'I will see you tomorrow when we interview everyone.'

The man's lip twitched once more, but he said nothing as he left.

Arnau slumped back to his pillow. Perhaps he would try to sleep early. Tomorrow looked like being a busy day.

CHAPTER SEVEN

FRIDAY MORNING

'So we know very little, in truth.'

Bernhard nodded. 'Respectfully, though, my men and I have had a great deal to do since the discovery, and little chance to delve. The disappearance of the will, your arrival and the various troubles that brought, the graf having largely shut himself away for the first two days, the laying out of the body and searching the castle. You understand.'

Arnau did. Events had somewhat snowballed since the death of Rüdolf less than four days ago, and Arnau and Felipe appearing had complicated matters and given Bernhard and the rest yet more to do. 'So you say that this Anna was the one who found the body and that it is believed that Graf Dietmar was the last to see him, with the exception of his killer, that is?'

Again a nod from Bernhard. 'The graf is expecting you, but I had Anna brought to the guardroom first. I think that is probably where to begin.'

'I think you're right.'

They strode into the room with its roaring fire, grateful to be out of the freezing air. Ever-present clouds were yet to drop today's deluge on the castle. A young maid was seated close to the flames and rose with a nervous start as they entered.

'Anna,' Bernhard said soothingly, then spoke in his native tongue, the only word of which Arnau caught being '*Tempelritter*'. The marshal would have to translate here.

'Tell us about finding the body,' Arnau said, calmly.

The maid began at Bernhard's invitation, hesitantly at first, and the marshal kept up well as he translated.

'It was Monday morning when she brought it to our attention, though it was the previous evening when she found the body, in a way.'

Arnau shook his head in confusion. 'What?'

She was still going, though, and Bernhard was translating the explanation. 'On Sunday eve she went to the well and tried to draw water for the kitchens, but could not raise the bucket. She returned to the kitchen and reported this, but all assumed that the ropes had frozen, which happens from time to time in the winter. It will often take two strong guards to free it then. So they used some of the water stored in ewers in the kitchen range. The next day, in the morning, she was sent to try again and the bucket was still stuck. She called for one of the guards, and Winrich helped haul the bucket up. The body came up with it.'

Arnau leaned back against the wall. 'How did he react? How did Anna?'

Bernhard rattled on once more, and then translated the reply. 'Anna was terrified. I can concur with this, for I saw her shortly afterwards and she spent the rest of the day in shock, with Father Oswald looking after her. She says that Winrich was so surprised that he let go for a moment and almost dropped the body back down the well.'

'Reactions that do not suggest involvement,' Arnau murmured.

'Quite.'

'When was it that she first encountered difficulty with the well, then. Do we know exactly?'

More translation. 'Mere minutes after the compline bell was rung.'

'Then we have a good approximation of time, given what you said earlier, though I think I need to see the graf to confirm it.'

'Of course,' Bernhard nodded. 'Will you require my presence?'

'No, I think not, for now. Can you have the rest of the guards and staff ready, and I'll update you then? I can't see we'll get much more of use from Anna for now. Can anyone speak for where she was before trying the well after compline?'

'She was in the kitchens preparing the evening meal for at least an hour. She will have been seen. Essentially, all the kitchen staff will have been working together.'

Arnau nodded. It was possible that one might have slipped away for a few minutes in the busyness of preparation, but that would be real trouble to reveal, and he'd already largely written out the guards and serfs from his list of likely killers. They would have so little to gain. Besides, a girl like Anna would be very unlikely to bring down a young knight and cut his throat. That would take strength.

'Very well, I'll see you back here in around an hour.'

Leaving the guardroom and the marshal, he strode back out into the cold, wrapping his cloak about him. Felipe was waiting by the far door, and fell in at his heel as they entered the main range. Up the staircase, they made their way to the graf's chamber, where Arnau knocked. He'd not sought an audience as such this time, but Bernhard had already spoken to the castle's master and Dietmar had agreed.

'Come,' called the graf's voice, and Arnau entered the cold chamber with his squire at heel. He bowed as he entered. 'I must apologise for this, my lord, but in order to do all I can to help find the killer, I need to know everything I can about the hours before and after Rüdolf's death.'

A look of pain crossed the older man's face, but he nodded in a resigned manner. He had set Arnau on this course, after all.

'I was in the hall downstairs on the eve of Sunday, and then in my room. I was speaking to Rüdolf in the hall, first. In fact, we were arguing. Things had become a little heated.'

'Might I ask what the argument was about?'

'Of course. The castle is undergoing something of a restoration. You cannot see much evidence of it at the moment, partially because it has only just begun, and partly because we simply cannot afford to do much. There had been a tremor in the earth a few years ago, and parts of the castle suffered minor damage. I have been living with it, and intended to continue doing so, but Rüdolf was insistent that work begin. He set Bernhard and his men to beginning work and had plans to bring in an architect from Sülz. I told him that we could not afford all of this, and we argued. He was adamant that the will would bring us back funds that had been given to your Order and that those funds would cover the work. He even waved the will at me angrily. I wish now I had snatched it from him. It might not have disappeared, and if it is the cause of all this, Rüdolf might still be with us.'

'So you argued over money and the will, but not enough surely to drive a wedge between you?'

Dietmar shook his head. 'No. We argue such on occasion. What father and son do not? But that was the last time I saw him, as he stomped from the room in fury. And I gather that was the last *anyone* saw of him.'

Arnau nodded. 'Might I ask if you have any idea what time this was?'

'I can say with certainty, for the compline bell tolled just as Rüdolf and I were at the height of our argument. The echoes still rang as he stormed out.'

Arnau chewed his lip. 'Then we know when the murder occurred, my lord. Rüdolf left you at the compline bell and Anna found the body just after it. It seems that we can rule out anyone who was at compline, which might save us some time.'

Dietmar shook his head. 'It will save you little. The only attendance Father Oswald ever gets for compline is Bernhard, and indeed it is Bernhard who tolls the bell. The evening meal is served shortly thereafter, and so the castle's staff are entirely busy preparing. My family habitually attend only one daily service, and it is never too early or too late in the day. The guards, of course, are busy much of the time.'

Arnau turned to Felipe. The squire had been to both compline services in the castle thus far. Felipe nodded. 'I have only seen Bernhard at the services.'

'Then that is little help. As long as Bernhard and Father Oswald can vouch for each other, I can rule them out. And if compline was imminent, neither would have time for the nefarious deed before the service. I presume you remained in the hall, my lord?'

'For a few moments only, once Bernhard visited me. I then returned here to my room where I raged, since the staff would be preparing the hall for the meal shortly after that. I left my room once more only in time for dinner, once I was sufficiently calm. I thought nothing of the fact that Rüdolf was not at dinner. I presumed him still in a rage, locked in his room.'

Arnau straightened. Likely someone would be able to vouch for Dietmar, and his grief spoke to Arnau of his innocence in any regard. It seemed that speaking to the castle's inhabitants was simply ruling people out. With luck he could rule enough out to be left with a clear culprit.

Thanking the lord, he bade farewell and withdrew from the room.

'Who next?' Felipe asked.

'Lady Gerdrut, I think. I am not looking forward to speaking to her mother.'

'Quite, brother.'

They found one of the servants and had him lead them to the room of Dietmar and Lütolf's sister. The serf knocked for them, secured admittance and opened the door. Arnau's spirits sank as the room came into view. It was a warm, bright and homely chamber, decorated with tapestries and hangings, with a fire blazing. The only chilling element was the *Grand Dame*, Ute, seated beside her daughter as the pair worked at embroidery hoops. Perhaps it was for the best, he decided. At least the younger woman might supply a little moral support against the old *dame*.

'I apologise for the intrusion, ladies. Has Bernhard spoken to you?'

Ute von Ehingen glared at him with her customary ice. Gerdrut nodded, however. 'You are here to find out about the evening Rüdolf died.'

'Yes. We have narrowed the time down to the compline service. I understand that neither of you attended?'

'No. No one does, in fact. Not from the family, anyway. If you are seeking to determine our whereabouts, though, I can speak for myself. I had bathed earlier in the day.' She gave an oddly embarrassed smile. 'I suffer rather from a stiffening of the joints, in winter especially, and a warm bath in camomile, breweswort and brown fennel once a week does somewhat alleviate my aches. It can be a lengthy business, and I was still plaiting my hair and dressing throughout compline and almost to dinner. If you speak to Katherine, my lady's maid, she will confirm all of this.'

Arnau felt an odd sense of relief. He'd greatly hoped there would be no reason to suspect the lady, and for a number of reasons, some of which were very un-monastic and he would have to do appropriate penance for in due course.

'And you, my lady?' he said quietly, turning to the *dame* and trying not to wince.

'If it is any of your business...'

'It is, Mother,' Gerdrut put in. 'My brother has tasked him with it.'

Ute harrumphed. She resumed in her scratchy voice, cold and hard. 'I was in the kitchens during the preparations for the evening meal. There has been a great deal of slovenly conduct of late among the servants. I have noted crockery and cutlery that have not been properly clean, the rushes on the floor not changed, fires unbanked and the like. I have taken, over the past few weeks, to overseeing activity and chastising those responsible for mess. You may ask any of the kitchen staff. I am certain that each and every one felt the lash of my tongue over the time of which you speak. And my own maid, Jutte, was with me too. So now you have the answers to your impertinent question. You should leave.'

Smiling at the apologetic look from Gerdrut, Arnau bowed, said farewell and departed.

'We are running low on suspects, Felipe,' he said out in the corridor. 'Dietmar might have had the opportunity, unless someone can vouch for him being in his room, though I cannot see why the lord might do such a thing. Ute was in the kitchens, and it seems likely that will be confirmed. The maid Katherine should clear Gerdrut. I am starting to become vexed by this. Come.'

It took directions from a serf to find the room of the Hungarian minstrel, Karolus Kovacs, which turned out to be the apartment next door to the graf, bringing them full circle. A brief knock and they were hailed in. The minstrel sat at a window, wrapped in a red and green shawl, peering at a paper covered in tiny writing. He put it down on the table as he looked up, placing a dragon-shaped paperweight atop it to stop it blowing away in the cold breeze from the opening.

'You are here to seek my whereabouts during Sunday evening, I presume?'

'If that is acceptable?'

The minstrel laughed. 'In actual fact, I was alone, but I think I can supply you with an alibi regardless. I am currently composing a ballad of a grand sort, telling the tale of the founding of this great fortress, Henry the Lion's dragon and Dietmar's family's part in it all. It is becoming troublesome, but it is progressing. Any time I am alone, you will hear me practicing and working. Sunday night I was obsessing over a refrain on my lute. I must have played a particularly vexing part of the air a thousand times that eve in a hundred different ways. I am certain that numerous folk would have heard me, including Dietmar.'

'You knew the graf was next door?'

Kovacs chuckled. 'Dietmar was angry. When he gets angry he throws things. Between every few bars of my melody I was given the percussion of a shouted curse or a thrown chair. Yes, Dietmar was in his room. And between his bouts of bellowed rage, I am sure he will have heard me in here.'

Arnau sagged. Again, like the lady, he had been hoping for some reason that Kovacs would prove innocent, but every confirmation he received ruled out more and more possibilities.

Thanking the minstrel, he made a brief visit next door once again to confirm with Dietmar that he had heard the lute being played that evening, which he had. Then they descended the staircase, grumbling.

'So Dietmar was in his room, as were both Gerdrut and Kovacs. Ute was in the kitchens. Two of those we have confirmed, and the other two we should be able to any time. Come, let us rule out two more before we meet those Bernhard has gathered.'

The pair marched down the stairs once more, out across the freezing courtyard and to the chapel. Father Oswald was busy at the altar, cleaning the surface with a light brush and Arnau called out to him gently, his voice quiet in the large room, and received no reply. As he crossed the church, calling out, he realised with interest that the priest was hard of hearing.

Finally, as they approached the altar, the old man with the white hair turned in surprise.

'All right,' he snapped in accented Frankish. 'You don't need to shout. I'm not deaf, you know?'

Arnau took a deep breath, pushing down the urge to argue.

'The compline service, Father,' he said, keeping his voice loud and his words clipped and clear.

'Yes?'

'Is it true that only Bernhard attends with you?'

The priest's nose wrinkled. 'Bernhard Bulstrich is the only attendant at *many* of my services. But yes, he is the only one at compline. He is a good Christian. Attends services at all times and helps me with my preparations and maintenance, for I am not as young as once I was. He was there that night as always. Prayed for the lords of Renfrizhausen, he did.'

Arnau nodded. 'I'll bet he did.'

'What?'

Arnau's voice rose again. 'I said I'll bet he did. And there is no way that the marshal could have been absent for even part of the service? He was there at the beginning and the end? There is no way you could be misled or mistaken?'

Father Oswald's brow folded into a severe, disapproving frown. 'As a purported soldier of God you would question the word of a priest? John four, Temple knight: "*We be of God and he that knoweth God, heareth us; he that is* not *of God, heareth* not *us. In this thing we know the spirit of truth, and the spirit of error.*"'

Arnau cringed at the admonition. 'I did not mean to imply that you uttered a falsehood,' he tried.

'No,' the priest snapped, 'Bernhard was there at the beginning, when he helped me prepare the altar, and ring in the service, and he was there at the end when he thanked me and we discussed the subject of fidelity, which had been the content of my reading. Bulstrich was with me throughout.'

'Thank you, Father,' Arnau said gratefully. 'I don't think I need disturb you further.'

They left the chapel once more and crossed towards the guardroom. 'So Bernhard and Father Oswald were together in the chapel, and I cannot bring myself to doubt the priest's word. With the exception of Michael Trost, we have accounted for everyone but the guards and serfs.'

The guardroom was warm and close, filled with men in chain shirts and the family's livery. In addition to Bernhard, there were six guards. Arnau strode across to the marshal and murmured in low tones. 'One at a time, I think.'

Bernhard gave the order, and as the men filed out into the cold courtyard Arnau updated him with what they had found out so far. Once the room had emptied, the marshal leaned through the door and beckoned to the first guard.

The following half hour was no more productive than the visits in the castle's main rooms had been. It continued to clear folk of suspicion, though that did little to help point a finger. Matthias and Wolf independently vouched for one another as they were the poor souls who had been on duty that night, marching around the walls of the castle. As such they had seen each other regularly. When asked about the compline bell, neither claimed to have seen anything in the courtyard, but explained that when walking the battlements there are large sections where the courtyard is out of view, behind buildings. The wall walk is designed, after all, for looking out and not in, as Wolf reminded them with more than a touch of sarcasm.

Otto had been off-duty in the guard house, along with Leupold. The pair had been playing dice by the fire when they heard the compline bell, and remained there until they attended the meal. They effectively ruled one another out.

Winrich had been theoretically in his rooms, for he'd been suffering a minor illness over the preceding days, but had actually snuck out and down to the buttery, where he and Conrad, the stable boy, had indulged in the mead kept there, since both were suffering. He had remained there for some time, the pair having fallen asleep through low-level inebriation, until he awoke deep in the night and snuck back to his room. As well as Conrad being able to vouch for him, several of the kitchen staff could too, he said, since they kept coming in and out for dinner preparations.

That left just one guard, for Renfrizhausen's military numbered only six. That last was Anselm, the man who had first admitted the Templars to the castle. Anselm had been on duty by the gate that evening. He had been in the small guardroom adjacent to the gate. No one could vouch for him, though he claimed to have left his post only once, to use the garderobe, and that visit had been seen by Matthias from the walls, suggesting that he was telling the truth. He had remained there, or so he said, until the morning. When Otto came to replace him on shift before dawn, he discovered that the door in the gate was unlocked. Anselm asserted that he had checked it when he first arrived for duty and it was locked, and neither man claimed to have unlocked it.

As the guards left to go about their duties, Arnau sat with Bernhard and Felipe in the guardroom, the door shut once more to give them privacy.

'We have ruled out the family entirely, and yourself and your guards can generally vouch for one another. Father Oswald is in the clear. The only blot so far is Anselm. Apart from his trip to the garderobe no one can account for him. And someone unlocked that gate. They had to have done that while he was at the garderobe, which was in the middle of the night.'

Felipe tapped his fingers on his knee. 'And that rules out any interloper coming in and doing the deed,' he muttered. 'The door would have been locked before the lord was killed. Being open afterwards is of no consequence.'

'Not so,' Bernhard replied. 'The door is open every now and then, for the gathering of kindling, or men going out into the woods around the castle to shoot birds or snare coneys or many other reasons. It is not impossible that someone might have come into the castle at an earlier time and lain in hiding, awaiting the chance. If he then committed the act, he might have slipped out of the castle once more that night, accounting for the open gate.'

Arnau frowned. It was feasible. It sounded a little farfetched, admittedly, but it was not impossible. 'What of the attempt on my life? Or the missing will?'

'What if the dog simply choked?' retorted Bernhard. 'And the lord had the will upon him. His attacker could easily have taken it.'

'If that *is* the case,' Arnau sighed, 'then we will never know the truth. The snow has come down many times since then, and any tracks will be long since covered.' He chewed on his lip. 'Still, that doesn't sound right to me. Someone would have had to hide in the busy castle for a time, waiting for his chance.'

Bernhard shrugged. 'There are many dark nooks in this place. It is not impossible. My men and I recently began surveying the structure of the castle for Graf Rüdolf's repair plans. You simply would not believe how many hiding places there are.'

'And that would mean someone lying in wait near the castle in the middle of a snowy winter, waiting for the opportunity when the door is unlocked and unguarded to slip inside. It sounds unlikely to me.'

'This I will grant you, but I have known Anselm for many a year, and cannot imagine him doing such a thing. Indeed, I cannot see what he might stand to gain.'

'And that is another problem. Who outside the castle might have such a grudge against the lord that they might consider such a thing? It sounds unlikely.'

Bernhard fixed him with a level gaze. 'More unlikely that an Iberian knight arriving in the middle of a blizzard with a will to contest?'

Arnau cringed. 'I concede the timing is odd. Perhaps we should see the kitchen staff and other serfs. After all, if that meal *was* poisoned, then it leads one to consider the possibility of their involvement. How many are there? I was surprised that you have only six guards.'

'The castle's staff is small these days,' the marshal admitted. 'Smaller than ever before. Under the graf's father there were almost twice as many, but the family's funds and lands have dwindled steadily. It is only my loyalty to the von Ehingen that keeps me in my post, for another man might well have left to seek a better paying position. But life is what it is, and I shall remain with the graf and his family until they are no more or they can no longer afford to keep me.' He sighed. 'Six guards and seven serfs. Anna and Hilde in the kitchens, Katherine and Jutte with the ladies of the house, Hugo and Gunther on general household duties, and Conrad in the stables. They are barely enough to keep the castle functioning, in truth.'

Arnau nodded. Only thirteen altogether. So at the evening meals that must be the entire staff at the tables with the family. He could remember only ten to twelve. Yes, five or six at each trestle. Undoubtedly the two kitchen staff ate separately after their duties were done.

'Only two in the kitchens?' Arnau frowned. 'The way the lady Ute spoke, it sounded like dozens.'

'Four,' corrected Bernhard. 'In meal preparation, Hugo and Gunther can be found there too. All the staff will be in the kitchens now, for I have sent for them all.'

The three of them left the guardroom and crossed the cold courtyard under the noticeably lower clouds, heading for the kitchen block. Four combined buildings, Arnau could make out. He'd been in plenty of castles and monasteries in his time, and though the detail might change from region to region, the root of it didn't. The bake house was identifiable at the near end from its several chimneys blackened with regular smoke. Next in line was the kitchen itself, with one very large chimney from its great roaring hearth. Third would be a cellar or pantry, he could see the change in stone where the rooms were divided off, but this stretch had no windows. Then another faintly visible divide before the last stretch, again with no windows, but with one wide, low door. Wide enough to roll a sizeable barrel through. The buttery, where the beer and mead and wine were kept.

With Bernhard in the fore, they entered the kitchen where all seven serfs waited. This time they moved into the buttery, where the serfs were admitted one by one for their interview. Anna was excused as she had already spoken to them, but the rest of the discussions were singularly unenlightening. Katherine had indeed been with Lady Gerdrut throughout her bath and all her ministrations from there to the meal. Jutte, the old *dame*'s maid, had been on her lady's tail throughout her time, which not only cleared Jutte, but also the old woman. Moreover, almost all the staff could account for Ute being present in the kitchens.

Hilde, Hugo and Gunther could account for one another's presence throughout, none having left the others' sight for more than a minute, not having to leave the block at any time. Moreover, having Ute's sharp tongue whipping them to a work frenzy allowed no time for dawdling. All that remained, then, was Conrad, though he vouched for the ill Winrich, just as Winrich had vouched for him.

They left the kitchen block perhaps three quarters of an hour later no wiser than when they had arrived. Arnau and Felipe hurried with Bernhard across the courtyard to find the only person in the castle to whom they had not spoken: Michael Trost. He was in the hall, seated at a table and working through documents with a quill. He looked up as they entered.

'You have come to question me now?'

Arnau nodded. 'It is necessary I'm afraid, if we are to uncover the truth.'

'And you will want to know where I was during the time the young lord was killed?'

'Yes.'

'Sadly, I can provide no witness to my presence, but I will say for the record that I was in the library, going through the family accounts. Anyone in the castle will tell you that this is my habit now whenever I can spare an hour. Graf Rüdolf had two weeks since set me the impossible task of squeezing the family's fortunes to provide adequate funds to begin the refurbishment of the castle. I have also been looking at the estates that were granted to your Order by Lütolf von Ehingen with interest.'

Arnau felt a sudden flutter of nerves. 'Oh?'

'Yes. The funds delivered we can do little about, but the estates granted consist of four good farming communities, all within a few days of here, including the graf's favoured vineyards in Württemberg. If I am correct, two of those have been sold to the Teutonic Order already, one sold to its workers, though how they managed to find the money I have no idea, and only one seems to still be held by the Temple, farmed by their tenants. No wonder you have been sent to contest the will. Should it be ruled that the lands be returned to the family, your Order would have astounding trouble doing so, my lord.'

Arnau felt that flutter again. He'd not looked into the matter himself, of course, beyond the fact that they'd been granted to the Order, and that suddenly made his mission all the more important. He frowned. Was he being thrown off the subject here?

'So you cannot provide proof of where you were?' he confirmed.

'No. But I am not guilty. I have served the family since the old lord's day and my loyalty has never been questioned. You may claim that I had the opportunity, but no *landgericht* will find me guilty, which is as it should be, since I am not.'

Arnau leaned back. The man was probably right. In truth, Arnau didn't really think the man was the sort to do such a thing. He had no clear martial training, a thin and light frame, did not habitually carry a weapon and was obviously much more at home with a quill than a knife. And if it came down to a trial, he could supply no actual evidence against Trost.

He sighed and turned to Bernhard. 'This morning has been singularly unhelpful. I begin to see why you have made no progress. I have an idea, though, which might shed further light.'

'Oh?'

Arnau nodded. 'I have in mind a reconstruction of the crime.'

CHAPTER EIGHT

FRIDAY EVENING

Arnau stalked through the falling flakes of white, Felipe at his heel. The rest of the castle's populace were about their normal business, and the family had been asked kindly to retake their positions as they were on the evening of the death. Most had agreed readily, for it was part of their general routine anyway, or at least no great deviation from it. The *Grand Dame* had been argumentative but after some convincing from her children, she had snorted and told them that she'd had the intention of watching the kitchen serfs carefully anyway. All was as close a facsimile as Arnau could manage to the time of the murder.

The sun had not been down for long, but already the darkness was becoming oppressive in the snow, especially with the heavy low cloud hiding the silvery light of the moon. It made Arnau shudder to think of the young lord's last hour in this place, and recreating it made it all the more immediate and real. He didn't like this one bit. He'd seen death often enough, and killed men in numbers in his time, but they had been enemies, face to face and on the field of battle. Murder was a different beast entirely.

Felipe huffed a cold breath. 'So I am Graf Rüdolf?'

Arnau nodded as they entered the main range once more. Reason told him that the murder had to have taken place here, somewhere, and not in any of the other buildings around the courtyard. The young lord had left the hall after arguing with his father. They might not know what had happened next, but the short time between compline beginning and the maid's trip to the well made it extremely unlikely he had gone anywhere else. He had left the hall and had died somewhere between there and the well, Arnau had decided.

He had been alive at the compline bell but dead, in Anna's words, *mere minutes* after the bell. There could only have been time to get from the hall to the well and die en route.

'Where do we begin?'

Arnau gestured ahead. 'Lord Dietmar is waiting for you in the hall. I want you to stay with him until the compline bell rings and then leave, walking purposefully towards the courtyard. Try and act as though you do not expect trouble. Angry and preoccupied. You will no doubt pick up a cloak for the weather on the way out.'

Felipe nodded and headed along the tapestry corridor, knocking at the hall door and entering. Arnau had perhaps five minutes until compline, for he had seen Bernhard cross to the chapel to help Father Oswald prepare just before they themselves had left the stairway a few moments ago.

Where, then? Where had the killer been? He looked along the corridor and wondered whether a person could conceivably hide behind the tapestry. It was certainly large enough, much taller than a man and many yards long. Gingerly, knowing its value, he stepped behind the near end of it, almost choking in the dust the movement raised. The thing needed beating badly. As he stood, covered by the heavy material, he looked down at his feet and shook his head. It mattered not that his feet would have protruded from the bottom, if he was any judge. Climbing back out, he went halfway along the passage to test his theory.

It was true. Any lump the size of a human behind the tapestry would stand out in the torchlight. Moreover, the difficulty he had emerging from it would make any surprise attack slow and clumsy. No, so that ruled out the corridor. And he was still convinced from his aerial view of the courtyard that it had been far too open for a struggle such as likely occurred.

A wise man hearing shall be the wiser; and a man of understanding shall hold governance.

Proverbs one, five. Give me such wisdom and understanding, Lord.

If the corridor and the courtyard were ruled out, then, that left just the antechamber in between. Grabbing the nearest torch from the corridor to provide extra illumination, he entered that small room. The corner to his immediate left was shadowed, as was the stairwell, and either could harbour a person unseen. He tried both and decided upon the latter. The corner was visible through the outer door from the courtyard. Too dangerous.

He was finally satisfied that he knew where the murderer had lurked.

Glancing out across the courtyard through the door, he saw the light in the chapel window glow brighter as Bernhard and the priest lit more candles for the service. Time was almost upon them.

Quickly, he searched the room. The castle was short on servants these days and Lady Ute was angry because the staff were pushed to keep things clean and working. No one had beaten out the tapestry in months, and with the extra duties like snow shovelling, Arnau would be willing to bet that the less lived-in areas of the castle were rarely cleaned these days. Places like this antechamber.

Holding the torch low, he went round the floor first, but there was nothing to see other than many wet boot prints. It was possible serfs had mopped the floor, of course. That was a quick job. The walls, on the other hand...

He began at the door, rising to his full height and dropping close to the ground like waves as he passed around the room, examining the walls. Nothing showed other than general dirt, and finally he arrived at the cloaks hanging on the pegs. Were the cloaks specific to owners, or just for general use of the castle's occupants when they emerged into the snow? Either way, they were regularly used, moved and removed and added to. The cloaks hanging there would have been different on that night.

Frowning, he swiftly unhooked the five cloaks that remained on the wall and dropped them in the corner. Bringing the torch close, he peered at the wall behind them. It took him just a few moments for him to spot it. He had seen the telltale spray of blood from a blow before, more than once. These marks were old, and the blood had gone dark brown over the past days of drying on the wall. The spray was only in two small patches, which meant that much had been absorbed by one of the hanging cloaks. That cloak had to have been removed, else someone would have noticed it.

And the second angel shedded out his vial into the sea, and the blood was made as of a dead thing, and each man living was dead in the sea...

With a shiver at the words of the Revelation of Saint John of the end times, he twitched, and then jumped at the sudden clong of the bell across the yard. Bernhard and Father Oswald had begun. In a flash he returned the torch to its bracket, then hung the cloaks back up and even as they swayed to a halt and he stepped back into the stairway, he heard the hall door open and booted footsteps in a stride. He wished now that he had insisted on seeing the young lord's body. It might have told him more about what happened, after all. But gentle probes had revealed that no one had visited the cellar where he rested since the laying out other than Graf Dietmar and Arnau doubted asking to examine poor Rüdolf would be taken well.

Still, he was now sure, looking at the marks on the wall, that the young lord was subdued here, not killed. The spray had not been cleaned. The killer must have thought it all caught on the cloak, yet there was nowhere near enough blood to be a cut throat. This was a smack on the head, he felt certain. He chewed his lip as he listened to the boots of the squire approaching along the corridor.

A wise man hearing shall be the wiser...

Where could the throat have been cut then?

The well, he realised. The torrent of blood would be lost there, unseen. Of course!

He braced himself, waiting and watching.

Felipe appeared, paused in the room and turned to the wall of cloak pegs. Arnau stepped out and reached up to the back of the squire's head, tapping him there with a finger. 'I have just struck you. Perhaps with a dagger pommel? Something hard enough to knock you down. That's how it was done, I'm certain. There will be moments passing now as you succumb to the blow, possibly struggling as I subdue you.'

The missing cloak, which would be spattered with blood...

He unhooked a cloak and as Felipe allowed his knees to buckle as though he'd been knocked out, Arnau gathered him in the garment. As the squire lay shaking in the fur and wool, Arnau grasped it and began to drag it out into the courtyard. With a little difficulty, for Felipe was farm stock and not small despite his youth, Arnau dragged the cloak across the snowy flags to the well. As he went, still counting, he looked about. Light was discernible behind many shutters, but only the chapel windows glowed. No one could see him. He even watched the battlements, but saw neither of the two guards who patrolled up there.

Reaching the well, he lifted Felipe up to the lip with grunts and a struggle.

'Here I lean you out over the well, cut your throat and tip you in.'

That being done, both men stepped back and straightened.

'Now I dispose of my evidence. I drop the bloody cloak and perhaps even the dagger into the well, where they may never be found. Indeed, had the body not caught on the bucket, it would probably have rotted in the water and never been found. Unpleasant for the castle's occupants but good for the killer.' He chewed his lip again, still counting. 'By now we have had time to return through a door and out of view of the courtyard.' He glanced up and saw the two guards on the walls emerge from behind roofs, circling and gesturing to one another, and then disappearing into towers once more. He then turned to the kitchens. 'Any moment now.'

Almost on cue Anna, the maid, appeared from the kitchens with her bucket for the well.

'Barely time to do anything,' Arnau sighed, 'other than get out here, do the deed, and return.'

'So can we rule out anyone?' the squire asked.

'I can tell you from experience now that no one small or weak could have done this. Dragging you in the cloak was tough work.

The ladies are in the clear, and I think Father Oswald too, as well as the smaller of the serfs. Both ladies' maids, as well as Anna, Hilde and Hugo could not have done it, I think. Gunther might be strong enough, and Conrad the stable hand. Perhaps he was not as ill as he made out, but if he was, along with Winrich, then neither of them could really have done it. Given the time constraints, Kovacs could not have done the deed and been back to his room swiftly enough, and I have listened to his lute. He would be audible from even the floor below, so I think we can be reasonably certain that he was in his room. The two men at the battlements could not have got down here, killed him, and returned to their place so quickly. And Bernhard was with the priest in the chapel.'

'Cuts down the number, does it not, brother?'

Arnau nodded. 'That leaves Graf Dietmar, though I cannot find it in me to consider him. But in the interest of objectivity, he did have the time to follow his son, do the deed and disappear back inside. He would only have to go back to the hall, for he didn't go up to his room immediately. The library is on the middle floor of the main range. If Michael Trost *was* there, he could not have done it in time, but we have only his word for that. And I have to admit that the clear suggestion is the guard Anselm. He was alone at the gate, and the guard post by the gate is just over there.' He pointed. 'A simple job to get in and out of there quickly.'

'Or an unknown character who snuck out through the door?'

Arnau turned to the squire. 'Do you believe that?'

'No, not really.'

'Neither do I. *"Come ye, and prove ye me, saith the Lord,"* as Isaiah says. So that leaves Dietmar, Trost, and Anselm as the only three people who had the time to do it, were not under observation of another, and cannot supply adequate evidence that they were where they say. Dietmar was in his room shortly afterwards, as Kovacs noted, but I fear he had the opportunity to do the deed first.'

'Only three, then,' Felipe mumbled.

'Quite. A father, which is too dreadful and unbelievable a notion for me, and I cannot see Dietmar killing his heir. Trost, though. He is a shady, defensive character, I think. I am not entirely sure he has the strength or martial prowess to do such a thing, however. I hover on dismissing him entirely. And then there is Anselm, the gate guard.'

He suddenly realised that Anna was still standing there, listening to them in curiosity, and panicked that he had said such things in front of her for a moment before remembering that she spoke only her native German tongue and would have no idea what they were saying.

'So, we need to re-examine those three, brother?' Felipe queried.

'I think so.' Arnau looked up into the falling flakes. 'Let's get inside and out of this weather. I suggest we speak to Anselm first.'

'Should we wait for Bernhard? He's the guards' commander.'

Arnau shook his head. 'Anselm should be able to answer some basic questions, even if it's with signs and gestures. If not, we'll wait for Bernhard, but I will not disturb a man busy at chapel for something that can wait. Indeed, had it not been for the necessary timings, we should be at that service too. Come on.'

Waving the maid back to her kitchen, Arnau led his squire across the courtyard, along one of the cleared paths that was already beginning to white over with fresh snow and towards the castle gate. As with most fortresses, the gate was protected from a small, flanking guardroom, which looked out on the space before the great portal through arrow slits and the inside of the gate by a window. Here was where the man on guard would stay at any time.

Pausing in the drifting cold flakes, shivering into his cloak, Arnau rapped on the guard house door. There was no answer. Frowning, he knocked once more, and was greeted by only silence. His heart climbed into his throat. No gate guard worth his salt would fall asleep on duty, since such a thing carried heavy penalties, and that suggested something much different.

Girding himself, he lifted the latch and swung open the door. The room's interior was dark, the torch having either died of its own accord, unattended, or having been snuffed out. He looked back. Torches guttered in other places, as they could see from the lines of gold around closed doors and shutters. Now certain of the worst, Arnau gestured to the main guardroom in the range across the courtyard. 'Go find a lit torch.'

Felipe nodded and scurried off.

Arnau took a step inside, steadying his breathing and coming to a complete halt so that all he could hear was the squire's muted boot steps out across the stone yard, muffled by the snow. Almost silent and now steady, he confirmed it. The room was quiet, but over the raw cold-hot breath of icy air, he could discern the metallic tang of blood in the air. Enough of it to fill the guardroom. And in the strange silence of snowfall, not a whisper of a breath from within the room. *A wise man hearing shall be the wiser.*

Damn it.

He waited, tense, cursing, until Felipe returned with the two men who had been in the guard house on both that night and this, Otto and Leupold. As the torch reached the room, and Felipe brought it inside, the guardroom leapt into golden, flickering visibility.

Arnau flinched.

Just as he'd anticipated, Anselm was no more. Girding himself even as the guards and the squire cursed in two languages from the doorway, Arnau crossed to the black-and-yellow-clad body slumped forward over a table that held just a mug of beer, sitting in the midst of a lake of crimson that had filled the surface and run down onto the floor to pool there

And the third angel shedded out his vial on the rivers, and on the wells of waters, and they were made as blood...

Damn the divine Saint John and his revelations.

Gingerly, he reached down and grasped the mail-covered shoulder, lifting the body back into the chair so that Anselm leaned back instead of forward. Arnau winced. The man was a mess. His face had been caved in with blows. Unless the killer had used a mace...

Maces. Sebastian on Bochard's rooms in Constantinople. A weapon of murder now...

He shivered. Unless it had been a mace, then it had taken multiple blows, and not one. He hadn't seen a mace in evidence around the castle, only swords, so the man had clearly been battered to death. Tentatively, he reached down and touched the blood on the table with his index finger. It came away tacky. He then cast a professional eye over the body. Mail-coated with leather gloves and big leather boots. A killing blow would be hard anywhere on the torso or limbs. Certainly there would have been a struggle. The only weak point was the unprotected head, the mail coif hanging down behind him and his kettle helm hanging on the wall.

'Either he was surprised, or he knew his killer,' Arnau said out loud. 'His blade is still sheathed and his knuckles unmarked. He never made to defend himself.'

'How long ago?' Felipe said, voice shaky.

Arnau shrugged. 'I'm not a medical man, but the blood is already getting sticky and stopped flowing. From what I've seen before, I might guess at an hour.'

'I think we've just ruled out our main suspect,' the squire said quietly.

'Yes,' Arnau agreed. 'And outside interference, too. If someone had killed the young lord and escaped through the door, then he would not still be around to do this. The killer is most definitely still in the castle.'

Something nagging at him, he examined the scene once more, holding the torch close. The body. The helmet. The table. The blood... He peered even closer, leaning towards the table. There was a shape in the blood pool that was too regular to be natural or accidental. Just a slight change in the density of the blood, but in a suspiciously rectangular pattern.

'Look at this, Felipe.'

The squire came closer and squinted at the table. 'There was something there. Something square.'

Arnau nodded. 'Something that was there when he was attacked but removed before the majority of the blood pooled, leaving only the faintest trace.' On instinct, he lifted the guard's right hand.

'Look: ink stains. The mark was left by a sheet of vellum. It and the ink and quill have all been removed.'

'The will?'

Arnau flinched. 'I cannot understand why he would even have the will, let alone be amending it, but that is most definitely a possibility, I'll admit.'

He turned and realised that only Leupold stood in the doorway now. Damn it. Of course, Otto would have run off to find his commander. Arnau braced himself. They now had another murder. And that meant another set of conditions that they might have to look at, but this time they could not easily narrow down the time of death. One hour had been a guess, but it could have been half that time or even maybe three hours. There would be no way of pinning down where everyone was this time.

Damn it.

Was the gate open this time, he thought on a whim? Had someone come in from outside and done this after all? Sliding past Leupold and Felipe, and handing his torch to the latter, he crossed to the gate and reached the door in it. Turning, he looked back and confirmed that a small window looked out over this spot from exactly where Anselm sat. He tried the door. It was still locked. Gritting his teeth, he pulled out the key and looked at it. It looked familiar.

'Felipe, run up to the room and fetch Lütolf's keys.'

Grateful to be doing something other than staring at a corpse, the squire grabbed the cupboard key from Arnau's other hand and ran off, passing a small group of men coming the other way. Otto had told Bernhard and Father Oswald, who were on the way from the chapel, and even now Arnau could see the guard heading into the main building. Graf Dietmar would have to be told.

Arnau cursed silently. This was getting messy.

Bernhard arrived a moment later, eyes wide.

'You found him?'

Arnau nodded. 'Just now. We had cut down the suspects to only three men who could have managed the killing and who had the opportunity. Anselm was one of them.'

'But why Anselm?' Bernhard fumed. 'This is the same killer, we presume?'

'I think so.'

'Then why? Especially if the man is already a suspect.'

'What?'

Bernhard spread his hands. 'Think. If he is not the killer, but he is a suspect, why would the killer remove him? It makes no sense.'

True. Absolutely true. He bit his lip again. 'Unless Anselm knew something. He was busy writing when he was killed and whatever he penned was taken by his attacker. If it was the will, then I think that is a ready-made explanation in some ways. If not... Perhaps he was going to confess, or to pass on some vital information? Something about the murder. Then the murderer knows we're closing in and has to kill the man to keep him silent.' He felt something click into place, and was sure he was on to something. 'I think that's it. I think we are pulling at an important strand and the killer was tying up a loose end before the whole thing started to unravel.'

He stopped and straightened, wide-eyed. 'I had not considered accomplices. I had assumed this to be the work of one killer. What if there are two? Then anyone whose alibi relies upon mutual attendance with another suddenly becomes a suspect afresh. Heavens above, but we might have to begin looking at this in a whole new light.'

As they stood there, silently fretting, Arnau heard numerous footsteps. Felipe was hurrying back through the drifting snow, and others were coming from the main building too.

Arnau drummed the fingers of his left hand on the doorframe as he held up the key from the gate in his right. 'This has something to do with it, even if only peripherally. Even if it was just an attempt to displace suspicion. But one thing is interesting.'

Felipe staggered to a halt, breathing heavily, and held out his hand. Arnau took the ring of three keys from him and held it up, finding one in particular. Beside the one he had removed from the door, they were twins.

'Lütolf's keys, from his personal effects. He had a key to the gate.'

'And therefore so did you,' Bernhard said suddenly, frowning.

'What?'

'You had access to the castle all along.'

'But I only just found out.'

'Perhaps.' Bernhard was looking at him oddly.

'But we only arrived after the event.'

'So you say.'

Arnau felt his nerves twitch. Damn it, but the marshal was right. He actually had as much opportunity and motive as anyone in the castle, and with what was happening with the will, a damn sight more than most.

'I am a man of God, marshal. A soldier of the Lord. You would do well to remember that.'

Bernhard fretted for a moment, then gave a nod. 'My apologies. Suspicion is a curse, and these are dark days. Though for the sake of impartiality, I must now append your names to our list.'

Arnau nodded. 'Yes. Agreed.'

Graf Dietmar was here now, with Michael Trost by his side, and Otto close behind. 'Anselm?' the old lord said, face pale.

'Yes, *Hochwohlgeboren*.'

'When?'

Bernhard looked across to Arnau, who sucked through his teeth. 'Our best guess is perhaps an hour, my lord, but it is too vague to get any real idea beyond that without a medical man's expert opinion.'

'Why Anselm?'

'Perhaps to silence him, my lord. Or perhaps because of the gate. This is the key your brother held in Rourell.' He held up the keyring. 'Are these other keys important?'

Dietmar and Bernhard both peered at the keyring.

'The one with the "T" shape in the middle is for Lütolf's apartment,' the graf said. 'The third I do not know. Bernhard?'

The marshal peered at them. 'I cannot say for what the third key is used. Perhaps it is from your preceptory?'

Arnau shook his head. 'I don't think so. Not in his shelved personal effects.' He turned back to Felipe. 'One thing is certain, I want these keys locked back up until we understand their significance, or lack thereof.'

The squire bowed his head, grasped the keyring and hurried off.

'How many gate keys are there?' Arnau asked.

Bernhard tapped his chin. 'Five, I think. That one of yours and this one that stays with the gate guard. I have one, as does Michael here, and of course, the graf.'

'And where are they kept?'

'With us, usually. This one here is accessible to most, though, as it spends most of its time in the lock.'

Father Oswald gestured to them to move aside, and by the light of the torch now held by Leupold he padded over to the body and began to perform the passagium for the poor deceased guard.

'What have you determined?' Dietmar said, looking back and forth between Arnau and Bernhard. The marshal remained silent, looking at the Templar, and Arnau sighed.

'The killer of both your son and Anselm has to be a strong person. I recreated the actions of that night, and even I, a martial man, found it difficult dragging a big man in a cloak across the courtyard. Your son, you see, was struck from behind as he reached for his cloak after leaving you. He was knocked unconscious, I believe. There are marks near the cloak pegs that confirm this. He was then dragged to the well on a cloak, which masked the worst of the evidence. That was where he was actually killed – the body, most of the blood, and the cloak all being dropped into the hole to hide them.'

The old man flinched as an arrow of sorrow thudded afresh into his heart with each detail. Arnau winced. He hated this.

'So that rules out anyone not strong enough for such an act.' He prepared himself. 'Only yourself, Anselm and the seneschal had the time to do it, and insufficient alibi to dismiss you.' He noted a raised eyebrow from Bernhard and swallowed. 'In the interest of openness, though I was unaware of it at the time, and was miles away, probably in Sülz or beyond, I had a key to the gate from your brother's effects. In essence, I had the opportunity, or would have done, had I been here.'

Dietmar simply nodded, nothing given away. 'Go on.'

'It now seems likely that the killer was known to Anselm as he did not try to defend himself, though that rules out no one. Possibly Anselm was killed because he knew something about the murder or was himself an accomplice to it. The key might be important, or it might not. I cannot say.' He sighed. 'And it has recently occurred to me that there might be two killers together. A pair in collusion. I fear we are going to have to look into this all afresh.' He rubbed his head irritably. 'Things become more cloudy and complex by the hour.'

Dietmar nodded curtly. 'Bernhard, have Anselm's body dealt with appropriately. As yet we cannot be certain that he was involved in my son's death, and he should be treated as an innocent for now. I am tired and shall not attend the evening meal tonight. I hope the two of you,' a quick nod to both Arnau and Bernhard, 'can work together swiftly to find whoever is responsible. This place is becoming a mausoleum.'

As Dietmar and Trost hurried off, and Otto and Leupold moved in at the priest's beckoning finger to help with the body, Arnau, Felipe and Bernhard stepped across to the cold shelter of the gate.

'This is becoming more appalling all the time,' he said. 'The other key, the one to Lütolf's room? It is not the only one?'

Bernhard shook his head. 'The graf also has one. His room has been kept since the day he left, though we searched it recently for the will.'

'I think we might want to look at it again tomorrow.'

The marshal nodded. 'And then we must present every fact we have and work through them. Between them, and combining the excuses of each of the castle's staff for the time of Rüdolf's murder, we should be able to narrow down the suspects once more.'

Arnau nodded and exhaled in frustration. 'A job for the morning, I think. My head is awhirl with everything right now. Let us have our evening meal, then retire for the night and think everything through. In the morning we will confer once more and begin afresh.'

THE WINTER KNIGHT

CHAPTER NINE

FRIDAY NIGHT

$\mathcal{I}$t was but the faintest of creaks, and it couldn't have been that which disturbed him. In fact, it was the change in the air of the room, a new current of cold wafting in and eddying, brushing across Arnau's face where it poked out from beneath the blankets, sending the hairs of his beard wavering very slightly.

Arnau's left eye flickered open just a crack, just enough to sense the change in the room's light.

Instinct told him that something was wrong.

Since the first night here, knowing that someone in the castle was a godless killer, he had taken the precaution of sleeping with his sword down beside his bed on the floor, unsheathed and ready for immediate use. His fingers probed out from the blankets and stretched, reaching for the weapon before he realised he would have to move properly to grasp it.

Even as that realisation hit him, he was moving. Despite being buried beneath seven layers, for there was precious little heat to be found in Renfrizhausen midwinter, he rolled off the edge of his bed and dropped to the floor where his sword lay. That simple instinct saved his life.

He turned in alert astonishment as the crossbow bolt thumped into the pillow where his head had been a blink of an eye earlier. The bolt passed straight through the downy pillow and into the wall with a muffled 'crack' as fragments of feathers suddenly bloomed up and eddied before beginning to drift down once more.

The beauty of that image was lost on Arnau, though, as his hand closed around the hilt of the sword and he rolled again, coming up into a crouch.

The shutter of their window clapped shut as whatever had been holding it ajar was withdrawn. Arnau struggled up at speed, turned and ran for the window as Felipe now sat bolt upright, woken by the thud of the bolt and the following violent activity.

'Wha...?'

At the window now, Arnau stepped carefully to the side, aware of ongoing danger, and undid the catch, which he now realised had been loosened enough to allow the opening of the shutter by just a couple of inches.

He was immediately dazzled as he threw open the shutters, still to one side in case the attacker had a second shot ready. During the few short hours he had been asleep, the snowfall had ceased and the clouds had scudded away on freezing wind to leave a sky that was oddly bright for the middle of the night, a glittering, moonlit silver-blue, reflected up from the world's blanket of thick white.

Blinking, aware that he needed keen eyesight right now, he gingerly leaned to the window and looked down to the courtyard. There was no one there. He frowned. He was on the second floor, above the courtyard. It had never occurred to him to expect danger from there. How had someone managed to get up to his window to shoot at him?

His gaze rolled inevitably side to side, and he spotted the figure. Hooded and swaddled in a nondescript cloak tied at the waist to keep it closed, a crossbow hanging from his shoulder on a leather strap. Along the whole range of buildings below his window ran a small ledge, just a few inches wide, a similar one above, just over the window. The figure was miraculously shuffling away, edging its toes along the lower ledge, fingers gripping the top one. He was good. He was also already out of sword reach. Arnau's gaze shot past him to the roof of the stables that abutted the end of this range of buildings. While this range had two storeys, the stables had only one, and he could make out footprints along the roof there, black in the crisp, white coating whence the man had clearly come.

He turned to see Felipe now up and with his weapon in hand.

'Someone's running. We need to stop them. Get your boots on and down to the courtyard, see if you can head him off.'

Felipe started to ask Arnau what to do, but the knight just waved his squire urgently towards the door as he darted over to the corner and slipped into his boots. What he was about to try was madness, though at least someone else had already proved it was possible. He pulled on his sword belt and buckled it swiftly, sliding the blade home.

In a moment he was climbing carefully through the window, only now beginning to worry about being in such an exposed position should his attacker manage to pause and reload. Fortunately he could see the figure still shuffling along the ledge. Taking a deep breath, he lifted one leg down until the toes of his boot touched the ledge, realising now just how precarious it was.

He felt a flutter of panic then, though it was somewhat overshadowed by the blistering cold. Even at his least prepared, when he'd first arrived, he'd only been outside in his chain coat and mantle, and since then had been sensibly wearing fur and wool cloaks too like the rest of the occupants. Now, he was wearing only his shirt, undershirt, hose and boots. He had never felt so cold.

As he lifted his other leg out and over, almost losing his balance and toppling to the unforgiving stone below, the icy fingers of the Swabian winter clawed up beneath his shirt, prickling his skin, and sending him into a fit of uncontrollable shivering. He almost fell again, then, gripping tight to the window frame for dear life as he fought to master his body. Shivering was an automatic response, but could be overcome with the mind. He pushed down panic, fright and uncertainty, locking them in a small box in his heart, sealing it with faith in the Lord, and settled to stillness.

For he delivered me from the snare of hunters; and from a sharp word. With his shoulders he shall make shadow to thee; and thou shalt have hope under his feathers. His truth shall encompass thee with a shield.

The ninety-first Psalm. A balm in times of such trouble.

The attacker was at the end of the wall now, almost at the roof of the stables. He had a strong lead on Arnau, but the Templar had an advantage and he hoped to see that advantage emerge from the bottom of the staircase any moment, raising the alarm and preventing the attacker's escape. Nothing had happened yet. Still, it had been but moments.

Thou shalt not dread of the night's dread. Of an arrow flying in the day, of a goblin going in darkness; of assailing, and of a midday fiend.

Gritting his teeth, he let go of the window frame with his left hand, reaching up, questing for that higher ledge. Finding it, he gripped as tight as he could and then let go with his right, doing the same again. He was on both ledges. Fortunately, the attacker's movements on approach and escape together had cleared the ledges of most of the snow, yet what was left was still wet and very cold stone, as slippery as an eel. Arnau regretted his impulsiveness immediately as first his left hand and then his right slid free of the stone, the left reattaching just as the right let go, keeping him up. He pressed tight with his fingers until his knuckles went as white as the ground below.

A thousand shall fall down from thy side, and ten thousand from thy right side; forsooth it shall not nigh to thee.

But please, Lord, don't let one of them be me...

He began to move, edging to his left as fast as he dared. He had no fear of heights, knew himself to be both strong and agile, and was going as speedily as any man might reasonably hope, but it was still too slow. His fingers were already going numb. Should he have worn his gloves? They would have protected him from some of the chill, but then he would not have had quite the grip his bare hands allowed.

Too late to wish now.

He moved on, carefully but with speed, edging along a foot at a time at most. Briefly he thought to cry out and raise the alarm. He was in only half a mind whether that might be a good idea. He was still fighting with the idea that there might be more than one killer, even after Anselm's death. Would it be a good idea when he was so exposed to draw further attention to himself? It was all moot anyway. His breath was coming only in short, controlled gasps. He couldn't take deep breaths, partially because of the biting cold, and partially because he needed to keep his chest as flat as possible against the wall as he shuffled along.

Felipe was still not in evidence, and Arnau began to worry that something might have happened to him. Again, though, there was nothing he could do right now. He was committed to a course of action.

He was catching up. The figure had stopped at the end for precious moments.

Shuffle. One foot, one hand. One foot, one hand. Shuffle.

His gaze remained locked on the figure. He couldn't see the face, for the attacker was well covered and shrouded against both cold and visibility. Even as he pursued, Arnau marvelled at the skill of his would-be assassin. It was bad enough climbing along these ledges, but to have held on with one hand while unhooking the window catch, slipping the tip of the crossbow through and loosing the missile, was a feat of almost superhuman dexterity. He had to be an expert marksman as well as agile and strong. Moreover he must have carried the bow loaded and ready, perhaps held in place with twine he could easily release? He had had only one shot, and the Lord was with Arnau in that he'd missed.

He watched, eyes wide, as the figure suddenly jumped, landing on the sloping, snowy roof of the stables. Even as he followed the man, shuffling and gripping his way along, he saw the assassin's first mistake. His gloves and boots did not allow much traction and as he hit the slates, he slid and slithered towards the edge. Still, he was considerably lower down now than Arnau, and could afford to drop to the ground without too much risk of broken bones or sprains or twists. The man gave himself to the fall, making for ground now.

Arnau, seeing his assailant escaping thus, felt a burst of relief as Felipe suddenly emerged from the stairway door into the courtyard, sword and shield on his arms, black surcoat proudly proclaiming the red cross. Arnau sighed as he realised there were rules in that little book of the squire's about bearing the cross when at all possible. The delay had been Felipe preparing himself and attiring himself correctly.

The squire ran out into the courtyard some way away from the building and turned to look back up. His gaze fixed on his fellow Templar edging slowly along the ledge, and if Arnau had dared allow his attention or grip to slip for a moment he'd have rolled his eyes and pointed at the fleeing man on the next roof. Instead he continued to edge along, willing Felipe to do something useful.

The squire's gaze tracked along the ledges and then finally fell upon the roof of the stables and the man sliding down towards the edge.

'Stop, fiend,' Felipe yelled in Aragonese, lapsing into his home tongue in the excitement. Arnau did roll his eyes then, though he continued to move.

'Doom shall be showed as water,' Felipe shouted, this time in Frankish, 'and rightwiseness as a strong stream. The justice of the Lord is coming to you, villain.'

To Arnau's mind it was somewhat elaborate as a threat, and smacked more of something that might arise in the midst of one of Kovacs' epics than a hurried imprecation in the heat of the action. Still, it seemed to have the right effect.

Where the attacker had been now controlling his slide ready to drop to the courtyard and escape, now he was scrambling back up the slates towards the apex of the roof, hurrying at a tangent, away from both knight and squire.

'Swine,' snarled Felipe, hurrying sideways across the courtyard and keeping level with the fleeing man as he ran. *That* sounded more like something Arnau would say.

The world suddenly tumbled as Arnau's grip on the slippery ledge above gave and his left arm swung out into the empty space above the courtyard. His stomach lurched as though about to disgorge its contents and he felt his point of balance changing, his mind whirling. His flailing left hand reached out, grabbing for anything as the fingertips of his right slid closer to the edge. Unexpectedly, they closed on a tiny hole, an imperfection in a piece of the wall's stonework, and two of his fingers dug deep and lodged there, allowing him precious moments to reattach the grip of his right on the ledge. Heaving in desperate, panicked breaths, he slowly recovered and once he was sure of the grip of his numb, frozen fingers he moved his left again back to the ledge and began to shuffle once more. He was almost there now.

He had no idea what Felipe was doing, for now all his attention was on the climb, and he could hear nothing, let alone the squire's words, over the thundering drums of his heart.

It seemed an age before he reached the corner, and it was a matter of astounding relief to do so. Looking around the corner, at the roof of the adjacent stable, he spotted the attacker, still too far ahead, a hooded shape rising to stand astride the apex of the roof at the other end. Despite his slide and recovery having taken precious time, he still had a strong lead.

Arnau wondered where he would go. His change of direction had already labelled him unwilling to drop and confront the squire, and Arnau was in dogged pursuit above. Felipe was shouting now, raising an alarm. The attacker was clearly still keen to hide his identity, and even though he might well think himself capable of besting the squire, it would take time and risk his being caught and unmasked. Hence he was still on the run from both of them. Where, though? Arnau couldn't see where he could go. There was a forty foot gap between the stables and the chapel.

The figure turned back towards Arnau, his face still hidden in the gloom of his hood.

He ran.

Arnau stared in shock as the man risked everything by breaking into an unsteady run along the apex of the roof, back towards Arnau's building. There was a chance to catch up with him now. Arnau looked across at the stable roof. Here, at the courtyard side of it, the slates were some six feet lower than the ledge on which Arnau stood, and sloped vertiginously, threatening to tip any occupant out into the air.

Taking a deep breath, he braced and threw himself across onto the sloping roof.

Immediately he was sent into a plummeting slide, and his boots and bare, numb fingers scrabbled for a hold as he descended. Still, he managed to grasp an edge and slow himself much faster than the other man had. He was gaining. Concentrating, he scrabbled back up the slates, slipping here and there, but managing with more success than he'd expected. He was vaguely aware of Felipe bellowing something, but his gaze slid up to the rooftop.

That was why the man had begun to run... to gain momentum for another jump. As Arnau approached the apex, he could see that the assassin had managed to jump and grasp the heavy iron gutter that ran along the end of the dormitory block. Even now he was hauling himself up onto the next roof, above Arnau's room. He was moving further away from Felipe and staying ahead of the knight.

Arnau grunted and clambered up to the apex finally.

My strength and my praising is the Lord; and he is made to me into health.

Lord, grant me this moment.

Taking a deep breath, he leapt up. The attacker was only moments ahead of him now, but that could still change. The hooded figure was up onto the higher roof. Arnau's fingers touched the gutter, despite the lack of a run-up, but he missed and fell. In a desperate panic, he landed astride the roof's apex, close to pulling muscles as his thighs strained. Yet he managed to keep his footing and steady himself. He blew on his frozen hands and rubbed them together, clapping them for warmth.

He looked up. The figure had vanished. He realised with dismay that the roof of this building actually abutted the castle's walls, and rose a little above them. The man had probably slid down and dropped onto the wall walk.

Arnau prepared himself for another attempt. He couldn't let the man get away and Felipe was now of little use down in the courtyard. As he flexed his fingers ready, a new voice cut in, shouting something in a deep Germanic voice. Arnau glanced over his shoulder. One of the guards had emerged from the tower above the chapel, likely drawn by Felipe's shouts. Clearly he had seen the figure for he barked a command and drew his blade.

Arnau jumped again.

This time, his fingers wrapped around the gutter and he heaved, pulling himself up. Now there were at least three of them chasing the attacker. Every advantage helped. For moments he hung there, drawing laboured breaths, knowing how much strain and effort it was going to require to pull himself up onto the higher roof.

That was when the attacker dealt with his new problem. There was a thwacking noise and a cry. Arnau turned to see the guard fall. He wasn't dead, or at least not from the crossbow bolt, for it thudded into his shield. However, the force of the missile threw the man sideways and he slid on the snowy stonework before plummeting over the edge, sword spinning away. He thumped into the stable roof hard and slid down it until he hit the angle where it touched the walls. There he lay, motionless.

Arnau snarled and threw his arm up, grasping the edge of the roof and pulling. He felt every muscle screaming, but he pushed on through the pain and discomfort. Too much rode upon this. His arm hooked over the roof, and he pulled himself up. In moments that seemed like hours, he managed to gain the range's roof and breathed, steadying himself. It was an easy enough job now to pull himself up to the apex.

As he reached the crest, he looked this way and that.

The attacker was no longer visible, though the doorway to another tower stood open and inviting. Arnau fretted. The man had gone into the tower. He clearly knew his way around the castle well, while Arnau had yet to visit the wall walk and had no idea what to expect. He could see two more figures now in the courtyard, a guard and a serf, drawn to Felipe, who was pointing up at the roof.

The other guard on patrol at the walls was coming now, at a jog, emerging from a doorway over by the main block of noble apartments, but running his way. The assailant might yet be trapped!

With fresh purpose, Arnau slid down the other side of the roof and dropped to the wall walk, drawing his sword immediately and breaking into an unsteady run towards that open door. As he entered the tower, he felt a moment's panic. His eyes were now used to the silver white of outside, and in this deep black gloom he was effectively blind. If his attacker was still guided by fight rather than flight, he could be hiding by the door, waiting to strike.

Arnau flailed this way and that in the darkness, sword wavering, but found nothing. Feeling his way forward he found another wall, and moving along it as he felt the first whisper of a breeze, finally found another door. Eyesight beginning to adjust, he ripped the door open and leapt through, sword sweeping this way and that in case of waiting killers.

The room was empty and lit at a comfortable level by three sources. Ahead, another doorway led out onto the next stretch of walls. To the right, a faint golden glow lit a spiral stairway that wound down into the tower's heart and up to the top level. And to the left, a window stood open and unshuttered, that and the doorway being the source of that breeze he had felt around the edge of the last door.

He paused, wondering. The stairs went up and down, and there was still the gatehouse tower between him and the second wall guard who would be running his way. It was then, as his gaze wandered in indecision, that he noticed the cloak.

Hurrying across, he peered myopically down at the heap on the stone-flagged floor. It was the figure's cowled cloak. He had shed his disguise. Arnau focused. Think. What might help? The footprints? He looked around the floor. There were wet boot marks on the cloak, but there were also wet prints all around the floor from where the wall guards had trudged back and forth over the past few hours. That would tell him nothing. And the man could now have relatively clear boots, having scuffed them on the cloak's dry inside. He didn't even bother examining the cloak. It would not contain any link to the killer, else he would not have shed it so readily.

He hurried over to the open window and looked down. There was no way the attacker could have left that way. A fall from there would kill the hardiest of men. Yet the window was open.

He grunted with unhappy realisation and squinted down. He could vaguely make out a mark in the snow below. The crossbow and quiver, almost certainly, discarded as evidence just as those other telltale items had been cast down the well on the night of a previous crime. No help there. The attacker would now look as he did any other day.

He ran over to the other side of the room and unlatched the hook on the shutter there, throwing it open. The courtyard came into view with an increased number of figures gathered in it.

Damn it. The gate tower along the next stretch of walls? Up the stairs? Down?

As he started down, he realised with further dismay just how easy it would have been for the figure to hide in any one of a dozen shadowed corners and allow his pursuer to slip past, then double back. Arnau had gone from close pursuit to looking for a single stalk of hay in a stook.

Furiously impotent and feeling the aches and pains of his exertions beginning to pull and claw at him, he slowly descended the steps and emerged finally, having checked every corner of both rooms on the way down, into the courtyard.

The castle's occupants were waiting for him. His tired and disconsolate eyes played across them, trying to spot an obvious gap. There was none.

Felipe stood there with Matthias the guard and the serf Hugo. Dietmar was staring at him in deep concern, wrapped in a thick night blanket, beside him Kovacs, shivering without one. Bernhard was there, talking to Michael Trost. Leupold and Wolf together in a pair. Conrad and Gunther together. Winrich was now emerging from the gate tower, the man who had just now been running along the walls to help. That left only Otto, and Arnau could hardly load blame on him, since he currently lay at the edge of the stable roof, either unconscious or dead from his fall.

Every figure who could climb, drag a body, or might claim any skill with weapons was here now, watching him. Briefly, he wondered whether he should ask them all whence they had come, but the attacker would lie, and all the rest would have had their gazes locked upon the action atop the walls. No one would have noticed the assassin slip back in among them, cloak and weapon discarded.

His gaze swept back and forth. All of them had damp footwear now, for they had been in the snow of the courtyard, and a mess of tracks led back and forth into most doorways. Few wore cloaks, for the excitement had drawn most of them too fast to spend time preparing. Besides, he couldn't rule anyone out on the basis of the cloak any more than footwear, since cloaks hung close to most of the castle's external doors and it would be an easy task for the killer to acquire a new one. The only person he felt inclined to rule out from this entire group was the graf, Dietmar. Being wrapped in a night blanket, that might have been hard to acquire in a hurry, and almost certainly stated his innocence in that he must have come straight from bed.

Damn it. So close.

He rubbed his temples. Bernhard and Michael were now organising things, dispersing the people back to their places, with the exception of two guards who were detailed to fetching a ladder to bring Otto down from the stable roof, whether he be alive or dead. The crowd began to break up and head for the doors. Arnau sighed. For a moment, he almost stopped them leaving. Someone here was a killer, after all. But there was no longer any reasonable way to identify who it was, so there was little point in keeping them around. As things began to settle once more, Bernhard crossed to Arnau, Felipe following, angry and unhappy at the way things had played out.

'It seems I may owe you an apology,' the marshal said quietly.

'Oh?'

'After you produced the gate key earlier, and it occurred to me that you could not prove that you had been far away, the possibility of your guilt had nagged at me increasingly. I was almost ready to go to the graf. Though I might respect those Templars I have fought alongside, your Order maintains a reputation as insular and somewhat secretive. The idea that you might stoop to such deeds to maintain those lands Lütolf had willed you had gained traction with me.'

Arnau nodded. It certainly made sense if you didn't know for sure that the two Templars had been far away when the young lord was killed.

'But I think this throws new light upon that matter. And also upon the possibility that someone fled through the gate. There is a killer still among us, and that killer has begun to target you now, clearing you in my mind.'

Arnau sagged. 'But despite this, I am no closer to identifying him.'

'Have you nothing new to go on?'

'No. Especially if there are two and they are working as a pair. But no, even solo I cannot identify him in a crowd. All I can say is at least one attacker is strong, dextrous, has no fear of heights, is skilled with a crossbow, and knows this castle well.'

Bernhard sighed. 'I shall go and speak to the graf, then check on Otto. I hope for the best there, but I fear the worst.'

Arnau watched him go and was left with Felipe as the courtyard cleared. He realised then that Father Oswald had not been there. He shook his head dismissively. The old priest was hard of hearing, and probably hadn't heard the commotion. Besides, he not only had a strong alibi, but could not possibly fit most aspects of the mould Arnau had formed for the killer.

'What now?' Felipe said

'Now, we go for a walk.'

Ignoring the quizzical looks from the squire, Arnau wandered over to the castle gate, where Wolf sat in the guard house. As Arnau approached, he realised the guard had two torches lit and the door wide open despite the cold. He was armoured with helm on head and sword bare on the table. Like all the guards, Wolf had taken to being prepared. What had happened to Anselm was not going to happen again.

Wolf spoke nothing but German, so Arnau pointed and made an unlocking motion. In moments, the guard had unlocked the door in the gate and the two Templars were stepping though it, confusion still reigning on Felipe's face. Arnau wished momentarily that the guard spoke enough Frankish to get ideas across, and instead used pointing and motions to try and explain that they were not departing for good, and to leave the door unlocked for now.

As it shut behind them, they began to circle the castle's walls, knee-deep in snow even at the lowest point. The sheer quantity of it confirmed the foolhardiness of any attempt to leave Renfrizhausen. Wading onwards, they passed away from the gate tower and to the next one, beside which the block housing Arnau's room would stand.

As they waded through the snow, Arnau fretted loudly.

'What is it, brother?' the squire murmured, shivering.

'This entire affair goes from bad to worse, Felipe. It may be our duty to help bring the ungodly to the light of divine justice, but we are still strangers in this place. Outsiders. Untrusted and often disliked. But despite the ill mood of the majority and the presence of an unknown killer, I had hardly expected to become a target myself. The incident at the meal might be explained away as mere chance, but not now a crossbow has been added to the arsenal being assembled against me.'

'You have endured *wars*, brother,' Felipe reminded him.

Arnau sighed. 'War is simplicity by comparison. Fighting for our lives in Rourell, or on Mayūrqa, or even struggling to survive in Constantinople was bitter and hard work, fraught with danger. But it was clear danger. It has always been a bared sword and a screamed curse and enemies rushing at me. Against an attack like that a man can defend himself. Against a knife in the night there is no simple solution. I am a knight of the Temple, not a creature of shadows and assassin's blades. I am not made for this kind of danger. And so we must identify the wielder of the assassin's weapon as soon as we can.'

In order to be certain, Arnau looked up. Sure enough a square of black lay in the grey stone of the wall perhaps three quarters of the way up, the only unshuttered window.

'Get searching in the snow,' he told Felipe.

'What for?'

'A crossbow. It's here somewhere.'

As the squire began to wade this way and that, getting into ever-deeper drifts of snow, so did Arnau. For perhaps a quarter of an hour the pair searched until Felipe gave a shout of triumph. Arnau pushed his way through the snow to the squire to find Felipe holding a crossbow.

'What about the bolts?'

Arnau nodded, and they spent a few more minutes hunting around until they located the quiver close by, three bolts remaining in it, the others likely lost somewhere in the fall, scattered across the snow. Gathering them together, Arnau took the bolts, examining them closely, but drawing no useful conclusion. He then looked at the bow. As he turned it over, he frowned.

'What is it?' Felipe said.

'I think we might finally have a useful clue to work from. I don't think this is a standard crossbow. Admittedly I've never seen a German crossbow before, but I presume they're similar to the Iberian and Frankish ones I know. This is different. More gracefully curved and ornate. This, Felipe, is a very individual weapon. With luck and the help of the Lord, we might be able to pin it to an owner.'

And with that, they turned, gripping their prizes, and began the difficult wade back to the gate.

CHAPTER TEN

SATURDAY MORNING

rnau sat at the head of one of the trestle tables in the great hall, Felipe in the next seat, their prizes on the clean timber surface before them. The serfs had been in and out, preparing for the day's first meal – a luxury that few managed, most relying upon noon for their first food, but one upon which the Ehingen lords insisted. Arnau and Felipe had not returned to their beds after their night-time adventure. Neither had felt a great urge for slumber, and both men were far too tense and alert for such, and so they had cleaned up and dried the items they had found in the snow and spent the next few hours fruitlessly going over everything they knew once more.

They had attended the morning service. Father Oswald rather slyly combined lauds with matins, given the late hour of dawn at this time of the year, and yet still apart from the two Templars, the only attendees were the priest himself and the marshal, a former Crusader whose devotion to the cross still drew him to each canonical service despite his current lay profession.

Three psalms, rote prayers, hymn, chant, reading and versicle, and Father Oswald had blessed them and released them once more to their worldly activities. The old priest had not been particularly pleased that Arnau and Felipe had brought a crossbow into the chapel, but had acquiesced eventually. The Templars were not about to let out of their sight the one piece of evidence they felt they could rely upon.

Following the service, they had returned to the hall and waited. The pair had sat as the places were set about them, comfortable that there was plenty of space for each occupant to sit at a table and still leave room for them. After all, Anselm would no longer need a place at table, and Otto would not be attending breakfast either. The guard who had fallen from the wall had survived, it seemed, and was in his rooms now, being tended to as best they could by the serfs and his friends. He seemed to have a broken arm and some damage to his chest, but his breathing seemed normal and no blood came with his toilet, so everyone was confident that unless some infection took him, he would pull through.

Still, he would not be here, instead being fed and watered in his room.

Gradually, the room filled with those attending the meal, each finding their seat in a strange silence, watching one another, but most particularly watching the two men who bore the red cross of the Order, gathered around the horrifying weapon. The details of what had happened during the night had filtered swiftly through the castle's occupants, and shock and distrust seemed to pervade the morning, filling the air. At least the snow continued to hold off, the sky a bright blue, cloudless but freezing.

Bernhard took his seat, as did Michael, Father Oswald, the remaining guards and those serfs not busily porting the food from the kitchens. Finally, as they were ready for the meal, the high-born joined them: Graf Dietmar, the ladies, Ute and Gerdrut, and Karolus Kovacs.

A serf tried to set a place hurriedly in front of the two Templars, but Arnau waved them away. He and Felipe had sought their own repast in the small hours beforehand. They were here not for sustenance, but for information. As the food was placed on the tables and the serfs seated at their own low stations, Dietmar gave some Germanic command that triggered the beginning of the meal, and in that same subdued quiet, the castle's populace began to eat.

Arnau waited for just a moment, and then slipped from the bench and rose, lifting the crossbow. Around the room, every hand with its hunk of wine-soaked bread paused, halfway from platter to mouth. The silence became even more strained.

'Lord Dietmar,' Arnau said, turning to the high table, 'were you aware of this weapon, might I ask?'

The graf, his expression unreadable, stared at the upheld crossbow.

'I do not mean this in accusation, of course,' Arnau added, just in case. After all, the lord was probably the only person in the courtyard last night that Arnau had dismissed as a suspect. 'I am simply trying to identify the owner of this weapon. I presume that no one is about to raise their hand and claim ownership?'

No hand rose, and though Arnau's keen gaze took in every visage, he saw no telltale sign of guilt, the reason for his confronting everyone unexpectedly and together. Graf Dietmar sat for a long moment, and finally shook his head. 'Such a weapon is forbidden for use against Christians by Papal Bull. Not only that, but from a Pope supported by the Empire and its master, Lothair of Supplinburg. There are no enemies of Christianity here, *Herr Tempelritter*. Why would anyone defy papal order and use such a thing. I would not have a weapon like that in my house.'

Arnau nodded. There was a vehemence in the old lord's tone that spoke deeply of conviction. His feeling that Dietmar was innocent found yet more traction.

'I believe you, my lord. Yet this very weapon was used against both Otto and myself last night, and has to have come from somewhere in the castle.'

Bernhard rose now, lowering his bread back to the plate. 'I cannot fathom where it came from. The castle has been searched thoroughly these past days, seeking the missing will. I am fairly certain that something the size of a crossbow would have caught our eye even though we were not looking for it.'

'Unless it belonged to one of the searchers?' Arnau noted. 'Who was involved in the search?'

Bernhard frowned. 'Myself, Wolf, Anselm and Otto. Everyone else had duties.'

Arnau nodded. 'Otto I think we can dismiss, given that he was a victim of it. Anselm could not have wielded it.'

'But it might have been his,' noted Felipe. 'Even if he did not use it last night, he might have deliberately overlooked it in his search if it was his.'

Arnau sighed. That was a possibility, of course.

'So despite this being a weapon with a papal ban, in a castle where the lord forbids such a thing, still we cannot hope to pin down its owner?'

Silence greeted this. Arnau turned the weapon slowly in the air. 'Then, perhaps someone knows something about it? I have seen crossbows in my time. Back in Iberia and in the east there are many enemies of the cross, and so these things are not so rare. But of perhaps a dozen or a score I have seen over the years of Aragonese or Frankish design, I can say that this is very different. More gracefully designed, with many curves, inlaid with patterns and with ornate plating. This is a loved and very individual weapon. In fact, it bears more resemblance to a Moorish bow than a Christian one. I cannot believe that such an unusual weapon cannot raise more than shrugs.'

Bernhard nodded. 'I too see the difference. In my years of travelling with the cross to Outremer, I saw Franks and Burgundians with their crossbows, but I have also seen weapons such as this and the men that carried them.'

Arnau felt his heart flutter. Bernhard recognised the design! Finally, perhaps they had something useful. The marshal turned towards the top table, but before he could say any more, Kovacs rose from his seat, dropping his handful of soaked bread.

'Before the accusation comes, I will confirm of my own volition that the crossbow you hold is of Hungarian origin. It is a nobleman's hunting crossbow. In fact, judging by the design and decoration, I would suggest it was manufactured by a Bosnian craftsman, probably from the Lašva region.'

The eyes of the room slid to the minstrel, standing with his hands raised.

'I suspect it will help me little to protest my innocence and claim no history of the weapon, though with my family's history I am familiar with the type. Indeed, I am no hunter and my aim is as poor as a blind mendicant's. Sadly, though, I am accused by the very object you hold, am I not?'

Arnau chewed his lip. Though the man had no better claim to innocence than many in the room, Arnau had already largely dismissed the Hungarian. He just simply didn't seem the type, and there seemed no clear motive for the death of Rüdolf, let alone of Anselm or Arnau. Still, the evidence was hard to dismiss. It was the first directly accusatory fact they had come across.

Dietmar rose from his seat, his face pale. 'I will say this to you all: I have known Kovacs since I was a boy. He was the first man to give a birthday gift to my son. I have never seen him wield a crossbow, and his disdain for the hunt I know well, for in three decades and more he has never joined me on one. The evidence you have points at my friend but I do not believe it.'

The silence in the room was all the more taut now, and Dietmar looked around at the eyes of all present. He might deny it all, but he had to do something. The level of paranoia and distrust among his people was growing by the day. The old lord sighed. 'I cannot... I *will* not bring this before the *landgericht*. Not until you bring me unassailable evidence. I am the law in Renfrizhausen.'

He turned to Kovacs, his expression slipping. 'But neither can I ignore what we have all seen. My friend, I have to ask you to leave my house. Return to your homeland, and when this is all done and your innocence confirmed, you will be welcomed back with open arms.'

Kovacs shook his head. 'My innocence will be proclaimed yet soon. Renfrizhausen moves from being a home towards becoming a mausoleum with every new death, and the next will clear me. Do not send me away, Dietmar. The journey in this blanket of snow will be hard and my home is far. Lock me in my chamber for now. I will go willingly, and stay there until someone else dies and my name is cleared.'

The pain in Dietmar's eyes was touching. He hated having even to constrain his old friend. But the people of the castle would feel just a tiny easing of their tension at the knowledge that the Hungarian was under lock and key.

'Very well. We will do just that. Thank you, old friend, and I pray that we catch the true culprit soon so that you can rejoin us.'

The lord nodded to Bernhard, who rose, gesturing to Winrich. The two escorted Kovacs from the room, the Hungarian's head held high, an air of injured innocence surrounding him. Arnau felt so bad for the man that he lowered his eyes as Kovacs walked past and only at the last moment reminded himself of two things. Kovacs was by nature and profession part actor and storyteller. If any man here might be able to conjure a mask of innocence and hide true guilt, it would be the minstrel. And Arnau also remembered that sudden flare of violent fury that had passed through the man at noon a few days ago, when the subject of Zadra and the Byzantines had come up. No matter how much he liked Kovacs, he simply could not dismiss him as a suspect. Especially with the evidence so weighing against him.

His eyes rose once more to the minstrel as he left the room under escort, and something odd struck him. He peered at the man's midriff as he vanished through the door, then back to the place setting at the top table. He frowned, trying desperately to replay an image of the Hungarian as he had risen and dropped his bread to claim knowledge of the weapon.

Yes, he was right.

He might just be able to either prove or disprove Kovacs' involvement. The room went back to the small meal in discontented silence, unconvinced still that what had just happened had ended it all.

'What will we do with the crossbow?' Felipe said.

Arnau drummed his fingers on the table edge. 'It needs locking away somewhere out of the reach of everyone, including us. So it cannot be kept in our room. I have an idea, though.'

As the meal drew to a close and Dietmar rose, signalling the end and allowing all others to similarly rise and depart, Arnau cleared his throat and turned to the top table once more.

'I realise that this is a painful subject, my lord, and I am asking much, but I feel that I might be able to progress the matter further or perhaps even prove your friend's innocence, but to do so, I will need to see Rüdolf's body.'

A flash of pain crossed the old lord's face, but he glanced momentarily at the empty seat close by, so recently vacated by Kovacs. Slowly, he nodded. 'I cannot join you. I cannot see him. Not now. But you have my permission, on the understanding that you will conduct yourself with respect and honour my son.'

Arnau bowed his head. 'Of course, my lord. Might I ask who has the key?'

Dietmar reached down to his belt purse. 'There are three keys to the cellars, but I have them all.' He produced one and held it aloft.

Arnau rose. 'I would also ask that I be permitted to leave the crossbow and quiver in there, under lock and key and away from all hands.'

A nod from Dietmar, and Arnau strode over to the top table. Before he reached it, the high lady, Gerdrut, had leaned across and taken the key from her brother's hand. 'I shall escort him, Dietmar.'

**

The steps down were slippery and bare, and Arnau descended carefully, torch held high, guttering and illuminating the staircase. Behind him, Lady Gerdrut followed at a short distance, keeping back from the flickering flame of the torch. Felipe followed on at the rear.

Arnau's sense of anticipation was rising with every step.

Six days or so Rüdolf von Ehingen had lain down here, awaiting the clearing of the weather so that he could be transported to the town and interred correctly. Arnau had been around week-old bodies once or twice in his short but colourful life and it was not something to wish for, but this was important. He had a theory and hoped it would – indeed, hoped it *could* – be borne out here.

Finally, the steps ended and opened out into a narrow corridor some twenty feet long. The ceiling was a mere foot above Arnau's head and now the confines made the heat and light of the torch unpleasant. He was forced to hold it forward, away from himself.

Ahead, he could see a door. Heavy and oaken, with a small iron grille in the top at head height. A lock sat beneath the handle. He paused as they approached, wondering for a moment how they were going to pass one another in the narrow space, but Lady Gerdrut simply passed the key forward, and Arnau reached down and unlocked the door.

'This is the cellars for the castle, then, my lady?'

Gerdrut's smooth tones washed from behind him. 'Yes. There is quite an extensive complex, but not a lot of it is used. None of it recently, in fact.'

Arnau pushed the door open and made his way inside. If anything, the air down here was even colder than the freezing world above. The room ahead was vaulted with a basic ribbing, quite large and with a stone flagged floor. A number of cupboards and shelves around the walls were picked out in the guttering golden light. Several large heavy tables were in evidence too, the one at the room's centre supporting a human shape draped in a cloth of black and yellow chevrons.

Around the edge, several large openings led off into other cellar spaces. Arnau's mind instantly, and unhelpfully, furnished him with images of those legends of which he'd been told the over the lunch when someone had tried to poison him. In the darkness, ghosts drifted and dragons slowly uncurled, the fire in their throats beginning to glow.

He shivered. This place was playing havoc with his imagination.

One other thing he noted about the room was several torches wedged in sconces around the walls. They had been used and extinguished several times recently, and he made his way to three of them, lighting them once more with his own torch, then placing that in an empty sconce near the door.

The room was gradually illuminated more and more with the golden glow of the flames.

'I cannot help but picture ghosts and dragons,' he admitted as he scanned his surroundings once more. Felipe, standing at the door, nodded vigorously and crossed himself, his eyes wide.

Gerdrut simply smiled. 'You are far from alone, Master Vallbona. Indeed, when the tremor shook the castle a few years ago, Rüdolf was initially convinced that it had been the dragon in the rocks below the castle, finally stirring from his slumber.'

Arnau shivered again, that image coming back in force.

'In a way, though, it was useful,' the lady said. 'It led my nephew to visit the cellars. They are hardly ever opened these days. With the diminished population of Renfrizhausen, we can store all we need in the ranges above, and the cellars were simply ignored. Then, after the tremors, Rüdolf came down here, seeking signs of the dragon. In doing so he discovered the damage the tremor had done to the foundations. Had he not done so, we might never have understood.'

Arnau suddenly felt a whole new oppressive worry. These rooms were damaged? And they supported the castle above? Claustrophobia bit down, and he shivered anew at the thought of all that heavy stone above him, held up by weakened foundations.

'I am beginning to understand why the young lord was so insistent on refurbishment and repair,' he said quietly, as though a loud noise might bring the whole thing crashing down.

'It has become something of a troublesome subject,' the lady sighed. 'Everyone in Renfrizhausen knows it needs doing, but Rüdolf advocated beginning the work as soon as possible regardless of the fact that the family simply cannot afford it. My brother agrees that it needs doing, but is also adamant that nothing can be done without sufficient funds.'

Arnau sighed. 'And here am I seeking to withhold money and land from the family for the Order. It is my duty to uphold the truth of the matter, whether it fall to the Temple or to the von Ehingen, but I have to admit a personal wish that I could abandon our cause here and give the money back to you. The Order needs funds to fight the Moor and the Saracen and to protect the pilgrims of the west, but what use are our efforts if we allow the houses of Christendom to crumble behind us?'

Gerdrut gave a sad little laugh. 'Do not trouble your conscience, *Tempelritter*. If it was Lütolf's wish that the Order have his inheritance, then none of us will stand in the way. You are but a messenger caught up in troubles not of your design. Personally, I fear that Rüdolf's new will is untrue, and that he might have found a dreadful way of funding his repairs.'

Arnau nodded. It was not to be condoned, of course. In fact, it was a damnably wicked notion. But he could also see how a desperate scion of a poor house might stoop to such in order to save his family. Who would not? Had he not fallen in with the Temple, Arnau too might have found himself considering similar to save his own impoverished estates.

'So the cellars are unstable, yet the young lord's body has been kept here?'

'This is the strongest of the rooms,' Gerdrut replied. 'The vaulting here is undamaged and we have been told that it is still good and secure. Many of the side cellars are dangerous, though. We have all been advised not to use them, as some tremble at even the tread of a boot.'

Arnau shivered again. 'Were they searched for the will, then?'

Gerdrut shrugged. 'I am not sure. But they were all thoroughly checked out months ago by Bernhard and his men, when my nephew set them to examining the damage.'

Arnau nodded. If they had been unused for decades and were shaky and dangerous, then it would be a very brave or foolish man who slipped into them simply to hide a will when there must be many better places in the castle for such a task.

'Let us turn to the reason we are here,' he said, and the lady nodded, joining him as he crossed to the body on the table. Felipe remained by the door gripping the crossbow and bolts tight, and carefully, as respectfully as he could, Arnau removed the cloth from the body. Struggling to fold it in the freezing room, he almost dropped the cloth, and the lady reached out and grasped a corner, helping him fold it.

Arnau's gaze slid to Felipe. The squire was watching them with an air of difficult disapproval. The fingers of his free hand went down to the book that hung in a pouch at his belt, and Arnau was suddenly reminded of how many rules in that book forbade contact with women. Arnau had always eschewed that side of the rules. After all, Saint Bernard might have laid that law down upon the Order at large, but it could never be the most enforced of rules in a house like Rourell, where Ermengarda ruled with a fist of iron.

Shaking off such thoughts, he turned from Felipe and to the body.

The family's similarity to one another ran true with Rüdolf von Ehingen. He strongly resembled Dietmar, though without the lines and the grey. His alabaster skin, mottled with black and blue, was youthful and unmarked. He had the physique of a soldier, but lacked the scars and stains of war. He was laid out in a simple shroud. Arnau walked to the head and peered closely. There were marks on the table under the head. With an apologetic wince at Gerdrut, he leaned over it and gently lifted the head.

Immense damage had been done to the skull at the rear. Not a mace, for the damaged area was small, if deadly. The pommel of a sword or knife, he suspected. Remembering his replaying of the murder, he could now picture the assailant's pommel coming down and striking, knocking the vital young lord from his senses.

He pictured Rüdolf being lowered onto the cloak, the blood from that head wound soaking into the wool and fur, leaving only that fine spray on the wall as evidence of the blow. Then dragged out on the cloak as Arnau had done with Felipe, across the courtyard. Lifted to the well, and then tipped over the edge. The knife across the throat, and then the drop, the cloak and probably the blade following.

He pictured the scene. This was important. Initially, the killer had hit Rüdolf from behind, as was evidenced by the wound. But the throat... would *that* be from behind too? Yes, he decided. It had to be. If Rüdolf had been facing his killer, the spray of blood from the neck would have soaked the man. He had bent Rüdolf over the well and then, from behind, drawn his blade across the throat. Had to have done. It was the only way.

He lowered the head gently back to the table, and then walked around to examine the neck. The wound was gruesome in the extreme. Arnau felt slightly ill at the thought. At least the corpse didn't smell. Despite being a week old, the cold of the cellar had kept him in good condition.

An idea occurred. 'Felipe? Run up to the kitchens and find a sizeable piece of meat. Pork if they have it.'

Frowning, the squire did as he was told, placing the crossbow and quiver on one of the shelves nearby and racing away up the stairs.

'Pork?' asked the lady Gerdrut, quizzically.

'To test a theory. Your nephew's throat was cut from behind. It had to be, or the killer would have been soaked in blood and instantly identifiable.'

Gerdrut nodded. 'I see, yes.'

'Look at the cut, if you can bear to do so.'

She leaned closer, nose wrinkling in distaste. 'I see it, but what am I looking for?'

Arnau mimed holding a man's head with his left hand and pulled his knife from his belt with his right. 'Watch.' He mimed dragging the knife across a throat, below the head he held. 'Does that seem natural to you?'

She frowned. 'I'm not sure about natural, but yes. I can picture it, although I would rather not.'

Arnau nodded. 'But look at the cut. The left end has a neat edge. The right is ragged. And in between, where it has passed through difficult matter, the pressure is from the left.'

'Yes?' she said uncertainly, her face paler now.

'Consistent, you think, with how I motioned the strike?'

'Yes.'

'I am right-handed. I used my right on the knife.'

'Yes?'

'Don't you see?' Arnau breathed. 'Kovacs is *left*-handed. I remember seeing him with his instrument, holding it that way. I thought nothing of it, of course. But when he left the room earlier, his knife was belted on the wrong side. And when he dropped his bread and stood, it had been in his left hand. Had Kovacs been the man to cut the lord's throat, it would be the other way around. *Reversed.* The blade would have made a neat entry at the right and ripped free to the left.'

She blinked.

'Kovacs did not kill Rüdolf?'

'No. Of that I am utterly convinced. I wonder if any other person in Renfrizhausen favours their left?'

'I have no idea.'

Arnau frowned. 'Please don't tell anyone about this. If the killer hears, they might try to feign left-handedness to remove themselves from the list of suspects.'

Gerdrut tutted. 'But that means Karolus will have to stay locked in his room.'

'For now, yes. But to be honest, in clearing him of this murder, I still have not cleared him of the crossbow. There is always the possibility of an accomplice.'

The lady sighed. 'Then this helps only a little.'

'Every little helps,' Arnau said in reply. 'For my part, I have removed Dietmar from my list, for he came straight from his bed last night. Now I have at least partially removed Kovacs. Slowly, but surely, I am piecing it all together.'

Felipe returned a few moments later with a slab of pig, which he manhandled, grunting, to another table. Arnau gestured to it and walked across. 'Let's confirm my theory.' Taking the meat from Felipe, he held it up, left arm wrapped around the top, and reached around with his knife, dragging it through the meat. When he had done, Felipe brought a torch closer and they peered at it. The marks in the cold flesh were remarkably similar to those in Rüdolf's neck.

'Now watch.'

He turned the meat upside down and repeated the process, but gripping the top with his right hand and rather inexpertly dragging the knife across with his left. The damage, when they examined it, was totally different.

'I cannot clear Kovacs of the crossbow use or Anselm's death, but I think we can say without a doubt that he was not the man who killed the young lord.'

They stepped back, lowering the pork to the table.

'Dietmar will be pleased,' the lady said quietly. 'Very pleased.'

Arnau nodded. 'I think I've learned all I can now from poor Rüdolf. Let us re-cover him and return to the world above before these creaky, damaged foundations bring the castle down upon us.'

As Arnau found the cloth, and with the lady's help carefully re-covered the body, Felipe grabbed the murdered pork slab and began to make his way slowly up the stairs, the crossbow now safely deposited on the shelf in the cellar. In moments, Arnau was extinguishing the torches once more with the snuffer in the corner, plunging the cellar into that cold, oppressive darkness. He then retreated to the stairs, locking the door once more and returning, shivering, to the world of men.

CHAPTER ELEVEN

SATURDAY NOON

Lunch was a subdued affair following the troubles of breakfast, leading on straight after the end of the sext service at which only the usual four had been in evidence. Arnau had positioned himself carefully to watch as many of the diners as possible, but had spotted no one favouring their left hand, and so had glumly concluded that no one else could yet be excluded from his list. Only two people were missing from the group in the hall, and Arnau felt he could readily disregard both of them anyway. Anna, the maid, was busy with fresh linens around the castle, but not only had she been the one to discover the body, she was also too small in frame to have committed the murder, and the chances of her having learned to fire a crossbow were laughable, too. The other, Winrich, was on guard, but he had been the other man on the walls running to help stop Arnau's attacker, so he seemed an unlikely suspect, also.

Felipe had eaten little and now, as the rest of them finished their repast, the squire continued to leaf through his ever-present book of the Rule instead. Arnau found his own appetite waning and finally, giving up, pushed his plate away. Bernhard, across the table, gave him a quizzical look, but shrugged and went on to demolish his own meal to the last crumb. Finally, when the man had finished and Dietmar signalled that the diners were free to leave, the marshal rose to depart, and Arnau gestured across to him.

'Can I beg a few moments, Bernhard?'

'Of course, *Herr* Vallbona.'

Arnau gestured to the corner with a nod of the head and beckoned to Felipe. Once they were in the corner, Arnau spoke quietly. 'Bernhard, I believe Kovacs to be innocent, of the death of Rüdolf at least. In fact, while I cannot disprove that the crossbow is his, I even think I could convince your *landsrict*—'

'*Landgericht.*'

'Yes, them. I think I could even convince them of his innocence. We've proof of a kind based on his being left-handed. I would love to tell Dietmar, but I want to talk it through with the minstrel first. Before I do that, though, I've checked everyone I can and it appears to me that the rest of the castle's occupants are right-handed. Have you any further information? Do you know if any of your guards favour the left? Even Otto or Anselm, since they would still have been hale and free at the time of Rüdolf's death.'

The marshal frowned. 'We have regular training sessions and practice bouts. The only man I have seen using his offhand is Anselm. He was naturally disposed to the left.'

'Then another suspect fades,' said Arnau. 'Anselm and Michael were the only two I could see having the opportunity to commit Rüdolf's murder, but if Anselm used his left, then he is not the man who cut the young lord's throat any more than Kovacs.' He sighed. 'Since I can gain nothing more here, I think I'll go talk through things with Kovacs.'

'The minstrel's door remains locked by the graf's order, apart from the delivery of meals. You will have to seek his permission, first.'

Arnau shook his head. 'I can talk to him through a closed door. I'm sure it won't matter.'

Bernhard smiled. 'The graf will be extremely pleased if you can clear his friend. In truth, I think we all will.'

Arnau gave a short nod and then joined Felipe and they exited the hall, strolling along the tapestry corridor towards the antechamber with the staircase to the second floor. Slipping up the steps, they emerged onto the floor with Kovacs' room and made their way along to it. The gentle melody of a lute issued from the room behind the door, and once again Arnau felt confident that anyone on this floor would know if Kovacs was in his room. His alibi still held up. If only he could be disconnected from the crossbow.

'Master Kovacs?' he said through the door.

There came a muffled reply and the lute playing stopped. Moments later footsteps approached the door.

'Vallbona of the Temple?' came a quiet voice, muted by the door.

'Yes. Can you confirm for me, just quickly, that you use your left hand in favour of your right?'

'I do. It is one of the reasons my father was always a little cold with me. He subscribed to the superstition that my favouring of the left put me somehow in league with Lucifer.'

Arnau snorted. 'Well if that is the case, then the Great Adversary might have saved you from the *landgericht*. "Thy word is a lantern to my feet and light to my paths," as the Psalm says. I believe we have proved that the young graf was killed by a right-handed assailant.'

Arnau could almost hear the relieved sigh through the door.

'Sadly, I still cannot disprove your connection with the crossbow, so securing your release might not yet be entirely feasible, but at least it is a step in the right direction.'

'It is something of a shame then that crossbows have not been designed to accommodate those who favour the left, is it not?'

Arnau shrugged. 'It matters not. Anyone trained with a bow or crossbow is trained with the right, whatever their natural preference. You cannot field a unit of archers who vary in how they hold the weapon. There would be chaos.'

'True, I suppose.'

Arnau fretted. That Kovacs had not immediately realised such a thing once again spoke of his unfamiliarity, and therefore his innocence, but it was far from proof.

'Karolus, please. I need to remove people from my list, and you and the graf are both so close to being clear. Is there anything you can tell me that will help me clear you of being the crossbowman?'

There was a resigned sigh. 'Sadly, I do not think so.'

Arnau cleared his throat. 'Then it is down to myself and the Lord God to do so. "And if any of you needeth wisdom, ask ye of God, who giveth to all men largely, and upbraideth not; and it shall be given to him." And if the Lord cannot grace me with an answer, I shall persevere regardless. I will speak to the graf this afternoon. I pray that soon we may open that door.'

'Me too, friend Templar. I pray that the Lord is listening, or if not, that at least Lucifer is kind.'

Arnau crossed himself vehemently and tried not to be offended. Minstrels had their ways and were not always known as the most godly of men. Leaving the door once more, they trooped back downstairs, seeking Graf Dietmar, who was still in the hall, the only family member to remain, as the serfs cleared away the meal around him. Michael Trost sat opposite, the two of them looking at a long list. As they approached, Trost removed the paper and stood, stepping back.

He retreated from the room as Arnau and Felipe reached the table.

'I would like to speak to you about Karolus, my lord.'

Dietmar nodded. 'Sit.'

As the two Templars did so, the graf pulled two unused glasses closer and filled them with wine.

'Despite impoverished circumstances,' he said, 'I maintain a few small indulgences. I insist on a morning repast for my people, for even Achilles insisted upon such before tackling the great walls of Troy. And I keep good wine. Sadly, I do not keep *large quantities* of it, and most of my people drink beer brewed in the village. But I always have a single hogshead of wine, preferably from the Württemberg winery. We must all have our little habits, must we not?'

Arnau smiled and tried the wine. It was truly excellent. Savouring the drink, he and Felipe spent the next half hour talking Graf Dietmar through everything they had done and discovered that morning. Finally the Templar sat back with a sigh and regretfully drained the last drop from his glass.

'That is where we stand currently. It is, of course, your decision whether Kovacs should yet be released. My instinct is that he is innocent of all three counts: your son, Anselm and the crossbow, but he can only be definitively cleared of the first.'

Dietmar sagged a little. 'Of course, I would like nothing more than to release my old friend. But it was the crossbow that put him in that room, and it would be remiss of me in the eyes of my people to free him until that can be at least *partially* disproven.'

Arnau nodded. 'The decision is yours, my lord. In the meantime, we have less than two hours before the bell for nones and we have been negligent of late in our training. Felipe and I shall be about our practice and I shall return after nones, by which time I hope to have more of an idea about how to proceed further.'

Taking their leave of the graf, they departed the now empty hall and made their way once more along the tapestry corridor. Pausing in the antechamber, they each took a cloak from the wall. Arnau automatically checked the room first and donned the garment with his back to the wall. Caution seemed sensible, given what he knew.

Appropriately garbed, they stepped out into the courtyard and shivered regardless. The sky remained blue, clear and crisp, though there was no sign of the snow melting. Indeed, the freezing temperature had given the blanket of white a strange echo of permanence, a hard crust. Where the paths had been cleared, they were now treacherous and icy, even where kitchen ash had been used – for once the ash cooled, the path froze over once more.

Across the glassy path they slid and skittered, heading for the stairs to their room. In his head, Arnau once more recalled the words of the apostle, James: *If any of you needeth wisdom, ask he of God.* He couldn't recall many occasions when he'd had *more* need of wisdom. *Lord*, he thought, *I am at an impasse. If, in your divine mercy, you might see fit to sending me a further sign, I would deem it the greatest of gifts.*

Ah well. The Lord might give, and the Lord might not. His ways were ineffable. In the meantime, he turned to his companion. 'I think we will find somewhere at ground level to spar today, eh, Felipe? I don't fancy the tower top with an icy surface.'

The squire nodded vigorously as they both pictured themselves sliding around and pitching over the edge of the roof. Focusing on the here and now, they crossed to the doorway and climbed the steps to the accommodation corridor. Turning left at the top, Arnau stopped suddenly, arm going out to restrain Felipe behind him.

'What is it?'

'Our door is open. Did you lock it?'

'As always.'

Arnau stepped forward slightly, hand going to the sword at his side and sliding the blade quietly free. Behind him he heard the whisper of the squire's sword similarly drawn. The two men moved along the corridor as quietly as possible. Neither was wearing their chain shirt, but the boots still clumped with uncomfortable volume. Gradually, they approached the door. Pale light formed an oblong across the corridor, and Arnau prepared himself. At least no one was standing in the doorway, waiting for them, for a shadow would tell that tale. Either side of the doorway, though...

The door opened inwards and to the right. Motioning to Felipe to stay back, he moved to the opening and then suddenly leapt into action. Springing through the door, he turned to the left, brandishing his sword where a figure could be hiding around the corner with ill will. As he did so, he backed hard against the door, sending it slamming against the wall to cause harm to anyone who might be lurking behind it.

Fruitless. No one hid around the left side, and the door slammed against the wall without a cry from a hidden opponent. Turning back to the room, his heart jumped and the hairs on his flesh rose on goose flesh.

Their room was a shambles, and a body lay in the centre. Arnau blinked. Too much to take in in one go. He focused on the body, naturally, his sword lowering. *Lord, I know I asked for a sign, but I may have been o'er hasty.*

'Check for anyone hiding,' he said to Felipe as he crossed to the heap on the floor. The squire ducked into corners and glanced under the bed, while Arnau bent over the body of the girl.

Anna. The girl who had found the body in the well, and who had not been at the noon meal, because she was attending to the changing of linen. Indeed, a pile of previously neatly folded sheets lay in a heap on the floor nearby, likely dropped as she was attacked.

She was dead. That was clear instantly, from all the blood. A jagged hole the size of a dagger blade sat in her lower back, soaked with crimson. The blood had bloomed across her grey dress and pooled below her. Before touching her, he looked her up and down. There were telltale marks on her lower skirts where the dagger had been wiped clean. There would be no evidence to be found on the weapons, then. The killer was too sharp for that.

She had been stabbed in the back, but that made no sense unless it was a secondary, killing blow. Her assailant had been here already, for it had not been Anna that had caused this mess. If Arnau was any judge, she had come here to make their beds and had surprised someone busily ransacking their room. He lifted her head gingerly and looked at her face, the eyes still wide in horror and shock. There were marks on her cheek and chin where she had been cuffed hard. He nodded and lowered her again, touching the pool of blood and then wiping his finger on her dress as the killer had done with the knife. Very recent. The blood was still flowing and red.

A shadow fell across him and he jumped for a moment before he realised it was Felipe.

'No one here, brother,' the squire said. 'Anna?'

'Yes. Came to change out beds and disturbed someone. It must have happened so quickly she didn't have time to cry out. That's why no one heard. A thump across the side of the face knocked her wits from her and she dropped her armful of linen. Then before she could recover, as she spun, he stabbed her here. A killing blow, straight into vital organs. This is, in ways, horribly reminiscent of what happened to Rüdolf. There is little doubt in my mind that the two murders are the work of the same villain. In fact, I am slowly coming to the conclusion that there is only one killer after all. Perhaps Anselm was in with him, but this death and Rüdolf's are similar, the brutality of Anselm's death and the sheer strength and guts it took to try and dispatch us with the crossbow... these are all the work of one man, and he is still around.'

Felipe sighed. 'On the bright side, your list of suspects diminishes with every death.'

Arnau flashed him a disapproving look. 'Hardly a subject for flippancy. But,' he said, rising slowly, 'this very much clears Kovacs, I think. He can be released now, for he could not have done this. It irks me that I never checked whether the key we had for our room was the only one. Now it seems obvious that at least one of the serfs or their masters would have a key for such duties as changing the sheets.'

'But she did not unlock the door. Not if she stumbled across someone in here.'

Arnau nodded. 'So there are *three* keys. She must have one, we have another and the killer has a third. Keys,' he said again, tapping his lip. 'Keys. It keeps coming back to keys.' He ignored most of the room's mess, well lit by the window whose shutters the killer must have opened for light. Reaching the chest where they kept their prized possessions, he tried it. It opened with ease.

'This was locked?'

Felipe nodded. 'Always.'

'Then either there is a second key for it, or someone is adept at opening locks without a key.'

Heart thundering, he began to go through the goods in there. He found Lütolf's old family surcoat crumpled into a ball and panic rose in him. Lifting it, he shook it out straight. The relief he felt as the document from Rourell fell from the folds similarly crumpled was probably the strongest he had ever experienced. If it was the documents the attacker was looking for then he had missed them in their hiding place. But he felt certain that it was not them for which the man had been searching.

Digging deeper, he found Lütolf's effects scattered among their things, tipped from the bag that had contained them. His fingers scrabbled around with ever-increasing tension.

'They're not here.'

'Sir?'

'The keys, Felipe, they're not here.'

He rose and turned. Felipe gave him a weird smile. 'Behold, sir.' The squire walked across to where his kettle hat hung on a nail in the wall. Lifting it off, he turned the helmet around. The ring with the three keys was tightly tucked into the leather band that ran around the inside of the brim.

'Felipe?'

'Well, you kept saying you thought they were important. It struck me that locking them somewhere everyone knew we kept the important things was a little foolish. The most basic place is the most often overlooked.'

Arnau blinked. 'You are a wonder, Felipe. I am almost certain it was those very keys for which the killer searched. Anna found him going through our chest and disturbed him. He was forced to kill her and, I presume, fled the scene immediately before he was spotted again, this time in an even more compromising position.'

'What value are the keys, though?' Felipe mused.

Arnau nodded, holding them up. 'One to the main gate. One to Lütolf's apartment. One nobody seems to recognise. It seems likely to be the latter, whatever it is. But the only solution I can see is to try it in every lock in the castle until it works. We may yet come to that. But firstly, I think perhaps it is time we looked at poor Brother Lütolf's room.' He looked down. 'Well, time *I* looked at it.'

'Sir?'

'We need to report this to Bernhard or to Michael and there will be explanations to give. I want you to secure Lütolf's effects and hide the document again, while I find someone and report this. Stay with our room and the body then until it is dealt with.'

Felipe looked uncertain. 'It might be better if you stayed too, brother.'

'This happened recently – the blood is still liquid – but our alibi is sound. We were with Kovacs and then Dietmar. There is no reason to accuse us of this. Just deal with things. I shall report this to Bernhard and then see to it that the graf sets Kovacs free. Then I shall look at Lütolf's rooms and see if I can identify any reason why the killer might want a key to them.' He paused. 'I think now that perhaps the killer never did want me dead. I fear it was just a way to get to what we had in our chest. Having failed to remove us from the scene entirely, he has resorted instead to simple theft. Wait here until someone comes.'

Leaving a worried-looking squire in their shambles of a room, Arnau hurried back along the corridor. Things were moving too fast. He barely had time to react to events before something else happened. How was he supposed to piece this together?

Crossing the courtyard, he spotted Michael Trost striding towards the stables with Conrad. Waving frantically, he ran over, slipping and sliding on the frozen stones.

'There has been another killing.'

Trost stopped in his tracks, turning sharply. 'What?'

Conrad, unable to comprehend Arnau's tongue, simply frowned in confusion. Arnau focused on the seneschal. 'Someone broke into our room while we were at lunch and in conversation with the graf. It would appear they were searching through our things and were disturbed by Anna coming to change the linen. I fear she was murdered to silence her.'

Trost blinked. 'I...'

'My squire is still there. Go and speak to him, Trost. I am going to see the graf once more.'

As the seneschal and the stable hand ran off towards his room, Arnau crossed the courtyard once more and entered the main block. Kovacs could be released, and Arnau needed to search Lütolf's room, but neither should be done without Dietmar's consent.

Entering the building, he hurriedly hung his cloak on one of the pegs and then turned and thumped up the staircase to the second level. At the top, he came to an immediate halt, swaying, unable to believe his eyes. Ahead, along the corridor, like a horrible reflection of what they had just discovered, a square of light fell across the corridor from Kovacs' doorway, and Jutte and Leupold stood there looking into the room.

'Heavens, no,' Arnau breathed as he broke into a run along the corridor.

'Has he…?' he began, but fell silent as he approached the door. Another body. Another soul sent to the kingdom of God. But it was not Kovacs.

The serf and the guard stared at him, neither able to speak a language he understood. Arnau pushed past them and peered into the room. The door was open and of Kovacs he could see no sign. Bernhard lay face down in the doorway, blood pooling beneath his head.

Arnau, heart thundering once more, reached down. As he touched Bernhard, ready to turn him and examine the wound, the marshal gave a tiny groan.

'He lives. He is unconscious, but he lives, thank the good Lord!'

Neither of the others might have a word of Frankish, but both clearly received the message. Leupold crouched to help Arnau as they carefully lifted and turned the limp form of Bernhard. The blow had been to his forehead at the hairline. Gently, Arnau touched it. The skin was broken, but he thought the bone still solid and unmarred. The man would have a demon of a headache upon waking, but at least he should wake. The blood was not as voluminous as he'd initially suspected, either.

'He was hit with something blunt,' Arnau said, largely to himself, since his audience were uncomprehending. 'Search for the minstrel,' he said. The maid and the guard looked at him in confusion. He pointed into the room. 'Kovacs. Understand?'

The pair nodded and carefully climbed around the scene, heading into the room.

Damn it, this was getting worse by the hour.

Rüdolf dead of a cut throat. Anselm, his face smashed to pieces. Anna stabbed in the back. Otto out of commission in his room with his broken bones. Now Bernhard attacked and Kovacs missing. Even a dog poisoned by accident. It was becoming hard to avoid the conclusion that Renfrizhausen was cursed.

The other two quickly reappeared, shrugging. Kovacs was clearly not in the room. How had Arnau been so wrong about him? Or was there yet more to this? Not for the first time, he wished he had access to the legal nous of Ramon or the subtle mind of Balthesar. He felt certain the two older knights would have had this entire matter resolved before even the second attack.

With Leupold's help, he lifted Bernhard up onto Kovacs' bed, laying him carefully where he could recover and closing the shutters to keep the room warmer. Arnau pointed to the fireplace. 'Light the fire,' he said to the maid. 'Understand? *Fuego*?' He made flickering flame motions with his fingers and pointed to the hearth. The maid nodded and Arnau turned to the guard, beckoning, leading him out into the corridor where they stepped around the small blood pool. Over to a window they went, and Arnau pointed at the main gate nearby.

'Make sure it is locked. Understand? Closed.' He mimed turning a key and trying to open a locked door. When Leupold nodded and hurried off to the stairs, Arnau stood and fretted, fingers drumming on his hip. Both these incidents were so recent that the blood was fresh. Where in God's name was Kovacs? Surely the Hungarian couldn't have managed to overcome Bernhard then cross to their rooms and search them in the time available, could he? They'd been... actually more than half an hour. Sadly, Arnau came to the conclusion that the man probably could have done it all if he'd moved very quickly. That would mean that Kovacs was the killer after all, and still somewhere in the castle. And if his identity as the killer had now been thrown open, he would have nothing to lose.

Arnau fumed. How could he have been so wrong? He'd cleared the man of the first killing based on the favoured hand, but what if Kovacs wasn't *really* left-handed? What if he was one of those men capable of using both hands with equal skill? What if he'd set this all up to give himself an alibi? And while he might claim no skill or history with a crossbow, he certainly knew more about them than most. He had the strength for all these things, and,

Arnau suspected, also the agility and subtlety. He was a storyteller and a liar by trade. Had he managed to fool even Dietmar?

It was infuriating. On one level, he didn't want to blame Kovacs. He'd liked the man, and had been almost entirely confident in his innocence. But now something had changed. All evidence pointed to the man, and his alibis were crumbling like old mortar under the blows of logic. Damn it. It wasn't as if Arnau even had another suspect he could consider.

Well, with Leupold locking the gate, Kovacs had to be locked in the castle somewhere. He would be found eventually.

Taking a deep breath, he returned to the stairs and descended, heading for the hall.

Graf Dietmar was still at the table, looking tired and staring down into his cup.

'My lord, it is my unpleasant duty to report new incidents.'

***

An hour later, Arnau was once more in his room. Felipe had tidied all their goods away, and the body of Anna had been removed. She and Anselm now lay wrapped in shrouds in one of the empty bedchambers close to Arnau's room. *Uncomfortably* close, in Arnau's opinion. It would not be seemly for them to share a chamber with Rüdolf, though.

The squire closed the door. 'I have two keys now, but it hardly seems to matter since we know the killer has a third.'

Arnau nodded. 'Nowhere is secure. Nowhere is safe. We need to keep the document and the keys hidden, I think. The rest matters not.' He sighed. 'I am in half a mind, Felipe, to leave this place now, taking what we brought.'

'You said it was our duty to help? To bring the killer to God's divine justice.'

Arnau nodded wearily. 'But the longer we remain and the more we investigate, the more trouble there is. The more people die or are injured. I started this with a clear plan, with ideas as to how we could perhaps make sense of this whole mess. Since then, though, events have run far beyond our control, and every turn takes us deeper into the labyrinth.'

'But you have a clear suspect, Brother Arnau.'

He sighed. 'I do. Everything fits Kovacs. He is the only one who was capable of doing each deed and, apart from the nebulous alibi of being in his room with his lute when Rüdolf died, he has few defences left to put up. And now his disappearance plagues me. Yes, everything says that Kovacs is our man. Why, then, am I uncomfortable with that conclusion?'

Felipe shrugged. 'Because he is a likeable man. Because sometimes it is only comfortable to face an enemy if he wears a devilish face.'

Arnau turned an appraising gaze on his squire. 'Very astute. And I fear you are right. I have been taken in by Kovacs' easy manner, just as has everyone else. And it would be nice, even so, to be able to say "here is an end to the matter", but we cannot. Not until Kovacs is found. There will have to be another search. And I still want to see Lütolf's rooms and try and identify this third key. But from this moment on, Felipe, no one is safe. The only thing worse than being trapped with a killer is being trapped with a killer who has nothing to lose. I have already warned Dietmar and Bernhard that everyone should sleep locked up tight and with a blade to hand.'

'How is the marshal?'

'Alive but sore. He remembers little. The speed of it seems to have overrun him. He went to take Kovacs his lunch, and as soon as the door was open... well, he doesn't know. He woke up some time later.'

'This place makes me nervous.'

Arnau looked across at the squire. 'Me too, Felipe. Me too.'

CHAPTER TWELVE

SATURDAY AFTERNOON

𝔄rnau sighed and, gesturing for Wolf and Felipe to join him, closed the door on Bernhard's room. Nothing. It was the last place. Kovacs had vanished into thin air. Arnau had wondered at times how the guards had managed a complete search of the castle for a will and turned up neither it, nor the crossbow they knew had been somewhere. He was beginning to sympathise, now they had searched the entire castle for a full-sized human being and turned up nothing.

And they couldn't realistically have missed anything. They had searched methodically, clearing one block at a time, while leaving people in the courtyard to make sure there was no sneaking around or doubling back. And no one could have deliberately missed somewhere from the search, for they had split into groups of three to do it, Arnau and his squire taking Wolf to search the kitchens first, while Leupold, Bernhard and Gunther had checked the ground floor of the guard range. Conrad, Winrich and Matthias had stood guard in the courtyard throughout. Then Arnau and his party had scoured the walls and towers systematically while Bernhard's group had searched the upper floor. They had paid a quick trip to the gatehouse and the chapel, and the well too, just in case, and then moved into the main range. With Winrich and friends watching the door and the courtyard still, Bernhard's team had begun in the cellars and Arnau's on the top floor, respectively climbing and descending until they met in the stairwell.

Nothing.

Kovacs was not in the castle.

They had then been to the gatehouse once more. Leupold had done as asked and had locked the gate, but just in case they opened it and checked the ground outside. Nothing. The pristine white carpet lay undisturbed, except for the tracks Arnau and Felipe had made returning with the crossbow.

Once more they reconvened in the great hall to discuss the matter: Arnau, Michael, Bernhard, Felipe and Graf Dietmar.

'If he is not in the castle,' the lord said with certainty, 'then he has left. It is that simple.'

'Unless he is not what he seems,' Michael Trost muttered.

'What?'

'Witchcraft. Devilry.'

Dietmar turned on his seneschal. 'I have known Karolus since we were young. *You* have known him almost as long.'

'But *have* we, my lord?' Michael responded. He turned to Arnau. 'What did John say in the Good Book? Chapter eight, verse forty-four?'

Arnau blinked, not because he didn't know the quote, but at being dragged into this uncomfortable position. He cleared his throat, but his voice was still hoarse when he spoke. '"Ye be of the father, the Devil, and ye will do the desires of your father. He was a manslayer from the beginning, and he stood not in truth; for truth is not in him. When he speaketh a lie, he speaketh of his own; for he is a liar, and father of lies."'

The table went silent.

Arnau fretted into the quiet. This was not productive. Whether Kovacs had been guilty all along and an excellent liar was a moot point. What was crucial was *finding* him, and while Arnau was ready to bend his knee to the Lord in the sure knowledge of his protection and the salvation of heaven, he was still sceptical on subjects like dragons, ghosts and vanishing minstrels.

'There are no other exits from the castle? No postern gates of which I am not aware?' he said, driving the conversation back to the useful.

'No.

'And no ground floor windows?'

'No. Only arrow slits through which a man could not fit.'

'Then we check the upper ones. We apply logic rather than biblical fear. We have searched the castle completely and he is not here. We know he did not leave by the gate, and that is the only exit on the ground level. So he must have exited by some upper level.'

'The fall would kill a man.'

'Not a clever one. The blanket of fresh snow will reveal whether anyone left that way.'

Bernhard nodded. 'Agreed. We have between two and three hours of daylight left. More than enough to simply circle the castle. It should be quite obvious if we find it.'

The decision made, they headed for the gatehouse once more. Leaving Conrad, Winrich and Matthias at the gate, they emerged into the knee-deep snow in the clearing before the castle, and Arnau shivered. Ahead, he could see the roadway leading off into the woods, along which they had arrived. Some thousand paces down there he had fought the last of the bandits.

''Til we meet at the far side,' Bernhard said, leading Leupold and Gunther off to the right. Arnau, drawn back from his reverie, nodded and gestured to Wolf and Felipe and the trio set off left, following their own tracks from earlier, heading for the crossbow window above their own apartment range.

They had not gone far before Wolf saw it. With no command of Frankish, the guardsman grasped Arnau's shoulder, shook it and pointed up. Arnau followed his gesture and nodded. 'Felipe, go back and shout Bernhard and his men. We've found it.'

As the squire ran back to fetch the others, Arnau looked up. A velvet drape hung out of the window below the one from which the crossbow had been flung. From there to the ground was perhaps twenty feet. Enough to deter an attacker, but low enough for a man to realistically shimmy down a rope and drop into soft snow the last ten feet.

Arnau pushed his way forward, with Wolf at his shoulder, and towards the ground below the window. As he did so, he realised the futility of further search. Still he got as close as he dared, and peered around at the snow. Wolf gave an irritable huff, and if Arnau could have conversed with him, he would have expressed sympathy. A few minutes of searching fruitlessly ensued before Felipe returned with the other three. They had not got far before being called back, due to the difficulty of wading through deep, fresh snow.

'An easy enough exit,' Bernhard noted. 'But then whence?'

'That,' Arnau fretted, 'I suspect we will never know. He chose his position well. Felipe and I had spent time searching this entire area earlier for the crossbow. From the walls to the woods is a complete mess of footprints and disturbed snow. A subtle man, and I would say Kovacs is nothing if not subtle, could use the existing marks to mask his own. In less than a minute he could have been out of the castle, down through the snow and into the woods.'

'We might pick up a trail in the woods, then?' Felipe said, hopefully.

Arnau shook his head. 'The floor of the forest will hide many things. In places the drifts will be very deep, but here the trees are thick, and the ground has barely any coverage. It would take a master tracker to even hope to find a trace. And, of course, there will be animal trails out here.' He paused, remembering that struggle in the road before the castle. 'And possibly desperate brigands.'

Fuming, he raced back over his connections, feeling he might have missed something. Kovacs and Anselm. An odd combination, but then they would have known one another for many years. Kovacs' motive remained something of a mystery. Could he have seen Rüdolf as a hurdle to be overcome? He was only a little younger than Dietmar, but he *was* a bastard from a Hungarian family from whom he would not inherit. He had no legacy to collect. The von Ehingen had little enough, but even that was more than Kovacs. Could he be hoping that with Rüdolf and Lütolf both gone, Dietmar would adopt him?

Stranger things had happened, of course. Why the attempts on Arnau's life, though? Unless it was about the Temple documents after all? Arnau blinked. Something slid into place. If Arnau lost the documents, the Order would have no real claim to the lands they now administered. If Kovacs had already secured the will, then the family would retake those lands and moneys.

Was Kovacs that shrewd? Probably.

But his plans had come to naught now. Discovered and imprisoned, he had taken the opportunity to flee, and all his hard work had come to nothing. Where would he go? Did he have other accomplices?

Again, his mind turned towards those bandits who had attacked him on his arrival. Were the bandits truly a chance meeting?

'There is nothing more to find here,' he grunted, and the six of them turned and made for the castle gate once more. Once inside, Bernhard gave orders that the drape be brought in and examined, not that they hoped to learn anything from it. Arnau chewed his lip. 'Bernhard, do you have much bandit trouble in the area?'

The marshal frowned. 'It is not something we struggle with as a rule. At times there have been troubles, but we are not on a major trade road or such, so we do not often attract that kind of problem.' He looked up at the ice blue sky. 'Mind you, this season brings out the worst. Hardship and hunger drive men to wicked necessities.'

'True. I have it in mind to head to the village and ask some questions there. Now that the weather has cleared, it should be possible, I presume?'

Bernhard peered at the sky again. 'Certainly there is little chance of you being caught in a blizzard. The going will be hard, though.'

'We will take the palfreys and leave my charger and the pack beast here. I hope to make it back by nightfall.'

Bernhard's face took on a look of concern. 'If there is any chance of not doing so, stay at the *kneipe*... the tavern in the village. Do not try to reach the castle in the woods in the dark, my friend.'

Arnau nodded his understanding. 'I intend to be quick. Can you give me good directions? We had trouble on the way here.'

'Would you like me to come with you?'

'No,' Arnau shook his head. 'Better you stay and keep things safe here. Directions, though?'

'Wait,' Bernhard said, and sent Conrad off to saddle the horses. Arnau and Felipe stood waiting near the gate and by the time the serf had arrived with their riding beasts saddled, tacked and ready, the marshal reappeared. With him, Hilde had a saddle bag, which she proffered. 'Some supplies, just in case,' Bernhard explained. 'And here.' He handed over a small sheet of vellum upon which he had hastily scribbled a map. Arnau smiled. Better than the directions he'd had from the gravediggers.

'Shall I warn the church of what will be happening in the coming days?' he asked, gesturing to the main block, beneath which Rüdolf rested in state, and to the upper floor of the range opposite, where Anselm and Anna lay.

'Better leave that to us,' Bernhard said.

'Very well. Thank you both.' The two Templars mounted their beasts, and Arnau hung the saddle bag from Canción and examined the map before folding it and tucking it away into his pouch. The gate was opened, and they emerged out into the snowy world. Felipe looked less than thrilled and, as he rode, he leafed through his book of the Rule. Arnau rolled his eyes, suspecting the squire was looking for some reason they had to stay in the castle and not brave the woods.

Certainly it was cold, and slow going, with the horses moving gingerly through the deep snow. They had only a general notion of the terrain below the crisp white surface, and the constant fear of rabbit holes that might catch a hoof and break a leg made it a nervous journey. Moreover, the dense heaviness of the snow tired the beasts quicker than a normal ride, and every quarter of a mile they moved through the woodland, they would have to pause for a time to let the animals recover.

Still, they were proving that it was possible. That, at least, came as something of a comfort. Having been trapped in the castle these past few days with little hope of making it to civilisation had added to the many levels of tension. Knowing now that at least it was possible to leave made them both feel a little happier.

With the afternoon sunlight and the dazzling white world, the journey seemed a great deal nicer than it had when they had arrived, for there was no low-hanging grey cloud and visibility was much improved, even if the snow was deeper and more troublesome.

Not far from the castle, they deviated from Bernhard's map, past a dead tree that rose, skeletal in the cold light, and moved around several side paths largely conjured from memory. With only two wrong turns and backtracks, they managed to find the place where they had been ambushed. Tethering the horses and searching the area, finally he found the telltale heap where the bodies of four bandits lay piled up beneath a blanket of fresh snow. The presence of animal tracks around and over the heap prepared Arnau for what he would find, and he covered his mouth and nose with one hand as he brushed away the snow with the other.

In the event, the bodies were nowhere near as bad as he'd expected. They had not begun to rot, for the constant cold had kept them relatively fresh. They had been partially consumed by hungry scavengers, but the difficulty of getting to them down in the snow had made it hard work, and only the top two bodies were properly disfigured, faces and extremities eaten away and soft tissue consumed.

Gagging a little, Arnau and Felipe pulled the mangled creatures away to reveal the two beneath who were better preserved and barely touched by hungry wildlife. The last time they had seen these men it had been late in the day too, but then it had been overcast and visibility poor. Now the world was bright and clear. He crouched and examined the bodies, moving limbs and turning them slightly to get the best view he could.

Fairly certain of his findings, he rose.

'These are not career bandits,' he said in a matter-of-fact tone. 'They bear scars and injuries, but not from battle. Their scars are more consistent with labourers and farmers.'

'I bear farm scars and yet wield a blade for the Lord,' Felipe pointed out.

'Yes, but you are an unusual example. These men are not bandits by nature. And I do not think this was an opportunistic assault. As Bernhard pointed out, there is no mercantile trail on the hill. In fact, the only termini of the road upon which we were attacked are the castle and the town. Why, then, would bandits lurk there? In such weather it could be days before anyone passed that way. I am now more or less certain that the bandits were waiting for us. Three of them attacked us while one went for the pack. I don't think they were just seeking coin and food. I think they were after something specific. Heavens, Felipe, but I think we were targets before we even arrived at Renfrizhausen.'

'But what were they looking for?' Felipe murmured.

'Possibly the documents from Rourell. We were expected, after all, or at least *someone* bearing those documents was expected, and soon. Desperate men might be induced to camp in the woods, even for days, and wait for us to pass by. I think a trap was set to seize those papers before we ever reached the castle.'

'Our enemy is clever and subtle,' Felipe noted. '"*The great old serpent that is called the Devil, and Satan, that deceiveth all the world.*"'

'Oh don't you start with the witchcraft and devilry,' Arnau sighed. 'He's just a dangerous man, not the Antichrist.'

With that, Arnau set to work once again, piling the ruined bodies on top of the better preserved ones, against the possibility that they might yet need to find them once more and check for something else later. Heaping snow over them, he stepped back, satisfied with his handiwork.

Before they departed, Arnau had a thought and scoured the area. Trying to place where everything had happened, it took him ten minutes to find it. Before the man he'd chased had broken cover and run for his life, he had discarded his bow and his arrows as too much of a burden. The bow sat propped against a tree, now half buried in snow. He grasped it and returned to the path.

Turning it over and this way and that, he showed it to Felipe. 'The man was definitely not a professional archer, nor a hunter.

This bow was not well kept and I suspect has remained strung for a long time.'

Felipe shrugged. 'It has been four days, brother.'

'I don't think this bow has been unstrung in weeks, and a trained bowman would unstring it for transport. A bow is only strung for use. This man might not have been a bad shot, but I don't think this was his bow, and I don't think he knows how to maintain one. Come.'

Task complete, they mounted once more, leaving the scene of the attack and taking the bow with them. It took perhaps an hour to descend to the town, or village as Arnau thought of it, of Renfrizhausen. Now, the sun was threateningly low in the west, plunging towards the hills fast. Perhaps Bernhard was right. Maybe they would need to stay the night. Reaching the church, he noted with interest the fresh grave, with the wooden marker, which had been a half-dug hole when they arrived.

'Where do we go?' Felipe murmured.

Arnau pointed at the church. 'It is exceedingly unlikely that we will find anyone in town who speaks a tongue we can understand. In retrospect, we should probably have brought the marshal with us, for translation purposes if nothing else. But if there is anyone in Renfrizhausen who might know something other than German, it will be the priest.'

They tied their steeds at the gate to the churchyard and entered, feeling an odd sense of peace settle upon them at crossing the threshold into consecrated ground. Arnau had not realised quite the level of nail-biting tension that had become the norm over the past four days until he felt it diminish. Walking along the path, they approached the church door and tried it. It swung open with a sepulchral groan and the two men entered an austere looking building, lit by four candelabra. The priest was near the altar at the far end, filling a bowl of water. He looked round at the noise and started in surprise at the sight of the two men, one in black and one in white, but both wearing the red cross of the Order.

'Do you speak French, Father?' he asked, slowly and carefully, in the Frankish tongue.

The priest frowned, then concentrated, his mouth working as though trying to form the words from carefully constructed thought, then strolled towards them down the nave of the small church. 'Little,' he said. '*Habst du keine Deutsche*?'

Arnau shook his head. Though he wasn't sure what the man said, he'd heard the word *Deutsche* often enough now to believe it meant German.

'My Frank bad.'

'Better than my German,' Arnau smiled. 'Might I ask you a few questions?' he said, once more, slowly and as clearly as possible.

The man frowned, working through a translation, then nodded.

'We are staying at the castle,' Arnau said. He pointed at himself and Felipe. 'At *schloss*. Yes?'

The man nodded, and Arnau eased into his subject, lifting the bow. 'We were attacked. Four days ago. Four men. One had this bow.'

'*Die jäger bogen*,' the man said, then thought hard. 'Hunter. In Renfrizhausen.' He pointed to the village outside. '*Ist verschwunden. Er... die* hunter, his bow gone. You.' He pointed at the bow.

Arnau nodded. 'A hunter had his bow stolen. We were attacked by four men,' He held up four fingers, then pointed at the bow, at the sword hanging at his waist, and up towards the castle on the hill, or at least where he thought it would be, through the walls.

The priest considered this for some time. 'Four men.' He nodded. '*Beschreiben. Er...* you describe?'

Arnau thought back as best he could. 'All perhaps between twenty and thirty years old. Poor. Hard workers, I think. Ragged clothes. Many scratches and marks. Two with red hair, two with black.'

The priest held out his hand to slow Arnau's description and the Templar repeated it, much slower this time. As he reached the hair colour, the priest's eyes narrowed. 'You know them?'

'*Ja. Ich verstehe. Ist* sons of Friderich. Live *hier*. See?' He beckoned them towards the door and pointed out across the graveyard at a low, poor-looking hovel close to the trees at the edge of the settlement.

'Sons of Friderich. Have they been missing... er, *verschwunden*,' he remembered, holding up four fingers, 'four days, yes?'

The man nodded. '*Fünf*,' he replied, holding up five.

Arnau turned to the squire. 'We are getting somewhere, Felipe. Four villagers stole a hunter's bow and have been gone for five days. I believe they camped in the woods waiting for us for a day or more, and then sprung.' He slapped his head. 'That coincides with the death of Rüdolf, does it not?'

Felipe nodded. 'So when the lord dies, Kovacs somehow gets these four men to wait for us, knowing that someone will be coming with the other documents. It makes sense.'

The knight turned back to the priest. 'Has Karolus Kovacs been in the village? Either five or six days ago, or today?'

'Ko-vacs?' said the man uncertainly.

'A minstrel,' Arnau explained, pretending to play a lute, then pipes, then dancing a little jig. 'Troubadour. Blue shirt,' he said, remembering what Kovacs had worn the past few days. He crossed to the wall, where exquisite paintings displayed scenes or saints and folk from long ago, and found a figure with a blue top. He pointed at it and then his shirt. 'Blue, see?' Then to something red and to his own legs 'Red hose and boots.'

'*Rot, ya*. No. I not see musician with blue *und rot*.'

Arnau sagged. 'No connection to be made here, then.'

'*Du solltest fragen Bulstrich.*'

Arnau blinked. He had no idea what it meant, but the name was familiar and unexpected. He frowned. 'Bernhard Bulstrich?'

The priest nodded.

Arnau felt his heart start to pound. 'Bulstrich was here?'

'*Ja, hier*,' the priest said, pointing at his altar.

'When? Five days ago?'

Again the priest nodded. '*Ja. Fünf.*'

Arnau turned to Felipe. 'Bernhard. Bernhard was here just before we passed through the village. A day earlier at most. After the young lord had died.'

'He never said such a thing,' Felipe noted.

'No. And unless it was him arranging a little welcoming party with the sons of Friderich, what in God's name could he have been doing here?'

Felipe shook his head. 'But Bernhard is innocent. He was attacked.'

'Was he?' Arnau said. 'Or is he *the great old serpent that is called the Devil, and Satan, that deceiveth all the world*'?'

The squire continued to shake his head. 'He is innocent. At least of Rüdolf's death. He was in the church. Father Oswald confirmed it.'

'Unless Father Oswald is somehow in on it?'

The two men shared a look for a moment, and Arnau sagged. 'No, I don't believe that either. But it's impossible to ignore that Bernhard was in the village at a very convenient time and has said nothing about it.'

Felipe tapped his lip. 'It is just a fresh puzzle on top of all the others.'

'No,' Arnau disagreed. 'This is a step towards solving it all. I feel we have everything we need, but I cannot quite see how they fit together. It is maddening, but we are close, Felipe. Very close.'

'What now?'

'Now we go back to the castle.'

'And confront Bernhard Bulstrich?'

Arnau sucked his teeth. 'I'm not sure. I don't think we want to reveal all our findings immediately. Let's hold our tongue for now and watch. See how things work out tonight and in the morning. I want to keep an eye on the marshal, for a start. And I think we might want to search again, but this time just you and I, without relying on Bernhard. If he is involved in all of this somehow, then even with others alongside, he might have deliberately overlooked things.'

'He might know how to use a crossbow,' Felipe said suddenly.

'What?'

'Bernhard had been on Crusade. He might well have acquired a crossbow and the skill to use it.'

Arnau nodded. 'He might, at that. But it is not proof and, as you pointed out, he still has an unassailable alibi for the night of the murder.'

Arnau felt the frustration building. They were tantalisingly close. Thanking the village priest, Arnau dropped a generous donation onto the platter near the door and the two Templars left. Hurrying down the path as the late afternoon light began to slide into sunset, they reached their horses and untied them.

'Should we stay in the village?' Felipe asked uncertainly.

'No. Things are coming to a head. We need to be in the castle.'

Minutes later they were departing the village and making their way back along the route they had used to reach Renfrizhausen. By the time they began to climb the true slope of the hill, the sun was gone behind the peaks to the west, and the light was fading.

'I don't like this,' Felipe muttered.

Arnau pointed onwards. 'Right now, I suspect we are safer here than in our room, but I want to get back regardless. A prolonged absence might be filled with any number of disasters.'

Slowly, they plodded through the snow, Arnau occasionally producing Bernhard's map and holding it up to attract the best possible light, then confirming directions and pressing on. Darkness had fallen by the time they reached the crest of the slope and began to make their way towards the twinkling lights of the castle. Approaching the gate, they were relieved when it was opened ready, figures awaiting them.

Inside, Bernhard, Conrad and Wolf stood in the shadow of the gatehouse, the latter closing and locking up behind them, while the stable hand took their horses and made towards the stalls for the night.

Arnau tried not to look the marshal directly in the eye yet. He didn't want to give anything away, and a flash of a glance at Felipe warned him too.

'Did you learn anything useful?' Bernhard asked.

Arnau painted an expression of vexed nonchalance on his face and turned. 'Not particularly. It does not appear that Kovacs has been in the village. What has happened to him, I cannot say.'

'But you found something?' Bernhard pressed. 'I can see it in your face.'

Damn it.

Arnau straightened. 'I have identified the bandits that attacked us. Four villagers, belonging to a poor family on the edge. It appears they stole a bow from the village's hunter. It seems that these conditions really do drive people to the most extreme acts.'

The marshal held his gaze for a while, then one eyebrow rose a little. 'Quite. Well, at least that clears one matter up. You need not fear the woods now.'

'No, although we will not be leaving yet. I still find myself half believing that Kovacs will turn up unexpectedly.'

'His murdering hide will be long gone.'

'I'm not so sure. Things remain shadowed in Renfrizhausen,' Arnau said.

'Then we must all look to our safety.'

'Yes. If you will excuse me, I think I need to change my sodden hose and prepare for compline.'

Bernhard nodded. 'I shall see you there.'

As the marshal turned back to Wolf, Arnau led Felipe away, across the courtyard and to the stairs to their chamber. Once they were safely in their room, the squire examined their things while Arnau locked up behind them.

'Someone has been here again,' Felipe said.

Arnau frowned, and crossed to the chest. Everything appeared to be perfectly in order. 'How do you know?'

The squire pointed at the chest itself. 'I plucked a hair, licked it and stuck it across the gap of the lid,' he explained. 'It has gone, fallen when the lid was opened.'

'Or spit is not an adequate adhesive and it simply fell?'

'No. Someone has been in it.'

Arnau frowned. 'The document? The keys?' He reached up and removed Felipe's kettle hat from the wall. He had not taken it with him to the village. It was empty, and Arnau's pulse quickened, but Felipe drew both the keys and the documents from his pouch. 'Nowhere was safe here, brother. You said so yourself, so I brought them with us.'

Arnau laughed. 'You are a marvel, Felipe.' The smile slid from his face quickly, though.

'Bernhard is guilty,' he said.

'You're sure?'

A nod. 'I have no proof, and cannot possibly approach Dietmar and accuse his right-hand man, who has a long history of loyalty to the family. But I saw the devilment in his eye when we spoke at the gate. He was waiting to find out what we knew. I suspect he had already feared what we might discover in the village.'

'But you told him nothing.'

'It was what I didn't tell him that he was busy reading in my eyes. I know Bernhard is guilty somehow. But the problem is that he now knows that I know. The next few hours might be a very tense game.'

'I am still at a loss,' the squire muttered. 'Bernhard stands to inherit nothing. Neither the will nor the Order's documents will make any difference to him. I do not understand what might have driven him to do such a thing?'

Arnau nodded irritably. 'There, of course, is another stumbling block, although the main such is the fact that Bernhard was in the chapel at the time and could not possible have done the original deed.' Arnau deflated with a heavy sigh and sank to the bed. 'This vexes me, Felipe. Somehow, deep in my gut, I know that Bernhard is guilty, but I cannot for the life of me fathom a motive, and he simply had no opportunity. He *did* it, I think, but at the same time he *cannot* have done it, and had no *reason* to do it. I shall keep a very close eye on him at the service tonight, on the assumption he is there. You, I'm afraid, will have to stay in the room and make sure our inquisitive friend does not rummage through our belongings once more.'

Felipe nodded, clutching his beloved book of the Rule tight.

'Tomorrow is the Lord's day,' he said.

Arnau nodded. He hoped so. Dearly, he hoped so.

CHAPTER THIRTEEN

SATURDAY NIGHT

𝔄rnau turned over in his blankets, shivering at the sudden intrusion of cold air into his world. His mind was churning, continually working things through and denying him any hope of sleep.

The service in the chapel had been exceedingly odd. Though on the surface nothing had seemingly changed, the few odd times that Bernhard and Arnau had caught one another's glance both men had been sizing each other up in a way that suggested the growing threat of violence. And yet both dangerous gazes had been fixed above deliberately easy smiles that no one else would possibly pick up on. Strained didn't even come close to a description.

Once the service had ended, Arnau had watched the marshal stride nonchalantly back into the main range and had fought for any realistic excuse to follow, but found none and had reluctantly returned to his own room.

He was certain that Bernhard was guilty. Of it all, in fact, and not just one part. But there was no evidence with which to approach the lord of Renfrizhausen, and the marshal had a record of decades of faithful service, while Arnau was an unknown and recently arrived outsider from a mistrusted group. He could only imagine how accusations would be met unless he could back them up.

And he couldn't back them up.

Bernhard could easily have dealt with Anselm, and he could have searched their room. He was a former Crusader, so acquiring and being familiar, and competent, with a Hungarian crossbow was not out of the realm of possibility. He was strong enough and possibly agile enough to have made that night attack on their room, and he knew the castle well enough to escape. He was right-handed and martial enough to have attacked young Graf Rüdolf. He could even have opened the door to Kovacs' room, done away with the man and then hit his own head and lay on the floor to allay suspicion.

But there was still a plethora of unanswered questions.

Firstly, and least importantly, where was Kovacs? Whether alive or dead, he still had to be somewhere. Secondly, what possible motive could Bernhard have? He stood to inherit nothing, so the document and the will seemed inconsequential. Even if he'd had cause to try and acquire Arnau's papers to save the family, why attack the young lord? Or was it something else? But what else connected Rüdolf and Arnau? He'd talked himself in circles all night on that one, even running through a list of everything they had in their pack. The one point he kept coming back to there was the keys, but even then he could not see how they fitted into the puzzle, and how they could connect him to Rüdolf.

But way beyond the missing minstrel and the motive, the biggest problem was how in God's name he had managed to kill the young lord, when he had one of the strongest alibis in the castle.

Until he could answer these questions there was absolutely no point in approaching Graf Dietmar and stirring up the hornets' nest. He would have to continue to work things out, easing pieces into place, all the time keeping an eye on Bernhard.

And so, after the service, Arnau had retired. As always now, he and Felipe slept with a blade down beside the bed, door locked and shutters latched, as if that would be enough. It had not taken the squire long to slip into deep slumber, but for Arnau sleep held off, pushed away by his busy, frustrated mind.

And if any of you needeth wisdom, ask ye of God, who giveth to all men largely, and upbraideth not; and it shall be given to him.

He'd begged the Lord for that wisdom, over and over again.

Finally, surrendering to inconvenient wakefulness, he pushed back his blankets, shivering at the sudden cold once more. As he rose and pulled on his mail shirt with some difficulty and more noise than he'd intended, Felipe stirred, opening one eye.

'Going for a walk,' Arnau muttered. 'I'll lock the door behind me.'

Felipe gave him a groggy nod and then rolled over. Arnau finished dressing fully and then crossed to the door, strapping on his sword belt. Opening the door out into the dim, empty corridor, he turned and locked their room behind him. His first point of call was clear. He walked along the corridor and down the flight of stairs into the courtyard and stopped there, wishing he'd put on one of the cloaks. Looking up, he realised that the silvery light was not there tonight. Clouds had begun to roll over Renfrizhausen, and snow was in the air once more.

Another irritation. He grunted. Not only would a fresh blizzard trap him in the castle once more, it would also erase all tracks and evidence, setting him even further back. Crossing the courtyard, he tried the chapel door. It opened readily, though only a single great tallow candle inadequately lit the large room. He approached the altar with the candle on it and kneeled at it like a knight at vigil.

There he prayed.

He prayed for wisdom and understanding. He prayed for better weather and the freedom to leave. He prayed that the wicked would suffer justice and that Bernhard would make a mistake. He prayed that Kovacs would turn up. He prayed, in short, for a solution. For some time, he prayed.

The Lord's favour having been sought yet again, he then returned across the chilly courtyard, grabbed one of the cloaks from the antechamber of the main range and began to climb the stairs, past the rooms of sleeping lords and ladies, emerging once more onto the tower. It had snowed since he'd last been up here with Felipe, and the door was difficult to push against the built-up drift outside. After some heaving and great effort, he emerged onto the covered tower top, the highest point in all of Renfrizhausen. Where else could he hope for a better view and potential clarity.

In actual fact, the cloud was only just above head level here, and gradually descending. Soon the tower would be within the murk.

Where was Kovacs? They had searched the castle completely and, even allowing for Bernhard potentially missing something on purpose, he'd not been alone. The very idea that he might also be in league with Leupold and with Gunther seemed too much. So where could the Hungarian be?

Fuming as he looked down from each edge, he settled once more on the courtyard. In his head he measured the distances from the door below to the well, and to the chapel, where Bernhard had been. But then he chided himself over wasting time. It wasn't a matter of Bernhard managing to slip out and do the deed. He had been in the chapel, and Father Oswald had confirmed it. The priest, Arnau was sure, was innocent. And he would in the course of the service turn his back on the marshal occasionally while facing the altar, but only for short moments. Not long enough for even the quickest man in the world to get to the main range and back, let alone murder someone and dispose of the body in the process.

Grunting with endless frustration, he turned away once more. Retreating to the warm and dark of the stairwell, he began to descend. He stopped on the top floor and looked around at the doors of apartments, remembering who was behind each, and then did the same on the next floor. None of it helped. Finally, he reached the ground floor and made his way along to the great hall. There he stopped, thinking fruitlessly again before beginning to explore the various nooks and crannies leading off the huge room, using a candle taken from the hall which had thoughtlessly been left burning through the night. He'd explored all these before, of course, during the search for Kovacs. They had even been thorough enough to prise up the wooden seat in the garderobe and check down the stinking hole in case the minstrel had decided he could fit down it in a bid for freedom.

Now, instead, Arnau was picturing Bernhard removing the seat and pushing the Hungarian down it. Still, he would not have fitted. It was fantasy and nothing more. Finding a familiar door, he descended to the cellar corridor and made his way along to the locked door at the end. He could see nothing within, even by the light of the candle, but the vaguest shapes of furnishings and the sad bundle that would be Rüdolf von Ehingen.

There he stayed for some time, sighing and trying to let his mind settle. It was still awhirl. Worse so now than when he'd been lying in bed. Sleep was still some way away, but he could no longer think what to fill the sleepless hours with, and instead he stood by the door to the young lord's body for some time, saying prayers of passage for Rüdolf and imploring the Lord for wisdom.

Finally, he sighed. Along with his visit to the chapel, he'd been out for over an hour now, possibly even an hour and a half. Dawn would come all too soon, and with it who knew what? Certainly, he couldn't imagine the coming day providing any improvement. With a heavy heart, he bade farewell once more to the lord of Renfrizhausen that he'd never met in life, turned and made his way back upstairs and to the world of wicked men. Out through the great hall and the tapestry corridor, through the antechamber and into the courtyard.

Nothing was stirring. Dark and oppressive, freezing and empty. He tried to imagine what it had been like for Rüdolf being smashed over the head in that room, dragged out here to the well, then thrown down it. Then he tried rather hard to *un*-imagine it, and vowed once more to avenge the young graf. He had no idea how, but he was going to make the killer – he was going to make *Bernhard* – pay for his crime.

Gratefully, he passed once more into the doorway and climbed the stairs, turning onto the upper corridor, and there he stopped, suddenly, flesh a-tingle and hand going to his sword. Their room's door was open again. Rather than leap into anything this time, he steadied his breathing as best he could and crept along the corridor quietly. There was no sound from the room, but that did not necessarily mean it was empty.

Reaching the door jamb, he peeked briefly round it, spotting no sign of movement. Quietly, he rounded the corner, sword held out in both hands, ready to strike in any direction or to block an unexpected blade. Nothing.

A quick turn revealed nothing hiding round the corner. Pushing the door back showed there was nothing in the way.

The room was empty.

Properly empty.

Felipe was gone.

Arnau allowed himself to breathe deeper again, but knew that something still was not right. It might look as though the squire had just stepped out to the privy, but Arnau knew better. He'd locked the door from the outside and taken the key with him. Felipe had not left. He had been taken.

Chewing his lip, edging towards panic and wondering what to do next, he crossed first to the window and checked the shutters as if they might have any bearing on matters. Then he checked through Felipe's gear. His boots, mail shirt, sword and everything were still here. He had been surprised, lacking time to even defend himself. Arnau felt a horrible lurch in his stomach, remembering Sebastian, Ramon's squire, who had met a grisly end in Constantinople through mere ill fortune.

Dear God, let that not have happened to Felipe.

The kettle hat still hung on the wall.

Arnau crossed to it and removed it. The leather rim band was empty. Nervousness growing with every passing moment, he dropped to the chest. Arnau had the key, not Felipe. He gently tested the lock, which stayed resolutely fastened, but with a frown, he scoured the lid for what he suspected to be there.

Nothing.

A swift search below and he found a single long black hair lying on the floor near the lock. He couldn't prove it, but it seemed highly likely that it had been another of Felipe's safeguards. Teeth gritted, he quickly unlocked the chest and checked through the contents. The documents had gone from the neatly folded surcoat. Panic rising now, he checked the bag of Lütolf's effects. The gold coin had gone, and there was no sign of the ring of three keys.

Arnau cursed then, words and phrases that would have him on his knees in a chapel begging forgiveness for weeks. An hour and more of moping around the castle, fuming over his inability to do anything about the crime, and all he had done was give the bastard ample opportunity to search the room again and deal with Felipe. And the castle was fast asleep, entirely unaware.

Rising, he set upon his next move. Somewhere, Felipe was still in the castle. He needed to find the young squire, and it had to be possible to do so. He was here *somewhere*. He tried not to remind himself that they had entirely failed to find a brightly-coloured Hungarian minstrel before now.

Leaving the room unlocked and with door open – there was nothing of value left to lose, after all – he pounded back along the corridor, then checked himself and repeated the process slowly, leaving their room, examining the floor and everything around him. Gently, he tried the doors of the other rooms, several of which belonged to guards he knew, and several were occupied by snoring owners. The only door that opened readily was the one to the vacant chamber currently being used as a chapel of rest for the two other corpses.

Arnau felt another coldness settle into him at the thought of adding the young squire to the population of the dour chamber. No, he had to believe that Felipe was still alive. Had to keep going and hoping.

The upper floor held no clues, and he descended the stairs to the courtyard.

Would someone be able to drag the squire out here unnoticed? Felipe would not submit without a struggle. He would have shouted and woken the castle. Arnau felt an unpleasant realisation sink in. So would Rüdolf. That was why he'd been knocked senseless first. Hopefully Felipe had escaped that. He'd been surprised in his sleep. He could easily have been overcome in the room by a strong man, silenced and gagged without the need for a blow to the head.

Arnau's hungry gaze swept this way and that. Could anyone possibly have witnessed it? They might not have seen Rüdolf's last few moments, but what about Felipe? Angrily, he concluded that the chances were minute. The castle was down by two guards until Otto's injuries healed and Anselm was replaced. The wall walk was patrolled by only one man now, and the gate only guarded when the manpower was available. Damn it.

All the more irritable, he realised that the lack of snow over the past few days made tracks far less likely to be left in the largely cleared courtyard. Where could he have been taken? His gaze swept this way and that, trying not to think about the well. Not the chapel. Arnau had been there, and there was always the chance of someone being present. Not the main block for the same reason. Fretting at the time he was taking, Arnau swiftly checked out the kitchen range, finding nothing there, and then the stables and the guardroom with similar results.

Heart in mouth, he quickly checked the well. The bucket moved readily on the rope and he could see nothing, so he presumed it to be clear, which was a blessing at least. On a whim, he hurried over to the castle gate. The key remained in the lock, but the guardroom was empty. With diminished staff, no one watched the gate through the night-time hours. Trying the handle, the hairs on his neck perked up as the door swung open. The gate was unlocked.

Heart pounding like a charger's hooves, he passed through the gate – sword still out, ready – and shut it behind him, then examined the snow. It was impossible to tell if someone had been out here recently and made fresh tracks, given the myriad footprints from the search for the bow and then the search for Kovacs.

His head swept this way and that, and he settled on heading left, purely for familiarity, that being the direction he had taken on both previous occasions. Out into the dark he trudged, slogging his way through the snow – still deep and difficult despite the tracks already carved through it. He swore that for just a moment he felt a flake of snow land on his face and he willed the weather to hold off. Now *really* was not the time. His eyes scoured the dull white world as he moved, roving across the surface and looking for new disturbances.

He almost fell over it before he knew it was there.

His foot nudged something as he pushed his way through the snow along tracks he had trodden earlier, and he almost pitched forward, face-first, attention locked on the world around him and not the ground directly below.

Staggering to a halt, his eyes turned downwards and his soul cried out in anguish at the sight of Felipe lying twisted in the snow, a dark stain barely visible on the black and red, but much clearer on the snow around him.

Oddly, as though the Lord above had chosen that moment to start paying attention and being helpful, a brief gap in the clouds suddenly bathed the body in moonlight, and Arnau flinched. Felipe had been killed with a single knife blow through the chest, directly over the heart. At least it had been quick, and not as grisly as Rüdolf's end.

The fury welled up inside him. He'd been adamant enough about bringing this wicked bastard to justice before, but now it had also become personal. He fought down the anger with some difficulty. One thing Lütolf had constantly laboured at was the need to be objective and alert, not to allow emotion and excitement to carry you in their wake, for that way impetuousness and failure lay.

James, three: wisdom that is from above, first it is chaste, afterward peaceable, mild, able to be counselled, consenting to good things, full of mercy and of good fruits, deeming without feigning.

Crouching, Arnau apologised to Felipe. He would deal with his poor, lamented squire in good time, but right now he had to find the missing items. Turning the body over, he quickly ran his hands across the young man, searching him. He was hardly dressed for the weather, and there was little to search. Just hose, a sergeant's black tunic and his belt. The killer had already turned his pouch inside out, dropping the contents into the snow. Arnau searched the folds of his clothes, and finally, miraculously, found leather amid the wool. Heart racing, he removed the documents from Rourell, tucked into the undershirt.

Miraculous was the word. Not only did he remove and unfold the papers from Rourell, but there was a second document folded within the first, and it was only as he spotted the seal of the von Ehingen that he realised it had to be the missing will. How had Felipe come across this? And how had the marshal missed them? Had he run out of time? Seen Arnau coming and fled the scene? Whatever the case, the Templar had retrieved the critical documents. Thank the good Lord for that. Sadly, he reached down and unclasped the book pouch from the belt. That also had been opened, but the killer had no interest in Felipe's copy of the Rule of the Temple. Arnau retrieved it. He had a duty to keep that, officially, but also as a duty to the squire. As he rose, still shaking with anger, the book fell open and Arnau marvelled.

In the centre of the book of the Rule, the squire had carved out a hole in the pages, and sitting in the gap, looking up at him, sat Lütolf's keys on the ring.

Bless you, Felipe, but to the very last you protected what we thought was important.

He felt a sudden wash of guilt then. The silvery glow faded as that gap in the clouds passed and the gloom encased the world once more.

What alerted him, he could not say. All he knew was that through instinct, or providence, or the sheer goodwill of God in his heaven, something made Arnau look up in time to see movement. It was hardly more than a shadowy shape flitting between other shadowy shapes, but Arnau turned and peered in that direction, eyes sharp, focusing. A figure beneath the trees, running, bent double, fast, through the wood.

Arnau's heart began to pound once more. The killer. Bernhard, surely. Arnau had been right. He had interrupted the man at his wicked work after all. The man had just moved into the woods as the Templar arrived, watching quietly, and then, when he'd seen Arnau stand again, he'd run.

Arnau felt the now familiar panic rising. The man was heading back towards the gate, and had a good, strong lead on Arnau. Moreover, the man was in the easier terrain beneath the trees, while the Templar would have to slog through deep snow. The bastard.

Arnau was running a moment later, book clutched in his hand, vital documents sandwiched between the pages, sword in the other, breath pluming constantly as he ran, struggling through the snow.

He shouted. 'Stop, Bulstrich. I know who you are.'

But it would be to no avail. Bernhard was way ahead of him, and was hardly likely to stop on command. And the castle would slumber. Only guards on duty would stand a chance of hearing a shout, but the one on the wall would have to be close by, and there was no one at the gate for the night. He could scream and no one would come, he suspected. Still, nothing ventured meant nothing gained, and he continued to bellow accusations and threats as he pounded through the snow after Bernhard.

He could swear he was gaining, but the sad truth was that the man was far enough ahead that they could probably circle the entire castle before the Templar caught up with his prey.

Damn the man's eyes, but this night was unfolding badly.

Arnau struggled around the corner of the corner of the gatehouse tower as he saw Bernhard approaching the gate itself. With a sinking feeling, the Templar struggled on, knowing it to be hopeless. He was less than halfway there when the killer disappeared through the door.

Arnau pushed forward and reached the gate shortly thereafter, heaving in breaths. Cursing and swearing like a costermonger at a poor trade, he fumed at the closed gate. Already expecting it, he hurried over and tried the handle.

Locked.

Damn and blast. Curses and God's bones. He was locked out. And now, with no witnesses to his deeds, Bernhard would be, once again, securing his alibis so that any accusation Arnau might level, on the assumption that he even managed to get back inside, would be seen as idiotic and malicious. Lord, but the villain was clever.

Without much hope, Arnau began to hammer on the gate with his fist and the pommel of his sword, calling for admittance. After a full minute of loud outrage, he subsided, half expecting to hear echoes bouncing off down the hillside. No echo came, for the cloud, the snow and the trees dampened too much of the sound.

No one appeared. No one would. Until the bell tolled for the servants to be up and about and preparing fires and the like, no one would hear a man outside the gate. Perhaps that one man on the battlements, if he was even there, but it was more than possible that Bernhard had somehow managed to move that guard away too.

He was locked out.

Fuming, Arnau did what he could – the *only* thing he could. He began to slowly circle the castle, heading the other way this time. Eyes on the walls and the shuttered windows, he moved slowly, wading through the deep snow. Briefly, he considered shouting up at these windows. These would be the ones to the apartments in the main range, and Dietmar, Michael and the ladies would be up there. He almost called out, but stopped himself in the end, and struggled on. He wasn't entirely sure what he could say. He was in something of a compromising position, after all.

He was outside the walls, beyond a locked gate, as far as the castle's population were concerned. Neither of the valuables he'd sworn to protect were missing, and Bernhard had now had enough time to slip back to his room and even out of his wet clothes. He would appear as innocent as always, and no matter what arguments Arnau might produce, he could prove nothing. Bernhard would have the high ground as he had all along.

For a moment, Arnau wondered what German law allowed. Was there a facility for bringing people to trial by the blade? At least that way Arnau would stand a chance of calling the man out.

But no. Right now, he had nothing to back up any accusations against Bernhard. Indeed, it might even appear to the common eye as though Arnau himself had chased his squire out into the snow and killed him.

Damn it. Damn it all to hell and back again.

By now he was opposite the kitchens, still slogging his way around. This far no one had come in since the last snowfall and the ground was an almost pristine blanket of white, undisturbed by no more than a hungry and inquisitive deer, who'd left prints here and there.

He pushed on, around the chapel, somehow desperately hoping to find a postern gate that no one had mentioned, and consistently failing to do so. Before long, he was passing his own apartment and the roofs and walls where he'd chased Bernhard the night of the crossbow attack.

That was when he saw it.

A drape hung from that same benighted window as it had earlier. They had thought Kovacs escaped down that makeshift rope, and only now that Arnau's suspicions had shifted to the marshal did he second guess that notion. Bernhard had put the drape there, surely, to lead everyone to that selfsame belief.

He struggled, now, with the decision. There were two ways back into the castle. Either he waited for the castle's inhabitants to be up and about and demanded admission to the gate, or... his eyes rose to the drape hanging from the window. That way lay horrible uncertainty. Images of Bernhard waiting with a blade beside the shutter leapt to mind. But it had to be done. If he just remained outside long enough, until the first guard heard him at the gate, then Bernhard had ample time to do anything he wanted. Arnau could hardly afford that. He needed to be in the castle. He needed to find a way to prove that it was the marshal who was guilty of every last evil in Renfrizhausen, and he couldn't afford to give the man any more time to cover his tracks than he already had.

With a grunt of effort, he trudged through the snow to the wall, passing both the twisted body of Felipe and the site where they had found crossbow and bolts. The drape hung low, and Arnau found that, with the additional height of the deep, thick snow, he was close enough. It was the work of little effort to sheathe his blade, tuck away his prized finds, and start the climb. The wall was easy at this low level, plenty of hand and foot holds, and Arnau managed the four or five feet above his head to the dangling drape with surprising alacrity.

His hands wrapped around the thick velvet, black and yellow like everything else that spoke of the family's arms, and with gratitude he began to climb. He was cold, but it hardly touched him now, the fires of anger and determination burning though him and keeping him going. Hand over hand, feet tight on the makeshift rope below, gripping the thing as he climbed.

Then he was there, at the window with the opened shutters. Trusting to luck, hoping that Bernhard wasn't waiting for him, he threw one arm over the sill, then the other, abandoning the drape. Then he hauled.

He was halfway through the window before hands were on him, grabbing, pulling, heaving. He felt himself dragged inside and then hauled upright, restrained. With impotent fury and strangled fear, he realised someone had taken his sword and his knife. He struggled, eyes adjusting to the room before him.

Bernhard stood in the doorway opposite, while Wolf and Leupold had him, and they were fresh and strong, while Arnau was exhausted and weak. He had no hope of fighting his way out of their grip.

'Lock him away,' the marshal said, with a snarl.

CHAPTER FOURTEEN

'**G**et your hands off me,' snarled Arnau, struggling, but Leupold had his left arm and Wolf his right, both men with grips of iron and faces of grim determination, while Arnau was ice cold and weak from his ordeals and lack of sleep.

'Stop struggling,' Bernhard said. 'Your guilt to me is clear, and I would have your life for your crimes even now, but Swabia is a place of law, and you will answer to the graf.'

Arnau frowned, blinking in surprise and shock. What was going on?

'*Ihn gebringen*,' Bernhard commanded, and Arnau found himself being manhandled towards the staircase. At the top, Wolf let go of him and took three hurried paces backward whilst drawing his sword and brandishing it. Once the guard's blade was on him, Leupold also let go and drew his own sword behind the prisoner. Thus Arnau was free to move, but unarmed and at the tip of two swords.

Still awhirl and confused, he was marched down the stairs between the blades, all of them following Bernhard out into the courtyard. Were these two in with the marshal? It seemed extremely unlikely. Wolf had been vouched for by Matthias during their initial investigations, and Leupold by Otto, who Arnau was also convinced was innocent for having been the man injured while trying to stop the crossbow attack. Since it seemed Anselm had been in league with the marshal and had paid the ultimate price, any further collusion suggested the entire guard were guilty, which was outrageous. Bernhard might command the guards, but for them all to turn their backs on the graf in favour of Bernhard was too much. No, Wolf and Leupold were not conspirators. They were simply following the orders of their commander, for *they* did not understand him to be a cold-blooded killer.

'You know me to be innocent,' Arnau said, to the two guards rather than the marshal, 'and this is wickedness once more. I am being set up, for certain.'

'*Schweigen!*' snapped Wolf, and Leupold shoved him roughly from behind as he staggered the last few steps and then out into the open. Arnau fumed. Both men spoke no Frankish, and the one man here who could understand him was never going to help.

In the courtyard, Matthias was hurrying from the guardroom, strapping on his sword belt, and the marshal rattled out German at him swiftly. The guard gave Arnau a disapproving look and hurried off towards the main block, shouting. Arnau's heart sank. The castle was being woken. And he was apparently apprehended for something of which he was yet unaware. Things were beginning to look bleak.

A Germanic command had Wolf and Leupold jabbing him into motion once more. He was bundled over towards the stairs to the rooms and held there at sword point as Conrad now appeared, looking shocked. Bernhard grabbed the serf and pointed at the main gate, rattling something else in German. Conrad ran off, unlocked the gate and hurried out, leaving it open behind him.

Sweet saviour, but this was going wrong. His eyes rose to where the heavens were, hidden by layers of threatening cloud. The words of the twenty-seventh Psalm rose to mind: *The Lord is my lightening, and mine health; whom shall I dread? The Lord is defender of my life; for whom shall I tremble? Noisome men nigh on me, for to eat my flesh. Mine enemies, that troubled me; they were made sick and felled down. Though castles stand together against me, mine heart shall not dread. Though battle riseth against me, in this thing I shall have hope.*

But hope seemed thin on the ground, right now. As he stood there, caught and fuming, nervous and uncertain as to entirely what was happening, Bernhard and the two guards spoke at length and speed in their own language. Arnau had no idea what they were saying, of course, but the tone of voice made it clear that they were asking questions, and the marshal was explaining. Arnau wished they could explain it to him. Or perhaps he did not.

Finally Matthias reappeared, with Graf Dietmar and Michael Trost at his heel, both wrapped tight against the cold darkness. Damn this night. Why could Arnau not have simply stayed in bed and slept? But then now that he had the measure of the marshal, he doubted that would help. He'd already faced poison and a crossbow bolt. Whatever came next would be unlikely to be much better.

As the three joined them, Bernhard gestured for them to move once more and they climbed the steps to the upper floor, then marched along towards Arnau's room, the door of which was still open. Arnau's heart sank ever further as he caught sight of the doorway momentarily, past Wolf and Bernhard. A figure lay in the doorway. A figure in red.

No... They stepped over the twisted body of Kovacs, the man's face locked in a rictus of agony, and into the room. Arnau cast a sympathetic look at the poor Hungarian as he passed, but then he was in his room, still at sword point and with Bernhard close by, Trost and Dietmar in the corridor, looking on in bleak dismay.

'This is not what it seems,' Arnau said hurriedly.

'Quiet,' snapped Bernhard.

'Explain,' Dietmar said quietly.

'The marshal is not—' Arnau began, but stopped as Bernhard cuffed him lightly across the jaw.

'He meant me, *Tempelritter*.'

The marshal turned back to Dietmar.

'One suspect we overlooked all along was the one you asked to help me investigate, *Hochwohlgeboren*,' he said. 'This Templar had your brother's keys, we know, though they are currently hid away somewhere. It is my assertion that he and his villainous squire are behind all of this, on the commands of their grasping and devious Order.'

'That's not true,' Arnau spat.

'My belief is that the Temple found itself in danger of losing lands they had already passed on, as Michael will attest from his investigations. They could not afford to do so, and so they sent this assassin to secure the will and remove any hope of the von Ehingen regaining their lands.'

'This is all lies.'

'Silence,' snapped Bernhard, lifting his gauntlet in threat once more.

He turned back to Dietmar. 'In fact, these men were in Renfrizhausen days before they knocked on our gate. I believe that they came here at night at the start of the week, unlocked the gate with their key and infiltrated the castle. Somehow passing Anselm – I suspect the squire had some part in that task – the knight here lurked in the shadows waiting for your son. When he appeared, the Templar attacked Graf Rüdolf, searched him and found the will, then dumped the body and left, locking the gate as he went.'

Arnau glared at him, aware that another outburst would earn him a slap, and would gain him nothing. For his part, he really wanted to point out the holes in the argument. Why had Anselm let them in, or how did they get past him? How had Arnau known where the graf would be? But he was on the defensive, fighting to hold a grip in this place, and any interjection was going to earn him pain and dismissal. No one would believe him, because he had nothing better to give.

'We discovered the body,' Bernhard continued, 'suffered our grief, and began to look into the matter. Then, lo and behold, the Templars suddenly appear in the wake of the tragedy, ready to examine a contesting will which you can no longer produce to stake your claim.'

Damn it, but it all sounded more plausible than it should.

'And the woman said to Elijah "*Now in this I have known: that thou art a man of God and the word of the Lord is sooth in thy mouth,*"' Arnau said suddenly. 'If you have any faith in the Lord then you should heed the words of the Book of Kings. And from our own Order's Rule, of which my beloved squire was so fond: "*By the clear judgement of our council, we command that if there is anyone in the parties of the East or anywhere else who asks anything of you, for faithful men and love of truth you should judge the thing.*" This is what Graf Dietmar asked of me, because I am a knight of the Temple and my word is my bond, for it is truth and must be so in the eyes of the Lord.'

He subsided, breathing heavily. Silence greeted him – and not a generally positive silence.

'What can you offer me in your defence?' the lord of Renfrizhausen said quietly.

Arnau, still shaking slightly, fixed him with a defiant look. 'Only my word. That and several uncertainties.'

'Words are like water in a swollen stream,' the old lord sighed, 'swiftly passed and soon forgotten. I would like to believe you, Brother Vallbona, for you have been unexpectedly sympathetic of our family's plight. But unless you can offer me proof that Bernhard is mistaken, then the law's verdict remains clear.'

'All I can give is that uncertainty. Anselm had no connection to the Order or myself. He was on guard and would never have let us in. For certain, when we *did* arrive he was reticent enough. And how might I have managed to fake a crossbow attack upon myself by an assassin who was witnessed by Wolf? No, this puzzle is far from complete. If you condemn me, then you give the real killer free rein.'

The lord turned to Bernhard again. 'You also believe he killed Anselm?'

'Yes, though as yet I am unsure why. Perhaps Anselm was even in on it. The *Tempelritter* says that Anselm has no connection to him, but do we know the past of every man? Maybe Anselm had been bought with Templar gold, for we all know how they are driven by avarice, and such sin passes from hand to hand easily like the plague. Perhaps Anselm had reached a point where he was going to reveal his information to us and had to be removed as an inconvenience. Let us not forget that we only found Anselm's body when the Templar brought us to it.'

Damn it, but that was true, too. Arnau had been the first to see Anselm.

'What of Kovacs?' the old lord asked, gesturing to the body in the doorway.

'Kovacs was about to be proved innocent. We had discovered that your son was killed by a right-handed man, and Kovacs was left-handed. Kovacs had been identified as the killer, and thus the blame had been laid and the Templar could relax. But when Kovacs was to be cleared, the Templar did away with him, so that we could not confirm it.'

'But why would he stay, if he'd secured the will?'

Bernhard grunted. 'Because until you, my lord, renounced any claim on the lands and signed a document to that effect, the *Tempelritter* could not leave and return to his fellow assassins. His job was not yet complete.'

'I am still unsure,' Dietmar said, his face troubled, for which Arnau felt tremendous gratitude. 'I do not understand what happened the night of the crossbow. Otto confirmed that someone shot at the Templar.'

'That,' Bernhard admitted, 'I cannot explain. I am sure the answer will come to light in due course, but for now I am still perplexed. What I can tell you is that I came to speak to the Templar this night. I could not sleep, and thought to examine what we knew together with a hope to uncovering something hitherto unnoticed, but when I got here I found this: no Templars, but Kovacs' body lying cold and dead. I sought Wolf and Leupold and sent them out searching. In just minutes, Wolf found a drape hanging from that same tower window as before and, when we looked down, we could see another body in the snow below. As we watched, the *Tempelritter* appeared from somewhere outside, swearing like an Austrian, and began to climb back into the castle. I believe the body to be his squire and have sent out Conrad to retrieve it. Why they fought I cannot say, but at least we now have only one villain to deal with.'

'This is all lies,' Arnau said again. 'Felipe was attacked and dragged out into the snow. I went to—'

He was stopped by a second slap.

'I warned you,' Bernhard snapped.

'Things do not entirely add up,' Dietmar said. 'I do not like this.'

'Then let us be sure, my lord,' Bernhard replied, and gave Leupold a command. The guard immediately sheathed his sword and began to search Arnau. It took only moments for him to locate the documents and withdraw them. Holding them up with a frown, the guard handed them to Bernhard.

'What do we have here, *Herr Tempelritter*?' the marshal mused, lifting the leather wallet of the Order's documents and sliding free the von Ehingen will. 'I cannot claim to be remotely surprised,' he added, and stepped across, offering the papers to the graf, who took them with a serious, unhappy expression.

Arnau stood impotent and furious, lip twitching, as Leupold continued to search him. His hands fell upon the book pouch and he removed the book of the Rule from it.

'That is the *Order's* property,' snapped Arnau, grasping it from him.

There was a momentary struggle for possession of the book until Arnau felt Wolf's sword tip touch the back of his neck and let go. Bernhard snorted and reached for the book.

'Your rules will not help you here,' he said, and as he did so, the book fell open and the keys dropped into his hand.

Arnau could not help but notice the blaze of triumph that flashed in the marshal's eyes for just a moment before he deftly dropped the keys out of sight and closed the book. The will and the document, then, had never been the focus. It *had* been the keys. But why?

'What do we do with him, my lord?' Michael Trost asked. 'The *landgericht*?'

Dietmar shook his head. 'It will be many days before the *landgericht* can meet, and even then I will have a say. Until then justice for Renfrizhausen is entirely in my hands and I do not relish the responsibility.'

'He should die a criminal's death,' Bernhard said, acid in his tone, 'his head struck from his body and displayed in the village.'

Arnau's heart skipped a beat at the words, and he risked a third blow by replying. *"'He that shall be slain shall perish from the word of twain, or of three witnesses. No man shall be slain for but one man saith witness against him."* Deuteronomy seventeen.'

An uncomfortable silence followed as all present digested the word of the Lord and matched it up against Bernhard's recommendation and their own opinions.

'Though *Blutgericht* be my right and my duty,' Dietmar finally agreed, 'while there is any doubt about the Templar's role in all of this, I am uncomfortable with ordering any such punishment. Unlike other killers, I will not commit blade to neck without proven evidence.'

Thank you, Lord. Arnau found that he'd been holding his breath.

Bernhard fixed his master with a stubborn expression. *'Hochwohlgeboren*, this man has killed with impunity. The castle houses not only the body of your own son and heir, but of Anselm and Anna, of Kovacs and even the *Tempelritter*'s own squire. This *cannot* go unpunished.'

Dietmar nodded, though his face was troubled. 'I agree, but the punishment will not be mine to give. While there remains any doubt, I cannot simply execute a man, and I can hardly imprison a foreign nobleman, as the Duke of Austria did with the English king. I cannot afford to start a war, after all.'

The marshal was fuming silently. His eyes announced his disapproval, and Dietmar shook his head. 'Remember, Bernhard, that while the Temple might have little influence here in the Empire, they are nonetheless a powerful organisation across Europe. It would be a foolish nobleman who earned their enmity by executing one of theirs without warning. The Order has the Pope's support, and to anger the Temple is to risk excommunication. No, I will not have Brother Vallbona's head. He shall be sent away. Let the Order deal with their own.'

Bernhard's eyes flashed. Arnau realised just how much he'd wanted the Templar to die by the graf's hand, but the man managed to restrain himself and nodded obediently. 'If that is your wish, my lord.'

'Wish?' Dietmar sighed. 'If I could *wish*, I would wish Rüdolf back by my side. But none of this can be undone. Let the death and the misery end here. Mourning will begin on the morrow when we carry the bodies to the town for burial. Let us put an end to this whole sorry episode.'

Arnau felt the tip of Leupold's sword being withdrawn. Dietmar turned to him. 'Let it be known you are banished from Renfrizhausen, Sülz and the whole of Swabia. You are welcome in neither my house nor my lands.' The lord stepped into the room and grasped the documents from Bernhard. Separating the two, he thrust the leather folder at Arnau. 'Take your papers back to the Order. I care not whether you believe my brother's donations to supersede this will. Given the damage done to my house and family, I expect the Order to relinquish all claim and to give to the von Ehingen that which is rightfully ours, and without question or delay. Pack your gear. You will be given bread and water from the kitchens to see you on your way. Once the weather is cleared and I have consulted with the *landgericht*, I will inform your superiors of events at Renfrizhausen and demand that they take appropriate steps.'

He turned to Bernhard again. 'See that all his horses are made ready. Have the body of his squire put over his horse and secured for the journey, for we will not bury him with our own. I want him out of the castle before daybreak.'

With that, Dietmar von Ow turned his back on the room and stalked away. Michael Trost lingered in the doorway for a long moment, his face radiating disgust, then followed his master. Arnau stood, glowering at Bernhard, whose expression was so unreadable that for a moment Arnau wondered genuinely whether the marshal actually believed everything he'd just said.

Bernhard barked out a series of orders to the two guards in the room, and both left, casting last disapproving looks at Arnau. He was alone in the room now with Bernhard, who moved to the doorway, stepping carefully around the body of Kovacs. There he stayed as the two men glared at each other, and finally leaned back, looking along the corridor, before peering at Arnau once more.

'You can thank that red cross on your chest,' he said, 'for saving your life.'

Arnau simply glared at him.

'Had you been a layman or a Swabian,' Bernhard continued, 'you would now be heading for the block and a blunt blade of three strikes. It is only the threat of your Order's power that preserves you. But you will gather your effects, mount your horses and leave, and you will follow the graf's command and persuade your Order to relinquish all claims. I personally will see you out of the gate and away from Renfrizhausen. You will be a fool in the extreme if you consider anything other than hurrying from these lands.'

'I have half a mind to draw steel and end you now to save the family future grief,' Arnau said in a low hiss.

'I welcome it. If you cannot restrain yourself then you prove me right and Graf Dietmar might well change his mind and send for the headsman after all. But before even that you must realise that I am a veteran of the arid lands of Outremer, and not some wet fool like your squire. You will find me a troublesome opponent. So run home, little knight, and give thanks to God that you were saved a Swabian blade.'

Arnau felt his lip twitching again. 'I cannot fathom how you did it, Bulstrich,' he said, 'and nor can I imagine *why*. But I know you *did*. And I know you have been behind every death since then, including Felipe's. I will go, not through fear, but through respect for your lord. Hear me, though, Bernhard Bulstrich, I will not rest until the truth is uncovered. Whether it be me or some other knight of the Temple, *someone* will come back to Renfrizhausen, and you will fall from your precarious perch and fall far, into the pit of hell.'

'Your words do not frighten me, *Tempelritter*.'

'Then you are a fool, Bernhard, for I am *Manus Dei* – the hand of God – and the almighty can see the guilt radiating from your shrivelled heart. Revel in the possession of those keys. I know not their value to you, but enjoy it while you can. You now walk a finite path, and at the end of it God's justice awaits you, wrapped around Iberian steel.'

The marshal sighed wearily. 'Are you quite finished? You are wasting precious time that you should be using packing for your journey.'

Grumbling throughout, Arnau moved around the room, gathering up everything of his and Felipe's and stuffing it into their travel bags and finally donning his mail shirt and coif. Once done, he realised that no one was going to help him with his burden and shouldered the packs with difficulty, almost crumpling under the weight. At a gesture from Bernhard, he stumbled from the room, along the corridor and then carefully, slowly, and with great difficulty, staggered down the stairs and out into the courtyard.

Conrad was there now with the four horses, while Leupold had the body of Felipe draped over his shoulder. Arnau, face grave, crossed to the group, struggling under his burden. The castle's entire living population were now gathered in the courtyard in the dark, watching with black expressions.

Arnau could feel the simmering hatred all around him as he slung the bags over the packhorse, then retrieved Felipe from the guard, lying him as reverently as he could over his horse and tying him there. It suddenly struck him that he had no idea what he was going to do with the squire. It would take around a month to travel back to Rourell, after all. Felipe would never make it back. Even with the winter weather, he would begin to decompose in a matter of days, and Arnau could hardly carry a rotting corpse home. He would have to be buried somewhere near, and soon.

Damn it, then there was the problem of returning to Rourell. He could hardly imagine how it would be received at the preceptory when they learned that not only had he failed to complete his task, but he had also lost a squire, been accused of heinous crimes and lost the Order its lands and funds. At the very least he would face losing his habit, and likely much worse.

He looked around as he pulled himself up into his saddle. The castle was still shrouded in darkness, but now lights shone from windows and doorways, the entire populace up and about, radiating malice. He sighed. Every stone of this place now carried some troubling mystery or gruesome memory

The building he had just left, where he'd survived an attempt on his life with a crossbow, where two innocent people lay dead, awaiting burial, where he had found their room searched repeatedly and where Kovacs' body had been discovered.

The chapel, which was the focus of the heart of his problem, where he had sought wisdom and guidance from the Lord and failed to acquire either. Where Bernhard had been at the time of the first murder, which made it impossible for him to be the killer that he so obviously was.

The main range, where Arnau had interviewed the lords and ladies of Renfrizhausen. Where he had survived a poisoning. Where he had examined a young lord who had met his untimely end, and where he had imagined dragons and ghosts in the bowels of the earth.

The gate, where he had found the ruined body of Anselm, where he had struggled over the significance of the key. Where he had been locked out while Bernhard had engineered his downfall.

The tower, where he had lost Bernhard on the chase. Where he had spotted the discarded crossbow. Where he had climbed the drape back into the castle only to be apprehended and accused of murder.

Every memory here seemed to be bad. He hated that fact, for in less than a week he had come to know the people of Renfrizhausen and was now surprised to realise that he liked them. With the exception of Bernhard, they had all been good people. Dietmar, the old noble lord, driven by honour and racked by sorrow for his son. Trost, sour-looking at every turn, yet devoted to his master, and sharp as a die. Ute, spiky and jagged, yet somehow demanding respect as the old *dame* of Renfrizhausen. Gerdrut, striking, friendly and helpful in spite of everything. Poor Kovacs, a man Arnau would have been proud to call friend. All of them, even the guards and serfs, he had come to like and wished to preserve and to protect.

But instead he was leaving the castle under a cloud – both literally and figuratively – with orders never to return. And the worst thing of all was that he could do nothing about what would happen thereafter. Bernhard had won, but Arnau had no idea *what* he had won. Would there be further losses to suffer for the lord of Renfrizhausen and his people before Bernhard was done?

It was infuriating, but there was simply nothing to be done about it.

With a sigh of finality, Arnau turned in the saddle to face the gate, took the reins of the other beasts in his left hand and kicked Canción's flanks, urging the steed towards the gate.

Seething with frustration, he left Renfrizhausen as the first flakes of fresh snow began to fall.

CHAPTER FIFTEEN

𝔄rnau realised his mistake just a few minutes out of sight of the castle. He had been so overcome with anger, wracked with disappointment and impotence, and blinded by the desperate urge to turn and accuse Bernhard that he had paid precious little attention to his direction. Thus it was that he had clearly taken a wrong turn several times while ranting to himself about his disastrous failure, and by the time he realised it, he was hopelessly turned around.

Earlier in the day, when it had been bright daylight and clear, he'd had little trouble making his way down to the town in the valley below. Now, in the dark, with glowering clouds overhead and a light but steady fall of snowflakes once more, things were very different. Every tree looked the same, every path identical. No sign of the village, no sign of the castle, just trees and narrow paths and the endless, accursed snow. Another thing to irritate him and weigh upon his already frustrated mind.

The problem was that he was on the very *cusp* of an understanding, and he knew it. He was now certain he knew everything there was to know, but had somehow just not quite put the pieces together yet. And if he could just do that, things would be different. As it was, how could he possibly go back to Rourell and announce his utter failure?

That was his first decision. He would spend the day in the village, and the next night there too. Though the graf had announced that they would bring the bodies down 'on the morrow', Arnau suspected he meant the next day, and even then the snow might yet hold them off again. Whatever the lord's intentions, he would be unlikely to bring the bodies to town until the start of the next week at least, and so Arnau would likely get a day in the town's inn to think things through. Perhaps without the constant distractions of the growing body count and the fear of assassination attempts, he might just be able to think more clearly.

He wondered briefly if he might be permitted to have Felipe buried in the village? He had been ordered away from the graf's lands, and this was still very close. Mayhap it was too close and not the most politic of ideas. Perhaps in Sülz, as he passed through there, would be better? Suddenly he wondered what the innkeeper in Renfrizhausen might say when Arnau had four horses and a corpse stabled for the night.

That was a wall to climb when he got to it. Right now it was bad enough that he was lost. At least he knew he was still going downhill, and if he continued to do so he would eventually reach either a valley or a river. Then he could follow it and find some sort of civilisation. And yet every step the horse took, nervous and slow in the snow and the dark, sent Arnau's mind racing again and again into the problems of the last few days.

The keys. It all had to do with the keys. Not the key to the castle, though. That was just a convenient aspect that Bernhard had built into his wall of lies. No, the castle key was one of several, many of which had been available to the marshal. And the second key? That had been to Lütolf's room. It was faintly possible that this key was what had so delighted Bernhard, but Arnau didn't think so. Dietmar had a copy of that key and his would be so much easier to acquire. Besides, Bernhard had been in that room during the searches of the castle. No, it had to be the third key.

He blew a flake of snow from the end of his nose where it had settled.

Just that one key. What on earth did it fit that made it so valuable to Bernhard and yet no one else seemed to know about it or have any interest in it?

Damn it, but he was on the very edge of an understanding.

He looked this way and that as he came to a crossroads of small trails. Here the slope seemed to have levelled out and it was rather hard to tell which way was down the hillside and which was up amid the trees. Left, right, straight on? He blinked a few times to rid his eyelashes of snowflakes and peered this way and that, trying to find a reason to decide upon one particular course.

His roving eyes picked out interesting features in the trees. The trails to left and right followed a contour. An embankment perhaps three or four feet high, partially hidden by vegetation and with trees growing from it, stretched to both sides, crossing the path before him and disappearing briefly as it did so. And just this side of the embankment a ditch of similar proportions running along both left and right.

Noting it with interest and figuring it as some ancient work of man he made his decision somewhat arbitrarily and rode on ahead, continuing along the trail upon which he'd been riding.

One key. Just one. And no one but Bernhard had been interested in it. Possibly Bernhard and Anselm, but Bernhard was the prime figure. And the marshal had not been interested in the Rourell documents or anything else in the pack.

He noted with further interest a second bank and ditch through which he passed, this time with the bank first and the ditch beyond. Despite the cold, the missed directions and the snow, he reined in. Something ran across his flesh, a frisson raising the hairs in anticipation.

The Lord was at work, he was sure. God's plan was unfolding on this bleak and freezing hillside. He had prayed again and again for wisdom and understanding, and finally he felt it was there, on the edge of his mind. He just needed to tease it out. Everything was there to be connected and this place... this place was the catalyst, somehow.

What was it? Part of the castle? Part of an earlier castle?

He pictured the mound and ditch he had passed a minute ago. This configuration was the reverse. That was because they were part of the same thing, surely. Whatever it was, he had first passed inside it, and now had left it. It was a fortification. A rampart with a moat, like a castle. A square, he decided, that he'd crossed two sides of. An *old* square, long pre-dating Renfrizhausen, he thought. Older than the castle, the village and the church. As old as time.

The hairs rose again, goose flesh puckering his skin.

A Roman camp. They were a semi-familiar sight in Catalunya and Aragon. Most had grown beyond being an antique fortress, becoming towns in time, the Roman walls supplanted with better, more modern ones. Others stood like sad ruins in the wilderness. Tarragona was one of the former. This was a rough equivalent, though. No great stone walls, just an earth bank. But it was, he was now sure, the work of the ancients.

What had he been thinking as he passed it?

Damn, but he couldn't quite tease it out. What *had* he been thinking? He slapped the side of his head in irritation. Come on, this was *important*. He'd been thinking about the key. The one key that was valuable to Bernhard, and not the other two. He'd got beyond that. Bernhard was not interested in the documents. Just the key.

Just the key...

Not just the key.

How in the name of all the saints had that slipped by him? The man had taken the keys, yes, but there was one other thing that had gone from Lütolf's effects. The gold coin. It was, of course, possible that he'd just missed the coin and it now lay somewhere in the snow where Felipe had been found, where Bernhard had rifled through his possessions. But no. Arnau didn't think so. It had been taken by the marshal deliberately, and Arnau could almost say why. *Almost.*

He'd been looking for the keys and had left everything else except the coin. He'd added the missing will to help frame Arnau, but the coin had been of enough value to take. Not just because it was gold.

The Roman camp...

A Roman coin...

The Roman *gold.*

With an overwhelming flood of recollection it all came crashing in. Kovacs' story. The Roman gold. The hoard of some emperor or noble who had been overrun by a German tribe. They had taken a vast prize back to their lands, and the legend had said that it was the source of the von Ehingen fortune. A fortune that now didn't exist, for the family were struggling to pay for...

The repairs to the castle. Arnau slapped his head again, chiding himself for his lack of vision and understanding. *Of course.* It all fitted together now. He understood at last why Bernhard was capable of such violence and cruelty.

"'For they that will be made rich fall into temptation,'" he bellowed triumphantly at the dark trees, *"'and into the snare of the Devil, and into many unprofitable desires and noxious, which drench men into death and perdition. For the root of all evils is covetousness, which some men coveting erred from the faith, and besetted themselves with many sorrows.'"*

The apostle Paul had had the crux of it in his letter to Timothy. Perhaps once Bernhard had been the staunch Crusader and loyal vassal of the family, but the love of gold had pulled him from righteousness. He may never stand to inherit anything from the family, but what use had he of a crumbling castle and diminished estates? A fortune in gold, on the other hand...

And the gold had been all but forgotten. It had become legend, like the dragon and the ghost. But one clue had remained. Lütolf had known the truth, for he carried one of the coins. Moreover, he carried the *key* to the coins. A key that Arnau had once possessed and, because of this, had faced death more than once. A key that Bernhard now possessed.

Arnau would be willing to bet all the gold in Renfrizhausen that young Rüdolf had also had a key. Every lock in that castle had more than one key, after all. And the young graf had died denying Bernhard the key.

Lord, but he was right, and he knew it. This was it.

He was about to turn round and race back to the castle when a cold realisation settled upon him. This changed nothing. For him it was epiphany, but at best it would thwart Bernhard's new riches and not the man himself. It would not see him fall, because it was only the *reason* it had all happened, and did nothing to explain *how.* Bernhard still had an unshakable alibi, and until Arnau could shatter that, there was no succour to be had in returning to face him. He had to have it all. A single blow would not be enough to fell the marshal. He needed to deliver the *coup de grâce.*

Fresh purpose was his now, though.

He had part of it. After days of bafflement, he had gained understanding by the grace of the Lord out here in the silent woods. Wisdom *had* been awaiting him, but had not been able to come while he was at the mercy of Bernhard's machinations.

How, though? *How* had Bernhard managed to kill Rüdolf von Ehingen while being at the service in the chapel. It was impossible. And at best, Anselm had been his companion in wickedness. No one else, Arnau was sure. Anselm? Yes, the guard had been Bernhard's creature. He had likely covered up so many small evils in the past days, but Anselm had not killed Rüdolf either. So how had it been done?

He rode on, down the slope. Now, though he was still lost, he did not care. This misdirection was the work of the Lord, driving him to the ancient ruins where wisdom had awaited. He was in divine hands, now. Oh, he had to use his brain, of course. The Lord would provide, but a man had to know what to do with those provisions.

He almost blinked in surprise as the trail turned a corner and suddenly opened out onto a wider road through the woods. He was in a valley. Only a narrow valley, but one used with some regularity, for this was not a trodden trail through the woods, carved out by beasts and their hunters, but a purposeful road. A logger's road, he suspected. From the village, men would come here to cut trees for construction and heating. And since it descended gently in what he thought to be a northerly direction, it had to lead to the settlement of Renfrizhausen.

The Lord had provided.

With a goal in mind now Arnau began to walk his horse, and lead the three beasts behind, along the wider road and down into the village. It now came as no surprise when he spotted the angular shapes of roofs and walls between the trees ahead a few minutes later.

The snow was still drifting down in light flakes. Nothing heavy, as though God himself held a hand above Arnau, sheltering him from the glowering clouds above. A few minutes later, he emerged from the edge of the woodland, into the open. The snow was still deep across the world, but the roads had been shovelled clear repeatedly down here, and more snow had been piled up on the already deep drifts to either side. Renfrizhausen had never looked so inviting.

Yet it was still night-time, with dawn more than an hour away, and the village was quiet and deserted. Would he find a roof beneath which to shelter while he thought things through further in light of his new epiphanies?

He rode on into the village. Houses remained dark and silent, the world hushed beneath the shroud of white and the ever-falling snowflakes. Two lights only showed as he entered the main square with its ancient stone cross and trough of frozen water.

One came from the church, sitting along one of the side roads, on the way to the castle that sat glowering on the hill above, now hidden in the snow and the trees. The priest would likely be preparing his services for the day, as the father at Rourell was wont to do.

The other light came from the inn. A low, heavy structure with sprawling outbuildings, it formed more or less one entire side of the square, the rear of its property butting up against woodland at the edge of the town. Unlike the general populace, but much like the priest, the owners of an inn would need to be up before the dawn, preparing food and hot water for guests.

Arnau crossed the square and approached the inn. He almost rapped on the door, but then decided that it might wake other residents and the world was already angry enough at him without inviting more. Instead, he dismounted and led the horses around the side of the inn towards the archway that led into a courtyard. The gates stood open.

A boy of perhaps nine summers was already at work in the dark, labouring by torchlight with a broom of twigs, sweeping the snow into the corners and keeping the flagstones clear for the day. The boy started at the sudden appearance of the horses, clopping hooves on the hard ground, and the knight bearing the red cross. Arnau smiled disarmingly and held up his hands.

'I realise that you will speak not a word of Frankish, and I have gathered but half a dozen of yours,' he said with a smile, but he was becoming an old hand at communicating with the Germans now. He pointed at the dormer windows of the inn's upper floor. 'Room,' he said, and then cast his mind back over five days of listening to the castle's inhabitants talking about his room. He thought he had it.

'*Zimmer*?' he said, hopefully.

The boy frowned, but then nodded. '*Ein zimmer. Ja.*'

Arnau smiled. Thank you, Lord. '*Ja. Ein zimmer. Und the horsen...* er... these,' he pointed first at the four horses and then at the stables leading off the courtyard. As he turned back to the boy, he noted the lad's eyes widen in horror and remembered suddenly the body draped over one of the horses.

'He is my friend,' he said, again holding out his hands.

'*Freund*?'

'*Ja*. Friend. He is dead. Err... *deaden*? I have to take him to the church. *Zum churchen*. For burial.' He pointed back across the square and then mimed digging a grave, a cross and hands pressed together in prayer. It took a few moments for the boy to put the gestures together, but finally he nodded, still looking nervously at the body.

Arnau chewed his lip. He was now changing his mind about where to take Felipe. With his fresh determination to see this through, he would not pass through Sülz just yet. Not until he had put this all right, at least. If he tried and failed, then he would probably be joining Felipe shortly and wouldn't care too much where they were interred, and if he succeeded then there would be no impediment to burial at Renfrizhausen anyway.

Decision made, he untied the squire's horse from the others and handed the reins of his own three beasts to the boy. 'I shall return soon. Stable these and I will be back when it gets light.' He knew the boy had no idea what he was saying, but it mattered not, for the lad took the reins and started to lead the horses into the stables. For a moment, Arnau laboured over whether to remove his packs from them first, but he decided against it. There was nothing there more valuable than his travelling funds now, the Rourell documents secured about his person, so let the lad stow the gear while he stabled the horses.

Nodding his thanks to the boy, he turned and led the squire's horse back out through the archway. The world was still dark and bleak, the square's edges difficult to make out in detail through the drifting flakes of white. At least he could see the church tower, and he set his gaze upon it, crossing the square and making his way along the side road.

Reaching the gate of the churchyard, he carefully urged the horse through the covered wooden gates and onto the path that led to the church's closed door. The light from the windows was not a bright, golden glow, but a gentle, soft flicker, indicating that only a few candles at most lit the interior. It did at least mean that the priest was there, and Arnau remembered with relief that the priest spoke a little Frankish.

At the door, he tied the horse to a stone bench's leg within the porch, keeping them sheltered from the thickening snowfall. With pangs of regret for the loss of the young farmer, and some reverence, he brushed the worst of the fallen snow off the body on the horse's back, and then turned and knocked on the door.

The priest opened up a few moments later, his face a mask of surprise at being disturbed at such a time of the day.

'*Ja? Ah, die Tempelritter aus schloss, ja?* Hello. You *bist* early *hier, ja?*'

Arnau smiled. 'I am sorry to bother you so early, when you must be busy. I intend to stay at the inn for the day.' He noted the confusion on the priest's face and checked himself, repeating the words but slower this time and with greater clarity, allowing the man time to translate as he went.

'*Ja. Ich verstehen,*' the priest answered finally. 'Understand.'

'My squire. My companion. He has died. I wish to say the viaticum and have him buried here. Money is not a problem.'

The priest frowned. 'Viaticum. Is before dead, *ja?*'

Arnau nodded. 'I know. I understand. But he is recently dead and I could not be there for his passing. I know that life has fled him, but unless you can say for sure that his soul has already fled the shell, I cling to the belief that the viaticum can still be said.'

This seemed to give the priest some trouble, though whether through translation or wrestling with his conscience, Arnau couldn't quite say. Finally, the man seemed to give Arnau an appraising look up and down, and nodded. He was, after all, a man of God every bit as much as the priest, for all his mail shirt and sword.

'Come,' the man said.

Arnau nodded and made to follow.

'Bring,' the priest added, pointing at the body of Felipe. Arnau crossed to the horse and carefully untied the squire, fishing out the black mantle he had tucked into the saddle bag and carrying him gently through the church door, which the priest closed behind them. Along the nave he ported Felipe, and then to the altar. As he waited, the priest fetched the two supports and the heavy board he used to support coffins. Placing them before he altar, he gestured to Arnau, who gently lowered Felipe to them, crossing his arms and straightening him.

He looked serene, which went a little way to assuaging Arnau's guilt for having led his first squire to his death. As the priest nodded to him and then went back about his business, Arnau knelt before the body.

'*Pax huic domui, et omnibus habitantibus in ea,*' he said quietly. Somewhat redundant, wishing peace upon the house and its inhabitants, given where he was.

Suddenly the priest was beside him with a goblet. Gratefully, Arnau dipped two fingers in it, nodding his thanks as he sprinkled the cross on Felipe's forehead.

'*Asperges me... dealbabor.*
Agnus Dei, qui tollis peccata mundi, miserere nobis.
Agnus Dei, qui tollis peccata mundi, miserere nobis.
Agnus Dei, qui tollis peccata mundi, dona nobis pacem.'

Skipping the bulk of the service, in which Felipe would be expected to take part on his death bed, Arnau gently opened the squire's mouth, placing a sacrament therein, handed to him by the helpful priest.

'This is the Lamb of God who takes away the sins of the world. Happy are those who are called to his supper.'

Leaning over the squire, he retrieved the black mantle from the step nearby, unfolding it and draping it over the body so that the red cross faced heaven. He stepped back, sadness threatening to overwhelm him.

'You, me wait,' the priest said from by his shoulder, and Arnau turned, frowning. The man was holding out both hands flat, as though patting something, in a gesture that Arnau translated as 'wait for me'. He rose, glancing at the squire again momentarily, and then watched the priest.

The priest walked to the other end of the nave and reached for a rope fastened to the wall. Untying it, he hauled on it. The church's bell clanged once, muffled and mournful, but as the priest continued to haul and let go, haul and let go, it began to clang loud and clear despite the snowfall. His work done, the priest hurried back along the nave, pointing at the body on the trestle.

'Apology. Need *schnell, ja? Rasch...* er... fast. Clear *für* lauds.'

Arnau nodded. He would have to clear the body away and place it somewhere, resting out of sight until a coffin could be acquired and the body interred. And it would not be appropriate to have a corpse lying before the altar at lauds.

He frowned. Turning, he hurried over to one of the windows further from the candles and pushed his face to the glass, squinting. It was dark outside, still. Of course it was. He'd only been in the church less than a quarter of an hour. But lauds wasn't due until first light.

He hurried back to the priest, pointing at the window.

'It is still dark. Dark, yes?'

The priest nodded.

'Lauds?' Arnau prompted.

The priest gave a low chuckle. '*Vier* people, *ja*? Four *komme für* Lauds, *ja*?'

Much like in the castle, of course. A minimal congregation 'Ja?'

'I... bell early. Much warning, *ja*? *Für* old men to get church, *ja*?'

Arnau smiled. Bright. Ringing the bell early so that the more devout villagers had sufficient warning to get to the service.

He stopped.

His heart was suddenly pounding.

The bell was early. It was the bell. The bell was the key.

Suddenly, he was moving again. Pointing at Felipe's body, he turned to the priest. 'Sorry. So sorry. Have not got time. I have to go. I know how the bastard did it.'

And with that he was running along the nave and out of the door. No time to go to the inn for Canción. Instead, he untied the squire's horse and led him out of the porch into the increasing snowfall and pulled himself sharply up into the sodden saddle. In a heartbeat he was racing away from the church, ducking as he passed through the gate and out onto the road.

Could he remember the way to the castle? It was still dark, but the sky was changing colour gradually. By the time he reached the top of the hill, it would be light. He would have to trust in the Lord. After all, tomorrow was Sunday. The Lord's day. God had saved him, brought him every revelation he'd needed, and now he had to stop Bernhard. All could be put right.

With furious urgency and the power of God's justice coursing through him, Arnau rode for the castle.

CHAPTER SIXTEEN

He'd been hammering the edges of his theory flat throughout the ride and was now content it was as perfect as he could hope to get it. God was with him, and he knew that beyond doubt, if for no other reason than the ease and alacrity with which he returned. The snowfall had gradually increased as the sky turned from black to purple and from purple to a strange pre-dawn violet colour with a golden band just visible at the horizon, and yet it hampered him not. Despite the conditions and the ever-troubling nature of this forested hillside, he turned that last corner to the castle swiftly, and without having suffered even one wrong turn on his ride.

As he approached the castle, he slowed his beast and marshalled every argument, every fact, every detail he had. Bulstrich was going to face justice, and for the first time in a week, Arnau knew why and had the truth of the matter.

Dismounting, he led Felipe's horse, whose name he couldn't remember, the last few steps and hammered on the gate with purpose. Most of the castle would be up by now even on a normal day, and many might still be up from the events of the night before. It mattered not. They *needed* to be up. Everyone needed to understand what had happened for – with the loss of Rüdolf, Anselm, Otto, Kovacs, Anna and even the dog – most of them had been affected in some way by the nightmare events in Renfrizhausen.

He stepped back, preparing himself, drawing his knife from his belt but keeping it hidden by his side in the folds of his mantle.

The door in the gate crept open finally, a black line in the dark wood, interrupted by a sliver of a pale face. Matthias. Arnau winced. Not the best choice of guard to deal with. Still, needs must when the Devil drives.

'Take me to Graf Dietmar.'

Matthias' one visible eye narrowed dangerously.

'Not welcome. Go.'

'The graf will want to see me when he hears what I have to say. Take me to him, or fetch him here, Matthias.'

The door slammed shut, but Arnau was ready for that. His dagger lanced out, not at Matthias, but into the gap, preventing the door from closing entirely. Arnau winced again as he heard the blade snap, but its remains kept the door ajar.

'Matthias…'

The door was flung open wide now, and the guard stepped forward. 'Go or I hurt.'

'Matthias, I know who killed them all.'

'You.'

'No it wasn't, and if you search your soul, you'll know that. If you take me to Graf Dietmar now, I can explain everything. If you do not, then the villain responsible for this all will get away with it, and might yet kill again.'

'No.'

'For the love of God, Matthias, you can even take my blade. Walk me there at sword point if you must, but let me end this.'

There was a strained silence. The burly, red-bearded guard glowered at him, and Arnau was preparing himself for another attempt when the man finally gave him a single, dour nod and stepped to the side. Relief washing through him, Arnau stepped in through the door, still leading the horse, who, being smaller than Arnau's riding animal and *far* smaller than his charger, could make it through the lower door with just a ducked head.

Inside, Conrad and Leupold were already hurrying across the courtyard, surprised in the extreme to see Arnau back at all, let alone so soon. The other guard rattled off something in German, sounding half panicked, half incensed, and Arnau was surprised and more than a little pleased to hear Matthias respond in his own tongue but clearly, from his tone of voice, defending his decision to admit the Templar. A short exchange took place, and finally the two guards clearly came to an agreement. Conrad was told to take Arnau's reins, which he did, leading the animal away towards the stables, while Leupold pointed at Arnau's sheathed sword and held out his hand.

Arnau drew his blade, which instantly put both men on the defensive, but turned it, offering the hilt to the guard. He took it with a nod, and then pointed at the broken knife in Arnau's other hand. This he passed over also, leaving himself unarmed. At least now he might be able to speak to the lord.

As Matthias led him towards the main range, Leupold following on behind with the weapons, Arnau prayed silently that Bernhard not appear from some doorway. He'd find a way to reach Dietmar, of course, but the marshal's appearance would certainly make things difficult. He was immensely relieved when they passed inside, into that antechamber, and then climbed the stairs all with no sign of the marshal. On the upper corridor, they made their way along to the graf's apartment.

Matthias took a deep breath. Dietmar was not a natural early riser. He never attended the morning services, after all, and he was not a young man, never having had the martial life that his brother endured and therefore having felt the onset of age in ways that Lütolf had not. Matthias was hesitant over knocking on his master's door before even the dawn sun had graced the rooftop, not that it would be particularly noticeable amid this latest blizzard.

Finally, the guard rapped on the door sharply, three times, and then stepped back. After a pause, a muffled voice called out in German. Matthias replied and the only word Arnau caught and recognised was '*Tempelritter*'.

Another pause followed, and Arnau could almost have cut the air with a blade had he still possessed one, such was the sudden tension. A few moments later, Dietmar spoke again, and the guard opened the door.

The lord of Renfrizhausen was standing, wrapped in a cloak, by his bed. His expression was not conducive to friendly banter, and so Arnau simply bowed his head in polite respect.

'I banished you from my lands.'

Arnau straightened. 'My apologies, my lord. Had this not been a matter of the utmost importance—'

'I could have your head struck off now, and be well within my legal right. I cannot begin to tell you how tempting a notion that is. The outspoken audacity of the Temple is infamous, but even then I would never have expected you to simply ignore my commands.'

'My lord, you may send me away again, or even order my death, but I beg you to hear me out first.'

Another long pause. Dietmar's eyes weighed him up, calculating, deciding. It seemed an age before the older lord nodded.

'Very well. Say your piece.'

'My lord, you are aware that I continue to protest my innocence over the dreadful incidents at Renfrizhausen this past week.'

'And what murderer does not protest his innocence?'

Arnau nodded. 'Granted, my lord, but when Bulstrich had me restrained, you yourself expressed doubts. There were things that didn't add up, as you noted. My lack of motive for Kovacs. Why I might even think of the death of my own squire. Most of all, the fact that Otto can vouch for the fact that someone else shot at us with a crossbow.'

Dietmar seemed to subside a little, losing some of the stiffness of his posture.

'Go on.'

'My lord, I have been puzzling all week over not only who committed these barbarous acts, but also why and how. Those last two have been the bugbear in my reasoning. It took the clarity provided by nature and distance – a lack of distractions maybe – and most of all the providence of the Lord, to finally piece together this puzzle. But now I have it. I know everything, and I would have all of Renfrizhausen know the truth, but you, my lord, most of all.'

Now, he had the graf hooked, and he knew it. Dietmar nodded for him to continue.

'It is a long tale, and quite complex. And to prove its veracity, I would like to walk you through it all, so that you might see with your own eyes how all the events unfolded. Would you do me that honour?'

Dietmar frowned. 'Very well. Allow me time to dress.'

Arnau rubbed his chin. 'Might I also ask that the people of Renfrizhausen be brought entire to the great hall? Once you have the truth of it, I would have all present understand, and condemn he who has brought us to this place.'

The graf paused once more, and then nodded, gesturing at Matthias and issuing a command in German. Arnau was then ushered from the room once more and the door closed behind him. It did not take long for the lord to dress, and Arnau stood as patiently as he could in the corridor with Leupold as he waited. Finally the door opened once more and Dietmar von Ow appeared in his fine black and yellow tunic, gesturing for Arnau to continue.

'Very well, my lord. Perhaps we might best begin downstairs.'

At a gesture, Leupold led them down the stairs and into the antechamber. Arnau stepped from there into the corridor. For the first time since his arrival, he took the time to look closely at the tapestry. Of course, the dragon at the root of the family's myth was present in several guises, along with the somewhat fanciful history of the dynasty and their castle, but no sign of the other legends of Renfrizhausen. Still, had he spent time examining it earlier, perhaps it might have jogged his thoughts in the direction of the truth.

Ahead, the hall door stood open and largely empty, barring the sound of someone moving furniture, setting it up for the day and for the lord of Renfrizhausen's traditional morning meal. Good. He could rather do with avoiding the inevitable confrontation with Bernhard until the lord of the castle knew the truth.

'I think perhaps it is best to begin here,' Arnau said, coming to a halt in front of the far end of the tapestry.

'Here?'

'As I said, this is a long story, and it goes back far beyond Monday. To understand everything, we have to look back into the legends of the family and of the castle. At the meal, not long after I arrived, Kovacs told me the tales of the castle. Of the ghost that some deny and some claim to have seen. Of Henry the Lion and the killing of the dragon. Of the family's ties to the Welf and the Hohenstaufen. But more interestingly of the Roman gold.'

'All of these are known to the family, and all are legends, Vallbona.'

'Legends traditionally contain a grain of truth, my lord. It is a universal fact. In this case, though, it contains considerably more than a grain, I now realise. There must indeed have been some battle in antiquity in which the Romans were overcome by Germanic warriors and had gold taken in quantity. That gold came to Renfrizhausen. I cannot say how, whether it was discovered here, or perhaps given as a reward for fealty from your patrons in those older days. But the gold exists, and in quantity.'

'How do you know this?'

'Simply because of a coin that we carried in Lütolf's personal effects, my lord. It is my belief that the graf of Renfrizhausen has always known of the gold and has relied upon it. Your grandfather and your father both knew, and when it came to him, your brother knew. When he left under a cloud, he took a single coin with him, along with the secret of its location. The rest is still here.'

Dietmar shook his head. 'We would have known. We would have found it. Or my father would have told me. *Lütolf* would have told us. What use would the family's fortune be to him, after all?'

'I fear that your brother continued to disagree with your loyalties and withheld knowledge of the gold so that it could not be used in support of the Hohenstaufen when it was the Welf who lifted the family to power. And so the gold remained hidden in Renfrizhausen while the family diminished and your brother simmered in resentment in Iberia.'

'Very well,' Dietmar said doubtfully. 'But what has this to do with more recent events?'

'Everything, my lord. To continue, will you accompany me to the cellars?'

Dietmar's face soured. 'I... I do not wish to...'

'This is important, my lord. And it is equally important that Leupold be with us.'

Unhappily, the lord nodded his assent and they made their way through the great hall, around the corridors that led off it and to the stairs that led down into the dark bowels of the castle. Arnau reached for a torch and the guard motioned him away from it with a sword. Arnau threw an appealing look at Dietmar, who nodded. 'We will need light. Go ahead.'

Grasping the burning torch, Arnau led the descent towards the heavy door into the cellar. At the bottom, he gestured at the heavy oak portal with an iron grill in it.

'The cellar door. I believe you have a key, my lord?'

Dietmar nodded and produced the key. 'Briefly, my lord,' Arnau added, 'I might point out the difficulty of getting past such a door without the key? The hinges are on the far side, and there is no other way of access barring the key, lest a man bring several heavy bodies and a battering ram?'

'Yes, it is a solid door, as are all the important ones in Renfrizhausen.'

'I would like you to bear this in mind, my lord.'

Taking the key, Arnau unlocked the door and swung it inwards, into the dark large cellar hall. Leaving Dietmar and Leupold in the entrance, he moved around the room, lighting the other torches so that the room gradually came into view. Dietmar flinched, unable to tear his eyes from the covered body of his son. Leupold looked nervous.

Striding back over to them, Arnau gestured to the guard.

'When we searched the castle after Kovacs disappeared, the lower floors of this range were searched by Bernhard, Gunther and yourself, while I was upstairs with others. Might I ask if you searched together, or split up down here?'

Leupold frowned in incomprehension until Dietmar, eyes still on the body, translated. After a reply in German, the lord explained. 'The three of them separated, each taking parts of the cellars. They are something of a warren, and not often visited. And, of course, they are now unstable.'

Arnau chewed his lip. 'Which way did Bernhard begin his search without you?'

A little translation later and Leupold led them to the archway on the far right.

'I know these tunnels are dangerous,' Arnau admitted, 'but I beg your indulgence. Please do follow me.'

Torch held up, he moved into the arch and began to walk around the vault and the various corridors and chambers leading off. He was searching still, but he now felt certain of what he would find. After perhaps a quarter of an hour, the lord was clearly beginning to wane in his support. Leupold was grumbling quietly, but Arnau smiled grimly.

'This way. Can you not feel it?'

As if to threaten him, the stones above gave an ominous groaning noise, and even Arnau swallowed nervously now, looking up. 'Please, indulge me. Can you feel it?'

'Feel what?'

'The air. The cold air.'

'The entire cellar is cold.'

Arnau smiled. 'But not breezy. We are underground. Where is the breeze coming from?'

Dietmar frowned, realising they were standing in a cold draught.

'Come,' Arnau said with renewed enthusiasm.

Now he was looking at the floor as they went. Decades of dust and fallen mortar fragments covered it, highlighting the marks of footsteps in it. Two things he sought, and the draught would lead him to one, the footprints to the other.

Four more turnings, following the breeze, and he found it. Dawn light, despite the clouds, filtering into the darkness. Dietmar stared in wonder as they approached the hidden entrance. A sally port, or postern gate, absent for many years. The end of the corridor as it led out to the white world was shaped for a door that no longer stood there. Snow had drifted inside.

'This will be important later. But it is only *one* of the secrets Bernhard has been keeping from you down here.' He turned, hurrying now, following the footprints. It did not take long. Again, the ceiling groaned, and all three men looked up nervously, but finally they reached Arnau's destination.

A heavy oak door, bound with iron and containing a grill just like the main cellar door. Again, it was recessed to open inwards, no sign of the hinges visible.

'Bernhard's great secret, my lord.' He held out the torch.

Slowly, tentatively, the lord took the burning torch and approached the door. It took some work to position it so that he could see through the grill by the torchlight without setting fire to himself. The lord of Renfrizhausen gave a startled, strangled sound.

'Gold, I presume?' Arnau said behind him.

'So *much* gold. And silver, too. How did you know?'

'Lütolf's coin. That, and a series of connections. The Lord God led me to a Roman camp when I left here, and it was only when I put that ancient Empire together with your brother's coin, which had been taken when my squire was killed, that I realised the motive behind this all. The coin was taken, I think, not out of greed. Why would a man who had all this need one more coin, after all? It was taken to prevent the likelihood of anyone else making the connection that I did.'

'Bernhard?'

'Yes, my lord. He is a man who has given you a lifetime of loyal service, and I feel confident that he would have continued to do so, had he not discovered the gold. I imagine he wrestled with his conscience for some time before deciding not to bring it to your attention, but instead keeping it for himself.'

'But how?'

Arnau smiled. 'The tremors in the rock. A few years ago, they damaged the castle. They made the cellars unstable. Your son came down here to check the foundations. I am not sure whether he found the gold or not. I suspect not, else he would not have produced his fake will.'

He winced at that. The accusation was an unpleasant one, even against a dead man and without the will here to examine, but it was an important point, nonetheless. A dark look passed across Dietmar's face, but the unfolding tale was too absorbing to interrupt for propriety's sake. Arnau cleared his throat and continued.

'He set Bernhard to examining the cellars further. Bernhard did a complete survey down here. You can confirm this with Leupold, but I am confident that the man he brought down then was Anselm. The two of them discovered the gold entirely by chance. I fear that Anselm was easily bought, and Bernhard offered him a large enough share that he kept his silence... for a while.'

Dietmar checked this in German with Leupold, who clearly confirmed it.

'But though they had found enough gold to make both men rich for the rest of their lives, there was a problem: the locked door. You saw the cellar door, and you see this one. No hinges to remove. Only a key will open this door. I suspect he even considered ramming it, but with the stones as unstable as they are down here, and the groans from above, I know that *I* would think twice before delivering damaging blows down here. No, he needed the key.'

'The set you had,' Dietmar said in realisation. 'My brother's key.'

Arnau nodded. 'Unfortunately, I think that was an afterthought. At first, Bernhard began to try and needle information from your son. As the lord of Renfrizhausen, every key to every room was his, after all. Bernhard had to reason that Rüdolf had a key to open that door. I imagine he searched your son's rooms time and again, without success.'

They turned away from the room, Arnau leading them back through the cellars as he talked.

'He became more and more frustrated. It was only a matter of time before someone else found the gold or Anselm talked. And with Rüdolf preparing to have the works done, soon there would be workmen and architects down here. Speed was of the essence.'

He sighed. 'I am not sure whether he ever intended to kill your son, but I suspect that was always his plan.'

They passed through the main cellar and Arnau led them up the stairs once more.

Moving into the great hall, Arnau looked around at the now-gathered populace of Renfrizhausen. All faces were filled with concern and disapproval, but also with curiosity. All bar one. Bernhard Bulstrich watched him with narrowed eyes, barely concealing the hate within. Arnau tried not to smile at him. The man's time was nigh.

'So on Monday...' Dietmar began.

Arnau swept an arm around the room. 'You and Rüdolf were in here arguing over money and the castle's repairs. I believe that Bernhard heard the arguing.' The marshal flashed a look of intense anger at him, but Arnau ignored him. He was ascendant now, and Bernhard was sliding from favour with every word.

'He heard you argue and snapped. He now decided that he had to move, and that the time had come. He hid in the antechamber and waited. Come.' He made to leave the room, but Dietmar shook his head.

'Not yet.' He turned to Wolf and Winrich, both of whom stood nearby, and barked commands in German. They marched over towards Bernhard, who stood close to the family. His lip wrinkled.

'This is a web of lies, and I will prove it once the *Tempelritter* fails to prove otherwise,' he snapped. Still, Wolf and Winrich disarmed the man and stepped back, their own blades now drawn and held out at their commander, watchful. Dietmar nodded his satisfaction before turning back to the Templar.

'Tell me of my son.'

Arnau beckoned him with a crooked finger and walked from the room, the lord and Leupold following him. He stopped in the antechamber with just the two of them. 'I am so sorry, my lord. Sorry to make you see this in your mind, but it is important that you know the truth. Here, hiding in the shadows of the staircase,

Bernhard waited. As Rüdolf emerged, angry and not particularly alert, he reached for a cloak, the marshal struck him on the back of the head. With Rüdolf's senses scattered, Bernhard lowered him onto the cloak that had taken most of the blood from the blow, leaving only two small marks on the wall. As quickly as he could, Bernhard searched your son for the key, but with increasing frustration failed to find it. He then dragged him to the well.'

Leading the others out into the snow, Arnau crossed to the well. 'Here, it is my belief that knowing he was undone if Rüdolf lived to accuse him, he gave a last quick search, found nothing, then killed your son and dropped him down the well, along with the cloak and the blade he used.'

Dietmar shuddered. 'But Bernhard was in the chapel,' he said. 'He always is, and we know this.'

Arnau shook his head. 'But he *wasn't*. It took me a long time to understand. Bernhard helps Father Oswald with his services. He is the man who rings the bell, for a start. I have seen him do it at each service. But on that occasion, he hurried to the chapel while you and your son were arguing in the hall. He snuck inside and rang the bell, perhaps ten minutes or more before the service was actually due. Then, when everyone in the castle assumed the service to be in progress, with no others attending as usual, Bernhard killed Rüdolf. Once the deed was done, he casually entered the chapel and there helped Father Oswald as always, the priest who could legitimately confirm that Bernhard was in the chapel for the service.'

'But the bell?'

'Father Oswald would not hear the bell even if you rang it using his head,' Arnau explained. 'He did not hear it when Bernhard rang it early, and assumed all to be normal. Then, when the service was beginning, Bernhard pretended to go and ring the bell. As far as everyone was concerned, even Father Oswald, the marshal was in the chapel when your son was killed. The matter with the bell's timing was the critical one that kept me halted in my investigation, and it is the work of a twisted genius. Bernhard is clever beyond words. Bernhard had given himself a ten or fifteen minute window in which to do the deed. And he knew where everyone would be. Indeed, he even knew the routine of the men on the walls, so could time his murder when no one was watching the courtyard. The only man who could have seen him was Anselm, who had as much of a wicked stake in this as the marshal.'

He turned, a fait accompli. Dietmar stepped back, reeling. 'It is a masterpiece of evil.'

Arnau nodded. 'But Bernhard was thwarted. All he had managed to take was the will, which was of no use to him. But he then discovered that there would be another chance. He realised that Lütolf would have had a key, and he knew that someone from Rourell was coming to contest the will. It was a natural assumption that Lütolf's personal effects would be brought, likely including the key. The keyring that had three keys, one for the gate, one for your brother's rooms, and one that no one recognised which would open that crucial door in the cellars.'

'And then you arrived.'

'Almost. In the day or so in between, Bernhard rode quickly down to the village. He could hardly risk repeating his crime in the castle, so he hired four desperate paupers from the village to attack my squire and I as we arrived, and to steal the key. Fortunately, we are no strangers to the sword, and the men failed. They were no bandits, but hirelings of Bernhard's, as the priest in the village church will confirm for you.'

'Come, let us return to the hall,' Dietmar said, and Arnau nodded, shivering in the cold as the snow continued to settle upon them. Entering the building they passed once more along the tapestry corridor and into the hall, where everyone waited expectantly, the marshal still at sword point.

'I understand now, Bernhard,' Dietmar said quietly. 'I understand, but I cannot forgive.'

'It is all lies, and I can prove that,' the marshal snorted.

Arnau shook his head. 'From there it becomes at once simpler, and yet more complex. Remember that Bernhard, as the commander of the castle's security, has keys to almost everywhere, except your family's rooms and the one door he needed to open.

You set me to helping Bernhard discover the truth, which gave him ample opportunity to cover it up as we went about our investigation.'

'Lies.'

Arnau ignored the man. 'Having failed to kill us outside, he managed to slip something into my meal either in the kitchen or as it was brought into the hall. Choking on my food would seem natural, and when I died he would be at leisure to take the keys from my gear. Indeed, at times he has searched my room again and again, failing to find them, largely through the shrewd mind of my squire, who out-thought him at every turn except the last.'

He scratched his chin. 'I fear that all this had become too much for Anselm. We were closing in on him as a suspect, and he would almost certainly have sold out the marshal to save his own skin. Thus Bernhard was forced to deal with his accomplice, who had been complicit in everything since they found the gold. I think that if you investigate the searches of the castle they had carried out, Bernhard had been with Anselm throughout. Anselm had overlooked the crossbow that had been in Bernhard's room – for the marshal, I suspect, has had one secretly all this time – brought back from the Holy Land where he had become proficient using it against the Turk. So Anselm died, and it was us who found him.'

Bernhard snorted. 'That you killed him yourself and are now attempting to clear your name is obvious to me.'

'Bernhard then made another attempt on my life, with that crossbow. He is one of few men in the castle with the strength, agility and knowledge of the place to have carried out that attack. And he got away, discarded the crossbow and his cloak and joined you all in the courtyard waiting for me to emerge. It was Bernhard who then identified the crossbow as Hungarian, which he knew because he had long ago received it from such a man in Outremer. And the blame was conveniently shifted to Kovacs, who we locked in his room.'

Dietmar rubbed his scalp. 'This all rings true, surely, but it is also fantastical in its intricacy.'

'Such is the mind of the killer,' agreed Arnau. 'That afternoon, while I was distracted, Bernhard searched our room once more. Unfortunately for him, Anna came across him doing so, and in his ever-growing criminal desperation, he was forced to kill her too. Leaving her body to be found, he hurried away and waited. We found Anna in our room and, as we were raising a commotion over it, Bernhard – now starting to panic as things unravelled, and knowing that Kovacs was on the verge of being proven innocent – set about further deflecting suspicion from himself. He went to the minstrel's room, unlocked it and killed Kovacs.'

'But what about the body?'

'That took me some time to figure out. I now realise that he dropped the body out of a window, where it fell into a snowdrift below, just as he'd done with the crossbow. He then smashed his head on something and feigned unconsciousness in the doorway.'

'It is outrageous.'

'But the truth. Now we were once more blaming Kovacs and hunting for him, and Bernhard had framed himself as the innocent and injured party.'

'What happened to Kovacs' body though?'

'Whilst we were searching the castle, Bernhard, I suspect, slipped away from his search team as they searched the cellars and retrieved the body, stowing it somewhere until he could safely hide it away in the cellars using the postern that only he knew about. He had already dropped a drape down from the window so that we would presume Kovacs escaped from there. The truth was safely hidden now.

'I believe that the truth might, in fact, never have come to light. Kovacs was presumed guilty and would never be found. Bernhard would have eventually succeeded in acquiring the key somehow, then he would gradually move the gold to somewhere else and depart a rich man. But unfortunately the truth was niggling at me now, and I would not let go. I went to find the men who had attacked me. I traced them back to the town, and there the priest told me about Bernhard coming down to the village just before I arrived. I realised then that the marshal was guilty, though at the time I could not decide how or why he had done it, so I kept my peace. That was my undoing.'

He gestured at Bernhard. 'The next few hours were uncomfortable. I knew he had done it, and he knew that I knew. Unfortunately, he moved again before I could prove anything. He tried to take the key the most direct way while I was busy stalking the castle, trying to work it all out. In almost a repeat of your son's death, he took Felipe while he slept, murdered him and dragged him out into the snow. There he searched him. Miraculously, he was frustrated yet again, finding only our Templar papers before my arrival disturbed him. Also Felipe had hidden the keys in a most cunning fashion.

'I then spotted Bernhard in the trees. He ran, and I chased him back to the castle. He made his way inside and then locked me out. I did not know of his secret doorway and panicked a little. He had hung a drape from the window once more. The first time we had bought his lie that Kovacs had gone out that way, and now you would buy that I had done the same. Meanwhile, Bernhard retrieved Kovacs' body from the cellars, knowing that it was night-time and the castle was almost entirely abed. Timing it so that the man on the walls would not see, he lugged Kovacs to my room and left him there.'

He folded his arms. 'It took but moments for him to *discover* the body and send out an alarm. As I climbed back inside I was apprehended. The rest you all know. I had had the blame laid at my feet by a most cunning adversary.'

Dietmar swayed. 'It is almost too much to believe.'

'But it is the truth,' Gerdrut said from across the hall. 'You know it. We all do. Bernhard has been loyal for many years, but he is poorly paid for a man of his rank and ability. You know that. The lure of gold is enough to overcome even a stout heart's objections to base acts.'

The graf nodded. 'All of this over money. It is a poor thing. A poor thing indeed.'

It happened so fast that Arnau almost missed it. Quick as a flash, Bernhard acted. He was undone now, and he knew it. There would be no more shifting the blame. No more dissembling. The guards here were strong enough, and trained as soldiers, but Bernhard was a Crusader, a man of true war experience with skills continually honed through exercise and training.

He spun sharply, bringing the heel of his boot down on Wolf's toes, breaking bones. Even as Wolf stared in shock and fell away, Bernhard had continued to spin, elbow thudding into Winrich's stomach and winding him instantly. As the two guards staggered, Bernhard plucked Winrich's blade from his hand and spun again, bringing it down flat on Wolf's forearm, breaking the bone and making the second guard drop his sword.

The room burst into sudden activity, as Leupold and Matthias drew their own blades and moved on their master, and Michael Trost shouted orders while the serfs fled the scene of violence.

But it had all happened in mere moments, and before the other guards could get to the marshal or the two wounded ones recover, the situation had changed. Bernhard stood behind the lady Gerdrut, his arm up over her shoulder, a razor-sharp knife blade at her throat while the sword bobbed around, threatening anyone who came close.

'Sadly, I feel it is time to change employment,' Bernhard said in an almost casual tone. 'And one thing you never worked out, *Tempelritter*, is that I can use both my left and my right hand without difficulty. As I might do any moment if a single one of you comes any closer.'

'Back,' Dietmar ordered everyone. 'Back, I say. Bernhard, you can go. Run as far as you can and I will not hunt you, if you now let my sister free.'

'That would be foolish of me, Graf Dietmar. With the lady here as my hostage, I can still have it all. I have the key and can have the gold. And now that I do not need to sneak around, time is no longer an issue. The lady and I here will make our way down to the cellars. You will have my horse and three pack beasts made ready. Once the gold is loaded on my animals and we are safely away from the castle, I will release the lady. I have no wish to kill her. I never wanted to kill *anyone*, in fact. I just wanted what I was owed. A remuneration of my worth.'

'Let her go and we will talk.'

Bernhard shook his head. As the two guards took a single step forward, the marshal pricked the lady's neck with his blade, sending a tear of crimson down her throat. 'Ah, ah, ah. No closer. You know how ready I am to kill to get what I want. I presume none of you need to be reminded to that. My horses?'

There was a tense pause, and finally Dietmar nodded. 'Conrad, have the horses readied and brought out to the courtyard. Bernhard, if you hurt Gerdrut, I will hunt you down to hell and back, stripping the flesh from your hide.'

'If all goes as planned, there will be no more harm,' Bernhard said. 'Now, we are going down to the cellars to gather my gold ready. I trust no one will be stupid enough to pursue me?'

In the silence that followed, Bernhard slowly backed from the room into the doorway that would lead him to the cellar steps, blade always at the lady's throat, moving very carefully. Gerdrut von Ehingen stood defiant and proud, her expression almost challenging her brother to do something. All watched, breathless, until the two were out of sight.

'Leupold? Matthias? Guard the stairs behind them,' Dietmar barked in German, watching Wolf and Winrich helping one another upright. The lord turned to Arnau, ready to throw out a new command.

But in the excitement no one had noticed the Templar leave.

CHAPTER SEVENTEEN

SUNDAY MORNING

𝔄rnau fumbled with the key, his cold, numb fingers struggling. Had he had time, he'd have hurried back to his room and collected his gauntlets, but time was of the essence, and he was going to get colder yet. Much colder.

Yanking open the door in the castle gate, he stepped out into the snow outside, a fresh deluge falling now and turning the world into a hazy white fleece. Time might be of the essence, but so were stealth and preparedness, a three-way balance to be maintained. He readied himself.

He had a sword, despite the fact that his own weapons were in the possession of a guard back in the main hall. He knew well enough that, as well as a small rack of weapons kept in the guard house in the range in which he'd stayed, a sword and a mace were also kept hanging on the wall in the guardroom by the gate. Briefly, he'd considered the mace, but he had not been able to pick up such a weapon since the day Sebastian had died in Constantinople. Instead, he'd ducked into the guardroom, grasped the sword – not bothering with belt or sheath – and hurried on to the gate.

He'd left the main hall while the argument was still going on, before even Bernhard had made any demands. He'd known exactly what the marshal would want, and what he would do, so there seemed little point in sticking around before he acted. The man would want the gold, and for that he would need horses. He had

Gerdrut hostage, and no one would move against him and endanger the lady.

Almost no one.

Bernhard would have to retreat away from everyone to the cellar. There he could prepare, away from danger, gather his gold and plan his departure. But Arnau was not about to let the man get away now. There was, after all, another way into those cellars.

Outside the walls, ignoring the gate and leaving it open, for the grave danger was already inside the castle, he began to slog his way around the outer ramparts. As he moved, as fast as he could, he began to discard his excess apparel.

First to go was the chain coif that had been tied about his neck and hung down the back. Gripping his borrowed sword tight in the freezing knuckles of his left hand, he wrenched the head protection clear and dropped it carelessly into the snow. What he was about to do relied at least as much on speed and secrecy as being protected, and chain was heavy and loud.

The voluminous white mantle was easy enough to remove, and it gave Arnau more of a jolt than he'd expected to leave the glorious symbol of his Order lying discarded in the snow as he staggered on. Numb fingers then gripped the hem of his chain hauberk and, as he passed beneath Dietmar's window, the heavy shirt gradually came up, peeling off his torso and up to his head. It had taken him years to become proficient enough to don and remove the hauberk without aid, but even then doing so with one hand was troublesome. In the end, he had to pause, slam his sword point-down into the earth, and use both hands to peel the shirt over his head and cast it aside.

Unarmoured, he now grasped the sword once more and slogged on, shivering constantly. The flakes settled on his hair and shoulders, filling his beard and soaking his linen shirt, which was far too inadequate protection for weather like this.

Still, it had to be done. Tunnels and cellars amplified sounds, and the noise of a man in chain mail was both loud and very uniquely identifiable. Bernhard would hear him coming long before he got there in a hauberk. Better to face the cold and hope for an element of surprise. Besides, the marshal was unarmoured, dressed only in his tunic and under-tunic. They would be equally matched, in those terms at least.

For a while he fretted that he might never find the entrance. After all, the mouth of the forgotten sally port had been hidden sufficiently that no one had noticed it for decades, and he'd only seen it from the inside. Finally, making his way to the bottom of the wall below Kovacs' window, he found disturbances in the snow and identified where the corpse had landed after being cast out. From there it was not difficult to follow the trail left by Bernhard as he'd carried the body back inside the castle. Fresh snow may have fallen, but not sufficiently so to mask the passage of a man through two- or three-foot deep snow.

It was cunning, really. Three shrubs had grown on the rocky hillside, much like their kind all around the castle, but their positioning entirely hid the entrance unless one knew it was there. Perhaps their placing had been happy accident, or perhaps decades ago someone had purposefully hidden the doorway with their planting.

Shivering once more as the spindly branches dropped yet more snow on him, he pushed his way between the shrubs and to the postern door into Renfrizhausen. As he approached, he slowed, forcing his breathing to calm and become level, rather than the bellows blasts he'd been heaving as he pushed through the snow.

Now, he had to be quiet. Along with his calming breath, he forced himself not to shiver. He'd realised long ago that shivering may be an automatic reaction, but it was also partially a conscious thing. All it took was a little effort of will and a man could stop himself shivering. It did little good in mitigating the cold anyway.

Philippians four: I may do all things through him that strengtheneth me.

Clenching his teeth, he began to step slowly into the tunnel mouth. The snow had managed to drift inside for some distance, and his footfalls were naught but the very soft crunch of snow under pressure. Still, aware that the lady of Renfrizhausen's very life might depend upon his stealth, he slowed and moved toe then heel, toe then heel, toe then heel, one careful pace at a time into the cellars.

Hurriedly, he wracked his brain for memories of this corner of Renfrizhausen's underworld. He had only been here once, after all, and had had a lot on his mind at the time. The tunnels were not lit with torches, and he had no such light source with him, and the deeper into the passage he went, the worse the gloomy visibility became.

The first bend removed almost all light. As he turned that corner the darkness enveloped him, and the last of the snow disappeared from underfoot. He was properly inside now. Time might be important, but he felt that he had at least a *little* leeway. It would take Bernhard precious time to sort his chests of gold, whatever he planned to do with them, and the lord would not send his men down for fear of his sister's life.

Care. He paused for a while, allowing his eyesight to adjust. Once he could make out vague shapes in the darkness, he decided that this was sufficient and began to move again, one pace at a time and very carefully, wincing with every crunch of fallen masonry in the thick dust. Still, he reminded himself, he was being quieter than he had been in the snow, and a thousand times less audible than a man in chain. He had to hope that the marshal would be too intent upon his task to catch notice of the Templar's approach. He would not have to be making too much noise to mask Arnau's movements.

Reaching a T-junction, he chewed his lip. He knew this one. Right would take him back towards the heart of the cellars and the great vaulted chamber where Rüdolf lay in sombre state. Left headed out further to the scarce-visited tunnels where Bernhard and his hostage would now be.

A slow but deep breath. He had no idea in truth what to expect, and therefore had been entirely unable to plan ahead. He had to trust in the Lord and in his own skills for what was to come. He was a trained warrior of God, his skills honed on the field of battle. He tried not to remind himself that so was Bernhard. Moreover, the marshal might have a decade on Arnau, but he had far from let his abilities slide. That rooftop chase around the castle had made it clear that Bernhard was faster and stronger than Arnau. The man was an expert marksman, and he regularly trained his men, so his sword skills would be good.

Shut up, he told himself, silently. He would only make himself nervous going on like this.

Show thy works to the Lord; and thy thoughts shall be addressed.

Gripping his sword tight, he blew gently on his knuckles, warming them as best he could.

Another corner. Another junction.

When he first caught the flicker of golden light, his heart leapt. Bernhard was ahead with a torch.

He pictured the scene as he'd observed it when he had been here earlier with Leupold and Dietmar. Ahead, the corridor turned a sharp right into a wider one, more a room than a passage, perhaps ten feet wide and thirty long, three doors leading off it on the far wall, the middle of which contained the gold.

The light was dazzling after so much gloom, but Arnau concentrated. How much light did a torch give off? Was it just around the corner or further along? Close by, he decided, and given the reflected glow, close to the corner where Arnau would enter. The marshal couldn't be holding the light source, for he would be busy with the gold, and he would not trust Gerdrut with it, for she would certainly make to thrust the torch in the villain's face if she could get her hands on it.

The villain had to have managed to secure the lady somehow. He couldn't hope to work while keeping a blade at her throat. Damn it, Arnau huffed silently. Too little information to plan adequately.

Slowly, breath coming now in tiny puffs to avoid betraying his presence, Arnau stepped towards the vaulted chamber where Bernhard would be working with the gold. As he approached the corner, he could hear low voices now.

The marshal was constantly chattering in his own language, incomprehensible to Arnau, though some rhythmic part of the monologue that kept making an appearance suggested counting. Occasionally, Arnau could hear the acidic thrust of Gerdrut's tongue, lashing the man for his betrayal, and every time, the marshal snapped back angrily at her.

Slowly, infinitely slowly, Arnau approached the chamber, moving along the right-hand wall.

At the corner he stopped and inched forward, moving one eye out to the golden glow, taking in the scene. The torch was indeed on the wall a couple of feet to his right, and stupidly he looked at it, half-blinding himself for precious moments. The room was precisely how he remembered, except that now the central door on the far wall was open. Another torch had been lit inside that sub-chamber, and another golden glow issued from the vault.

Even as he espied it all, the marshal stepped into view from that room, chattering in German and carrying two heavy hessian bags tied together over his shoulders. Arnau ducked back into the shadows, but not before Gerdrut saw him.

The lady was almost opposite Arnau and the torch, by the nearest of the doors on the far wall. Bernhard had lashed her wrists together with his thick leather belt and tied them to the grille in the door. She was bound and incapable of stepping away from that fastened door. The lady spotted the movement in the corridor just as Arnau pulled back and he sent her desperate silent pleas not to give the game away.

Gerdrut was sharp, though, at least as clever has her brothers, and she simply gave the tiniest of nods, letting him know that she had seen and recognised him. Arnau breathed the tiniest sliver of a sigh of relief.

He ran his mind over what else he had seen in that momentary glance. A pile of hessian bags, undoubtedly full of gold and silver. They had been gathered in pairs, attached to one another with twine so that they could be slung two at a time over the shoulder to be carried and then, tellingly, over a horse's saddle or blanket for transport.

Bernhard was preparing the gold to take it away by packhorse. Either the bags had already been in the room, since the days Lütolf had been in there, or Bernhard had been well prepared, the bags ready in some other chamber nearby, simply awaiting the chance to do this. Now, he was decanting the coins from the chests that no man alone could move into bags that could be readily taken away. He might not be able to take it all, but even what he'd already moved would be sufficient to keep a man in luxury for the rest of his life.

Arnau pictured the scene in the castle above. Gerdrut had not been taken hostage purely to keep Bernhard from harm. She would be his insurance until he was away from this place and to safety. He would have told Dietmar to have horses ready upstairs, to which he would need to move the gold. He could have made it easier by having the horses brought round outside to the postern, of course, but that would have drawn unwanted attention to the secondary exit, and the marshal was likely keeping that as a last resort escape route.

No, he would slowly port the gold through to that main cellar room, and then he could simply stand there with his knife at Gerdrut's throat while the castle's staff loaded his horses for him. It was the only realistic way to get away with the gold.

Arnau chewed his lip again. He had been almost ready to go for the man, but with this fresh realisation, he was swiftly changing his mind. If he waited until Bernhard was ready to take the gold to the main cellar, he might be able to get the man by surprise and without endangering Gerdrut further.

Nodding to himself, he stepped back quietly. He would bide his time and do this more carefully than simply trying to surprise the man now. Retreating slowly and quietly, he returned to the junction and ducked around it, lurking in the shadow.

He did not have long to wait. Bernhard had clearly almost finished his work. Only a few minutes later the noises from around the corridors changed and then, as Arnau held his breath and waited, Bernhard passed the end of the junction, heading for the main cellar.

Arnau cursed silently. The man had not now left the lady tied to the door as he worked. Instead, he had draped two heavy sacks of coins over her shoulders, leaving her hands tied, and sent her on ahead, another pair of bags over his own shoulder, but with his sword out and pointed at the back of her neck.

Another curse. Arnau couldn't jump the man now, for he had Gerdrut at sword point. Fuming, he carefully stepped along the passage, back to the junction. As he did so, he brought his footfall into sync with the marshal's, his steps hidden beneath the sound of Bernhard's own boots.

That way, carefully and hanging back in the shadows, Arnau paced along, following the marshal and the lady back to the central chamber. As they approached, he could now hear other faint sounds. More voices, but muffled and distant. The others, he realised, would be up above, beyond the steps down to the cellar.

As they closed on that archway that led out into the main chamber, Arnau paused once more. The other two disappeared around the corner, the lady taking the opportunity to glance back for a fraction of a second, spotting the pursuer in the passage.

Arnau crept forward to the corner as he'd done at the other room. The cellar was just how he remembered it, with the shrouded body on the central table. The four sacks of coins had been dumped on the floor, and as Arnau watched, the marshal looped the belt that secured Gerdrut's wrists over a sconce to restrain her further, then moved around the room, lighting the other torches.

This was it. He had to move now. Ready...

He waited until Bernhard had moved around and the only torches left were the two near this archway. As the marshal approached, and would surely notice the figure lurking in the arch at any moment, Arnau moved.

He leapt from the doorway, sword held out to his right in both hands, to counteract the weakness of his numb, cold grip, his arms bringing the blade around in a wide sweep even as he leapt. He had been right to rely upon surprise. The marshal had been entirely unaware of him and, far from meeting his blade with a prepared block, he staggered backwards desperately, out of the range of Arnau's swing.

Keep him on the defensive. It was something he had learned early. With a well-trained opponent, you could not afford to allow them the time and leisure to regain the initiative. Thus, he brought the sword around in another swing. This time the marshal was beginning to recover from the shock and, though he leapt back, his sword came down and caught Arnau's in a parry.

The Templar forced the marshal back another step across the cellar, away from the gold, mercifully past the restrained figure of Gerdrut. For a moment he almost told her to free herself and run, but it would have been redundant. She was already struggling to try and escape the bonds. She was no dullard, after all. Her chance had come and might vanish again at any moment.

Arnau felt the initiative slipping as he thrust again and had his blow turned aside. Both warriors were unarmoured, and both fought to wound with intent, parrying and dodging with the urgency of men who both knew that the first blow to land true would probably end the fight.

Gods, but the marshal was good. Arnau cut up and right, bringing his sword up with every ounce of strength in his arms, but the marshal knocked the blow aside almost negligently, his sword strong and swift. Then Bernhard was suddenly on the attack. For every step he had been forced back by Arnau, he was now treading forward again with determination, blade lancing, swiping, probing and chopping with astonishing speed and strength.

Arnau found himself retreating back towards the arch now, past the struggling figure of Gerdrut once more. His chance came then, and only because of the lady of Renfrizhausen. As Arnau fought for his life, Bernhard advancing with grunted oaths in German, Gerdrut paused in her struggles and thrust out a leg, tripping the marshal as he passed.

With a sharp cry, Bernhard tumbled forward, sword sweeping out as he did, forcing Arnau to leap back or take the blow on his ankles. By the time he was moving again, the marshal had begun to recover, rolling out to the side and coming upright with dazzling speed for a man of his years.

Arnau took the lead once more. No quarter and no chance to recover, this time. He slashed and jabbed, leaping forward a pace at a time, forcing Bernhard back, always on the attack. This time they were retreating across the room, towards the stairs and past the shrouded body on the table. Every blow Arnau landed was cast aside by the master swordsman that was Bernhard, and he realised that he would have to be incredibly fortunate to be the one who came out of this fight the victor. Any blow that struck home would likely be a killing or incapacitating blow, the way both men were attacking, and it was becoming obvious that despite Arnau's training and experience, the former Crusader was still better. Stronger, faster, and more skilled.

Damn it.

"*Dread thou not, for I am with thee,*" he snarled, quoting Isaiah and feeling the word of God flow through him, bringing with it fresh reserves of energy. "*Bow thou not away, for I am thy God. I comforted thee, and helped thee; and the right hand of my just man uptook thee.*"

Feeling the small burst of fresh strength, Arnau forced the man a little further and a little further. His sword suddenly struck home. Just a little nick, but tellingly below the shoulder of the man's sword arm. Arnau felt the thrill of victory swell for a glorious moment, and then felt it slide away once more as Bernhard leapt back again, swapping his sword to his left hand. Of course, the man was equally able with both.

The onslaught that came then had Arnau close to panic. Bernhard came on with a vengeance, blade whirling, slashing, stabbing and all at lightning speed. Moreover, the left-handed attack was something with which Arnau had little experience, and he found himself misjudging his enemy at almost every turn. Once more the Templar was being pushed back across the chamber with strength and force.

Knuckles white and with rising dread, he faced the most dreadful attack, then. The marshal slammed his blade down hard, and Arnau's own sword was knocked easily aside. A second chop, and the only way Arnau could stop the blow cleaving him in two was to grip his own sword at both hilt and tip and thrust it in the way. The swords met and the reverberation shot up both the Templar's arms to his shoulders. The marshal was so fast now, so fierce, that Arnau could do little more than back down and desperately keep the sword in the way, blocking those hammering blows with the flat of his blade as his fingers became more and more numb.

A particularly powerful blow sent Arnau down to a knee, bending upwards, holding his sword sideways above him to protect his body from the repeated chops of Bernhard's blade. He was going to die at any moment.

Then his sword broke. Whether the marshal was super-humanly strong, or perhaps there was some imperfection in Arnau's borrowed sword, it snapped in two, and Arnau narrowly avoided being split like a log by rolling away desperately, discarding the broken blade, eyes darting around, looking for a replacement.

It was then that he saw the others. Figures were at the grille in the cellar door, having come down the stairs. Someone was trying to unlock it. Help was on the way, if only he could hold out long enough. Arnau scrambled away, fresh hope filling him. Perhaps it was not over quite yet.

He was up and running now, backing away at speed, keeping the table with the shrouded body between him and Bernhard, buying time. A sudden realisation struck him, filling him with relief. There was no sign of Gerdrut. She had freed herself and managed to slip away. There was still some struggle going on with the keys. Damn it, but they had to hurry.

Arnau backed away again and as the marshal advanced on him, cursing in German, he spotted a figure in the shadows. The lady Gerdrut emerged from the archway. For a dreadful moment, Arnau thought she would attack Bernhard, but she was unarmed and far from stupid. She had no such notion, but she was motioning at Arnau. He frowned, lacking comprehension as he lost sight of her again, circling the table and backing away from the snarling marshal. Another half circuit and she came into view once more.

What was she doing? She was standing straight, legs together, face serene, hands folded over her chest. What...

Realisation dawned in that moment. The *clever* woman. Arnau's hand reached out, gripping the white shroud over Rüdolf's body and knotting it, pulling and hurling it aside. As was only appropriate, the young Graf lay in state with his sword held tight, laid vertically on top of him, hands over the pommel just as they would soon be in the stone monument that would be placed over his tomb.

With a silent apology for impropriety, Arnau grasped the sword from the dead noble's grip and pulled it away just in time to use it to block a blow from Bernhard. It would still not be enough to win the fight, though, even if it had saved his life for now. Bernhard was better. Moreover, the man was well rested, warm and sufficiently-clad, while Arnau was exhausted, freezing and enduring the cold of the cellars in a simple linen shirt.

Arnau backed away as he deflected blow after blow.

He was losing. Any moment now.

And then the marshal's sword was up, ready to fall and end him, while Arnau was still reeling from the previous assault, his sword down to his right, too far away to even hope to block the coming strike.

There was a thud, a crack, and a scream, and Arnau blinked in shock as Bernhard's raised left arm suddenly shattered at the elbow, a crossbow bolt wedged into the bone. Somehow, even as the ruined limb dropped the blade, the marshal managed to grasp it with his slightly wounded right, backing away, tears streaming from his eyes to match the blood gushing from his arm. He was moving away, out of danger.

Even as he advanced once more, Arnau glanced over his shoulder. The cellar door was open and Leupold and Matthias stood flanking Dietmar, who was looking at the crossbow in his hands with wonder.

'I never knew you had mastered the crossbow, my lord,' Arnau said in awe.

'I was aiming for his head,' admitted the graf.

Arnau laughed, then, and pressed forward.

Bernhard was retreating to the archway. He almost stumbled over the pile of coin sacks on the floor, but realised at the last moment and skipped around them.

'Your time has come,' Arnau snapped, advancing on him implacably.

Bernhard, suffering and beyond words, failed to respond, simply backing away once more, heading for the arch. What was he hoping for? To escape Renfrizhausen through his sally port perhaps? He would never survive the journey to somewhere his wound could be dealt with. He was going to lose the arm at the very least, anyway.

No. He was going to lose a lot more than the arm, vowed Arnau, speeding up his pursuit.

As he turned into the archway into which Bernhard had retreated, the Templar felt a moment of fresh panic. Two figures stood a little way back, illuminated by the glow of a torch. Gerdrut was now free, holding the burning light, and beside her stood Matthias, covered in snow, but with a feral expression and a sword and shield at the ready. Matthias, the man who had hated Arnau from the day he had arrived. The man who had once told him that he was innocent of the poisoning because if he wished Arnau dead, he would come at him face to face, with a sword.

That panic subsided in a moment of considered logic. The guard was not here for him. Matthias was with Gerdrut, and had come for the marshal. Dietmar must have sent the guard out to find the other way in, just as Arnau had done.

Bernhard now realised the fresh danger and stopped, trapped and sorely wounded in the wide passageway. His left arm hung useless at his side, blood pouring down it and running from the tips of his fingers in a small cascade. Without help the man would bleed out soon, but that would not satisfy the people of Renfrizhausen.

Bernhard was white-faced now, struggling to lift his sword with his right arm where Arnau's cut below his shoulder leaked crimson. The Templar stepped forward to finish it. He raised his sword.

'Stop,' called a voice from behind.

Arnau glanced over his shoulder to see Dietmar in the archway behind.

'He must die,' Arnau said, defiantly.

'Yes, but not now. Not like that.'

'My lord?'

'I am law in Renfrizhausen. It is my place to condemn and sentence the vile monster that has been lurking beneath my roof all this time. The man who killed my son deserves to suffer so much more than a soldier's death. He shall be broken on the wheel.'

Arnau shivered at the thought. To be killed thus, strapped to a cartwheel while all and sundry took clubs and broke first hands and feet, then shins and wrists, working in until the man was pulverised beyond hope, and then leaving him, broken, to die slowly and in agony over days, while birds pecked out his eyes.

Lord, but what a punishment.

Bernhard had clearly decided the same. Before Arnau could stop him, the marshal, defiance still painted across his face, cast his sword aside, drew the dagger with which he had threatened Gerdrut, and ran it across his own throat in the blink of an eye.

As Bernhard toppled, blood fountaining across the stones of the cellar floor, Arnau found that despite everything, he was grateful the bastard had done that and avoided the grisly spectacle of the wheel.

'The murderer is finished,' he said with a relieved sigh.

Dietmar approached, towering over the shaking, dying form of the marshal even as the last bubbles of air formed at the rent in his neck. The old graf put his boot down on Bernhard's neck and pressed down with all his weight until there was an unpleasant and very audible crack. If Bernhard, still slightly conscious, could have screamed through his ruined throat, he would have. At least the lord of Renfrizhausen had had the last blow.

'*Per istam sanctam unctionem ignoscat tibi Dominus quicquid peccaveris sive deliqueris,*' Arnau said with quiet reverence, and went to bend over the body, but Dietmar's hand came down and grasped his shoulder, stopping him.

'No last rites for this man. No confession. Let him suffer and burn for eternity in the fires of hell for what he has done.'

With no argument to be raised against the condemnation, Arnau simply nodded silently, and then staggered back against the wall, freezing and exhausted, shaking through exertion and cold in equal amounts. It was over. Guards were with him then, helping him, holding him upright, taking away the sword and throwing a cloak over him.

The murder of Rüdolf von Ehingen had been avenged.

CHAPTER EIGHTEEN

I saw under the sun unfaithfulness in the place of doom, and wickedness in the place of rightfulness. And I said in mine heart 'The Lord shall judge the righteous, and the unfaithful; and then shall be the proper time for each thing.' I said in mine heart of the sons of men, that 'God should prove them, and show them that they be like beasts.'

Ecclesiastes 5:16-18

𝔄rnau had been preparing it for a while, and the von Ehingen were beginning to look impatient when he made his way into the hall, shaking the snow from his shoulders and squeezing the water from his hair.

'I must apologise for my tardiness. I had something to attend to.'

Striding forward, he took the seat being offered opposite the lord of Renfrizhausen. There were four of them at the table. The castle's staff were busy preparing a late lunch, Father Oswald was at work in his chapel, and the guards were about their duties, but Graf Dietmar and the ladies Gerdrut and Ute sat at the table, along with the seneschal, Michael Trost.

'It occurs to me,' Dietmar said quietly, 'that I have yet to officially lift the charges laid against you and renounce any punishments. You are no longer under banishment, *Herr* von Vallbona.'

Arnau smiled at the honorific which sounded odd with his name. He smiled at the lord of Renfrizhausen. He smiled at

Gerdrut, who smiled back. He smiled at Michael Trost, who nodded a recognition of value and friendship. He smiled at the *Grand Dame* Ute, who regarded him as though he were something fished out of the garderobe. Ah well. You couldn't win every battle.

He'd arrived less than a week ago, convinced that the entire Germanic people were dour, unfriendly, unforgiving and held a searing hatred of the men of the west. That week had changed his opinion greatly. He had warmed to this insular but caring and principled family and to their people, almost all of whom had a strong code of honour and a tight bond with their lord.

'While it is exceedingly unlikely that the Order will send me here again,' he replied, 'it is pleasing to know that I would be welcomed if it happened. And in truth, *should* that happen, I would be most pleased to do so.' He grinned. 'Perhaps next time I will prove the existence of the ghost or the dragon instead?'

This raised a chuckle from all but the old *dame*.

'Michael has made a cursory count of the coins,' Dietmar said. 'It would appear that they are of an unusually high content of gold and silver, and altogether they represent a solid foundation for a family's finances. They will pay for the repairs to the castle and will allow us to acquire certain local estates and positions that will ease the family's fortunes considerably.'

Arnau nodded. The family would no longer struggle. He prepared himself. 'What will you do with your vote upon the next occasion? Are you for the Welf or the Hohenstaufen now?'

The tension that filled the air he entirely expected. Really, it was none of his business. Lütolf and his brother had quarrelled over the matter so much that the first lord had ridden away to join the Order rather than split the family. Arnau had no vested interest at all, he was simply curious.

'I fear that depends upon who is the master of each house in the coming years, and upon how they treat the von Ehingen. Beyond that I cannot yet say.'

Arnau nodded. Fishing in his belt pouch, he produced the article he had been preparing in his room. Two of them, in fact; identical documents. He laid them on the table, each penned with great care in black ink and with a quill he had acquired from Katherine. He rarely had cause to write, and it had been a painstaking job, especially to get it so neat and perfect. He'd not been involved in writing legal documentation before, and he was convinced it would be legally binding, but it had needed to look as official as possible.

Graf Dietmar frowned and picked one up, angling it so that the light from a nearby torch illuminated it as he read. Gradually, his eyes widened.

'We cannot substantiate this, you realise.'

Arnau smiled. 'That's the beauty of it. The will disappeared in the troubles, did it not? But I saw it before its disappearance, and can vouch for its veracity. After all, that was the whole reason I was sent to Renfrizhausen, to do just that.'

'And your Order will accept this?'

'The Order will follow the law to the letter. They would prefer to keep *everything*, of course, but I was told from the outset that if I found the evidence to be in the favour of the von Ehingen, we would renounce our claim without argument.'

'That is uncommonly generous, *Herr Tempelritter*.'

'It is a small thing among the estates.'

'What is it, Dietmar?' the lord's sister cast across impatiently.

'Brother Vallbona has given us back the vineyard at Württemberg. My favoured wine.'

Arnau shrugged. 'As I say, it is a small thing in the grand scheme. I cannot defy the Order in toto, especially when dealing with the donatives of your brother. I would not insult his memory any more than I would cheat my preceptrix, but there comes a time when a man can see where true value lies, and the value of Württemberg for you as your family's hereditary winery is far greater than to the Order as some penned line in a ledger that brings in coin. According to the will, which I verified as true, all estates should be retained by the Order, barring the vineyards of Württemberg, which had already been transferred to the ownership of Dietmar von Ow, and were therefore not Lütolf's to grant. My affidavit says as much, and the Order will accept it without question.'

Even old Ute gave him a nod of gratitude for that.

'Then perhaps,' Dietmar said, 'we could indulge in a few flagons of the produce tonight to celebrate.'

Arnau chuckled. 'I fear I should be heading back to Rourell soon.'

Folding one of the documents, he lifted the candle from the table and dripped a small puddle of red wax onto the fold, holding it shut and then pressing the ring on his middle finger into the soft seal, leaving an imprint of two men sharing a horse and a lance. With Dietmar's copy, he appended the seal to the bottom to give it the Order's authority and handed it back. The von Ehingen would have their vineyard and, with the treasure from the cellars, the future looked bright once more.

'You would be foolish to depart in such weather,' Dietmar noted, gesturing to the window. Outside the snowfall had become somewhat intense.

Arnau chewed his lip. 'I fear you may be right. And the snow looks as though it might be set in for some time. When will the roads be clear, do you think?'

'June,' smiled Gerdrut, and Arnau chuckled.

'I fear the preceptrix might expect me back *before* summer. Iberia gears for war against the Moor again. The Almohad menace have been concentrating on putting their own house in order, but once more their gaze turns north towards Aragon and Castile.'

'The moors have other conflicts?'

Arnau snorted lightly. 'Endlessly. Much like the kings if Iberia, sadly. If only Aragon, Castile, Leon and Portugal could put aside their own arguments long enough to draw swords together, so much might be achieved. But yes, the Almohad leader Al-Nasir has spent much of the past decade defending his territory in Africa from Berber invasions. Now, though, that is dealt with, and he can once again look to his conquests in Iberia. I fear he has spent that time itching to repeat his success at Alarcos.' He straightened a little. 'My preceptrix believes that Aragon at least will lead a push back and that perhaps Castile might join the fight. The Order will, of course, be drawn into that.'

'A Crusade?'

'Life in Iberia is one long Crusade with short breaks to draw breath,' sighed Arnau. 'But the kings of the north reeled for years after their defeat at Alarcos, and they long to take the field once more and avenge themselves.'

'Then it is all the more important that you rest and recuperate here for a few weeks,' Dietmar smiled. 'And in the absence of some of our livelier fellows it would be good to have the company. I shall miss my old friend almost as much as my son.'

A cloud of sadness drifted over the table, but Arnau was grateful to note that it passed quickly. The lord would mourn Rüdolf and Kovacs for some time, but the death of Bernhard had been cathartic, and had begun the healing. One thing that Arnau wondered, and had been trying to work out how to ask without causing offence, was the future of the family. With no young heir now, who would inherit when Dietmar passed on? Presumably there would be some cousin somewhere.

'Your Order does not frown on carousing? On drinking wine, then?' Gerdrut murmured.

Arnau smiled. 'All things in moderation, my lady. *"Therefore this seemed good to me, that a man eat, and drink, and use gladness of his travail, in which he travailed under the sun, in the number of days of his life, which God gave to him; and this is his part."* Ecclesiastes chapter five.'

'Does anyone ever renounce the cross and return to laity?'

Arnau was slightly thrown by the non-sequitur of a question and frowned. Something about the way the lady Gerdrut was looking at him made him feel distinctly uncomfortable, and the words of his vow of chastity floated through his mind like a warning. 'It is not common, my lady.'

He tore his gaze from the lady and shuffled in his seat, looking at Dietmar once more.

'I left my horses in the inn at the village,' he said, 'and the body of Felipe at the church. The poor priest will be fretting over what is to be done, and the innkeeper will want money for stabling at least.'

Dietmar waved it aside. 'The next time the snowfall eases, I will send Conrad and Matthias to deal with them. Your squire requires nothing unusual for burial? No specific Templar rites?'

Arnau shook his head. 'A simple service and a simple burial is all that we require.'

'Then it would be my honour to see that he is interred with the family and with my dear friend Karolus at Renfrizhausen. His shrewdness and stalwartness saved our family's fortune, after all, and he died for our good, not his own.'

Arnau nodded. 'That would be most kind, my lord.'

He tried not to look at Gerdrut, but could feel her eyes on him.

'When will the services take place?' he asked.

Dietmar sighed. 'In truth the body of my son could have been taken down to the village any time the snow stopped this past week, but I have been loath to part with it. Saying farewell to a child is a hard thing, master Templar, but I fear the time has come. The next time the clouds clear we will travel to the town with Rüdolf, Karolus, Anselm and Anna, and attend to their burials. The priest will see that things are done swiftly. But though we may easily reach the town between storms, I would still advise against travel beyond there. Some of the passes to the west will be closed for weeks yet.'

Arnau nodded. It looked as though he would be spending some time in Renfrizhausen before he returned to Rourell. Fanciful notions of discovering the dragon hidden in some great cave beneath the castle or lurking in the hall at night and waiting for the ghost danced through his imagination and he smiled. The smile slid uncomfortably as he caught Gerdrut throwing him an oddly predatory look.

These it be, that be not defouled with women; for they be virgins. These follow the lamb whither ever he shall go; these be bought of all men, the first fruits to God, and to the lamb.

The Revelation of Saint John.

A few weeks in Renfrizhausen would be pleasant, though he had a feeling they might bring with them their own personal difficulties

HISTORICAL NOTE

The fourth book in the Templar series was not originally intended to be a murder mystery. In fact, it was intended to be a political thriller based around the troubles between the Welf and Hohenstaufen dynasties. The simple truth is that the more I looked at the location, the history, and the situation in the series, the more this story began to take shape in my head.

Winter Knight I will admit leans more towards the fiction side of historical fiction than either *City of God* or *Daughter of War* did, but that is the nature of the beast when dealing with crime writing, I think. As far as possible I have rooted fact into the tale, though, as I'll explain below.

Ever since the first book in the series, I have wanted to explore the past of some of the supporting characters. In *Daughter of War* we got to know our hero, Arnau de Vallbona, who has grown over the series, and we were introduced to his fellow knights with an explosion of personality, but with only tantalising hints beyond the present.

Thus, when I moved on to book two, I delved into Balthesar's fascinating past, which had something of a parallel with the life of Rodrigo Diaz (El Cid) in that he was as often a warrior for the Moors as he was for the Christians. In book three, I rounded out Ramon's character and his past a little with a legal background. But I had left one character untouched from book one.

Lütolf von Ehingen was a highlight for me in writing *Daughter of War*. He was different from any character I've ever written. He was aloof, haughty, lacked much of a sense of humour, was not particularly sympathetic, and so on. And yet, I think (and I hope you do too) that somehow he still came across as likeable, a character with whom readers empathised. And I included right back at the start some tantalising hints of the dubious past of this character that had been deliberately left hanging as loose threads. The reason for this is that before I even started on a second book, I planned in a few years to come back and unravel some of the mystery of Lütolf.

This, then, is as much a homage to that character as it is a murder mystery.

To the location and the family, then. I had placed Lütolf's family in Swabia back at the start of the series. At the time, I had no idea how complex high medieval southern Germany was, and there have been times in the recent months when I have cursed my decision not to place the family somewhere with which I am more familiar – perhaps Wensleydale. But the fact remained: They are the von Ehingen.

Here is where I hold up my hands and admit that because Lütolf was a supporting character with no future in the series, I had originally plucked a name from a hat. Ehingen I chose because it is in the right area, is old enough to have such links, and has no dreadfully famous noble sons with whom I was going to interfere.

Then I decided to write this book and looked into it further. And it turned out that the von Ehingen did exist. In truth, though, I am writing in a time before their prominence. The family become a fixture in southern Germany in the later Middle Ages, with Georg von Ehingen (the son of another Rüdolf, by pure chance) in the early fifteenth century travelling all over Europe and the Middle East on political missions for the Empire, dealing with noble unions and joining the Order of the Holy Sepulchre in Jerusalem. But there were scant references to the family in the early thirteenth century. It took some research and the aid of a stalwart German friend to work out some details that allowed the tale to be told.

I had worried that the von Ehingen were a later family and had no roots in my period, but then stumbled across one Markward von Ehingen, born in 1220. They were there. The family *were* around in my era. In some respects I had a green light. Whose child Markward might be, I leave it to you to speculate. For my part I hope that Gerdrut remarried and had a new heir, though not one with Vallbona blood, I can happily confirm.

My German friend helped me piece all sorts of things together thereafter, and of the castles within the holdings of that family, from Sülz to Rottenburg and beyond, few fortresses existed as early as my date. We looked at half a dozen potential castles. The one that did work was Renfrizhausen. Standing on a forested hill above the eponymous town, the castle existed as a holding of the von Ehingen at the time Arnau would be there and, perhaps best of all for me, there are *very* few remains and little record of the place. A few fragments of walls and ditches among the trees means that I was free to build Arnau's Renfrizhausen how I wished, which was extremely useful when I needed to plan hidden movements, secret entrances, locked cellars and the like.

To some extent, the castle is based upon various others. Richmond in North Yorkshire has its influence in the buildings and ranges. Bran in Romania (the popular 'Dracula's castle' that really isn't) gives it its flavour, being a gothic pile on a rock in a snowy, forested valley. The Wawel castle in Krakow, Poland, has a 'dragon' cave that opens out by the river way below the castle. My

Renfrizhausen is a composite of many such sites, built to allow the action to happen.

Navigating the nobility of medieval Germany is troubling. I will apologise now to any German reader who gets this far and is grumbling about the nuances of noble titles and legality, etc. I delved as far as I could. At least the black and yellow chevrons of von Ehingen are based on their actual arms, displayed above, at the start of this section.

The character of Karolus Kovacs, who is an important 'third party' in the story, is in some respects my homage to the great Guy Gavriel Kay, whose Italianate minstrel Rudel in *A Song for Arbonne* remains an all-time great character. His nationality as Hungarian was drawn from the need to have a hook into Arnau's past (the city of Zadra) and yet someone removed from both the western Church and the Germanic political system. The crossbow is loosely based on a beautiful Hungarian survival: the crossbow of Matthias Corvinus. Look it up. It is an astounding item.

Needless to say, as a largely Roman-based author, the connection of the Roman gold was a natural fit for me. Coin hoards have been found through history, some of incredible value. For this to be the financial root of a family in this area was feasible. Indeed, though the Roman temporary camp through which Arnau rides is fictional, there are almost certainly such sites awaiting discovery in the area. At Sülz close by is the site of a Flavian fort, and the entire area is part of the *limes*, the frontier of the Roman world, from which we get the modern word *limit*. The Roman connection was added with relish. The ghost was an idea that arose from the story of the 'grey lady' in the old hall in my village. The dragon tale is a real legend based around Henry the Lion, combined with the dragon of the Wawel in Poland. I needed several legends in order to absorb the gold into the story and not make it stand out. Part of any good whodunit is the addition of red herrings and distractions, after all.

In the thirteenth century legal recourse in Germany came down to the regional assembly of the *Landgericht*, and in between times each local lord would hold legal right to try and punish, which made it very easy to have the cut-off, snow-bound Renfrizhausen as something of a closed entity, not reliant upon some distant court or legal unit.

Many minor facets of this took some of the most unravelling and the deepest research of all. One is how the local churches maintained the traditional liturgy of the hours in winter when the second service (lauds) would be held at dawn (eight a.m.), and the third service (prime) would be held several hours earlier. Hour-based routines are at odds with the shortening of the day in winter, after all. Another is the meals and foods consumed in medieval Germany. Breakfast is not a thing in the medieval era, but I made it one for Renfrizhausen for plot purposes. The foods served, though, are based upon regional, medieval choices and availability. Another small factor is the wine, which has actually very little point in the plot, but occupied much of my time. Dietmar has a favourite wine that they keep, and Arnau makes sure in the end that they retain that vineyard. This is based upon a list of the family holdings, which confirm that they owned a vineyard in Württemberg in 1294. Guess what? It turns out that not only was Swabian wine considered some of the best in the medieval era, but in Britain it is currently a very sought-after, up-and-coming wine region.

On to the Order, then.

The Knights Templar had less connection even with Germany than they had with the Fourth Crusade from my previous book, which is at one and the same time a blessing and a curse. It means one has to be very careful how one slots the story into the historical framework without seeming forced or artificial, but it also means that if one can do that, one has almost free rein.

The Templars were largely French in origin. They were founded in the Holy Land by Frenchmen, supported by the Pope, and their spiritual heartland might have been Jerusalem, but their political and administrative one was Paris. We know that parts of Italy held Templar lands. Spain and Portugal also had Templar holdings, although they are less noted and researched (hence my use of them in the series). Britain, of course, had plenty of Templar influence. The Germanic world, though, had hardly any. It is interesting to note, however, given how I started this series, that the only recorded Templar nunnery was in Austria, at Mühlen. Regardless, Germany had little contact with the Templars.

There are many convoluted reasons for this. Germany was an oddity in the medieval era in that it was a kingdom whose king was elected, and those electors were drawn from both noble and religious positions. Thus the monarchy was a constant tug-of-war between church and state. The king was also, of course, the Holy Roman Emperor, crowned as such by the Pope. A weird situation, and one in which the German lords and bishops were hardly going to allow any powerful religious group like the Templars to gain any influence. The Templars were not encouraged within the Empire. Indeed, the German knights had been insular throughout the Crusades. Under Frederick Barbarossa they had signed up for the great expedition, but had not reached Jerusalem, as their lord died in Anatolia en route. They turned round and went home after some trouble with the Turks. The German knights who could be found in Jerusalem worked around a religious hospital of their own, and eventually evolved into the Order of the Teutonic Knights.

And so Arnau and his Order were not universally popular in Swabia.

One last thing remains to be said, and that is a huge thank you to two people in particular. My old university friend Dominic von Stösser helped me a great deal with the early research for the book, and also kindly agreed to read through the finished draft to check my German language and Germanic facts. Thank you Dom. I owe you beer! And thanks to my wife Tracey, who read through the story as I wrote it, whose comments I used to tweak and cut as required to keep the plot tight and inscrutable. These two have been invaluable in the writing of *The Winter Knight*.

I think that I have now covered almost everything I needed to say. I hope you enjoyed Arnau's time in Germany. I did. Our young Templar will return, and what's more, he will return to Iberia for the next book. The war against the Moor in Spain is reaching a crescendo and Arnau, of course, has a place in that. Thank you for reading, and a nice, frothy German beer to you all.

Simon Turney, August 2019

Thank you for reading The Winter Knight, I hope you enjoyed it. Please consider taking a few moments to leave a review online..

If you enjoyed The Templar Series why not also try:

The Ottoman Cycle Series

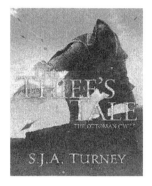

Book 1. The Thief's Tale

Istanbul, 1481. The once great city of Constantine that now forms the heart of the Ottoman empire is a strange mix of Christian, Turk and Jew. Despite the benevolent reign of the Sultan Bayezid II, the conquest is still a recent memory, and emotions run high among the inhabitants, with danger never far beneath the surface.

Skiouros and Lykaion, the sons of a Greek country farmer, are conscripted into the ranks of the famous Janissary guards and taken to Istanbul where they will play a pivotal, if unsung, role in the history of the new regime. As Skiouros escapes into the Greek quarter and vanishes among its streets to survive on his wits alone, Lykaion remains with the slave chain to fulfill his destiny and become an Islamic convert and a guard of the Imperial palace. Brothers they remain, though standing to either side of an unimaginable divide.

On a fateful day in late autumn 1490, Skiouros picks the wrong pocket and begins to unravel a plot that reaches to the very highest peaks of Imperial power. He and his brother are about to be left with the most difficult decision faced by a conquered Greek: whether the rule of the Ottoman Sultan is worth saving.

The Tales of the Empire Series

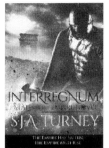

Interregnum by S.J.A. Turney

For twenty years civil war has torn the Empire apart; the Imperial line extinguished after the mad Emperor Quintus was burned in his palace, betrayed by his greatest general and oldest friend, Kiva Caerdin.

Against a background of war, decay and violence, men who once served in the proud Imperial army now fight as hands for hire, little but fodder for greedy lords fighting over the remnants of more glorious times.

Kiva's memories of the Empire are reignited when fighting alongside a fearsome mercenary unit, the Grey Company. Forced to face a dark and shameful past, he struggles to put his life back together. To achieve redemption, he and his men must defeat an ancient, cunning and bitter rival. Only then can the Empire be unified and become reborn…

The Praetorian Series

Praetorian by S.J.A. Turney

Promoted to the elite Praetorian Guard in the thick of battle, a young legionary is thrust into a seedy world of imperial politics and corruption. Tasked with uncovering a plot against the newly-crowned emperor Commodus, his mission takes him from the cold Danubian border all the way to the heart of Rome, the villa of the emperor's scheming sister, and the great Colosseum.

What seems a straightforward, if terrifying, assignment soon descends into Machiavellian treachery and peril as everything in which young Rufinus trusts and believes is called into question and he faces warring commanders, Sarmatian cannibals, vicious dogs, mercenary killers and even a clandestine Imperial agent. In a race against time to save the Emperor, Rufinus will be introduced, willing or not, to the great game.

The Damned Emperors Series

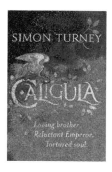

<u>Caligula by Simon Turney</u>

The six children of Germanicus are cursed from birth. Father: believed poisoned by the Emperor Tiberius over the imperial succession. Mother and two brothers arrested and starved to death by Tiberius. One sister married off to an abusive husband. Only three are left: Caligula, in line for the imperial throne, and his two sisters, Drusilla and Livilla, who tells us this story.

The ascent of their family into the imperial dynasty forces Caligula to change from the fun-loving boy Livilla knew into a shrewd, wary and calculating young man. Tiberius's sudden death allows Caligula to manhandle his way to power. With the bloodthirsty tyrant dead, it should be a golden age in Rome and, for a while, it is. But Caligula suffers emotional blow after emotional blow as political allies, friends, and finally family betray him and attempt to overthrow him, by poison, by the knife, by any means possible.

Little by little, Caligula becomes a bitter, resentful and vengeful Emperor, every shred of the boy he used to be eroded. As Caligula loses touch with reality, there is only one thing to be done before Rome is changed irrevocably.

Printed by Amazon Italia Logistica S.r.l.
Torrazza Piemonte (TO), Italy

10976093R00166